STORK BITE
A Novel

L.K. Simonds

STORK BITE
A Novel

This novel is a work of fiction. Names, characters, places, and incidents are either products of the author's imagination or used fictitiously.

Lyrics from "Fence Breakin' Blues" attributed to Ed Schaffer of the Shreveport Home Wreckers quoted herein are public domain.

Excerpts from "Birches," "A Boundless Moment," and "Stopping by Woods on a Snowy Evening" by Robert Frost from the book THE POETRY OF ROBERT FROST edited by Edward Connery Lathem. Copyright © 1923, 1969 by Henry Holt and Company. Copyright © 1951 by Robert Frost. Reprinted by permission of Henry Holt and Company. All Rights Reserved.

Edited by:
Katherine Rawson

Cover Design by:
Kristie Koontz
KK Designs

ISBN: 978-1-7362030-0-2

www.lksimonds.com

For Mabel

Your eyes saw me when I was still an unborn child.
Every day of my life was recorded in your book before
one of them had taken place.
Psalm 139:16

BOOK ONE
DAVID WALKER

Chapter One

1913

When David Walker was seventeen years old, he killed a man.
A white man.

If David had taken the pig trail—his usual path—that Saturday morning, he wouldn't have been on the highway when a rusted Ford Runabout passed, driven by a man who glared and scowled. The motorcar disappeared around a curve. David heard the engine slow. He stopped walking, and his dog, Huck, sat at his side. The car's engine revved and grew louder again.

Bourbon Democrats. That's what Gramps called the rural whites who despised their darker neighbors. They were sprinkled through the countryside.

"Stay away from them," Gramps said.

"How will I know them?"

"You'll know."

Before that October day, the center of David's secluded, rural life was his maternal grandfather, Gramps, who called David "Big Man." David was not a big man. He was tall but thin as a rake, so thin he might've toppled over in a stiff breeze if the air could've gotten hold of him at all.

Gramps had been a sharpshooter in the Union Army's 7th Louisiana Regiment during the Freedom War. By the time Gramps was seventeen, he had killed many men. But that was war. Afterward, David wondered if war made it easier or if the man's face haunted you just the same.

When the war ended, Gramps did not go home to Port Barre. Instead, he landed on the staff of his former captain, first in Shreveport, then in New Orleans, where Captain C. C. Antoine served as lieutenant governor for four glorious years that were heady with promises of equality.

David had killed his first deer with Gramps's Sharps rifle. He patiently fixed the sight on the crease behind the buck's shoulder and held the long barrel steady, arms burning, until he had a clean shot. He squeezed the trigger. The hammer and the deer seemed to drop at the same time.

"That's a better use for this gun," Gramps said.

Gramps was the reason David hunted ducks with a .22 rifle.

"Ain't nobody hunts ducks with a rifle," the white man had said.

"I do," David answered.

That seemed to set him off.

When David heard the Runabout turn around, he said, "C'mon, Huck." He and the dog hurried into the woods and crouched behind a bramble. The Runabout passed by slowly, the white man half-standing in the vehicle, peering toward the woods. Toward them.

David put his index finger to his lips. "Shhh," he breathed. The dog looked up at him, his pale blue eyes luminous in the gloom, and licked David's hand. Huck was a Catahoula Hound, obedient only to David.

The car rolled out of sight. "Let's go," David whispered. They made their way to the pig trail they often followed on their reconnoiters. It meandered through the woods for miles. The previous Saturday, David had followed it farther from home than ever—across the Arkansas line—and discovered an oxbow lake that swarmed with mallards.

By the time they reached the lake, David had forgotten all about the Runabout and its driver. There was a pirogue overturned on the shore, with a long paddle tucked beneath it. He wrestled the boat over and laid his rifle and haversack in it. He pushed it to the water's edge, took up the oar, and prepared to shove off. As soon as he turned to call Huck, he saw the white man step out of the woods. The man wore a pistol on his hip and a badge on his shirt.

The man walked to the boat and raised one boot onto the gunnel. He removed his spectacles and cleaned them with his handkerchief, taking his time about it. He looked over David and Huck and the contents of the pirogue, then he put his glasses back on, hooking a wire arm over each ear.

"Why you takin' so much trouble to dodge me, boy?" the man asked.

David looked at the ground.

"Say," he insisted.

"Didn't mean to be dodging anybody."

"You're lyin' on that count." The man kicked the pirogue with the side of his boot. "This here boat's for whites only."

"Didn't know that," David said. "I was just gonna use it, the way folks do."

The man squared himself on both feet and put his hands on his hips. "Matter of fact, this here county's pretty much whites only. I know all the coloreds around here, and you ain't one of 'em. You musta come up from Lousy-ana."

David did not answer.

The man reached into the boat and fetched out the rifle and the black-tarred haversack. The haversack was Union army issue, surplus gear Gramps had brought home from the war. It had been packed away for many years until Gramps gave it to David on his thirteenth birthday. For the first time in his life, David was thankful no insignia adorned it.

The man sighed. "Reckon I better take you in for trespassin'. You and that Leopard dog."

Fear thrashed in David's gut like a pain-savaged animal. He tightened his grip on the long paddle, feeling his knees might give way.

"This is pretty good stuff," the man said. "Might be enough to pay the fine for you. It ain't enough for you *and* the dog. He'll have to come with me." He looked David up and down. "Ain't you a dandy? Outfitted real nice, ain't ya? New boots. Store-bought clothes. Looks to me like you got money to burn. Where'd ya get all that money?"

"I don't have any money. You can check."

"I ain't checkin' nothin'! They ain't no reason for you to be up here poachin' white folks' game, now are they? Wha'chu huntin' anyway?"

"Just ducks."

"Ain't nobody hunts ducks with a rifle."

"I do."

The man looked at him sharply. "Well, you is just full a cheek, ain't ya?" He dropped the haversack and took a step forward, lifting the rifle. "Get on the ground!"

Huck barked and rushed him.

The man swung the rifle toward the dog, and David swung the paddle toward the man. The blade of the five-footer left the ground and landed on that milky temple with such swift force that the oar broke into two pieces. The splintering wood sounded like a shot, and David smelled gunpowder. He turned toward Huck.

The dog was down, lying on his side. David ran to him. Fell on him. Blood bubbled from a wound in Huck's chest. David sat cross-legged in the dirt and pulled the dog into his lap. Huck's eyes were open but unseeing. David pressed his hand against the hole to stop the blood and air coming out of it. He held it there tightly while the dog panted. With his other hand, David traced three long, bald scars on Huck's hind leg, healed gashes from an alligator's teeth.

David had foolishly taken the yearling puppy hunting during their first autumn together, before the water cooled and the alligators became indifferent. One came out of nowhere and yanked Huck under. The dog bobbed to the surface, paddling frantically, and David pulled him into the boat before the monster got hold of him again. Watching that pup fight his way clear, watching him cry and tremble and bleed afterward, had torn David up. He'd felt so remorseful that he would've done anything to keep Huck safe after that.

David touched a jagged tear in the dog's right ear, made by an angry raccoon. David shot the raccoon and cured the pelt, and Huck had slept on it every night since. The hound wore other scars too—as did David—each calling up a memory from their seven years together.

Huck stopped breathing, and David gathered him into his arms and cried. He rocked and sobbed and wailed.

When he had worn himself out, David looked toward the pirogue—only a few paces away—where the man had fallen against its bow. The man's head was cocked at an unnatural angle that reminded David of the fossils in his mother's textbooks: lizards imprinted in rock, their necks curved back sharply in death. The man's eyes were open and startled—absent the spectacles that had flown off—and they were almost as blue as Huck's. A blotch of deep red bloomed on his pale temple.

David eased Huck off his lap. He went to the man and knelt beside him. He laid his palm on the quiet chest, next to the badge. The badge was a ruse. It was tarnished and worn almost smooth, except for a faint imprint: Texas Ranger.

David sat on the ground beside the dead man and wondered what he should do. All the warnings his mother and father had given him: *Don't eat! Don't say! Don't touch!* Not once had they warned him this could happen. Never once had Mama said, as he was on his way out the door, "David, honey, don't kill anybody while you're out today."

David's parents didn't need to tell him not to kill. God Almighty warned against it. "Thou shalt not kill." Thou shalt not even kill a man who abused you. *Especially* not a man who abused you. The Bible said to pray for those who despitefully use you.

The man surely would've abused Huck too, if he'd gotten the chance. Terrible images had flashed through David's mind when the man said he was taking Huck. When the rifle swung toward the dog, David felt his fear coil and strike before he could stop it.

The only thing David knew for certain was that he couldn't leave the body for the whites to find. He knew this instinctively, before he took time to reason it through. David had been seen on the road that morning. A family in a wagon had passed him and Huck. The daddy's thickly bearded face was partially hidden beneath his hat brim, and the mama's red hair was tied up in a glory knot. She smiled, her eyes kind, and David smiled back. A passel of children lazed in the wagon bed. They stared, slack-jawed and snaggletoothed, as the wagon rattled past.

"Close your mouth, David," His mother had told him often enough when he was young and given to sitting around with his jaw hanging open.

The family in the wagon were white. When word got around that a man was dead, they'd tell about seeing a dark stranger and his merled dog on the highway. The whites would assemble a posse and begin a manhunt that would end at his family's front door. Then David wouldn't be the only one they took.

The motorcar on the road had to be reckoned with. If left there too long, it might provoke a passerby to investigate. David got to his feet and pried his rifle from the man's clenched hands. He walked to the highway and turned south, making his way through the trees alongside the road, hiding himself and his bloodied clothes. He went about half a mile but saw nothing. He turned and walked north, eventually coming to a break in the trees across the road. He looked each way and hustled across. The car was there, on a dirt track that angled into the highway. David reached inside, released the brake, and pushed the car far enough from the road to be hidden.

He trudged back to the lake. From a distance, Huck looked peaceful, as if he were dozing in the sun. David almost expected the dog to raise his head and hail him with a soft woof. He walked directly to the pirogue, passing Huck without looking down. The sun was high and hot, and flies crawled across the man's open eyes. David knelt and closed the eyelids with his fingertips. He laid his rifle aside and unbuttoned the man's shirt. He undressed the dead man completely, an awful violation that felt more shameful than striking him, which David had done before he had a chance to think about it. The corpse lay naked, white flesh exposed to the afternoon sun, and David wondered if the skin would sunburn, even now.

He gathered some stones and put them in the man's boots, and then he set the boots in the bottom of the pirogue. He spread the man's shirt on the ground and laid in its center the spectacles, socks, drawers, and undershirt, the empty holster—not the pistol—and a large rock. He wrapped the shirt around it all and tied the sleeves. In the man's pants pockets, David found a folding knife, some coins, and a money clip stuffed with banknotes. These he put into his haversack, along with the pistol. He knew he shouldn't keep the gun, but he did. David wrapped the pants around the shirt and secured it all with the man's belt. Then he placed the bundle in the pirogue next to the boots.

David took off his jacket. He got behind the man and pushed and heaved until the body was sitting up. The man reeked of body odor and another smell, like potatoes gone bad. David put his knee against the man's back and sloughed off his own shirt to keep the man's stench off it. He took a deep breath and wrapped his arms around the man's chest. David had never embraced another human being, flesh to flesh, as intimately as this dead man. The skin was dry, and the body was without resistance, the muscles having let go of their vigor. David wrestled him over the gunnel of the boat and laid him flat in the bottom.

He shoved the flat-bottomed pirogue through the mud until the water finally got up under it. He retrieved the blade end of the broken oar, stepped over the body into the boat, and pushed off. He paddled to the middle of the lake and dropped the man's possessions into the water. They sank out of sight. He turned the pirogue toward a grove of towering cypress, beneath which the water's surface was choked with yellow-flowering bladderwort.

In the shadows of the cypress, David rolled the body out of the boat. He held onto one suntanned arm and reached into the warm water to cut the throat. Black blood seeped from the wound, and strands of bladderwort clung to David's arm and the man's pallid skin. He punctured the abdomen and the chest, driving the knife to the hilt. He couldn't have the corpse gassing up and rising in a day or two if the alligators didn't take it. David had seen a bloated pig float like a cork for days.

David let go and the body sank, leaving an empty space in the black water where the plants had been disturbed. He rinsed his knife and sheathed it. He churned the water with the paddle then stopped and listened. There was a splash and another one close behind it. He churned some more then paddled a little distance away to wait and see what the alligators would do.

David swatted at the mosquitoes and listened to the swamp sounds. Birds and insects sang cheerfully as on any other afternoon. A breeze lifted the curly gray beards hanging from the bald cypress. Gramps was the reason David knew Spanish moss wasn't really moss at all. David and his grandfather had explored Caddo Parish with Gramps's field guide: *Flora and Fauna of Louisiana*. David could distinguish the calls of blue herons from those of great egrets. He knew the trilling insects were cicadas, and he could diagram their life cycle.

"Folks who don't understand their world are given to superstition," Gramps always said.

David didn't let himself think about what he was actually doing. Instead, he gave his mind over to the familiarity of sitting in a pirogue among cypress knees, waiting for an alligator to take bait. He'd done it many times before.

Sudden roiling erupted—gray-black armor and white flesh twisted in a churning whirlpool. Two of them were rolling the body.

David had seen enough. He turned the pirogue and paddled back to shore. He pulled the boat onto the bank, dragged it to the spot where he'd found it, and turned it over. He gathered the two pieces of the broken oar and carried them into the brush, shoving them under the first log he came to. He went back to the clearing and looked around. Every trace of the man was gone, and the lake was undisturbed except for Huck's gunshot corpse.

David knelt beside Huck and pressed his hand against the dog's flank on a patch of fur that wasn't stiff with blood. "I'll come back for you," he said.

He stood. Retrieved his shirt and put it on. He picked up his jacket, rifle, and haversack, with its unfamiliar weight. The shadows were long, and David thought about his mother. She'd be wondering if he'd fallen asleep in the warmth of the Indian summer afternoon.

He looked at the oxbow lake for a long time before turning and walking away.

Chapter Two

David walked to the motorcar and sat with his back against a wheel to wait for nightfall and think about what he'd do next. He had a strong desire to get rid of the car quickly, thus doing away with the last trace of the hateful stranger. He knew just the place, a few miles to the east, where a twenty-foot bluff overhung the Red River's sucking eddies.

The bluff was upstream from an inlet where David, his father, and his grandfather had camped during many overnight fishing trips. Gramps called their excursions bivouac. David called them heaven. Every trip, before they put a line in the water, David and Gramps walked north from camp to a bluff that had once overhung a vast raft of fallen trees that spanned the river from bank to bank. David's grandfather had not only seen the bridge of packed debris, he had walked across it. "All the way to Bossier in dry boots," he said.

Gramps was there when the Corps of Engineers dynamited the logjam. "The dynamite smelled like ripe bananas," he said. David had eaten a banana once. It was as sweet as candy.

David wanted to hear the deep boom of the exploding dynamite and feel the ground jolt under his feet. He wanted to watch the muddy water geyser skyward, launching whole trees into the air. To smell the sweet dynamite and see the white smoke linger over the water. To watch the river rush through the breach afterward and hear the joyful roar of waters homesick for the sea.

They always caught plenty of fish on their camping trips, enough for supper and breakfast the next morning. David and his daddy liked the sweet crappie, but Gramps was partial to catfish. They dredged them in cornmeal and fried them with potatoes and onions in a skillet over the campfire. Even Huck lay out with a full belly when supper was over.

After sunset they sat around the fire, talking and watching the sparks fly up. The previous summer, the campfire talk had rolled around to college. The family had decided David would attend Wiley or Bishop, both in Marshall, Texas. There had been much discussion over the pros and cons of each school. David liked the idea of college—of being on his own for the first time in his life—but not for months on end. He would miss home too much. No fishing or hunting or hikes through his woods with Huck at his side. David had broached the idea of continuing his education at home with flattery, telling his mother that she could teach him as well as any college professor.

"Just let that thought roll right out the other ear," his mother had said. "You could use the exposure."

Again and again, David found himself turning to speak to Huck. He was used to those glass-blue eyes looking up at him. Huck hung on his every word, as if David's voice was the only one worth listening to. It felt wrong to leave him, even for a while, as if he'd meant nothing.

David worked through how long it would take him to hike back from the bluff on the Red River, collect Huck, and carry him home to be buried. Hours. It would take hours. Maybe until daybreak if he waited for nightfall to set out. David imagined himself arriving at the doorstep of his home in the early dawn. Dead Huck in his arms. His mother's face appearing behind the screen door.

Every time he got to that part—his mother's face, the worry and love and relief in her eyes—his thoughts turned away sharply. He could not rein them back to find out what happened next.

When evening set in, the sky became gray with clouds and lightning flashed in the northwest. David counted, "One potato, two potato, three potato, four—" Thunder rumbled. He'd be wet soon. He got up and wrestled the Runabout's convertible top over the worn seat, then sat with his knees sticking up on either side of the steering wheel. Overhead, light shown through many gashes in the fabric and long threads hung down and caught on his hair.

David slid off the seat and went around to the cargo box, thinking it might hold a tarpaulin. He lifted the lid on squeaking hinges. Inside was a plaid wool jacket, bunched as if it had been tossed in hastily. An afterthought. Had the man's wife brought it out of the house—screen door banging—as he was about to drive away? Had she called out to him? "Here, honey, take your coat. It's October, after all."

David pushed aside the jacket and the image of the man's wife. A dozen boxes of .22 caliber cartridges nestled in folds of white cloth. He gathered the ammunition and stacked it on the wool jacket.

When the cartridges were out of the way, a vacant-eyed white hood stared up at him, lying atop a white cloak with Klan regalia on its breast. David stepped back. He took a deep breath and then another. He stepped forward again and touched the cloth, timidly, as if it were enchanted. It was shiny, brilliant white, and very tightly woven.

The storm grumbled again.

David hastily pushed the hood and cloak aside, which seemed like an impossible thing to be able to do. Yet there they lay, bunched to the side of the cargo box, wrinkled and harmless. David looked up and scanned the forest around him. He imagined a horde of Klansmen in tall white hoods, watching from behind every tree, waiting to fall on him and avenge their brother. But no one was there.

A leather pouch tied with a thin strap and a pair of brown leather gloves, the knuckles stained dark, had fallen from the folds of the robe and lay atop a weathered tarpaulin. David took the leather pouch and the tarp and closed the cargo box. After he'd arranged the tarp over the tattered roof, he settled in the seat and untied the pouch, reached inside and brought out an envelope and a sheaf of crisp banknotes, fastened with a paper sleeve. The notes were hundred-dollar certificates, issued by the United States Treasury.

David's experience with paper money was limited. The customers in his father's general store unpocketed coins and an occasional threadbare dollar bill, if they paid with cash at all. The white man's banknotes were as crisp and clean as the pages of a new book, and the thought crossed David's mind that they might be counterfeit. He counted them, growing ever more alarmed as the numbers ticked higher, ". . . ninety-eight, ninety-nine, one hundred."

Ten thousand dollars!

The bundled stack was less than an inch thick. Surely, the money was not real.

The last of the daylight was fading fast. David picked up the envelope. Someone had written on the front in decorative script, such as he'd seen on important documents in history books, *Non Silba Sed Anthar.*

The envelope was sealed with crimson wax imprinted with the letters KKK inside a circle. David stuck his thumbnail under the wax, opened the envelope, and pulled out a letter dated mere days before. It was addressed to the "Grand Dragon, Realm of Louisiana." He read the letter slowly, taking in every word. It was an exhortation to the "Good Citizens of Louisiana" to uphold the "Tenets of the Christian Religion and White Supremacy, Just Laws and Liberty, and Pure Americanism."

On and on the letter went with high talk, affirming that "every true, red-blooded, native-born, white Gentile, Protestant American Citizen" was with them. "Please accept the offering this letter transmits as a blood-bond between the Good Citizens of Louisiana and their brothers in the Realms of Arkansas and Tennessee. The bearer of this covenant risked life and limb to place it safely in your hands." The letter was signed "Grand Wizard of the Invisible Realm."

It did not contain a single person's name.

The storm's first gust sheared the tarpaulin off the roof of the Runabout. David dropped the letter and leapt from the seat to run after it, as if his life depended on catching that thin scrap of protection before it flew away.

Chapter Three

David sat in the motorcar wrapped in the tarpaulin while cold rain drove in great blowing sheets. In his lap, under the tarp, were his rifle and haversack, and the dead courier's package. He had not drunk a drop of water since leaving home that morning, and his tongue cleaved to the roof of his mouth. He drank from his canteen and refilled it with rainwater by creasing the tarp. Drank again. Refilled it again.

David thought about the rain pounding Huck's body into the mud. He had an urge to go and get him and bring him under the tarpaulin, just until the rain stopped. Then he could wrap Huck's body in the canvas and carry him home in it.

No, he couldn't. The tarp would be too hard to explain.

Once again, David imagined himself at home, but this time he was seated at the kitchen table with his family. Huck was lying out in the yard. David could see him through the screen door, just lying there with his stiff fur, waiting to be wrapped in the old raccoon pelt and buried near the people he had loved.

"We'll get to Huck soon enough," David's family said, all in unison. They were all around the table—Mama, Daddy, Gramps—and they were all looking at him. "Tell us everything that happened," they said. "Start at the beginning."

And David said . . . what? What might he say? That he accidentally shot Huck while aiming at a mallard? Gramps wouldn't believe that for a minute. David could say the gun discharged on its own. He'd say he fell asleep at the lake, sad and exhausted, and had to wait for first light to make his way back. That's why it took him so long.

What if he told them the truth? That a Klansman attacked him. Wait. It was Huck the man attacked, not David. He would tell them it was an accident. He killed a man—a very bad man—accidentally. Then he fed him to some alligators. On purpose. Maybe he wouldn't mention the Runabout, that he drove it to the Red River and pushed it into the muddy current.

"I'm proud of you, Big Man," Gramps might say. "Chip off the old block."

No, Gramps would not say that.

David imagined spreading the Klan's letter and the banknotes—*ten thousand dollars!*—on the table for his family to see. As evidence of the man's wickedness. The thought of the blood money and the terrible, awful letter on his mother's kitchen table chilled David to his marrow.

In his mind's eye, the horde of tall-hooded white savages he had imagined in the woods rushed the front porch and broke through the screen door, with their bloody-knuckled gloves, their ropes and guns and knives. They filled the kitchen and grabbed his family. Dragged them outside to the yard—

David inhaled sharply.

There were so many trees in the yard. So many live oaks and pines with thick, high branches.

What had he done?

How had this happened?

David's mother had quoted Jeremiah 29:11 so many times that David always said the words with her, partly to make her stop and partly to keep her going.

"'I know the thoughts that I think toward you,' says the Lord, 'thoughts of peace, and not of evil, to give you an expected end.'"

Maybe killing the man was David's expected end—his destiny. What if he was God's instrument to stop the Klan's devilment? Gramps had killed many such men in the Freedom War. He had leveled the sights of his Sharps rifle—at their heads? their chests?—and squeezed the trigger. On purpose. Wasn't David's violent encounter a war too, after all? David wasn't sure if he might be right or was so terribly wrong that he no longer knew the difference.

Surely the Lord knew this day was coming all along. Surely God had anticipated it, while David headed blithely toward it, hapless and hopeful. Every single day of David's naive, sheltered life was another step closer to this evil, inevitable moment.

Was it inevitable?

David had been raised to believe he always had a choice. His family didn't cotton to notions of predestination, at least not when it came to a person's behavior. His mother quoted Proverbs to make her point. Not as often as she quoted Jeremiah, but often enough. "A man's own foolish choices make his life hard," she said, "but he blames God."

David wrapped his arms around himself. The rain had stopped as suddenly as it began, and cold wind gusted from the north, tugging at the tarpaulin. He imagined his mother at home. Oh, how he wanted to be with her! To hug her and feel the safety of her embrace. He imagined their warm kitchen and his mother sitting at the table, a steaming cup of tea in front of her.

But he was not imagining anymore. He was remembering. They all sat around the kitchen table for a family meeting when David was eight years old, nine at the most. He and Gramps had returned from Shreveport, where they'd gone to pick up supplies at the train depot for the Walker General Store. It was David's first trip to Shreveport, his first brush with the world outside the sanctuary his family had built in the deep piney woods of Caddo Parish.

They had passed a sign on the way to the train depot. It was hanging in the dusty window of a ramshackle store on the highway, just north of town. A large white board—too large for the size of the window—suspended by ropes. Painted on it in angry black brushstrokes were two words: Whites Only!

"Why is that sign there?" David demanded as they drove past.

Gramps shook his head. Said nothing.

"Somebody needs to tell him to take it down. *We* ought to go back and tell him that's not right."

"You listen to me, Big Man. When we get to the train depot, there'll be white folks there. You don't speak to them. You don't even look at them, you understand?"

"Why not?"

"These white folks aren't like the white folks you know. They're looking for an excuse to make trouble. Big trouble. Don't you give it to them, hear? I mean it. You look straight at the ground. Do you understand me, boy?"

"Yes sir," David said, chastened. He sulled up then and wouldn't get out of the truck at the depot. He sat and stared at his boots while his grandfather and the porters loaded crates of canned goods, flour, sugar.

When they returned home, Gramps told David's parents the trip had not gone well, and David's father called a family meeting. His mother made herself a cup of tea, and they all sat around the kitchen table

"We've been too protective," his father said. "These are dangerous times, son, the worst we've ever seen. I fear we haven't been wise to hide them from you."

"What about the Freedom War?" David said. "You said we won."

"We did," Gramps said, "but you wouldn't know it. It's worse now than it was before the war. At least, for the freedmen. And it's far, far worse than during Reconstruction. We were making progress, real progress, but they snatched it all away. Seemed like almost overnight."

"Who snatched it away?" David asked.

"We can't vote anymore," Gramps said, as if he hadn't heard. "God help us if we look at the wrong white the wrong way. My God! We are *all* subjugated now!" Gramps raised his fist, then unclenched it and put his palm on the table.

David's throat closed at his grandfather's frustration, at the powerless words coming out of his mouth, when he'd seemed all-powerful before.

David's mother said, "This conversation can't be all about the whites."

"They are the problem," said Gramps.

"Not all whites see us as inferior. Many of them sympathize with our situation, but they can't change it any more than we can. Besides, the real problem goes deeper than race. Even if you could drive down to Shreveport and vote in the next election—"

"That would be nice," interrupted Gramps.

"Yes, it would. But *I* wouldn't be able to vote, now would I?"

"Well, that's a different discussion."

"I think it's the same discussion."

David's mother turned her attention from her father to her son. She pushed her cup and saucer across the table toward him. The silver tea ball and its thin chain rattled against the china.

"Take the tea out of the water, David," she said. "And put it back in the infuser."

David looked at her, confused. Finally, he said, "I can't."

"That's right. You can't. No more than you can drive all the evil out of the world. There's only one person who'll do that, and even he can't do it until the trumpet sounds. In the meantime, you have a choice to make. You can fight against it every day of your life, if that's what you choose to do. But I suspect in doing so you'll only add to the evil, not take it away."

David looked down into the milky tea. He wanted to sling the cup and saucer across the room and hear the bone china shatter against the plaster of the wall. Watch the tea streak down it like muddy water.

"Or you can choose peace. We chose peace, David. We chose to overcome evil by doing good, to the extent we can. That's what we do with your daddy's store. With my lessons. With your grandfather helping the neighbors."

"Gramps fought," David said.

"There's a time to fight," Gramps said. "But this ain't the time."

David's mother pressed her lips. Looked at Gramps.

"*Isn't* the time," Gramps said.

She reached across the table and laid her hand on David's. "Today is a crossroads for you, son. Are you going to meet the wickedness in the world with anger and frustration, or will you find another way? There are already too many angry people in the world." She slid the cup and saucer back to her and sipped the cooling tea.

"We believe in you, son." David's father put his arm around him. "Maybe we have protected you too much, but only to give kindness a chance to take root." He put his heavy warm hand on David's chest. "In here, where it counts."

David believed his family had tended him like a beloved garden, trying to grow only good things. Up until that morning, David had believed he was a kind person. A good son. But when push came to shove, he did not choose peace. Or kindness. Nor did he choose to overcome evil with good.

The storm dragged behind it a cold wind that did not let up. David sat in the car for a long time, waiting for the night to grow deeper. Waiting to wake up from the nightmare. He waited and waited, but nothing happened. Nothing changed.

The stars came out, and the moon rose large and bright above the pines. There was plenty of light for driving and plenty of light for anyone he passed to see him. He shrugged off the wet tarpaulin and made his way to the trail to see if it was passable. The track was deeply rutted and soft with mud, so he paced off a path between the trees to the highway. He returned to the car and opened the cargo box. He took out the wool jacket and put it on over his own lightweight jacket. It was heavy and roomy, and David felt warmer right away.

He lifted the white cloak and ran his fingers across an embroidered patch on the left breast. He held it up to the moonlight. It was dark and round with a white cross in the middle. Had the man's wife sewn it on? He imagined a woman—a mother?—now a widow, stitching the patch by the light of a kerosene lamp. Maybe she didn't know what it meant. Or maybe she was all for it.

Before he thought about what he was doing, David slipped the cloak over his head. He stretched out his white-clad arms in the moonlight. He laid his right palm over the patch, as if to pledge allegiance. He felt the same as he always had, and he knew then and there that the robe was not enchanted at all. It was merely cloth and thread, and all the hate and fear it carried came from the man inside. He grabbed the hood and closed the cargo box.

Despite the motorcar's sorry condition, the engine caught on the second crank and ran smoothly. David got under the wheel and eased the vehicle between the trees and brambles until he reached the edge of the woods. There he stopped and picked up the conical hood. Slid it over his head. Aligned the eyeholes.

David breathed in the rotted potato smell of the man. He made himself eat the stench in deep, slow breaths, as if he were swallowing sin itself. As if he were a scapegoat onto which the rancid hood transferred everything that might bring harm to his family.

He drove out of the woods onto the road and looked to the right, where the highway cut through the pines all the way to the Red River. Then he turned left, away from the river. He straightened the wheel, opened the throttle, and clutched. The tires slipped and caught, slipped and caught again. The Runabout flew down the highway, carrying him toward the wilderness of Caddo Lake. Carrying the day's sin and death far, far from home.

Chapter Four

David stood on the ferry landing on the north shore of Caddo Lake, studying the choppy water. Wondering how deep it was. The ferryboat itself was half a mile across the lake at Mooringsport, whose buildings rose white above the dark shore. Here and there, welcoming lights glowed in windows, despite the late hour. White-frothed waves broke around the dark timbers of oil derricks between the town and David. He could not hear the waves, only the wind flapping the cloak around him. How he must have looked, standing alone, aglow with moonlight like haint.

He walked back to the Runabout's cargo box to see what was left. Inside a valise were wadded clothing, two bottles of Tennessee whiskey, and an oilcloth bag. The bag held several paper-wrapped portions of cornbread and ham. David pinched the cornbread and put some in his mouth. Although he had not eaten in many hours, the bread was no more appetizing than sand. He wrapped it again and put it back in the bag. A rope lay coiled in the bottom of the cargo box. David did not touch it, fearing he would find it dark and greasy with blood, like the gloves.

He put one bottle of whiskey in the oilcloth bag with the cornbread and ham. He slipped off the hood and cloak and stuffed them into the valise and closed it. Then he closed and latched the cargo box, checking and rechecking the fasteners until he was satisfied they would not open of their own accord. He cranked the engine, got under the wheel, and backed the Runabout away from the landing far enough to get up a head of steam.

Oh, how he wanted to turn the car around and go home! How he longed for the comfort of his bed. For a hot breakfast at the kitchen table. Might he still go home and hope for the best? Did the Runabout have enough gasoline to make it back to the Red? What if it ran out of gas on the road? For all he knew, the car was running on fumes.

He had to rid himself of the man's car. Here. Now. But that didn't mean that he couldn't go home later. He had time.

"Slow down, Big Man. You've got all the time in the world," Gramps said when David hurried through a chore. There was time to think things through and sort them out. Time to make a plan, or at least come up with a story he could stick to.

David clutched and started the Runabout forward. The car picked up speed and bounced wildly when it hit the bump between the road and the ferry landing. David felt himself lift off the seat entirely, and the car came down hard and veered left. He straightened the wheels and threw himself out the side. He tumbled and scrambled to his feet in time to see the car belly flop onto the lake.

The Runabout nosed over amid bubbles and smoke. It quickly drifted away from the landing, its cargo box riding high like a buoy. David watched with panic as the cargo box disappeared and reappeared among the waves.

"Mooringsport!" he cried.

David saw himself shrugging off the wool jacket and stepping out of his boots. Diving into the cold, black water and swimming to the car. Climbing onto the cargo box until it filled with water and sank.

And then it was gone.

David paced back and forth across the landing, watching for the cargo box to reappear. It did not. He strained to see moonlit waves breaking against anything other than the oil wells.

Nothing.

David collected his things and made his way toward the railroad trestle, coming to a large open space where the trees and brush had been cleared to bare dirt. "The bridge," he said aloud.

The area had been cleared for construction of a new drawbridge. David and Gramps had made plans to watch it being built. The bridge was to follow a new design that raised a horizontal section between stanchions. Gramps had sketched the design on paper for David to see. "Vertical lift," Gramps said. "It's right clever."

They had made plans to visit Caddo Lake every Saturday after construction began. David had imagined himself leading the bridge-building crew. Directing the work. Shouting orders. Standing tall.

David crossed the clearing and came to the railroad trestle. The timbers angled out from the tracks into the rough water. He knelt and laid his palm on the cold, smooth rail. No vibration. He started across, hurrying in long strides that skipped crossties. The air over the water was noticeably colder, and the wind gusted with fresh enthusiasm. He reached the middle of the lake and stopped. Knelt and again laid his palm on a rail.

All quiet.

David stood and looked to his left, where Twelve-Mile Bayou, shining silver-black, snaked southeast through dark bottomland. He looked to the right, where Caddo Lake stretched to a distant tree line. He turned around and looked at the railroad tracks behind him, glinting in the moonlight. David dropped to his knees and closed his eyes. The haversack slipped off his shoulder and swung down between the crossties.

In that moment, he did not believe he would lay eyes on his family again. Not until he was gathered to his people at death, as old Father Abraham had been gathered to his people. David imagined Abraham as a very old man with a long gray beard, walking slowly into mist shot through with light, as the morning sun illuminates white fog lying in bottomland. He imagined Abraham's people appearing within the mist and moving toward him. Gathering around him to welcome him home. But would David be gathered to his people when he died?

He opened his eyes. He heard the wind again. He felt the cold. He stood and hurried the rest of the way across the lake, reached the south shore, hopped down, and crawled under the tracks into the tight space where the trestle met the bank.

The roar of the morning train overhead woke David abruptly. Dirt and pebbles showered him until the train passed and the trestle stopped its shaking. Nothing else smelled like a locomotive. Sparks and metal and oil and power.

David wiped his face with his palms and looked around, stupefied and innocent in the moment before he remembered. The sun was bright beyond the black timbers of the trestle. It was Sunday morning, and everyone was in church. Everyone except his family, who would be searching for him. He could hardly bear to think of them hoping to find him when there was no hope. He rolled to his side, tucked his knees to his chest, and slept again.

David woke a second time with the ham and cornbread on his mind. He raised himself under the low crossties and ate all the food, even though the bread was dry and the ham was going rank. He drank all the water in his small canteen and was still thirsty. He crawled to the water's edge, hidden within the timbers of the trestle, only to find the water covered with shimmering rainbows that ran up the timbers with each wave. The water had been spoiled by the oil wells and wasn't fit to drink.

Despite his thirst, David returned to the space where the trestle met the bank. He opened the haversack and emptied its contents. The man's money clip was stuffed with banknotes and bore the same symbol as the red wax stamped on the envelope. There were some forgotten venison strips his mother had packed, but he was too thirsty to chew them. Instead, he put a few pebbles in his mouth, as Gramps had taught him.

David took the folded banknotes from the clip and slid them into his boot. He used his knife and fingers to dig a hole at the base of the first timber. When the hole was deep enough, he laid the bottle of whiskey in it. He slipped the leather pouch and money clip into the oilcloth bag, wrapped the bag around itself, and placed it in the hole on top of the bottle. He raked the loose soil on top of it all, smoothing the dirt with the flat of his hand over and over again, until the ground appeared undisturbed.

Chapter Five

Thirst drove David into the open as soon as it was dark. He tracked westward along the shore, sampling the water along the way until he reached a place where there was no taste of petroleum. There he drank his fill and filled his canteen.

Late in the night, David reached a clearing on a low, broad point. The brush and trees he had been picking his way through gave way to a vast lawn on which stood a two-story house. It was a fine place with a deep porch that wrapped all the way around it. A colossal white dog lay on the porch at the front door. There'd be no getting around him.

A few pirogues had been pulled onto the grass at the water's edge. David watched the dog for a long time, but the animal did not stir. David didn't know if the dog cared about the boats or only about the house. One thing he knew for sure was that the dog knew he was there and was waiting to see what David would do next. Dogs were patient that way when they wanted to be.

David considered whether or not he could get the boat off the shore before the dog reached him, if indeed the dog did care, and he decided that he could. He shouldered his gear and marched quickly and with feigned confidence toward the nearest boat, watching the house in his side vision. The dog's head came up. He issued a low woof, but he did not growl or get up. David pushed the boat into the water, stepped in, and looked back toward the porch. The dog watched him paddle into the lake. He was a good dog, and David wished he could bring him along.

The lake was flat calm, all the previous night's wind spent. Sound traveled a long way on such a night, but the only thing David heard was his paddle breaking the water's surface and occasionally scraping the side of the boat. The moon was just coming up behind him. The passing of a day had lopped a corner off it, but it still cast plenty of light and made a pretty white stripe across the water. Ahead of him, the bald cypress left the shore and marched into the shallow water. David paddled on until the open lake gave way to a labyrinth of sloughs and channels.

He passed under a bough from which hung an old boot. "Trotline," he whispered.

David paddled to the cypress and felt around its sinewed trunk until he found a slimy line under the water. He cut the line, then clenched the knife between his teeth and pulled. The first snood came up with a fair-size channel catfish. The fish had been on the line too long and was in a sorry condition, but at least it was alive. He continued pulling the boat along the trotline and brought up two more catfish, both dead. He cut them loose and tossed them in the water. A few empty snoods later, he was at another cypress, from which he cut the other end of the line. The line lay in a tangle in the bottom of the boat, and the catfish flopped half-heartedly at his feet.

David paddled along in the shadows. The trees became thicker, and the water was so shallow in places that his oar hit the bottom. When the first solid ground presented itself, David stepped out of the boat and pulled it ashore. He killed and cleaned the catfish and wrapped it in the paper he had saved from the ham. Then he lay down in the boat and fell asleep.

Chapter Six

The summer when David was twelve years old, he found a book about the Caddo Indians in the library on Texas Avenue in Shreveport. He read from it to Gramps during the drive home, describing the dome-shaped grass huts the Caddo constructed and the tools and weapons they used. At one point, David opined that the Caddo Indians were "simple, primitive people."

"Why don't we build a Caddo house?" Gramps said.

"Think we could?"

"You said they were simple."

"The people, not the huts." David was sorry the minute he heard the words come out of his mouth.

"No difference in meaning," Gramps said.

Using only axes and knives, which were the closest they had to the tools used by the Caddo builders, David and his grandfather hacked down pine saplings and stripped them of their branches. They spent many days of trial and error assembling the long poles into a framework for the hut. Gramps finally agreed to use leather straps to tie the poles at the top because they could find no grass or bark or reeds strong enough to hold them. They wove river cane between the poles to hold them in place and support the grass thatch.

By the time they got to chopping and bundling sheaves of switchgrass, then tediously fastening them to the hut's frame, David had grown weary of hut building. He begged Gramps for time off to play before summer ended and he had to go back to his studies. Gramps insisted they finish the project, even if it took the rest of the summer. Which it did. By late August, David and his grandfather had sweated their way through building an off-kilter but waterproof Caddo hut in which they could both stand upright.

The hut became David's home away from home that fall and winter. He decorated the interior with his arrowhead collection and wheedled some old blankets from his mother to lounge on. He even dug a firepit in the center, as the Caddo had done. He and Huck spent many winter evenings in the hut, warm and cozy beside a dancing fire that threw their shadows onto the grass wall.

A spring storm knocked the hut whopper-jawed, and Gramps told David not to go inside anymore. Later that year, another storm flattened it altogether.

By the time David had been on Caddo Lake a fortnight, he had found a permanent campsite on which he was building a squatty Caddo hut. He dug a firepit deep in the loamy soil to keep the flames from threatening the grass thatch overhead, and he lined the pit with rocks to catch and radiate the heat.

Every afternoon, David went out in the pirogue, paddling aimlessly amid fiery red and yellow foliage that, at evening light, looked as if the entire forest had been set ablaze. From time to time, he came across signs of human activity but none of the humans themselves.

In one place, an abandoned houseboat listed with half its deck underwater. Inside, David found some fishing line and hooks, a rusted tin cup, and a cast-iron pot, nasty with old grease. In another place, a dilapidated duck blind hung precariously between two dead cypress. David climbed the makeshift ladder of boards nailed to one of the tree trunks but found nothing of use in the blind.

A wood stork started hanging around camp, and David named him Old Gourd because of his cobbed head. David didn't know if Old Gourd hung around because he had taken a shine to the catfish offal David threw his way, or if the old bird had been ostracized by a colony of storks that lived in a nearby myrtle. Either way, David was glad to have the company, even if he was a bird.

David marked each day's passing with a notch on one of the hut's poles. On the first day of November, he scratched an "N" beside the cut. The white man had died on October 18, a Saturday. By the time November rolled around, David's memory had rendered all the messy, troubling details of that day into four impartial words, "The White Man Died." Like a headline in the *Shreveport Journal*. The story under the headline—how David made it home again—had not been written. Nor did David seem to be any closer to writing it.

Days passed—another month's worth—and David scratched a "D" beside the notch for December. He sat back on his heels and studied the notches marching down the pole. Whereas they had been marching away from a day—The Day the White Man Died—they now marched toward a different day—December 20. His birthday.

David was to have received his own deer rifle for his eighteenth birthday. A rite of passage. He had pored over the Sears and Roebuck catalogue for months, comparing models, and finally settled on a Winchester 94. As far as David knew, the rifle had been ordered as soon as he made his choice—his parents weren't prone to procrastinate—giving Gramps the sad chore of picking the gun up at the Shreveport depot after David disappeared.

On the heels of David's birthday came Christmas Day. At Christmastime, David's mother decorated every room with pine boughs and bundles of herbs, filling the house with the fragrance of holiday cheer. Daddy and Gramps strung lanterns from the corners of the house to the trees, and from tree to tree. Every night of the week before Christmas, scores of little oil lamps lighted the entire yard.

On Christmas eves past, all their neighbors gathered at the Walker home for a potluck supper, which they ate on wooden tables in the brightly lit yard. Their friends brought hams, fried fish and fried chicken, tubs of spicy red crawfish boiled with corn and potatoes, and pots of steaming vegetables that had been put up the summer before. They brought so many pies and puddings, cakes and breads, that the sweets had a table all to themselves.

David's mother had a gramophone she set in the window to play Christmas songs, and David always manned the machine. He loved turning the tiny crank—like a toy compared to a motorcar's. He lowered the sharp needle onto the spinning disc carefully. One wrong move and the recording would be ruined. The instant the needle settled into a groove, music bloomed from the gramophone's big horn and spilled into the yard, magically released from its dark prison like a princess in a fairy tale. Everyone danced. Stomping, whirling play that left the grown-ups laughing and panting.

But David's family would be too sorrowful to decorate this year. Too sad to host a potluck supper and make merry. By now they would have searched for him long enough to find Huck. David imagined Gramps standing over the dog's rotting corpse, hoping he would not see his grandson's body hanging from a nearby tree. David's only consolation was that Gramps would not face the sight he surely feared the most.

Thinking about his birthday and Christmas churned emotions that tossed David back and forth like waves. Had he done the right thing? No, he had not. But had he at least chosen the best course afterward? Should he have gone straight home, confessed, and let his family help him? Or had he spared them by not doing so? He did not know. Back and forth he went between waves of regret and reasoning and indecision.

David was beginning to believe he might never know what he should have done or what he should do now, despite the Bible's claim that the wisdom of the prudent was to understand his way. He was tired of vacillating. Sick of agonizing to no good end. He stopped staring at the notched pole, got up, and walked outside. He looked up, beyond the tops of the bald cypress, into a blue winter sky.

"I don't know what to do," David called in a loud voice.

Old Gourd tossed his head and clattered his long bill.

David opened his mouth to scream at the stork. To scream at God. But instead of yelling, he choked on his own spittle. He bent over, coughing and sputtering. When he had finally cleared his throat, he straightened up.

"I don't know what to do," he said again, quietly this time.

He paced back and forth across his campsite, repeating the phrase. The Bible was full of stories about God speaking to all kinds of people in all kinds of ways. One time, God even loosed a donkey's tongue to rebuke a wayward prophet.

David stopped in front of Old Gourd. "You got anything to say?"

The stork tossed his head and flapped his wings mightily. He lifted from his perch, and David watched him glide away among the trees.

David truly believed God was all around him and even in him. Like air. The Apostle Paul had written, "In him we live and move and have our being." Words David had loved since he was a young boy.

He sucked in a long, deep breath and exhaled slowly. "I don't understand," he said aloud. "I don't understand how this happened or why it happened. But you understand everything. You know all about everything and everybody, and you even know the future." He stopped and waited, listening to his own breath. In and out. In and out.

"I can't carry this burden anymore. It's too much for me. It's too heavy and so big I can't see the edges of it. So I'm gonna lay it down. Right here. Right now. Until you show me how to pick it up again." He waited quietly to see if anything would happen. When it did not, he went back inside his hut.

He made no more notches on the pole after that.

Caddo Lake settled into winter. The bald cypress shed their needles, leaving only the Spanish moss that hung from their branches like great hoary beards. The ancient gray trees towered around David, as lifeless and grand as columns in a cathedral. Sometimes he stopped paddling and laid the oar across his knees. He sat as quietly as he could and tried to hear something besides the calls of coots and egrets and herons, but he never heard anything other than his own breathing.

Winter deepened, and the lotus and lilies rotted and disappeared below water that had gone as black as onyx, as shiny smooth as marble. David dipped the paddle, and the pirogue slid along slowly as if through mercury.

Yet even in the dead of winter, the swamp yielded bountifully. Catfish, perch, and crawfish; rabbits, turkeys, and squirrels; wild sweet potatoes, onions, and garlic were abundant. David harvested persimmons and dried them on a rack he fashioned in the top of his hut. He collected acorns and pecans. He used hickory nuts to flavor the meat and fish he cooked over smoldering embers.

A family of beavers captured David's interest. Their dam had formed a pond from which David caught crappie, and he watched the beavers for hours while bank fishing with a cane pole. The mama and daddy grew used to David and stopped slapping their tails to signal their kits to head for the lodge when he came around.

One morning, David paddled the pirogue to his trotline and retrieved two small catfish. Back at camp, he cleaned them and gave Old Gourd his portion. Then he wrapped the fish around wild onion and garlic and drove whittled spits through the tough skin. He went into the hut and built up the fire.

David sat cross-legged, listening to the sizzle and smelling the char come on the tough skin. He absently combed through his hair with the fingers of his free hand. It was a habit he had taken to as his hair grew longer than it had ever been before. The sprouts on his chin and cheeks, though sparse, were getting long enough to tug and twist when he wasn't fiddling with his hair.

Suddenly, without any warning at all, he had a vision of a future David with a thick, heavy beard and matted, wild hair, sitting at the same fire cooking the same meal, and he knew he had to get himself moving again.

Chapter Seven

1914

David paddled into Texas on Big Cypress Bayou sometime in February, by his estimation. The bayou turned every which way through the cypress brakes until the channel finally settled down and carried him into open country. All the trees had been cleared, their stumps bristling in fields that once had been forest. The pirogue glided along the sluggish water, and David was sheltered from view between canebrakes, grasses, and useless scrub oaks that had escaped the saw.

Big Cypress Bayou entered Jefferson, Texas, eventually. David had traced the waterway on Gramps's maps many times, and he remembered seeing smaller towns along it, east of Jefferson, but he did not remember where they were. He wasn't ready to face town people just yet.

He put in at a dense canebrake and pulled the boat deep into the thicket. He shouldered his rifle, haversack, and canteen and took off on foot across a field stubbled with flat-topped pine stumps. In the distance he saw two men and a mule, and two young boys playing nearby. They were not white, so David continued toward them and saw that the mule was harnessed to one of the stumps. When he was within earshot, they still had not seen him, so he put down his gear and sat on a stump to watch.

The older man clucked and coaxed the mule. "Heh! Gee up. Come on, now." The animal leaned into the collar, but the stump did not budge.

The younger man yelled angrily, "Pull! Damn ya!" He picked up a rock and threw it hard, with fast ball accuracy, at the mule's rump. The animal bawled and kicked, threatening to tangle its hind legs in the traces.

The young man was going for another rock when his father—surely, he was the father—hollered, "Sherman!" He hurried to the son, caught his hand, and spoke to him. David couldn't hear them, but he could imagine what was said. The son dropped the rock and hung his head.

David realized the young boys had seen him, as had a hound dog he had not noticed before. The dog tore across the field toward him. David had never seen an animal run so fast. Lightning fast. He stood and braced himself, ready to push the animal off when it lunged. But the hound stopped short. It sat and looked at David with worried eyes.

David had never seen such a dog in the flesh, only in books about old English breeds, sight hounds whose names he could not recall. The dog was not large, weighing maybe forty or fifty pounds. His slick coat was brindled where it was not white. He was long in the legs, thin in the flank, and deep in the chest, and his delicate head was disproportionately small. The dog's neck arched in a noble line, and he was as out of place among these farmers as an aristocrat among peasants. His long ears flopped upright when he tilted his head back, and his eyes were bright and intelligent.

David sat down again and dug in his haversack for a piece of dried rabbit, which he offered with outstretched hand. "Friends?"

The hound slinked forward and stretched his neck until he could snatch the meat. Then he took off.

They were all looking at David now. He stood, shouldered his gear, and raised a hand. "Can y'all use an extra hand?" he called.

The father removed his worn and faded hat and rubbed his shaved head. He looked fierce and very strong, with the muscular build of a prizefighter. But he smiled at David.

"Reckon so. Can you handle a shovel?"

"Sure," David said, looking into the hole they had dug around the stump. "Looks like y'all are gonna have to dig to China to free those roots." He smiled and looked up into their blank faces.

"Wha'chu say?" growled the young man. The violent one.

"What?"

"Wha'chu mean? Dig to China?"

David realized they had never heard of China and any attempt to explain would only mock their ignorance. He shrugged and forced a laugh, "I dunno what it means. I just heard it all my life."

The father settled his hat to his head. "Well, it's a right funny sayin'." He handed David a shovel. "I'll unhitch the mule. You start diggin' on the other side, and Sherm, you git the axe after them roots some more."

David and the father dug, and Sherman hacked with the axe. The stump jerked every time the blade broke through a root.

"What will you do with the stump after you get it out?" David asked.

"We gots to let it dry out good. Then burn it."

The whack, whack, thump of the axe stopped, and Sherman climbed out of the hole.

"Papa, can he spell me?"

"You mind?" asked the father.

"No. Happy to."

David accepted the axe, and Sherman met his eye impassively. David looked into the hole at the perfectly cut roots. Sherman had not wasted a swing; every single cut had landed in the chink of the one before it.

David planted his feet, heaved back the long handle, and swung the heavy head in an arc. The blade landed on a root but bounced off without making a cut. He looked up in time to see Sherman glance at his father, who had stopped digging and was leaning on his shovel, watching. David widened his stance and took another swing. This one landed in the dirt, near the root.

Sherman pointed, slapped his knee, and guffawed. The younger boys came over to see what was funny.

"Dang, son," said the father. "Ain't you never swung a axe?"

"No sir."

"Well, I'll be."

"He cain't even hit the root, Papa!" hollered Sherman. Loudly. The boys giggled.

"That's enough," said the father.

"Gimme it," Sherman said, "or we be here the whole damn day."

"Go on now, son," the father said to David. "It's all right. They's plenty a diggin' to do."

David handed Sherman the axe, looking him in the eye. *How about we see how you handle that rifle?* David thought. *I bet you couldn't hit the side of a barn.* Of course, the last thing David wanted to do was hand a gun to this guy. Fury simmered in Sherman's eyes, fiery as magma.

They worked all afternoon, and the younger boys played. At one point, David straightened his back, wiped his sweating head, and looked across the field. There were hundreds more stumps like this one. Finally, the poor mule dragged the rootless mass out of the hole. The gray-muzzled animal dropped its head at the end of the ordeal.

They untied the ropes around the stump, and David gathered his things.

"Come on up to the house for supper," the father said. "You earned it."

"Thank you. If you have plenty."

The father clapped David on the shoulder and stuck out his hand. "Sherman Tatum. Folks call me Big Sherman." David shook the man's hand and glanced at the son.

"I ain't Little Sherman," he said.

"The two young'uns there is Zachary and Luke," said Big Sherman.

They looked at David expectantly.

"I'm Tom," David said. If they had asked for a last name, he would've said Sawyer.

"You talk funny," said Luke, the younger of the two, a tiny boy whom David judged to be six or seven.

"He talks like a white man," said Sherman.

After a pause, David said, "Well, you can see I ain't white."

Big Sherman laughed. "I reckon you's dark enough. Come on, boys. Mama's waitin' on us."

The house and small barn were unpainted and badly weathered. The family appeared to be barely scratching out a living from the hard-packed earth, practically with their bare hands. David thought about how ungrudgingly Caddo Lake had supplied him, even in winter, and he wished he could load the Tatums into the pirogue and take them to his camp, where life was easy. "Rest yourselves," he would say. "Let's live among the cypress and the myrtle and leave the thorns and thistles behind."

A petite woman in a faded dress, her head wrapped in a red bandanna, appeared in the doorway when they reached the yard.

"Gots company for supper, Audie," called Big Sherman.

"Pleased to meet you," David said.

Audie looked at David and then at the rifle. She said nothing.

"This here's Tom," said Big Sherman. "He helped us dig out a stump. Took all afternoon."

"Much obliged," Audie said.

"Well, alrighty then," said Big Sherman. "I's gonna tend to this old fella." He turned and led the mule toward the barn. The two young boys pushed past their mother into the cabin.

"Sherman, y'all wait out here for your papa," Audie said.

"Yes'm," said Sherman.

Audie went inside and closed the door. David and Sherman stood in the yard. Not speaking. Not looking at each other. Dusk was coming on, and without the distraction of activity, David felt the chill. He imagined Sherman was even colder, in his threadbare jacket, though neither of them would have admitted it. The hound came trotting from the field, and the chickens scratching in the yard scattered. The dog wriggled under the low porch.

Big Sherman came from the barn. "Reckon we better lay off them stumps," he told his son. "Cain't affords to wear the old boy out before we git the crop in the ground."

"We need us a new mule," said Sherman.

Big Sherman put his hand on his son's shoulder and said, "Let's git on inside. Mama's waitin'."

Chapter Eight

David followed Big Sherman into the cabin and stood awkwardly inside the doorway, letting his eyes adjust to the dim light. His Caddo hut had been dark too, when the fire was low, but its close, thatched walls made it as cozy as an animal's den. By comparison, this one-room cabin was only dreary. Old newsprint had been pasted to the boards like wallpaper. Even so, David saw the evening light coming through in many places. There was one glassless window with its shutter closed against winter.

A large blanket hung from the rafters, forming a partition beyond which David glimpsed an iron bed. A rolled pallet lay under the blanket's lower edge. To David's left were a fireplace and a wooden rocking chair, and to his right a table and a sideboard. The sideboard was very old and finely made, with scrollwork and claw feet. Its wood was black and shiny in the low light.

"Sit yourselves down," Audie said.

A round of yellow cornbread cooled on a plate in the center of the table. The rest of supper was in a pot hanging on an iron arm in the fireplace. Audie used a bunched-up rag to lift the lid, then she spooned red beans into enamel bowls while the menfolk patiently waited and watched.

David fought the urge to help, as he would have helped his mother, but he could see it was not their way. He would've offended them by offering to carry bowls back and forth, as if Audie were too slow. So he sat and waited with the rest of them. After Audie had filled her own bowl, she took a battered pan from beside the hearth, ladled beans into it, and set it on the mantle to cool.

"For the dog," said Big Sherman when he saw David watching Audie. "I reckon we's just happy Whip don't eat first."

"Hush now," said Audie. "Mr. Tom, would you ask a blessin'?"

"Yes ma'am."

They all bowed their heads, and the two little boys carefully folded their hands between their chins and their bowls of beans.

David recited his family's mealtime prayer, "Lord, thank you for this food. Bless it and the hands that prepared it, in Jesus's name. Amen."

"Amen," the Tatums echoed in unison.

Big Sherman picked up the plate of cornbread and handed it to David. There were no knives on the table, so David tore off a piece. The bread was dense cornpone—made with hot water rather than buttermilk—such as he had seen the poorest families bring to Sunday dinner on the grounds. Usually, they were families whose food he avoided. But on this night, Audie Tatum's cornpone looked and smelled plenty appetizing. He took less than he wanted, but he hoped not more than his share, and passed the plate back to Big Sherman. The plate made the trip around the table, last of all to Audie. After she took a piece, they all began eating.

"Those chickens sure took off when Whip came around," David said.

"Him and Audie been round and round about them hens," said Big Sherman. "I thought she was gonna wring his neck and fry him up for supper before it was all said and done."

"He's a fine dog," said David.

"He belongs to Mama," said Sherman, as if David were trying to claim the hound.

"I can see that."

"He's a Whipper dog," said Big Sherman. "That's what they called them dogs because they's fast as a whip. White folks used to raise them fancy dogs on a cotton plantation round here. Plantation long gone, but we think he come from that stock."

"He just showed up?"

"Yes sir, couple a year ago. He was just a pup, but we never seen a mama dog or any other pups. Just him."

"Mama say Whipper was the white people's name," said Luke. "That's why them dogs is called by that name."

"Well now, son," said Big Sherman, leaning forward over his bowl. "That there's a point a contention betwixt me and your mama. I say the name come from the dog bein' fast."

Luke looked at his mother.

"Your papa's most always right," Audie said.

"Listen to your mama now, son."

Audie went on, "It don't matter if'n he be wrong on this one occasion. Besides, Papa know very well that the man that owned the plantation was called by the name Whipper. Ever'body round here know that."

"Whippet," David said aloud. He had been racking his brain for the name of the English sight hounds. The dog was a Whippet.

"No. Whipper," corrected Big Sherman.

"Yes sir," said David.

"Mr. Tom, where is your home?" asked Audie.

"Missouri."

"Don't reckon we know anybody from over that way," she said. "What your business here?"

"Wiley College in Marshall. I want to get a job there and take some classes."

Audie smiled thinly, and Sherman glared at him.

David was suddenly embarrassed. Here the Tatums were, most likely illiterate and barely getting by on red beans and cornpone, and he was going on about taking college classes. Mama would not have been happy.

"Be careful what you say, David," she once told him. "Not having things doesn't make a person poor, so don't make them feel as if it does. The Lord himself didn't own a pot to pee in or a window to throw it out of, and he's the king of all creation."

"Miss Audie," David said. "This is the best meal I've had in a long, long time, since I ate my mama's cooking. I sure appreciate you giving me a place at your table."

"You's welcome to stay the night," said Big Sherman. "You can bed down there beside the fire."

"Thank you. It's pretty cold out there."

"Very well, then," said Audie. She rose and cleared away the empty bowls.

David lay awake after the family had gone to sleep. Their breathing and snoring filled the cabin, making it less forlorn. The wood floor was hard, and cold air seeped between the planks and through the thin blanket Audie had given him to wrap himself in. David unrolled his jacket, which he had used as a pillow, and put it on. He could not help wishing for his cozy thatched grass bed at Caddo, next to the fire pit that radiated heat all night.

The Whippet hound lay a few feet away in front of the cabin door, his head resting on his front paws. David was surprised when they let the dog in for the night, but Audie seemed to prize him. Whip watched David wrestle with his jacket and the blanket, and he continued watching after David became still again. They looked at each other for a long time, and then David lifted the blanket, as he had lifted his blanket at home many times to invite Huck to snuggle on cold nights.

The dog raised his head.

David clucked softly.

The dog rose and took a step forward, his head low.

"Here, boy," David whispered.

That was all the encouragement Whip needed. He ducked under the blanket, made three quick turns and curled up against David's stomach. David was so happy for a warm companion that he didn't mind when, deep in the night, Whip dreamed of running and punched David with his quick and powerful hind legs.

The next morning, David and Whip slipped out before daybreak to shoot some game for the family. They walked a long way to reach woods that had not been cut down, but they were rewarded with plentiful squirrels. Whip stole the first kill. He ran and hid to eat it but was back in time to get the offal of the next one. By late morning, David had shot and cleaned a mess of squirrels for the family. He hiked back to the house, and Whip trailed behind, tail low, full as a tick. As soon as they reached the dirt yard, the dog found a sunny spot beside the barn to sleep it off.

David stood in the front yard, uncomfortable approaching the house if Audie was alone. "Hello!" he called.

Big Sherman opened the door. "We thought you was gone."

David held up the squirrels. "I shot these for you."

Audie appeared beside Big Sherman in the doorway.

"Do you like squirrel?" David asked.

"Course we do," Audie said. She squeezed around her husband and took the game. "You best come on inside."

"Leave that long gun by the door," Big Sherman said. He stood aside for David to enter. David propped the .22 inside the doorway, and Big Sherman closed the door behind him. Audie laid the squirrels on the table.

"Where are the boys?" David asked.

Audie picked up a paper from the sideboard and handed it to David.

"Is it you?" Big Sherman demanded.

The corners of the paper were notched, as if it had been torn from a wall it was tacked to. "MISSING" was printed in large letters across the top. Beneath that was a likeness of David. He recognized it from a photograph his mother had taken the summer before. His name was printed below the likeness.

David sat down, his haversack and canteen still slung across his chest. Under his name the paper bore instructions about who to contact with information. David recognized the name and address as Gramps's lawyer in Shreveport. He had just come out of hiding yesterday, and already these people—people who lived in another state and could not even read—knew who he was.

"Where did you get this?"

"You didn't answer my question. Is it you?"

"Course it's him," said Audie. To David she said, "I remembered this paper the minute I laid eyes on you. Big Sherman went over to the church this mornin' and took it off the wall. We been prayin' for you at the church ever' week, David Walker, cause a that paper. Pastor say somebody is lookin' mighty hard for you to send such a paper as that ever'where. It say you's missin'. Right there." She pointed to the word.

Big Sherman's hand came down firmly on his shoulder. "Son, what did you do?"

There were railroad tracks north of the farm. David had crossed them on the way from Big Cypress Bayou. He could walk north and follow the tracks until he found an opportunity to jump a train and make his way to Kansas City or Chicago. He had seen men jump trains in Shreveport. He would figure out how to do it, and he would get out of the South altogether.

"I have to go," David said.

Big Sherman's heavy hand remained on David's shoulder. "I keep thinkin' about our boy Sherman," he said. "If'n he run into trouble, would he find a friendly face?"

David reached into his pocket and took out two hundred dollars he had separated from the banknotes in his boot. He could not think of a better use for the Klansman's money than helping a poor black farmer. He placed the banknotes on the table and said, "For a new mule. I hope it's enough."

Big Sherman pulled up a chair and sat in front of David, knee to knee. "They was a young fella named Pete lived near here," he said. "Sherman and him was friends. Pete was a good boy. He was a real good boy, always lookin' to help out. He done some work from time to time for a white fambly had a farm betwixt here and Marshall. About a year ago, the fambly's youngest girl turned up with child. Told her daddy it was Pete had gone and forced hisself on her, and she been too scared to confess it."

"No," David said. He did not want to hear this story.

"A bunch of 'em dragged poor ol' Pete into Marshall and hung him from a tree next to the post office. Sheriff stood there a watchin'. Didn't lift a finger to stop 'em. They say the sheriff run with the Klan at night. Reckon it's so."

David did not want to picture the mob or the frightened boy yanked to death at the end of a rope slung over a limb. He surely did not want to think about the sheriff approving it. No trial. No justice. No mercy. He thought about the men who rode the trains, men made hard for want of mercy.

"That night the Klan burned out Pete's fambly, the house and ever'thin' in it. The barn. They shot the mule."

David wasn't listening anymore. He thought about the railroad men who patrolled the cars, looking for tramps. They carried wooden batons. The cruelest among them carried lengths of iron pipe.

"Sherman took it hard. Real hard. He ain't been the same since."

"I can't tell you what happened," David said. "For your own good."

"Turned out the girl had her a sweetheart in town, a white boy, and the baby was his all along." Big Sherman looked at Audie. "We sure could use a extra hand around here, Mama. Reckon we could work somethin' out?"

"If'n you think it best."

"Ain't nobody around here much, 'cept us."

Audie nodded, and Big Sherman turned back to David. "Reckon you could use to stay on with us for a while? We can feed you and give you a place to sleep."

"Maybe for a few days. Until I figure out what to do."

"Reckon you best put that paper away," Big Sherman said. "Now about this money—"

"Please keep it. Let it do a little bit of good in a whole world of wickedness."

Chapter Nine

Audie shaved David's face and scalp. The Tatums did not own a mirror for David to examine himself, but Audie said he looked swept clean.

Big Sherman accepted the two hundred dollars David offered and bought a gigantic, snow-white mule. David thought Big Sherman would've been surprised—frightened?—to learn that a Klansman had funded his purchase. "I ain't ever seen such a mule," Big Sherman said. "He pull a load like he don't even notice it."

The Tatums did not name mules, but David named the new white mule Pegasus, and he told Zach and Luke about the winged horse of Greek mythology. David renamed the hero who captured the mythical horse Zacharias because he thought the Tatum's shy middle son could use a boost in confidence. Zachary beamed, and even Sherman, leaning against the sideboard with his arms folded, smiled a little.

David told them that Zacharias rode the flying horse to the top of Mount Olympus, where the Greek gods lived, to slay a fire-breathing monster. The boys listened, spellbound by David's description of a monster with two heads, one a lion and the other a goat. David couldn't remember how the fable went, so he improvised. He had the lion breathing fire and the goat spitting lightning. He rolled Medusa into his tale, telling the boys the monster's gaze turned folks to stone and the lion's mane was made of snakes.

"What's a mane?" Luke interrupted. "Preacher talk about lions, but he ain't never said nothing about manes."

Before David could answer, Zach asked, "They's other gods besides the Lord?"

"No sir!" Audie snapped. "They ain't no other gods. Just forgit that part. I reckon that's enough for one day."

Big Sherman said the white mule would be called Big Peg and Zachary would be the first to ride him, which David could tell pleased the boy to no end. David asked Big Sherman for the old mule, mainly to save him from whatever terrible fate awaited farm animals who'd outlived their usefulness.

"You know anythin' about mules?" Big Sherman asked.

"No sir, but I can learn. I can use him to bring venison back from the woods. I've seen plenty of deer out there."

"Alrighty then," Big Sherman said. "He's yours."

David named the mule Methuselah, whom the family knew was the oldest man recorded in the Bible.

The first farm chore David was given was chopping firewood. He was clumsy with the long-handled axe, even after Big Sherman demonstrated how to handle it. The tool seemed to animate in David's hands, as if it had gone insane. The heavy blade slung itself all over the place, and the family kept their distance when he was at the woodpile.

David's next assignment was harnessing Big Peg to the wagon. The mule's complicated harness confused David, and the leather straps twisted themselves into hopeless tangles that could only be sorted out by a Tatum. Even little Luke could make sense of them, but it was quiet Zachary who showed David the sequence that kept the traces straight. After David harnessed the mule, Big Sherman drove to town and came home with a wagonload of supplies, including a brown felt hat for David.

"Now you look like a farmer," Big Sherman said.

David did not feel like a farmer. He felt as if he stuck out like a sore thumb. He seemed to go about everything contrary to the Tatums. He spoke differently. He ate differently. He laughed at things they did not find funny and he failed to see the humor in things they did. The only boost to his confidence during his first weeks on the farm was his aim with his rifle. He went hunting every morning, and he always brought back something.

David took Methuselah to the woods and found the old mule tolerated the sound of the .22. The gun was too light for hunting deer, but David reasoned he was shooting well enough to kill a small white tail if he had a clean head shot.

One morning, a little doe wandered into a clearing where David sat with his back against a pine tree. David raised his rifle slowly and waited while she foraged ever closer. When she was less than a dozen yards away, he shot her between the eyes. She dropped instantly. David tied a length of rope around the deer's neck, threw the other end over a branch, and heaved the carcass off the ground.

He field-dressed her, then walked Methuselah under the branch and laid the deer across the mule's back.

David and the Tatums ate like royalty on the tender venison. Big Sherman traded some of the meat to a neighbor who had a dairy cow, and Audie made two pans of buttermilk cornbread as good as any David had ever eaten. They ate the bread steaming hot and slathered with fresh butter.

"You's good luck," Big Sherman told David while they lazed around the cabin after supper.

"No sir. I ain't lucky," David said.

Audie always knew when it was Sunday, even though farm time, like swamp time, did not march to clocks or calendars. David no longer bothered keeping up with what day it was, but he wondered how Audie managed it. "She gots a way," Big Sherman said.

One evening David saw Audie pick something from a chipped teacup on the sideboard and deposit it in another similar cup. When she wasn't around, he examined the cups and found seven dried peas divided between them. He watched her after that and learned that when one cup was empty and the other was full, off the Tatums went to the church house.

On Saturday afternoons, Audie commanded the men and boys out of their clothes and into blankets. They took turns bathing in a large washtub filled with water heated in the fireplace. The fire was stoked to blazing to keep everyone warm, especially the boys. David was the last to bathe, and by the time his turn rolled around the water was as thick as pot liquor. Audie scrubbed their clothes on a washboard on the porch and hung them to dry from the rafters inside.

On Sunday mornings, the Tatums put on their clean clothes and left the farm for the weekly church service. David did not attend, which troubled the younger boys.

"Why don't he come?" Luke asked.

"That his business. You young'uns leave him be," Audie said.

"Ain't he saved?"

"That be his business too," Big Sherman said. He playfully swatted the boys on the behinds. "You two go on now and quit wartin' ever'body."

Next Luke announced that he and Zach would stay home from church with David.

"No sir," Audie said, and that was that.

The constant demands of the Tatum farm pulled David's life out of his head, except on Sunday mornings when, idle and alone, he daydreamed as he had at Lake Caddo. For those few hours, David was himself again. When time neared for the family to return, he retreated to the barn to tend the mules and steal a few more minutes by himself.

Peg and Methuselah had fallen in love with each other. The animals loved David too, and they made an impressive variety of honks and snorts and bellows whenever he approached. When David went to the woods to hunt, he gathered into his haversack a few handfuls of whatever caught Methuselah's fancy and gave it to Peg.

Audie sewed for David a thin mattress of hay-stuffed ticking. Every night, he unrolled it near the hearth and was asleep as soon as he was prostrate. He often woke up before anyone else and lay in the darkness with Whip curled close against his side. In the respite of those quiet mornings, David allowed his thoughts to dwell on his own family.

David had a recurring dream that first appeared during his time on the Tatum farm. He dreamt it several times while there, and many more times in the years after. The dream always had the same beginning, middle, and end, like a book that never changes no matter how many times it's read.

The dream was about tornados.

When David was a boy, a tornado had come through, barely missing his family's home and their general store. The twister traveled all the way from Shreveport to Texarkana, skipping along and wreaking havoc wherever it touched the earth. One town in particular, Gilliam, was leveled. Only two houses remained, and many people were injured or killed.

The spring storm hit around suppertime, which may have accounted for so many folks being caught unaware in their homes. It knocked out the telegraph wires and washed out the railroad tracks. Reports of the disaster spread by word-of-mouth from town to town, and the next morning someone brought the news to the Walker's store. David's father and Gramps loaded provisions onto the back of the Mack Junior, then swung by the house to pick up David and his mother.

The trip was very exciting because David got to ride with Gramps in the back of the truck. The morning was bright and warm—it was May—and he and Gramps sat behind the cab on stacks of boxed goods. The wind roared in their faces as David's father barreled down the dirt road. Twice along the way, they passed the twister's path. Neat swaths crossed the road and bent into the woods as if a drunken giant had run a plow through the forest, uprooting the pines and leaving bare earth.

David's excitement collapsed when they reached Gilliam. For once, his imagination fell short of reality. He had imagined an orderly catastrophe, in which they repaired the damaged homes and filled them with supplies from the Mack Junior. He imagined a convivial gathering, like Sunday dinner-on-the-grounds.

Instead, they came around a curve into a battlefield. Debris from inside the homes draped the tattered pine boughs, as if each house had been turned inside out and its contents blown skyward like tufts from a dandelion. A naked man, torn and limp as a rag doll, was caught in a web of branches overhead. Another pine held a dog in similar condition. A dismembered leg hung by a shoe that was still on the foot, wedged in a fork of two branches. David was gaping at the trees when they drove into the clearing where the town had been.

"My God," Gramps said.

The houses were not damaged. They were shredded.

People had laid the dead in a row in the shade of the pine trees. The people who were hurt—some badly—but still alive were lying or sitting in another shaded area away from the dead. Survivors picked through the rubble, but most of them seemed too dazed to know what they were looking for.

David and his family worked until dark, doing whatever they could to help. They rode home that night in exhausted silence. They returned to Gilliam the next day, and the day after that. Then the trains started running again, bringing relief from the abundant resources of Shreveport, and David's family returned to their lives.

Afterward, Gramps showed David a book he had about the war. "I was gonna wait 'til you were older to show you this, but I reckon it's time since you've seen so much already."

David turned page after page of photographs that told the story of war. Soldiers from each side stood proudly beside their respective flags. Officers in Union blue sat or stood in front of white tents, while others in Confederate gray stood in front of identical tents. There were photographs of battlefields filled with men on horses and men on foot. There were pictures of cannons, the men standing by them ready to light the fuses. There were photographs of the dead too. One showed scores of dead soldiers laid in rows.

"Just like we saw in Gilliam," David said.

"Except these were soldiers, and they knew they might die. The Gilliam folks were sitting down to supper. They didn't expect anything bad to happen."

"It's not right," David said.

"No sir. It is not."

In David's tornado dream, he was back in Louisiana, except the land looked like East Texas. The sky was wide, and everywhere he looked tornados writhed beneath black clouds that hung low over stump-studded fields. The twisters skipped every which way, raising great clouds of dirt.

The storms converged on the Walker home, drawn to it as if by gravity. David ran, trying to beat the storms to the house and take his family to safety, but his feet tangled with each other, and he fell again and again. There was too much ground to cover, and the tornados raced ahead of him.

Then, suddenly, David was standing amid the trees in the yard at home. The front door stood open, and he ran through it into the parlor and from there into the kitchen. He ran to his parents' bedroom, to Gramps's room, and to his own bedroom. All the furniture and rugs and bric-a-brac were gone. Every room was empty, and every window was wide open.

The wind roared through the house like a freight train. David darted frantically from room to room, calling his family at the top of his lungs, but the howling wind drowned out the sound of his voice. He stopped running and stood in the middle of the parlor. The wind ceased, and the house fell silent. Then the rain came. Drumming, deafening rain.

David always woke up when the rain began, and he lay very still until he could no longer feel his heart beating.

Chapter Ten

One day Audie told David, "Them boys is askin' me if you's deef."
"Why?"
"Because you ain't respondin' when they call you Tom."
Big Sherman solved the problem by giving him a new name that, to David's dismay, stuck to him like glue. This came about after a Sunday sermon about Jacob, who worked on his Uncle Laban's farm to win the hand of his daughter Rachel. Laban employed scheme after scheme to keep Jacob working for him longer than he'd agreed to. Laban did this because he believed Jacob was blessed, and as long as Jacob stayed with him, Laban was blessed too.
"You's my Jacob," Big Sherman said. "You's bringing us blessin's."
David did not want to stay on the farm for a long time. He wanted to be among people with whom he had common interests, people who listened to him and understood his ideas, as Gramps had. The Tatums were too wrapped up in their God-awful farm for such foolishness. David thought about leaving constantly, but where would he go?
One afternoon, Big Sherman took David out with him to walk the length and breadth of the farm. "My daddy bought this farm," Big Sherman said as they hiked across the fallow acres. "When he died, it was split betwixt me and my brother, Ben. Ben passed two year ago, and I bought his portion."
"What happened to him?"
"Dunno. He got sick and couldn't git well. His wife didn't have no way to keep the farm goin', so she found work in Marshall and moved her chil'ren there."
Big Sherman stopped and removed his hat. They had come to an unplowed corner of the farm where the grass, still lifeless from winter, was undisturbed.
"This here's Ben," he said, pointing to a low mound of rocks David had not seen amid the tall grass. Crumbles of dried flowers

were caught between the stones. "And this 'un over here's Daddy." Big Sherman pointed to another, similar mound.

David followed as Big Sherman led him past one unmarked grave after another, pausing beside each flower-sprinkled mound to call the name of the person buried there and their relation to him. None of them were Audie's people, except the children. Six graves belonged to little ones he and Audie had lost.

"This 'un here's Millie. Little Millie didn't live to see the mornin'. And this 'un over here's name Ben after my brother. Little Ben was about yay high," Big Sherman waved his hand a few feet above the ground, "when a fever come through. Like to killed us all."

"I'm sorry you lost them," David said.

Big Sherman, ever the father, put his hand on David's shoulder. "Reckon we gonna have ourselves a big fambly reunion on the other side," he said.

David remembered when he was a boy and he realized that all their neighbors had at least half a dozen children, armies of them who stormed his father's general store, always hoping for a bit of candy.

"Where are my brothers and sisters?" David had demanded of his mother.

"It's a miracle we have you, honey," she said, as if his parents had managed to order David from Sears and Roebuck, just in time, before they ran out of children.

"This here creek marks the property line," Big Sherman was saying. "My daddy used to bring me and Ben fishin' down here. Used to be more water back then—dunno where it all went."

Big Sherman and David stood side by side a while, looking into the meager stream. Then they settled their hats back on their heads and continued their hike, eventually coming to the field where David first happened on Big Sherman and his sons.

"Last year, this land come up for sale. Forty acre. Cheap land cause it ain't been cleared. But it's good soil." Big Sherman turned to David. "Say, where you come from that day?"

"Lake Caddo. Do you know it?"

"Heard of it. Ain't been there."

"We'll go sometime. We'll go fishing."

Big Sherman smiled. "That sounds right fine."

They walked the length of Big Sherman's second forty acres. The whole of it was riddled with stumps.

"I been in hot water with Audie ever since I spent the money we was saving toward a mule on this land. Poor old Methuselah—" Big Sherman laughed. "Dang you, Jacob, you done got me calling that mule by name."

"You can call me David out here."

"Best keep the habit. Anyways, that poor old mule give his best ever' day, but I knew they weren't no way he was gonna get a crop in the ground. He's plumb wore out."

"Methuselah seems to be doing better. I think he's put on a little weight."

"I reckon the rest done him good, but he ain't up to spring plantin'. I didn't know what I was gonna do. It was a terrible worry. Only God knows how many a night I laid awake worryin', with no answer in sight. Then here you come outta nowhere, with more'n I coulda hoped for."

"Best to figure it came from the Lord," David said. "I'm just the messenger."

"I told Audie you might be a angel."

"What'd she say?"

"Well . . . ," Big Sherman looked down. "She don't much think so."

After their walk across the farm, Big Sherman introduced David to cotton farming. The first day David spent behind the heavy turning plow, he gripped its wooden handles so hard and for so long that they rubbed the skin off his palms and fingers. By late afternoon, water-filled blisters had formed and broken. The skin peeled away, leaving spots of painful red flesh. That night, Big Sherman showed David how to coat the burning sores with axle grease, which they also applied to Peg where the collar and harness had rubbed his hide raw.

The next morning, David asked, "What about gloves?"

"Don't need 'em," Big Sherman said. He held out his palms and showed David the thick, brown calluses that padded them.

David sighed and curled his hands around the wooden handles, wincing at the pain.

Sherman and the boys followed behind the plow, breaking up the clods of dirt with rakes. The boys collected arrowheads and an occasional coin and deposited their prizes in their deep pants pockets.

During the first week of plowing, David was too tired and irritable to pay any mind to the treasures the boys had found. But he perked up the second week and told them stories about the Caddo Indians and about the hut he and Gramps had built. Zach and Luke were giggly and wild after listening to David's stories. They threw themselves against him to provoke wrestling. They preferred to roughhouse with David rather than Sherman because David let them win, as Gramps had done when he was small.

It took David and Big Peg three weeks to break up forty acres of fallow East Texas loam. By then, they both had thick calluses the color of axle grease.

"Me 'n Papa coulda done it in two weeks," Sherman said.

"That would've been fine with me," growled David.

It rained for three days after they turned the fields, which Big Sherman took as a sign the coming season would be prosperous. When the sun returned, out came another plow.

"This here's the furrin' plow," said Big Sherman.

"More plowing?" David asked.

"We's just getting started."

Big Sherman and Peg made an arrow-straight furrow with the plow to demonstrate.

"It's a furrowing plow," David said.

"Furrin' plow," Big Sherman corrected.

David said nothing more.

Big Sherman plowed two more long furrows parallel to the first one before turning the reins over to David. While David plowed, Big Sherman walked in front of Peg. He clucked and sang and occasionally raised his hands in what David inferred was overwhelming gratitude for all his blessings. Peg followed his new master, his long ears twisting, pulling the lightweight plow effortlessly and so quickly that David had to jockey the handles constantly to keep the blade from bucking out of the ground. It was mind-numbing work, but if he let his thoughts wander, the plow jumped off course.

David's parents had given him a bicycle on his thirteenth birthday, and he rode it everywhere for months, with Huck trotting behind. One afternoon, David tried to cross the creek near their home on rough gravel that had been put down for the wagons that forded there, to keep them from miring in mud. David was pedaling fast, and the bicycle's front wheel bounced crazily when it hit the rocks. He held on tight and fought the handlebars to keep from losing control. Plowing furrows was like riding that bicycle across gravel from sunup to sundown, six days a week. At the end of each day's work, David's arms trembled from the strain.

After Easter, Big Sherman put the cottonseed in the ground, which was hardly any effort at all compared with preparing the fields for it. When the planting was finished, Big Sherman cleaned the turning plow, the furrowing plow, and the planter with coal oil and put them away in the barn. David was thrilled. That night, over a supper of beans and cornbread, he said, "It sure feels good to have the cotton laid by. I'm going hunting in the morning to celebrate."

The Tatums stopped eating and looked at one another.

David looked around the table. "What? Big Sherman, you've been talking about having that cotton laid by for weeks. 'When the cotton's laid by, we can pick up work at the sawmill.' 'We can clear more stumps when the cotton's laid by.' 'Ain't no breaks 'til the cotton's laid by.'"

Big Sherman coughed and choked on his cornbread. Then all the Tatums got tickled, and the longer they howled, the funnier the joke became to them. Even David's little buddy Zach covered his mouth with his hands, over which his eyes sparkled and crinkled.

"Okay, okay," David said. "The joke's on me. Tell me, what's so funny?"

Audie wiped her eyes. "Oh Lordy, you gonna see. You gonna see real soon."

Early one morning, David and Big Sherman walked side by side down the rows, where lines of new leaves had pushed through the soil in crowded clumps.

"That planter put too many seeds in the ground," David said. "The plants are too thick. They'll choke one another out."

Big Sherman stopped walking and looked at him. "Dang, Jacob. Where you come from? Ain't you never heard a choppin' cotton?"

David had heard of it. When he had grumbled about chores, Gramps's typical answer was, "Beats chopping cotton." David had seen people with hoes working cotton fields plenty of times, but he had not had an appreciation for what they were doing out there or the length of time they were at it. He lifted his eyes and looked over acre after acre of young plants racing one another for a future. He looked at the rising sun—already hot on his face—its arc climbing higher and longer by the day. "Cotton is a labor-intensive crop," he said, quoting one of his mother's textbooks.

Big Sherman laughed and shook his head. "Lordy, Jacob, the things you come out with."

Not only did the cotton plants race one another, they raced the Tatums too. Six days a week, the entire family and David, armed with hoes, went out to the fields at daybreak to thin the young plants and chop the weeds and grass that sprang up overnight. Everyone had to bend into the hoe, but David had the disadvantage of being unusually tall. His lower back burned as if a hot brand had been put to it.

"We gots to git you a longer hoe," Audie said as she worked the row next to David.

"Before next year, for sure," called Big Sherman from the row beyond Audie.

"Not gonna be a next year," David muttered, and he kept right on hacking away.

The Tatums and David spent days upon days, from dawn until dark, chopping every unwanted thing from the fields. In the beginning, they left groupings of three or four young cotton plants. Later these were thinned to single plants spaced a couple of feet apart. Within a month of the first sprouts breaking ground, there marched across the Tatum farm an army of evenly spaced, green-leafed survivors.

"That's a fine stand," Big Sherman said. They all stood at the edge of the field admiring their handiwork and passing around water ladled from a bucket.

And still they were not finished.

Big Sherman took from the barn the last farm implement Peg would pull, the cultivator. Despite the rising midday temperatures, David found walking behind the cultivator was pleasant compared with the backbreaking hoe. The whirling mechanism uprooted weeds and widened the furrows, banking loosened dirt against the growing cotton. Peg and David completed their circuit in a few days, only to repeat it within a week or two, depending on rainfall. This they did, while the cotton plants grew taller and sturdier.

"That's enough," Big Sherman called one morning. He followed behind David and Peg as they started down a furrow. "You's gittin' into the roots."

David looked behind him and saw frayed white capillaries poking out the sides of the mounded earth. He and Peg backed out of the field, and David removed his hat and wiped his sweating head. It was early, but already the morning was hot and sultry. David estimated it was sometime in July, or maybe early August. "What now?" he asked.

Big Sherman put his hand on David's shoulder. "Now the cotton's laid by." He whistled for Peg to follow and headed to the barn.

Over the next few days, the Tatums discussed what to do with the idle weeks until time to pick the cotton. The options were pulling stumps or picking up extra cash at the sawmill in Baldwin, an hour's walk from the farm.

"We gots us a opportunity we ain't never had before," said Big Sherman. "Me 'n Sherm could do some loggin' this year. If'n Jacob stay here with Mama and the young'uns, we wouldn't have to come home ever' evenin'. Loggin' pay a lot better'n the mill."

"Ain't no reason for him to lay off workin'," said Sherman. "Why ain't he goin' with us?"

"Because somebody need to stay with Mama and the young'uns."

"They been by theirself before."

"Not durin' the night. Don't want 'em here alone at night, way things are these days."

"Papa's right," said Audie, and that was that.

The next time they were alone, David thanked Big Sherman for not pressing him to leave the farm.

"I reckon we best not be traipsin' you all over creation," Big Sherman said.

Chapter Eleven

After the men left for logging camp, Audie was dressed and out of the cabin every morning before David and the boys woke. David didn't know if she felt as awkward with him as he did with her or if she was just taking advantage of the early dawn.

When David had arrived on the farm in winter, he had thought the Tatums were too poor-minded to throw away the many dirt-filled tubs and troughs in various states of ruination that were scattered around the yard. Or to tear down a dilapidated arbor that surely would've collapsed were it not for the dead vines climbing each side and intertwined across its arch.

But as soon as the days grew warm, colorful flowers spilled from every tub and trough. The vines on the ancient arbor budded as suddenly as Aaron's rod, and soon the arbor disappeared beneath a canopy of heavy purple wisteria blossoms that perfumed the entire yard. The boys and Whip spent hot afternoons dozing in its shade to the white noise of bees buzzing overhead.

Tall sunflowers sprouted up alongside the walls of the cabin and the barn, and along the split-log fence that surrounded Audie's garden. The furry plants wove themselves between the rails, and the fence seemed to come alive with rough green leaves and dish-sized yellow blossoms.

Audie fertilized her flowers with chicken droppings and watered them every morning, lugging bucket after bucket from the well, a chore David helped with when he rose early enough. She swept the fine, khaki-colored dust of the yard daily, leaving brush strokes as elegant as an artist's.

Rabbits and squirrels were abundant, as was David's ammunition, and he hunted every day. Audie panfried the game David shot and made luscious gravy from the drippings. They had so much food that she frequently sent Zach and Luke off to one neighbor or another to share the bounty. There seemed to be plenty of everything, including time, with the Tatum men gone.

David helped Audie carry boxes of canning jars from the barn into the cabin. He looked suspiciously at the clouded, chipped glass and the discolored tin lids. His mother's canning jars had been crystal clear, and they had equally clear glass lids that fastened down with wires.

David remembered a cash-strapped family who had paid his father with food preserved in a jar such as the ones Audie had. The blackish contents inside were almost hidden by thick red wax that covered the top. "No telling what's in there," Gramps had said, holding the jar up to the light coming through the window of the general store. He handed it to David. "Go empty it in the woods for whichever of God's creatures is brave enough or hungry enough to eat it. And don't let Huck get at it."

David picked up one of the jars Audie had set on the table. "Looks like this one might have a hairline crack. Just there," he said, holding it up.

Audie snatched the jar from his hand. "Is you gonna stay un'erfoot all day? Ain't you got chores to do?"

"I thought you might need some help."

"You can help me by gittin' outta here. Now shoo." She swiped at him with her rag and ran him out the door.

On Sundays, when Audie and the boys headed across the field to church, David walked with them as far as he could without being seen. He stopped in a stand of oak trees, where he watched them join their neighbors. When the service began, David sat with his back against an oak, listening to the congregation sing.

Some days, David could hear the preacher's deep, booming voice well enough to catch snatches of the sermon. On other days, he made do with hearing the gist of the message from Audie and the boys when they met him and walked home together. After dinner, Audie, David, and the boys sometimes sang the hymns the congregation had sung that morning. None of them could carry a tune in a bucket, but the old songs made David feel good anyway.

One day Audie opened one of the sideboard's drawers to take something out, and David saw a massive, ornately embossed Bible.

"Audie, is that a Bible? Can I see it?"

She lifted the book from the drawer and placed it on the table.

"Why didn't you tell me you have a Bible? Surely you knew I can read."

"Yes sir. I knew it." She sat beside David on the bench. He opened the cover and turned to the births, marriages, and deaths.

"Are these your people?"

"No sir. They the people my granny—" Audie stopped. "My granny brought it from Virginie."

"These dates go back to the seventeen hundreds, almost to the Revolutionary War."

"If'n them young'uns find out you can read, they be all over you to read to 'em."

"I can teach *them* to read," David said.

"We cain't pay you back, and we's already indebted."

"Pay me back?"

Audie pursed her lips. "Didn't mean no offense," she said.

"I can teach you to read too, Audie," David said quietly.

She hesitated, then said, "We'll see."

In the late afternoon, Audie called the boys in from playing. David was waiting for them at the table with the big Bible open to First Samuel. Audie busied herself while David read the story of David and Goliath to the boys.

"And David said to Saul, 'Let no man's heart fail because of Goliath. Your servant will go and fight with this Philistine.' And Saul said to David, 'You are not able to go against this Philistine to fight with him, for you are only a boy, and he has been a man of war since he was a boy.'"

"Hold on," Audie interrupted. "Where's the thees and thous?"

"What?"

"Where's the arts and eths? You ain't readin' it right."

"I'm changing it to the way we talk today."

"No sir. You gots to read it like it's writ."

"The old King James English is a relic," David said, quoting his mother. He turned to the Bible's title page. "See, sixteen eleven. It's three hundred years old. People don't talk like that anymore."

Audie pointed to the Bible and said, "Ain't one jot nor tittle a that book'll pass away before heaven and earth pass away."

"Yes, but—"

"Ain't no buts. You gots to read like it's writ. Or else you ain't gonna read it at all. Un'erstand?"

"Yes'm," David said.

He continued reading the story of young David's rise to fame, including every jot and tittle of the King James lexicon.

When Audie went outside to fetch something or other, Zach leaned toward David. "Welcome to the fambly," he whispered.

A week later, David told Audie the boys needed easier books to read. "Your pastor might have some books we can borrow."

"What books?"

"Well, there's *Tom Sawyer* or *Huckleberry Finn*. Either one of those would be real good. Or *Treasure Island*. I could write them down if we had a pencil and paper."

"We ain't got no pencil or paper."

"That's okay. Zach can remember the titles. He has a good memory."

"Lemme think about it," Audie said.

Audie surprised David the following Sunday afternoon when she said the pastor would bring her some books. "If'n we borry them books," she said, "we gots to take real good care of 'em. We gots to give 'em back in the same condition they was in when we got 'em."

"We'll be careful," David said.

Late Monday morning, when David was walking back from the woods with a few rabbits, he saw a strange horse tied to the wagon. The cabin door stood open, as it always did to catch any breath of wind. He wondered if he should turn around and go back to the woods before he was seen. Instead, he decided to hide in the barn, where he could keep an eye on things.

David hung around inside the barn for a while, but he became worried about Audie and the boys. Some kind of watchman he was, only worrying about his own skin. He picked up his rifle, squared his hat on his head, and marched through the open door, gun at the ready.

The preacher—David recognized him—sat at the table with Audie, Zach, and Luke. David stopped, suddenly embarrassed at having entered so brusquely. He removed his hat quickly and placed the rifle by the door.

The preacher stood. "Howdy do," he said.

The boys jumped up and ran to David, holding up books.

"This is Jacob," Audie said to the preacher. She looked annoyed.

"Jacob ain't his real name," confessed Luke.

"Luke, mind your business," said Audie.

"Papa call him Jacob because he carryin' a blessin'," explained Luke. "Like Jacob in the Bible."

The preacher said, "It's right nice to know somebody's taking my sermons to heart."

If the preacher recognized David from the paper that had been posted at the church, he did not let on, and he did not ask questions. He stuck out his hand and said, "Mo Rawlins."

"Pleased to meet you, Pastor Rawlins."

Mo Rawlins smiled, and deep crow's feet beveled the skin between his eyes and his gray hair. He was a slight man and much older than David had imagined from the fire and brimstone he thundered on Sunday mornings.

"Just passing through, Jacob?"

"Yes sir. I'm staying 'til the cotton's in."

"You ain't said nothin' about leavin'!" cried Luke.

Zachary ducked his head. His arms went limp at his sides, and his lower lip came out. David knelt and took the book that dangled from Zach's hand. "Whatcha got here, Big Man? *Call of the Wild.* Looky here. This book is about a dog."

The boy refused to look up.

"Hey now. I'm not going anywhere. We've got too much reading to do." David turned to Luke. "And what've you got there?" Luke stuck out his book, *The Eclectic First Reader.* "Well, now. How about this? My mama taught me to read from this book."

Zach's and Luke's eyes widened. "How'd the preacher get hold of it?" Luke asked.

"Luke!" cried Audie.

David laughed out loud, as did Pastor Rawlins.

David said, "Well, see, they usually make more than one of a book. Sometimes they make a whole bunch of them so lots of children can learn from them." David looked up at Pastor Rawlins. "Does the church have any extra pencils and paper?"

"We don't get much call for such things, but we might be able to scare something up."

"We don't wanna put you out none," Audie said quickly.

"But the boys could sure use something to write with besides a stick and Audie's yard," David said without looking at her.

"I'll see what I can find," said Pastor Rawlins. "Reckon I better get going. Got a couple a more houses to visit. Pleased to meet you, Jacob."

After the preacher left and the boys went outside to play, David said, "Maybe I can go to church with you and the boys now."

"Lots a waggin' tongues there," Audie said.

"I just thought . . . now that the cat's out of the bag."

"What cat?"

"Never mind," said David.

Chapter Twelve

One afternoon Big Sherman and his son walked onto the farm from the direction of the woods where David hunted. David looked up in time to see Audie drop the bucket of water she was carrying and run to greet them. Big Sherman picked up his wife and spun her around, while Sherman stood by awkwardly until his mother freed herself and hugged him too.

They all sat under the fragrant wisteria listening to logging stories. Big Sherman was no worse for the wear, but Sherman had lost half of his left pinky to a two-man saw. "Ain't no matter," Sherman said. "Didn't use it no way."

The boys were keen to examine the nub, which was capped by a ball of pale scar tissue marked with a black X, where the camp's de facto doctor had pulled the skin together, stitched it closed, and covered the whole affair with axle grease. The men had been paid two dollars a day each and three on Sundays, and they returned home with a small, unobligated fortune.

"I ain't gotta turn around and hand it to the general store," Big Sherman said.

When Audie went into the cabin to get supper going, Big Sherman wanted David to walk the cotton fields with him. David had watched the cotton bloom white. Afterward, the blossoms turned bright pink then deepened to almost red. Their beauty surprised him and softened him a little toward the crop. The blossoms dried and fell off the plants, and David watched the bolls grow round and eventually burst with fluffy white lint.

"It's time," Big Sherman said.

After dinner, as David and the boys had rehearsed countless times, Luke stood and announced that he had something to say. He spread his feet, placed his hands on his hips, and sang the alphabet song, finishing with,

Now I know my ABCs
Next time won't you sing with me?

He then took the *Eclectic Reader* from the top drawer of the sideboard, opened it, and read,

The dog ran.

He turned the page and read a little more haltingly,

Is the cat on the mat?
The cat is on the mat.

He closed the book, took a bow as David had taught him, and sat down. Big Sherman looked at Audie, who put her finger to her lips. Zachary stood in Luke's place and took *Call of the Wild* from the open drawer. He opened the book and read,

Buck did not read the newspapers, or he would have known that trouble was brewing, not alone for himself, but for every tide-water dog, strong of muscle and with warm, long hair, from Puget Sound to San Diego.

"Buck's a dog," Luke said.

Zach did not stumble over a single word, even though *Call of the Wild* was too advanced for beginning readers. But it was what they had to work with, and better than King James English, in David's estimation. Zachary had proven to be a quick study when it came to phonics and recognizing words by sight, but David had been most impressed by the boy's comprehension, especially since he had almost no experience with the world outside the farm.

"I want to see that place," Zach had told David one afternoon while they were mucking the barn.

"What place?"

"The place where Buck was. The Yukon."

"You will one day," David said. He might've added that he wanted to see it too, except he felt as if he already had.

Zachary took a bow and sat down, and Big Sherman looked at Audie, who nodded.

"Whose chil'ren is these?" Big Sherman asked.

"These is *your* sons," Audie said.

Big Sherman opened his mouth to speak, but his eyes welled up. He pulled both boys to him and held them close. Even Sherman, who David thought would be jealous and small about it, smiled. "You boys done good," he told his little brothers.

"Can you teach 'em to cipher too?" Big Sherman asked David.

"I sure can."

"Well then, I reckon ain't nobody got nothin' on the Tatums."

Chapter Thirteen

Big Sherman spent three of their hard-earned dollars on a new scale so they could weigh the sacks of cotton before emptying them. He commandeered one sheet of the paper Pastor Rawlins had supplied and told David to keep a tally of what they picked. Big Sherman watched as David drew six columns and wrote each person's name at the top. He had never seen their names written before, and he took the paper from David's hand and studied it for a long time.

Sherman attached sideboards to the wagon, doubling its capacity and cutting in half the periods of respite David had looked forward to while Big Sherman and his eldest son hauled the cotton to the gin in Baldwin.

Audie outfitted David with a nine-foot pick sack that hung from a shoulder strap. The first boll David touched broke the skin of his fingertips with its thorn-sharp points. He pressed his forefinger against his thumb and watched a droplet of blood form.

"Hurts, don't it?" Zach said.

"It surely does."

David gingerly closed his fingers around the cotton, avoiding the boll's sharp points. He tugged until the lint came loose. He picked another the same way. It wasn't too bad, but it was too slow. David quickened his pace, his arm jerking back reflexively every time the bolls stuck his fingertips. He inched down the row—doubled over to reach bolls that were mere inches from the ground—dragging the pick sack behind him. The strap rubbed against David's neck, and he constantly tugged at his shirt collar to try and keep it between the rough fabric and his skin.

Big Sherman called David to the scale every time a pick sack was filled. Big Sherman hung the bag on the hook and watched while David slid the pea across the iron bar until it was level. David wrote the number on his paper, then stuffed pencil and paper back in his pocket and returned to his own pick sack, lying in the dirt between the rows. Big Sherman was a cotton-picking wonder. His pick sacks consistently topped a hundred pounds and he filled three bags for everyone else's two.

At midday, they ate cornbread and peas that had been warmed by the sunshine and lounged in the shade of the wagon until their food settled. They picked through the afternoon to the hum of katydids. When the cotton reached the top of the wagon's sideboards, David copied down the last weights of the day and tallied them. He was ashamed that his total was hardly more than Luke's, but at least none of the Tatums knew it.

"How much is it?" Big Sherman asked.

"One thousand, eight hundred and thirty-two pounds," said David.

"That don't figure," said Big Sherman. "Fifteen hunerd make a bale. A wagonload most always make one bale."

"It's more than fifteen hundred this time. Quite a bit more."

Big Sherman took off his hat and rubbed his head. He told Sherman to go and fetch Peg, then he said, "Jacob, you's comin' with me. And bring that paper."

David hesitated.

"Go on now. Climb up."

"Yes sir," David said. He stuffed the tally sheet in his shirt pocket and climbed onto the seat about the time Sherman returned with Peg.

"Where you think you's goin'?" said Sherman.

"Jacob's comin' with me," Big Sherman said. "I need him. You can go next time."

Luke and Zach climbed onto the back of the wagon and wriggled into the soft white lint. "You boys don' go to wrestlin' around and knockin' that cotton out," warned Big Sherman as he climbed onto the seat beside David and took the reins.

"How much will you get for this?" David asked.

"Depend on the year. Last year we got sixty."

"That sounds pretty good."

Peg picked up speed as they approached a low, washed-out stretch in the dirt road. "Smart mule," said Big Sherman. "He know he gots to get this load up the other side." He gave the mule his head. Peg was trotting by the time they reached the gully, and the wagon lurched and rocked dramatically as they rattled through it. David turned quickly to grab for the boys in the back lest they be tossed out. Luke and Zach were still on board, wide-eyed and buried in white lint up to their chins.

The wagon made it to the other side of the gully upright and in one piece. Big Sherman reined Peg to a stop, jumped down and walked around, inspecting the wheels and axles. "Don't reckon we's any worse for the wear," he said as he climbed back on. He turned to the boys. "Y'all don't say nothin' about this to your mama now, hear?"

"Yes Papa."

"You neither," he told David.

They rode in silence, and after a while David asked, "How much did you say a bale weighs?" he asked Big Sherman.

"Five hunerd pound."

David turned around and looked at the cotton, which appeared to be pretty clean. The boys were fast asleep on a bed much softer than theirs at home.

"So, only a third of what we picked is cotton? What's the rest of it?"

"Seeds 'n trash."

"That doesn't seem right."

Big Sherman shrugged. "Just the way it is," he said.

When they came into the gin yard, Big Sherman guided Peg behind the last wagon in a long line. "Sump'n goin' on," he said.

White men armed with rifles and sidearms swarmed the yard, and many of them wore badges. They moved up and down the row of wagons and congregated at the gin stand. David felt as overwhelmed as a startled doe. He pulled his hat brim low over his eyes, gripped the wagon seat, and fought the urge to jump up and run.

Zach and Luke scrambled over the sideboards and ran to play with the other children, whose innocence permitted them to run around the yard without so much as a glance from the ragtag deputies. A white man approached the wagon, and David lowered his gaze to the floorboard.

"Evenin'," Big Sherman said.

"Just stay in the wagon," the man said. "Follow the line right on through."

"Yes sir."

"After y'all make your sale, head right on outta the yard. Ain't no hangin' around nor loiterin' permitted."

"Yes sir."

In his peripheral vision, David saw the white man's gloved hand resting on the wagon. A tarnished badge was pinned to his shirt pocket.

"Price a cotton's down," the man said. "They's a war pullin' it down."

"How much?" asked Big Sherman.

"A good bit. Down to seb'm cent a pound."

"Lordy."

"We aim to keep things peaceable, so don't make no trouble at the stand, y'all hear?"

"Yes sir."

The man removed his hand from the wagon, and Big Sherman clucked at Peg to close the gap that had opened ahead of them. "Seb'm cent," said Big Sherman. "How much we git for a bale now, Jacob?"

"Thirty-five dollars. Just over half of what you got last year."

"How we gonna make it?" Big Sherman said.

David watched under his hat brim as the wagons ahead of them pulled under a breezeway next to the gin. A black man holding the end of a long pipe suspended from the ceiling jumped into each wagon bed and sucked up all the cotton with impressive speed. Normally, an operation like the gin would have captured David's interest and imagination, but he could not enjoy it because of the armed white men everywhere. And a war! Who was fighting? *Where* were they fighting? What had happened in the world while he was sequestered on the Tatum farm?

They moved forward in fits and starts, and soon Peg pulled the wagon under the breezeway, which felt like a box trap to David. A white man with a clipboard stood on the platform, his boots at David's elbow. David watched the boots move back and forth as the man shifted his weight impatiently, waiting for the cotton to be sucked from the wagon. A newspaper lay haphazardly on a stool behind the man. The front page had fallen onto the platform, and David could read the headline. *FRANCE HALTS GERMAN INVASION.*

"Europe," David whispered.

"Fifteen hunerd pound," said the man with a clipboard.

Big Sherman elbowed David. "Give him the paper."

The man knelt, and David fished the paper from his pocket. The man's face was red from the heat, and he grinned at David through thick white whiskers. "Well, well. What do we have here?" he said, taking the paper. "You done learned to cipher, Big Sherman?"

"My man here. He ciphered it."

"Is that right?" The man looked at David. "You can cipher, boy?"

"I bought us a scale," said Big Sherman. "We done weighed ever' sack, and he ciphered it."

The man read the paper. He worked his mouth. Finally, he stood. "Alrighty then. Eighteen hunerd pounds. Now move on through."

Big Sherman dragged David to the general store in Baldwin, where he did business. "Mornin', Mr. Stark," Big Sherman said to the storekeeper. "I come to pay up."

Mr. Stark pulled a metal box from under the counter. "Let's see . . . Tatum . . . Tatum. Here you are." He pulled out a paper and handed it to Big Sherman. "Most folks cain't pay in full, but I'm gonna have to charge extra interest to carry it over to next year."

David's father had not charged his customers interest, even though some of them were never able to pay their bills in full. David's family were happy to supply their neighbors' needs and preserve their pride. As he matured, David had realized the Walker General Store was, in fact, a charity funded by his grandfather's wealth.

Big Sherman handed the paper to David.

"Who's this?" asked Mr. Stark.

"This here's my hired man," said Big Sherman.

David looked over the bill, to which Mr. Stark had added twelve percent interest. The items listed were things he'd seen Big Sherman bring home from his monthly trips to town. He handed the paper back to Big Sherman. "It looks right. The interest is twelve percent."

"Alrighty then," Big Sherman said. He pulled his hard-earned cash from his pocket—everything from the cotton crop and a good bit of the logging money—and placed it on the counter. David watched Mr. Stark count out enough to cover the bill and push the rest back toward Big Sherman.

When they left the store, David said, "That interest was almost five bales of cotton. That's five acres of your forty just paying interest."

"The other stores in town charge black folk twenty percent," said Big Sherman. "Say we's high risk. Mr. Stark charge black folk 'n white folk the same."

"Then why'd you bring me?"

"Just makin' sure."

"It'd be good to get out from under that interest, Big Sherman, and pay as you go."

They were at the wagon. Big Sherman hoisted himself up, and David climbed onto the seat beside him.

"Yes sir, it sho' would," Big Sherman said. He sat holding the reins loosely but made no move to set Peg going. "How you reckon I can git out from under the interest if'n sump'n happen to stop me ever' time I's about to get ahead?"

David felt tension in Big Sherman. He felt frustration. "I don't know," he said.

"I ain't never done nothin' just cause ever'body else done it. Folks think the way things has always been is the way they gots to be, but I don't believe that."

"Things like farmers having to use credit?"

"Yes sir." Big Sherman clucked for Peg to get moving. "Things such as that."

Chapter Fourteen

1915

David thought about his mother, his father, and his grandfather every day, and his guilt over helping the Tatums while his own family suffered grief was overwhelming. Every morning, he beseeched God to whisper to them that their only son was alive and well. He prayed that his family would hear the Spirit's witness and believe—even though they could not see—as they believed in heaven.

The months on Lake Caddo and the Tatum farm had not brought David any closer to knowing how to go home. In fact, his regret and shame had only compounded with each month that passed, during which he could have—should have—found a way to let his family know he was alive and did not.

David found a friend in Pastor Mo Rawlins, who sent word by Audie one Sunday for David to meet him at the church house that evening. Pastor Rawlins brought David a copy of the *Marshall Messenger*, and they talked about the war, which had dug into the French countryside like a tick on a dog.

After that, David walked to the church house every Sunday evening, and Mo met him there with the newspaper. To his credit, the pastor never mentioned David's absenteeism on Sunday mornings. If he recognized David Walker from the handbill he had tacked to the church door months before, he kept it to himself.

David always sat on the first pew, and Mo sat on the altar. They were warmed by a potbelly stove in the corner, into which Mo fed pieces of kindling that caught fire quickly in the embers from the morning service. Mo and his flock were foot washers, and washtubs hung on pegs above the tall windows along each side of the sanctuary. David tried to imagine Big Sherman washing Audie's feet, and Audie washing her husband's. David would've been embarrassed for anyone to see his bare feet, much less wash them.

Mo wanted to start a school, but it had been impossible to round up the local children. He had loaned David the textbooks he'd acquired to that end. "You're doing a good job teaching Zachary and Luke," he said.

"I can't teach Zach fast enough," David said. "Luke, well, he tolerates his lessons, more or less." Luke had managed, finally, to master the *Eclectic First Reader*. He could count by ones, fives, and tens as high as his impatience allowed. And he could add and subtract. David thought these skills were enough to run the farm, which Luke swore he would never leave.

"I want Zach to go to college," David said. "In Marshall."

"That would be a first." Mo nodded toward the paper. "*Messenger's* got a story this week about Americans going to France on their own, to fight the Germans." He pulled the paper apart and found the article. "Says they're signing up with a French outfit called the Foreign Legion. Real interesting part here about a colored fella—a boxer from Georgia—who's been in the fighting since it started."

David had imagined finding a way to Europe to fight in the war. Becoming a soldier like Gramps, maybe even a sharpshooter. He took the paper and read the paragraph Mo pointed to. "He was already over there," David said and put the paper down.

"Yes sir."

Neither spoke for several moments. A stick of overheated wood cracked in the potbelly stove. "My grandfather fought in the Freedom War," David said. He wanted to tell Mo everything.

"That so? What regiment?"

"Louisiana 7th infantry. He was a sharpshooter."

"From what Big Sherman says, you're a pretty good shot yourself."

"Yes sir. Thanks to my grandfather."

"So, you're from Louisiana?" Mo said. "Where abouts?"

"Port Barre," David lied.

"Don't know it," said Mo.

"No sir, not many people do."

David lingered in the church house after Mo went home to his family. He read the paper. He thumbed through the hymnals and sang a few songs. He walked around the sanctuary, examining the washtubs. Trying to imagine the foot washing part of the service. When he got sleepy, he blew out the lanterns and walked outside, shutting the big oak door behind him. The churchyard was bright with fallen snow, and the air was thick with silently falling flakes.

David stood his threadbare collar up around his neck and walked toward the live oaks where he always waited for Audie and the boys when Big Sherman was away. He stopped under their evergreen boughs, the bare ground black beneath his boots. He removed his hat and shook it, then brushed off the snow that had settled on his shoulders.

The snow on the rough fields was as pretty as freshly blossomed cotton. But looking at the fields made David feel lonely. Sitting in the church telling Mo about Gramps had made him lonely too. It had made him sick with desire to go home. He was a grown man, but he had no one and no place to call his own. For a brief moment, before he left the sheltering oaks and struck out for the Tatum cabin, David wondered if he was living under a cruel, slow-moving curse.

Christmas came, and the Tatum family sang carols at church with their friends while David hid among the live oaks, listening and singing along in a low voice. At Christmas dinner, the Tatums and David feasted on fresh pork from the annual hog killing. Afterward, Audie surprised them with a bread pudding laced with honey David had collected from a hive he found in the woods the summer before.

The family lingered around the table, drinking coffee with lots of milk and sugar, and David read aloud the second chapter of Luke's gospel. "Next year, you'll be the one to read it," he told Zachary.

"Yes sir. I'll be ready."

Zachary still read aloud haltingly, but his silent reading was fluent.

Mo had acquired a large dictionary for the church, and it lay atop an old pulpit that stood in one corner of the sanctuary. Zach copied new words and definitions from the dictionary every week and brought them home. The dictionary was slowly and steadily being transcribed onto scraps of paper that Zach kept in a drawer of the sideboard.

Zach read every word of the newspapers David brought home from his Sunday night visits with Mo, and he asked David many questions about the things he did not understand. David listened with fascination as literacy leached into Zachary's everyday speech.

David had studied the Tatum's one-room cabin ever since he moved in. He wanted to build a room onto the back of it—a bedroom for Audie. By the time a new year rolled around, David was ready to approach Big Sherman with the idea.

Big Sherman took off his hat and rubbed his shaved head. "Need to clear lots more of them stumps this winter." He put his hat on again, settling it on his crown with one big hand. "But I reckon me 'n the boys can handle 'em. They ain't no money to spare for lumber."

"I have a little money left."

"Why you wanna do this, Jacob?"

David shrugged. "Beats pulling stumps."

Big Sherman laughed. "Reckon it do, son. Reckon it do."

Big Sherman's eldest son was not as supportive of the project. Sherman caught David behind the barn the next day and pinned him to the rough, weathered wood with a forearm against his throat. "Wha'chu think you's up to now?" he growled.

David pulled on Sherman's arm with both hands, but Sherman leaned into him with all the force of his stout, muscular frame. David mustered everything he had, put both hands against Sherman's chest, and shoved him away. He was as surprised as Sherman that he was able to push him off. He rubbed his throat. "What's the matter with you?"

"You don't belong here. Ain't your farm. Ain't your house. Ain't your fambly."

"You think I don't know that?"

"You needs to go. Go on now, git the hell outta here."

"I ain't leaving. Not yet."

"Yeah. You's goin'."

David took a step away from the barn wall, and Sherman took a step forward too.

"I *will* go, but not yet," David said. "I'll go in my own damn time."

Sherman took another step forward, and they were chest to chest.

"I'm not gonna fight you," David said.

"You's gonna get a whippin' if'n you stay."

"I won't fight you, even though I want to. My fists are itching to hit your stubborn puss. But I won't take a chance on killing you."

"You is ignernt as a stump. You couldn't kill me if'n you tried."

"Killing folks is no trouble at all, Sherman. You of all people ought to know that."

The ferocity drained from Sherman's face.

"I'm sorry," David said quickly and walked away.

David had dreaded the day when Big Sherman would grow tired of feeding Methuselah, whose only contribution was carrying an occasional doe back from the woods. David did not want to put a bullet in the old mule's head, but he understood the hay and corn he ate represented money that was needed for a lot of other things. One day when he couldn't stand it any longer, he asked Big Sherman flat out how long he intended to keep feeding Methuselah.

Big Sherman looked surprised. "Methuselah *your* mule. I got no say in the matter. I reckon you's puttin' in enough work for the both of you."

"What if I leave and can't take him with me?"

"That ol' mule done give all he had, 'n then some. I reckon he earned his rest. My daddy give me that mule when I took my half a the farm. Did I ever tell you that? He give Ben a mule as well."

"He did? How long ago was that? How old is Methuselah?"

Big Sherman laughed. "Shoot, Jacob. I don't even know how old I am."

David looked down, embarrassed.

"No sir," Big Sherman went on as if he hadn't noticed. "I ain't never gonna lift a hand against that ol' boy. Me 'n him done made this farm."

Chapter Fifteen

1916

David put twenty dollars in his pocket and led Methuselah from the barn to the wagon. He thought the old mule would balk at the traces—it had been so long—but Methuselah was as docile as a lamb. He obediently backed up between the wagon shafts as if he had never missed a day in the harness.

David walked into the lumberyard at the Baldwin sawmill, and a bearded fellow—possibly older than Gramps—came out of a small shed to greet him. The old man said his name was Deet.

"I'm looking to add a room to a cabin, Mr. Deet," David said.

"Just plain Deet. You's free to look around." When Deet spoke, his jaw slid sideways so dramatically that his grizzled beard seemed to twist and writhe.

David wandered around the yard, looking for materials. He was determined to do better than the cabin's plank floor and walls, through which cold air seeped all winter, making it impossible to keep the inside warm. There were always drafts and cold spots, even with the fireplace blazing.

David's parents had laid down heavy carpets in the winter months, even though no air came through the polished floors. David missed swinging his feet out of bed and into the thick pile of the rug in his bedroom. It was as indigo as nighttime and covered with ivy leaves of pale and dark green. When the weather warmed, they rolled the carpets and stored them with mothballs, the smell of which was so sharp and unpleasant that David's mother aired the rugs for days before they were put down again. David wished he could afford a carpet for Audie's feet to land on when she got out of bed each morning, but the best he could do was to build a solid floor.

David came upon a pile of creosote-soaked beams. They were the perfect length and he wouldn't have to worry about them rotting. He studied the beams, considering how many it would take to build a foundation.

Deet shuffled up beside him. "Lookin' to put down some railroad tracks?"

"I think I'll get these for the foundation," David said.

"Smell'd run y'all out. Son, I don't wanna get up in your business, but has you ever built sump'n?"

"I built two Caddo huts."

Deet cocked his head. After a minute, he said, "Well, a house ain't no hut. Look to me like you got a whole lot a wanna 'n not much else."

David smiled, embarrassed.

"Ain't nothin' wrong with that, son. Ever'body gotta learn some way. You gots the right idea, just don't need no creosote." Deet led David to the rear of the yard where weathered lumber of various sizes and lengths had been discarded. "These here is free for the takin', and it ain't all trash."

Deet knelt in the dirt with considerable difficulty, and David knelt beside him. Deet drew in the dirt. A white patina of dry, chapped skin covered his hands, and his knuckles were swollen with rheumatism. He drew a rectangle in the dirt and bisected it with several lines.

"These here's your beams," he said. "Eight footers. You needs to set 'em down in the ground so that they's level. Un'erstand?"

"Yes sir."

"We gonna git you a bunch a one by sixes. Lots of 'em. They be for the joists and the floor." Deet described in detail how to build joists on the beams and lay the planks over them.

"Is there a way to fill the gaps between the floorboards? Too much cold air gets in."

"Yes sir, they's a way. Shiplap."

"Where can I get shiplap?"

"Don't you worry about that. You just go on 'n make all this like I told you. You nail them one by sixes onto the joists like I told you—that be your subfloor. I be workin' on the shiplap for when you come back."

"Thank you."

Deet winked at him. "You got you a bride you fixin' this room for?"

David's eyes widened. "No sir, I just—"

"Alrighty, alrighty. Ain't none a my business no way."

"No, I just . . ." But Deet had already walked away to gather lumber.

After hearing the condition of the old cabin, Deet counseled David to build a separate structure rather than trying to attach it. "Cain't put new wine in ol' wineskins," he said philosophically. He told David to build a breezeway between the two. "Ain't nothin' to that."

David left the yard with his twenty dollar note still in his pocket and a load of good lumber, which Deet had ordered his men to pull from various stacks—not the scrap heap. Deet gave David a hammer, a good saw, two short lengths of iron welded into a right angle, and a bucket of rusting nails that he said to soak in coal oil. Deet said to use the iron angle to square the corners. "Them corners gots to be square or the whole affair cain't never be right."

Methuselah dragged the wagon back to the farm at his aged pace, and David thought about building the bedroom, which—he had to admit—was solely for Audie's benefit. He thought about her all the time. This embarrassed David, even though he was the only one who knew it.

The spring before the white man died, David had overheard his mother and grandfather talking about him in the kitchen. He had almost walked in on them, but when he heard he was the topic of conversation, he hid in the dining room to eavesdrop.

"Leave him alone and stop teasing him," his mother said.

"He's gonna have to get over that shyness," Gramps said. "Ain't a girl worth her salt gonna chase after him. That youngest daughter of Mr. Dunbar's was in the drugstore today, and I can tell she's got her eye on David, waiting for him to make a move. She's got herself a wait because that boy just stands there like Old Dan Tucker."

"Are you talking about Josephine?"

"Yes'm. They call her Jo Jo. She's cute as a bug. Real pretty."

"He'll come around," Mama said.

"He's seventeen."

"Exactly my point. He's only seventeen. He has his whole life in front of him."

They were silent a moment, and David stood with his back against the wall beside the doorway, barely breathing. He was afraid the floor would creak and give him away if he tried to take a step.

"Daddy?" Mama said.

"What is it, honey?"

"Try not to say ain't."

Jo Jo Dunbar *was* pretty. David thought she was beautiful. She wore her hair pulled up into a puff on top of her head, and she wore a different color ribbon on it every time he saw her. She must have had dozens of ribbons because David never saw the same one twice. Jo Jo's neck was long, and it curved above the collar of her blouse. Her blouses—pink or white or pale blue—always had starched collars. Loose wisps of hair on the back of her neck floated above those collars, and David wanted to reach up and smooth them into place for her.

Jo Jo's eyes were startlingly green, and one glance from them turned him to stone as suddenly as if Jo Jo were Medusa. Though he was as dumb as a stump in her presence, the feeling David had on the inside was the same warm, liquid flush he got when he drank the steaming milk and chocolate Mama cooked on the stove on very cold days. It heated his belly and spread slowly all the way to his fingers and toes. David did not know what to say to Jo Jo besides hello. After he overheard the conversation in the kitchen, he asked Gramps how to talk to girls.

"Depends on the girl," Gramps said. They were sitting on the front porch, and Gramps was cleaning and trimming his fingernails with his pocketknife, which was as sharp as a razor. "You got any particular girl in mind?"

"I like that Jo Jo Dunbar pretty well."

"She's right pretty, that one." Gramps leaned back, folded his knife, and put it in his pocket. "There's no end to the things you can say to get a conversation going, Big Man. It ain't hard to talk to women. In fact, they're a sight easier to talk to than men."

"Seems like every thought flies out of my head when I walk into the drugstore and she's there. I can't think of anything to say that doesn't sound stupid or boring."

"That's just nerves. You'll get over that with practice."

"So what should I say?"

"How about asking her how she likes working in her daddy's drugstore? You could ask what her favorite flavor of malted milkshake is. Then offer to buy her one."

"That's good. Real good."

"You could ask her if she likes to read, and if she says yes, you can ask her *what* she likes to read."

"Maybe she likes the same books I do."

"Maybe so, but you ain't gonna know until you ask her, now are you?"

"No sir."

"You want to get to know her, don't you?"

"Yes sir."

"Then show some interest. I'm not saying to interrogate her. Just act interested. She'll start talking, and before you know it, you'll be over the hump."

David took Gramps's advice the following Saturday when they went to town, and he asked Jo Jo if she liked working in the drugstore.

She did. She told him she met a lot of people because someone new came in almost every week. That almost stumped him until he remembered the doorman at the York Hotel in his deep red uniform with shiny brass buttons. David thought the man—Mr. Samuel—was a soldier, an important one, until Gramps told him Mr. Samuel was wearing a hotel uniform, not a military one. After that, David noticed Mr. Samuel's threadbare cuffs and collar and the little grease spots on the heavy coat's wide lapels.

David asked Jo Jo if she had met Mr. Samuel. She had. David told her about thinking the doorman was a general, and Jo Jo said she had thought the same thing. That got them talking about the different people who worked on the Avenue. When Gramps came around to tell David it was time to go home, he and Jo Jo were chatting like two old friends.

David and Jo Jo visited every Saturday after that, and he learned more about her each time they talked. He thought Jo Jo liked him too, from the way she smiled when he came into the drugstore. He began to indulge in daydreams about making a home with her. Even having children. David could be a daddy—he *would* be a daddy—with lots of children to play with and spoil. Then October came, and one Saturday David went hunting instead of going to town with Gramps.

The thought occurred to David for the first time that his family might have held a memorial service, as Tom Sawyer's family had done when they thought he was dead. Would Jo Jo have cried for him as Becky Thatcher cried for Tom? Had she resisted other boys, clinging to hope that David would return? He settled into imagining the things people might have said about him at his funeral. He wished he could have been there and heard it, as Tom and Huck Finn and Joe Harper had done.

Finally, David roused himself from his deep reverie and looked around. Nothing looked familiar. In front of him, Methuselah's shoulders, dipping with every step as he slowly plodded along, were lathered in spite of the cool day. They had missed the turnoff to the farm, and no telling how far beyond it they had traveled. Was he a child? Daydreaming about Tom Sawyer and Becky Thatcher and Jo Jo Dunbar? Imagining his own funeral? Would he ever grow up and live in the real world instead of inside his own head?

"Whoa, boy." He reined Methuselah to a stop. The road was too narrow to turn the wagon around, bordered on either side by woods David did not recognize. His heartbeat quickened. He had not brought his rifle.

How had Methuselah missed the turn? Even without David's prompting, the old mule should have taken them home. He'd made the trip home from Baldwin hundreds of times, and mules were creatures of habit.

David looked around, and seeing no one, hopped to the ground and walked to the mule's head. "Hey old fella, you missed the turn." At the sound of David's voice the gray muzzle swung around. The mule's big eyes were as clouded as two cracked marbles. "Lord, Methuselah. When did you go blind?"

David took the reins and led the mule to a place that was wide enough to turn the wagon around, and then he led Methuselah home.

Chapter Sixteen

David's attempts to lay the foundational beams in a perfectly squared grid were futile and embarrassing. He worked all day moving the timbers around, hopping from one side to the other. Every time he squared all the corners, the ends were mismatched. When he shifted the ends of the beams to meet one another, the corners were off again.

When Big Sherman and his sons came in from pulling stumps that evening, Sherman said, "See Papa, I told you. He lazy as they come. Ain't no tellin' what he been up to all day."

Big Sherman waved his hand, signaling his son to go into the house. "Maybe that feller at the yard can help if'n you's havin' trouble," he said when Sherman was out of earshot.

David ducked his head. "I reckon I better go and see him in the morning."

Big Sherman put his hand on David's shoulder. "Ain't no worry, Jacob. You'll figure it out. I ain't seen nothin' yet you cain't do. Now come on inside. Audie's waitin' supper."

The next morning David sat for a long time on one of the timbers, studying the layout. Audie brought him a steaming cup of coffee, sweet and rich with sugar and cream. David said, "I guess I'm gonna have to go see Deet about these corners. Reckon that'll take all morning."

Audie stood beside him. She was a tiny woman, barely taller than he was sitting down. She said, "Wish they was a way to keep them corners from movin' about so."

David blew across the top of the scalding coffee and took a sip. He jerked his head up. "Oh, Lord! "

"Coffee too hot?"

"No ma'am. Coffee's good. I just figured out a way to keep the corners from separating."

"Well then, Mr. David Walker, I reckon it gonna be a real good day."

"Thank you, Audie."

She gave him a quick nod and returned to the house.

Before the sun reached its peak, David had not only secured the right angles with boards nailed diagonally across the beams, he had laid out a perfect grid. The solution had been so simple that David was glad he had not asked Deet, who might have lost confidence in him for not figuring it out on his own. David spent the afternoon leveling the beams by shoveling dirt out from under some and adding it under others. He used a bucket of water for a level.

When Big Sherman and the boys returned from the fields that evening, Sherman walked past David's work without a glance. But Big Sherman and the boys stopped to have a look. Zach and Luke hopped from beam to beam, balancing with arms outstretched.

"You done it," Big Sherman said. "Did you talk to your friend?"

"No, Audie showed me how."

"Well, I ain't one bit surprised. No sir, not one bit."

The next day David framed out the floor joists using one by six boards set on their edges. On the day after that, he nailed the boards of the subfloor across the joists. Everywhere he set a bucket, the water in it was level. The foundation was beautiful, and David walked around it again and again to admire it from every angle. He walked across it, enjoying the sturdiness of the smooth yellow pine and the hollow thump his boots made. The old cabin's splintered gray wood seemed shabbier than ever next to it.

Before David returned to the lumberyard for more supplies and instruction, he built a platform in the nearest oak tree with leftover lumber. The treehouse was smaller and simpler than the one David's father had built for him when he was a boy, but Luke and Zach were elated when they saw it.

"It ain't the Taj Mahal," David said.

"What's that?" asked Luke.

"I'll tell you about it after supper," Zach said, and David smiled.

David drove the wagon back to Baldwin with a pot of collard greens and a round of yellow cornbread on the seat beside him, gifts from Audie to Deet. Deet ordered two men to load the wagon with two by fours, as if David were a paying customer. He loaded David's head with instructions on how to frame the walls. Deet drew in the dirt again, showing the walls splayed out flat, as they would look before they were raised. Three of them had framed openings for windows, and the fourth had an opening for the door.

"That's a lot of windows," David said.

"Needs 'em to let in a breeze on hot days."

"But in the winter—"

"Glass'll block the wind. Got's to have glass in the wenders. I done ordered it."

"Deet—"

"Shiplap's on the way too. Be sure to say thank you to your lady friend for the cornbread and greens. Reckon I be eatin' like a king tonight."

That evening, David told Big Sherman he needed help to raise the walls after they were framed, which put an immediate halt to stump pulling. The next morning, David had more help than he could shake a stick at. His heart sank at having lost his solitary hours, but the work progressed rapidly, even without Sherman, who refused to help.

When they exhausted their materials, David returned to the sawmill and Big Sherman went back to pulling stumps. A north wind had come up during the night, bringing with it an azure sky and bitter cold that cut so deeply David threw an old blanket over Methuselah to keep him warm.

Deet invited David into the two-room shack he called home. The room was August hot, thanks to a potbelly stove that blazed with wood scraps. David quickly shed his coat.

"Sorry about the heat," Deet said. "Helps with the rheumatism."

"I'm cold most all the time, so I don't mind."

A beautifully ornate checkerboard and checkers waited on a barrel in the front room.

"I've never seen such a board," David said.

"Made it myself."

Their first game went quickly, and during the second, David heard a muffled snore from the shack's back room. "Who's that?" he asked.

"That be Mr. Joseph Baldwin the Third. The yardman."

"I thought you were the yardman."

Deet laughed. "Ain't never heard of a colored yardman. No sir, Mr. Joe, he the yardman. He gots the profit 'n I gots the work." Deet stood and pushed the door open. "There he be in all his glory."

The stench from the shut-up room—body odor, metabolized whiskey, floral perfume—rushed through the doorway. The man snorted as his breath caught on his drunkenness. David got up and peered into the darkness at a rumpled figure sprawled on Deet's bed.

One leg hung over the side, and the sole of his shiny new boot rested flat on the floor.

"Sometime Mr. Joe get on a mean drunk," Deet said. "Say he gonna fire ever' man on the yard. Say we ain't nothin' but white trash 'n niggers that ain't good for nothin' 'cept . . . well . . . I won't repeat the rest of it."

"Mercy."

"Sometime Mr. Joe get on a sorrowful drunk. Say he gonna make it up to me for coverin' for him. Say he gonna make it right cause I doin' all his work." Joe Baldwin stopped breathing. After a minute, he reared up, coughing and gasping. Then he rolled onto his side and faced the wall. Deet said. "Mostly, though, Mr. Joe just dead drunk."

"Baldwin?" David asked.

"Yes sir. His fambly own the whole town 'n there he lay, goin' to ruin. He a young man, 'n I reckon he gonna die young from a rotted gut or a bullet some lady husband put in his head."

"Does he know?" asked David.

Deet closed the door.

"Know what?"

"Does he know about all the materials you've given me?"

Deet motioned for David to sit down again. "Way I see it," Deet said as he studied the checkerboard, "them Baldwins owes they riches to the folks that's livin' around here. Most folks around here ain't hardly got a pot to piss in or a wender to throw it out of."

"Can't argue with that."

"Them Baldwins ain't much of a mind to give nothin' away, so I's helpin' a bit in that regard. Not so's they notice, mind you, but maybe enough for the Good Lord to take notice. Maybe when Mr. Joe show up at the pearly gate, he have a little more good works to his credit than he expected."

"I never heard of anybody having an idea like that, Deet."

"Well, a feller's got to think for hisself."

Deet supplied a great deal of shiplap and tar paper. "Tar paper keep the inside cool in the summer 'n warm in the winter," Deet said as the men loaded the long black rolls into the wagon.

Big Sherman and David tacked tar paper over the one by sixes of the subfloor, the walls, and the roof. Then they covered the subfloor and the walls, inside and out, with shiplap. Finally, they covered the roof in tinplate and sealed it with pale gray paint. Afterward, Big Sherman and David stood outside, admiring their handiwork.

"You done good, Jacob," Big Sherman said. "It be a sight to behold."

"We ain't done yet," David said.

Deet's men loaded onto the wagon a potbelly stove, which the Baldwin Hotel had mistakenly ordered. "Cost too much to ship it back," Deet said with a wink.

The final and most difficult part of the building project was framing and casing the windows. David and Big Sherman spent hours shimming the frames according to Deet's instructions. It was unforgiving work, but when they finished, each window sat in its frame perfectly and opened and closed without a hitch.

Last of all, Big Sherman and David painted the walls white inside and out and hung a varnished green door with a real glass knob, also courtesy of the Baldwin Hotel. Audie cried when she saw her new cottage, and she kept crying for a long time.

David still carried the twenty-dollar note in his pocket, thanks to Deet and Mr. Joseph Baldwin the Third, and he said a little prayer that Mr. Joe would indeed find mercy at the pearly gates.

After David discovered Methuselah's blindness, he paid more attention to the mule to see how he was getting by. Methuselah stayed close to Big Peg. They ate together. They drank together. They slept lying beside each other in the old barn, with Methuselah's head laid across Peg's rump.

Then one day, David found the old mule alone and confused behind the barn. On another day, he found him wandering in a field, far from the house. When David led him to the water trough, Methuselah dunked his gray muzzle and sucked water as if he hadn't had a drop in days. It broke David's heart to watch him, and he knew it fell to him to do the merciful thing.

David turned his face away while Big Sherman said goodbye to Methuselah in the privacy of the barn. The farmer wrapped his thick arms around the old mule's neck and hung there for a long time with his face pressed to Methuselah's hide. He spoke softly into the long ear, saying, "Me 'n you done it, didn't we, old feller? They weren't nobody but me 'n you 'n Audie. You's plumb wore out now 'n sufferin', I reckon. It be best this way. I know it don't seem like it, but you'll see. You gonna be a young feller again 'n they ain't gonna be no aches 'n pains. Ain't gonna be no blindness neither, nor any work at all. Just play. You be eatin' the softest, greenest grass you ever did see 'n when you's tired, you just lay down 'n have a nap. Ain't nobody gonna object. You'll see." Big Sherman laid his wet cheek against Methuselah's. "I ain't never gonna forgit what you done," he said, and then he slipped out of the barn.

Audie cried too, as did Zach and Luke when their turns came to say goodbye. Even Sherman—tough guy that he was—held the old mule's face in both of his hands and kissed him between the eyes. "Good mule," he said and bent his forehead to Methuselah's.

David took Methuselah to the woods on a summer evening when the air over the cotton fields had settled from its scorched frenzy. Because of the heat, they walked deep into the forest where the smell of the rotting carcass would not reach the house. Whip followed along, rooting under every log and bramble. David stopped at a maple tree and pulled from his pocket a bit of cloth he had filled with crusty sugar from Audie's store. He held it out and Methuselah licked until the sodden cloth had no more sweetness.

Tears ran down David's face when he hugged Methuselah around the neck as Big Sherman had done. He told the mule how much his family loved him and that Big Sherman was telling the truth about heaven, where all the days were sunny and warm, and all the pastures were thick with green grass and flowers. This brought the Twenty-Third Psalm to David's mind, and he quoted it to the animal. He told the mule that all his troubles and hardships were over. Methuselah's long ears turned this way and that at the sound of David's voice, and once he tossed his head the way he used to do.

Because the .22 was such a light gun, David shot Methuselah in his milky eye at close range. The mule dropped as readily as a deer, dead before he hit the ground. Whip ran to the carcass and sniffed all over it, as he had never been able to do when Methuselah was alive. The dog turned and looked at David with worried eyes, as if to ask, "Am I next?"

David sat down cross-legged and laid the rifle aside. He called the dog to him and hugged him tightly. Then David Walker opened his mouth and let loose a loud, suffering wail that had nothing to do with Methuselah.

Chapter Seventeen

By the time David's third winter on the Tatum farm rolled around, he looked like every other colored cotton farmer in Harrison County. Gone were the threadbare clothes, shiny from wearing and washing, that he'd worn when he paddled out of the Caddo swamp. In their place were other clothes the same dull, faded brown as East Texas loam. The gangly teenager who fled Arkansas was long gone, and in his place stood a man, weathered and worn in his twentieth year.

In December, for the first time since he had been on the farm, David accompanied the Tatum family to the annual communal hog killing. Hog killing coincided with the first freeze, which came late that year—it was nearly Christmas—and took place at the farm of neighbors who raised hogs rather than cotton.

Every spring, Big Sherman bought a suckling piglet from Old Man Barnes and notched its left ear with his mark. Barnes raised the piglet to an adult hog that weighed about the same as a bale of cotton. The animal never left the patch of ground where it was born and where it would die, the same as everyone else in the county.

The Barnes family supplied this service for a fee to their neighbors who, like the Tatums, were not set up for raising hogs. Even those who raised their own hogs brought them to be slaughtered during the annual event. David had stayed away, as he had stayed away from church and other social gatherings. But he felt it was safe at last to give in to the family's urgings and go with them.

It was a cold trip, riding in the back of the wagon with Luke, Zach, Sherman, and Whip, while Audie huddled close to Big Sherman on the wagon seat. They rode under a blanket of gray clouds that seemed close enough to reach up and touch. The Tatums were upbeat, singing and laughing, but David felt cold and gloomy. He was stuck in limbo, like the dull day that didn't even have enough gumption to cast a shadow, much less push it across the earth.

"Looky there!" Luke exclaimed. "They's startin' without us!"

He had been hanging over the side of the wagon, and now he turned to his brothers, his eyes sparkling with excitement. The wagon bed dipped, and Peg's hooves splashed in water. David raised himself and looked over the side at the stream they were crossing. The water ran bright red. The entire stream in both directions was as blood-soaked as Egypt's rivers, staining the rocks and dirt along each side.

David sat down and pulled his hat brim over his eyes. He tried to push away an image of other blood, black and thick, that curled and pooled in warm water. He had jerked his guilty arm away before it reached him and clung to his skin like the green bladderwort.

The smell of the slaughter reached them first. An aroma of rendering fat as appetizing as morning bacon frying in a pan, and Luke rubbed his belly. Dark smoke poured from a long, whitewashed smokehouse and collected in a layer beneath the clouds. The wagon rolled into the yard, and David saw men and women congregating amid long rows of tables.

Folks were in high spirits, talking and laughing. The boys, Sherman, and Whip hopped out of the wagon and disappeared before Big Sherman reined Peg to a stop. Even Audie climbed out on her own rather than waiting for her husband to help her down. David climbed out and went around to the front to help Big Sherman unhitch the mule. He took his time unbuckling the traces and looking over the hog-killing operation, which was much larger than he had imagined.

"C'mon 'n meet Ol' Man Barnes," said Big Sherman.

David followed Big Sherman to a fat man—a very fat man—seated on a ladder-back chair against the smokehouse. The legs of the chair bowed under the load, but Mr. Barnes appeared unconcerned, relaxing in a fragrant cloud of tobacco smoke that billowed from a bent pipe.

"Howdy do, Mr. Barnes," Big Sherman called as they approached.

"Mornin', Mr. Tatum. That ain't Sherman, are it?" Mr. Barnes squinted at David. His round cheeks pushed his eyes into friendly crescents.

"No sir. This here's Jacob, my hired man."

The introduction rubbed David the wrong way, even more than it had at the general store in Baldwin, and at the cotton gin before that.

It seemed to please Big Sherman to no end for folks to think he had a hired man.

"Pleased to meet you, Jacob," said Mr. Barnes.

David shook the fat man's soft hand. Mr. Barnes's lady hands were fastened to thin wrists at the ends of his roly-poly arms. David caught himself staring rudely at the delicate fingers curled around the bowl of the bent pipe.

Luke ran across David's field of vision, chasing three shrieking little girls. One of them slowed long enough to yell, "Meanie!" over her shoulder. Luke stopped and raised his arm. His hand clutched entrails that hung down to his elbow. He laughed like a lunatic, and David feared he was about to throw the offal at the girls.

"Luke!" he hollered. The boy stopped and looked at him, then tucked his arm and took off running again. He made a beeline to his brother and shoved the innards in his face, but Zachary only pushed his little brother away.

Zach sat on a stool facing a wall from which hung a row of hog's heads. He was one child in a line of children—boys and girls—sitting on stools in front of the decapitated heads, using paring knives to carefully scrape the hair from the disembodied faces. The hogs' eyes were closed, and their expressions were placid, like pudgy, wrinkled white men permitting barbers to shave their stiff, unwanted whiskers.

The grunting of the hogs, which had been a murmur under the voices of the crowd, erupted into panicked squeals, drawing David's attention toward the pen where the animals were held. A group of teenaged boys—Sherman among them—had separated one poor sow from the passel awaiting slaughter. The half-dozen young men pulled—by a rope and her tail—the frightened, screaming pig toward the creek bank. They laughed and tossed themselves about as if it were a game, while she desperately sought a way out of their hands.

Another young man waited by the creek with a sledgehammer, its iron head resting on the packed earth. He took a position at the sow's head and struck her more or less between the eyes. She shuddered and went down on her front knees. The teenager landed a couple more blows in quick succession, and she rolled to her side, jerking, her legs kicking weakly. He dropped the sledgehammer and sat on her while the others drove hooks into her hind legs.

The blunt noise of the sledgehammer on the hog's skull made David's stomach ball into a fist. Had he heard such a thunk when the oar struck the white man's skull? Did the man shudder as that poor hog had—already killed but not quite dead—before he fell against the pirogue? Was David remembering sights and sounds long forgotten, or was his imagination filling in the details?

Barnes said, "Jacob, I reckon a big feller like you could knock a hog clean out with one blow. You oughta pick up a hammer cause that 'un over there sho 'nuff makin' a mess of it."

The teenagers heave-hoed a rope attached to the hooks until the sow was hoisted from the ground and suspended upside down from a scaffold. The animal shook unnaturally while they cut her throat, and then she hung there trembling, occasionally convulsing, until she bled out.

The sow was carried away along narrow tracks that stretched across the yard, and the pigs still alive squealed again as the young men stormed the pen to catch another victim.

David saw now that the scaffolds rolled on these tracks, carrying the hogs through the butchery. The sow was moved over a steaming trough, where she was dunked and scalded. When her pale body came out of the boiling water, two men scraped the hair from her hide like moss. Her tender white skin showed through in stripes that grew wider and wider.

After that, other men hacked off her head and split her open from tail to throat. Her entrails spilled into a tub, and the fist in David's stomach clenched and threatened to cast out his breakfast.

"Jacob?" said Big Sherman. "You okay?"

"I can't do this." David turned and walked away, back toward the way they had come.

He heard Barnes's voice behind him, saying "Is your man squeamish?" But he did not care. He kept moving, head down, until he was across the bloody stream and could no longer hear the noisy death.

After the hog killing, David would not touch the ham Audie served at Christmas dinner. Its spongy pink flesh seemed unclean. No one commented on his abstinence, not even Sherman.

David knew his time to leave had come and if he waited until the turning plow came out, he would be on the farm another year. He told Mo Rawlins as much during their first Sunday evening visit of the new year. Mo said he had a friend in Marshall, a pastor, who might be willing to take David in for a while, at least until he could figure out his next move.

David invited Zachary to go hunting early one morning, just the two of them. This was a first because David had resisted the boys' pleas to go with him to the woods. Hunting was one of the precious times when David could be alone and feel like himself again. Zach accepted the invitation soberly, as if he understood the weight of it. "I'll be quiet," he promised.

"I know you will."

David showed Zachary how to clean the squirrels he shot, and they gave the offal to Whip, who carried it off to eat, as he always did.

"Would you like to try your hand at shooting?" David asked.

"At a squirrel?"

"Maybe we'll have some target practice first."

David taught Zach to shoot the same way Gramps had taught him when he was a boy. He showed Zach how to load and unload rounds, and when they got back to the cabin, David showed him how to clean the gun with coal oil. "My daddy gave me that gun when I was about your age," David said. "I've been carrying it ever since."

"I like this gun."

"Well, I'm glad to hear that." David put his hand on Zach's shoulder. "Because I need you to look after it for me."

"I don't want you to go away."

"I know. It's hard."

The boy began to cry. "Why can't you stay? Why do you have to go? Don't you like us anymore?"

"Of course I like you. I *love* you—all of you."

"Then stay with us. We *need* you."

"Zachary, listen to me. Do you remember what Jesus told his friends when he had to leave and they wanted him to stay?"

"No—I dunno."

David put his arm around the boy's shoulder. "He told them he was just going ahead of them, to prepare a place for them so they could come and be with him someday. You remember that, don't you? See, that's what I'm doing too. I'm going ahead to Marshall, and there's a college there. Do you know what a college is?"

Zach shook his head.

"It's a school, a really big school, and people come to it from all over so they can learn. And they live at the school. How does that sound to you? Think you'd enjoy that? Living at a college and learning all the time?"

Zach nodded, but his eyes looked doubtful.

"You might miss picking cotton," David said.

Zach grinned.

"I will come back for you. You just keep reading and learning. Pastor Mo will help you."

This was the first promise of any substance David had ever made to another human being, and the trust in Zachary's eyes frightened him. He didn't know how he'd ever keep his word, but he had to find a way.

Chapter Eighteen

1917

The Tatums listened solemnly when David told them he was leaving the next day. Even Sherman, leaning against the sideboard with his arms crossed, did not say good riddance or have a look of satisfaction.

"You know you's always welcome here," Big Sherman said. "You always gots a place to call home."

On the Sunday morning David walked off the farm, he woke early after tossing and turning all night. He stood and rubbed his face, stretched, and rolled up his pallet for the last time. Sherman was sitting at the table with a steaming cup in front of him.

"Want some coffee?" Sherman asked.

"Sure."

The young man who had been his enemy throughout his time on the farm motioned for David to sit at the table. He poured a cup of scalding coffee, added milk and sugar, and set it in front of him.

"Thanks."

Sherman hesitated a minute, as if he had forgotten what he was about to do next. Then he walked to the door, opened it, and went outside. He returned with one of the washtubs that hung on the porch. He carried the tub to the fireplace and ladled hot water into it from the pot that hung there. David sipped coffee and watched him.

Sherman carried the tub to where David sat and put it on the floor in front of him. The water steamed in the still morning air. Sherman took a clean rag from a drawer in the sideboard and picked up a bucket of drinking water that sat on the floor. He knelt and poured a little cold water into the tub and swirled it around with his fingers. Then he looked up at David.

David set his coffee cup down.

Sherman held out his hand. He wiggled his fingers. Finally he said gruffly, "Gimme." David lifted one boot, and Sherman grasped the heel and loosened the laces. He slipped the boot off and set it aside. Then he lowered David's bare foot into the warm water and ran his open palm along each side and across the bottom from heel to toe in a ceremonial washing. Then David's enemy laid one hand across the arch, so gently that it felt like a caress, and he said, "Beautiful on the mountains is the feet of them that bring good news. Lord, bless these feet."

Sherman picked up the rag and wiped the foot dry. He set it on the floor beside the washtub and motioned for the other foot, which received the same washing and blessing. When he was done, he rocked back onto his heels and said, "Reckon that oughta do it." Without another word he got to his feet, picked up the tub and carried it outside, balancing it against his hip as he opened the door. He shut the door behind him and did not return.

David slid his feet back into his boots and tied the frayed laces. He went to the fireplace and topped off his cooled coffee. Then he returned to the Tatum dinner table to sip the sweet coffee and listen to the sounds Zach and Luke made while they slept.

BOOK TWO
SHREVEPORT

Chapter Nineteen

1927

Cargie Barre was a twenty-three-year-old graduate of Wiley College when she took a deep breath and walked through the front door of Cole's Dry Cleaning and Laundry on Prospect Street. Mr. Cole stood behind the counter reading the *Shreveport Journal*. He looked up, and surprise made a quick trip across his eyes.

"Can I help you?" he said.

"I'm a bookkeeper," Cargie said. "I heard you need one."

"Well, I declare. How in the world—"

"I have reference letters," she said quickly, pulling three envelopes from her handbag. "Oh, and my name's Cargie Barre."

Mr. Cole raised the counter flap. "Mrs. Barre, please. Come through here."

He opened a door to a small room, into which had been crammed a desk and swivel chair, and many wooden crates stacked floor to ceiling. Piles of paper receipts overflowed the desk onto the chair seat.

"Oh Lord," Cargie whispered, too loudly.

"I know. It's a mess."

Cargie picked up the nearest receipts and looked through them.

"Centenary College," Mr. Cole explained, even though she had not asked. "We're picking up new business from the school every week."

The bell on the front door jingled, and a customer called, "Mr. Cole, are you in? Mr. Cole?"

"Be right there," Mr. Cole answered. "Excuse me, Mrs. Barre." He left, closing the door behind him. The bell jingled again and again as more customers came in.

Cargie brushed off the swivel chair and sat in it. She wiped a clean spot in the dust on one corner of the desk, took off her hat, and laid it there. The room was musty and sultry, despite the morning hour. She looked up at the single high window, in which a swamp cooler hung. "Well," she said disapprovingly.

Cargie straightened her back, scooted the chair forward, and began organizing the tickets. Soon she was lost in the ebb and flow of Cole's Dry Cleaning and Laundry. The receipts told her everything she needed to know about Mr. Cole's day-to-day business. Which days were busy and which were slow. Who brought in laundry, and who brought in dry cleaning, and how often. They tattled on Mr. Cole's turnaround times too.

Cargie had a talent for visualizing businesses by reading their accounts receivable and payable, and she remembered everything she'd ever read, even as far back as grade school. When Cargie was a child, she assumed everyone remembered things as she did. But when she got older, she realized that, given a little time, most people forgot almost everything except their names.

"It's a gift, baby girl," her mother had said. "You gots to take advantage of it."

Cargie's mother had put her money where her mouth was. She paid for Cargie's college with the dollars she had saved from her job as a maid for a rich family in Dallas. And she took in ironing to make up what was lacking.

Mr. Cole knocked on the door of his own office, twice. Then he opened it.

Cargie looked up. "Yes sir?"

"Looks like you jumped right in," he said.

"Yes sir. Plenty to do here." Cargie put her attention back on the receipts.

"Um, well, it's mighty stuffy in here. Want me to turn on the cooler?"

"Too damp," Cargie said. She waved an arm toward the window without looking up. "It'll have to go. An electric fan will do fine."

Mr. Cole stayed in the doorway long enough that Cargie looked up again. Why, he had not offered her the job yet! She felt a flush of embarrassment. "Excuse me, Mr. Cole. Does this suit you?"

He smiled. "Why yes, Mrs. Barre, very well. I'll have the boys take that cooler down."

And just like that, Cargie Barre had a job.

At midmorning, two men came and wrestled the cooler out of the window, and Mr. Cole brought in a small electric fan. Cargie plugged it in and set it on the windowsill, where it could pull in fresh air without rustling the papers below. She did not let it oscillate lest it crawl right off the ledge.

At noon, Mr. Cole knocked on the door again. "Mrs. Barre, it's lunch time."

Cargie hated to break her stride, but she would fare better through the afternoon if she ate a bite. There were restaurants nearby, but Cargie did not like giving her money to merchants who thought she was second class. No thank you, ma'am. She would take the streetcar to Texas Avenue and eat at the soda fountain. Anyway, she wanted to give Hennie Filbert the news.

"I'll be gone a while," she told Mr. Cole.

"That's okay. You've been at it all morning. Might be nice to stretch your legs."

"Yes sir, I believe it would."

Mr. Cole stepped back and motioned toward another door behind the counter. "Let me show you the cleaning hall on the way out."

Cargie had heard the machines all morning, but she was not prepared to be hit in the face with heat and chemicals when Mr. Cole opened the door. The acrid air did not *smell* of chemicals. It was saturated with them. She took a step back.

"It takes a little getting used to," said Mr. Cole.

"I reckon so."

The high-ceilinged, bricked hall housed tumblers and steam presses, washing and drying machines, and other machines Cargie could not decipher. Electric cords were everywhere, hanging from the ceiling and snaking across the floor. There were canvas bins lumpy with clothes, long tables piled with clothes, and steel racks on which hung cleaned and pressed clothes. A dozen sweating men and women toiled in the heat. Big windows lined each side of the hall, and oversized electric fans pulled in fresh air and pushed it across the room. Even so, the air was thick.

Mr. Cole motioned toward a doorway that led to the alley behind the tiny office where Cargie had been working. The evaporative cooler sat against the wall below the open window. The alley was short and ended on Line Avenue, where she could catch the streetcar.

"Take your time," Mr. Cole said. "We'll be here."

"May I bring you something?"

"No ma'am. Mrs. Cole packs me a lunch, seeing as I can't leave the counter."

Cargie had eaten at the soda fountain every day that week, and Hennie Filbert had served her. When Hennie had learned that Cargie was looking for work and not finding it, and that she was trained as a bookkeeper, he had a suggestion. His wife cooked for a white banker who was a long-time friend of Bill Cole, proprietor of Cole's Dry Cleaning and Laundry. Mrs. Filbert overheard the two men talking over lunch recently, and Mr. Cole said he needed to look into hiring a bookkeeper because his business was growing so.

Cargie had pursed her mouth at Hennie's idea. Her college professors encouraged their students to seek employment in colored-owned businesses. "Black folks cooking and cleaning and raising babies, that's fine with white folks, but they get a little particular when it comes to professional work," one professor told the class. "Why, the Protestants and Catholics and Jews won't even mix when it comes to business," he said with a chuckle.

Hennie thought Mr. Cole might be different. "It cain't hurt to ask," he said. "He ain't the type to make trouble."

Cargie said she would think about it. That evening, she talked over Hennie's idea with her husband, Thomas, who made no bones about being against it, although he stopped short of telling Cargie what to do. Cargie woke up the following morning and thought, *What have I got to lose?*

"I got the job," Cargie told Hennie as soon as she perched her narrow behind on a stool.

Hennie grinned. "Well, how about that?"

"Yes sir. You tell Mrs. Filbert I said thank you, now, hear?"

"I sure will. How about that?" Hennie patted the counter. "She'll be tickled pink. Egg salad and Orange Crush?"

"Yes sir. And I believe I'll have a slice of that buttermilk pie to celebrate."

"Comin' right up, Miss Cargie. Comin' right up."

At closing time that evening, Mr. Cole opened the office door without knocking. "Front's all locked up," he said. "Let's go out the back."

Cargie stood and retrieved her hat. It would be nice to hang a mirror behind the door to check herself. She had a way of becoming disheveled while she worked. She picked up a slip of paper from the desk and handed it to Bill Cole. "Mr. Cole, we could use these things."

"Four double-entry general ledgers," he read.

"I can pick them up in the morning on my way in. I think it'll be best to plan one ledger for each quarter, way your business is picking up."

Mr. Cole reached into his pocket. "I'll give you some money."

"I'll bring the receipt and take it out of petty cash."

"Petty cash?"

"Next thing on the list. We'll need a money box to keep cash for small purchases."

"I usually just buy the small things myself."

"Muddles everything. Best to keep business funds separate from personal money."

"Okay. Petty cash box. And three fireproof, four-drawer file cabinets?" he said.

Cargie tapped her toe against one of the crates of solvent, on which "FLAMMABLE" and "STODDARD SOLVENT" were stenciled in large black letters.

"Of course," said Mr. Cole.

"This place is a tinderbox."

"God forbid."

"Yes sir. God forbid. Sears and Roebuck will have the best prices on cash boxes and file cabinets. I'll look at the catalogue tonight and bring you numbers and prices tomorrow."

"Thank you, Mrs. Barre. I believe the business is in good hands."

"The best," Cargie said.

"It ain't bragging if it's true," said Mr. Cole. He motioned toward the open doorway. "After you, Mrs. Barre."

On the streetcar going home, Cargie was lost in her thoughts about the next day's work and missed her stop to change to the Hollywood line. She had to backtrack and wait for a long time for another car, and it was almost dark when she walked the last few blocks to the house. She smelled supper before she reached the back door that led directly into the kitchen.

"Was getting worried about you," Thomas said when she opened the screen door. "Thought you'd run off with another man."

"Can't anybody fry chicken like you, Thomas. You know how I feel about your fried chicken." Cargie slipped off her shoes right there in the kitchen and sat at the table. She picked a drumstick off the cooling platter. "Mm, mm! Fried green tomatoes too? You outdid yourself tonight, sir. Where'd you get the peas?"

Thomas sat down across the table from Cargie. "Mrs. Bishop," he said. "I mowed her yard this afternoon. Your turn to say grace."

The couple bowed their heads. "Dear Lord," Cargie said, "bless this food we're about to receive. Bless the earth that provided it and the hands that prepared it. Oh, and thank you for giving me a job today. In Jesus's name. Amen."

"Looky here, what's this?"

"Yes sir. Worked all day." Cargie took a bite of peas and a bite of hot water cornbread. "Thomas, you make the best cornpone I ever put in my mouth. Better than Mama's." She bit into a fried green tomato, crunchy corn meal crust around firm, buttermilk-soaked flesh. "These are delicious."

"Go on now. Where's the job?"

Cargie glanced up at him. "Steady now. Cole's Dry Cleaning."

"No. You don't say. The white fella?"

"Yes sir. Marched right through the front door and went to work like I owned the place."

"You did not."

"No, I mean it. I just sat right down without even asking and went to work."

"*Cargie Barre!*"

"I don't think Mr. Cole knew what to do with me."

"Lord God Almighty! Who would?"

They both got tickled then and could not eat their food for laughing. "Stop! Stop it, now!" Cargie cried. "I'm starved. *Honestly!*"

"Cargie Barre, you tell me right now that you did not go in there and start bossing that white man around."

Cargie wiped her eyes. "I surely did."

"How much is he paying you?"

Cargie's hand flew to her mouth.

Thomas howled. "Oh Lord, girl! They only made the one of you. You won't do. You just won't *do!*"

"I forgot to ask about the wage!"

They hardly got through supper for all their laughing.

Chapter Twenty

1928

Cargie was working in the third general ledger for Cole's Dry Cleaning and Laundry when she came to terms with being pregnant. She'd been hoping against hope that it wasn't so, despite missing her cycle twice. But when her lean middle rounded out with a mind of its own—even after she'd cut out pie in desperation—there was no denying it. She was with child.

Cargie told Thomas over breakfast on a Friday morning. She looked down at her plate, where the yolks of her half-eaten eggs ran up against the grits. For the first time in Cargie's life, sunny-side-up eggs repulsed her. "I thought I might escape motherhood," she said without looking up.

"Oh, Cargie."

Thomas got up and came around the table to kneel beside her. He pushed her plate away, as if he knew it made her sick, and took both of her hands in his. Cargie looked into her husband's face. He grinned and said, "It'll be an adventure."

Cargie laughed, but tears spilled down her cheeks. "For you, maybe," she said. "For me it'll mean quitting my job, and I don't want to quit working. Not ever." She put her hand on Thomas's cheek. "I'm sorry, honey. I know how I feel isn't right. I don't know what's wrong with me."

"It's okay, Cargie."

"No, it isn't. I should've told you I didn't want children. Before, I mean."

"Do you think that would've mattered to me?"

Cargie looked away, her face hot with a fresh wave of tears.

"I love *you*, Cargie," Thomas said. "With or without children." He took her in his arms and held her tightly. When he released her, he said, "You won't have to quit."

"That's sweet of you, honey, but how am I gonna have a baby and nurse it and go to a job every day?"

"We'll get your mama over here from Dallas to help," Thomas said. "And I'll help."

"You can't nurse it," Cargie said. She felt frustrated rather than comforted. "And neither can Mama."

Thomas took her hands in his again. His hands were so big, so skilled at seemingly everything. "We'll find a way," he said.

"I don't see how."

"There's always a way," Thomas said. "You'll see."

"Do you really think so?"

"I know so."

Cargie sighed and squeezed her husband's hands. She forced a smile. "Thank you, honey. You're so good to me. I need to wash my face and get going."

"Go on then, and I'll wash the dishes this morning."

The little office at Cole's Dry Cleaning and Laundry was not recognizable from the first day Cargie had walked into it. Neither was the dry cleaning and laundry operation, for that matter. Cargie had shaken the inefficiencies out of it as one shakes dust from a rug.

The crates of dry cleaning solution had been moved to the cleaning hall where they belonged, and Cargie's fireproof filing cabinets were installed along one wall. She turned the desk around to face the door and replaced the cumbersome swivel chair with a ladder-back that took up much less space. In the corner was a newly purchased combination safe so Mr. Cole did not have to tote money to the bank every day. The electric fan still perched on the windowsill and circulated the air over Cargie's head. When the weather turned cool, Mr. Cole removed the fan and brought in an electric space heater.

Mr. Cole had taken to going out for lunch every day, and Cargie worked the counter while he was away. Thomas packed her a pail of food every morning, and he always put in a little something extra. Sometimes, he scrawled a line or two of poetry on a slip of paper. Sometimes, he clipped a flower for her or put in a piece of chocolate. Chocolate was Cargie's favorite surprise.

If Thomas was feeling full of himself, he wrote a riddle, and Cargie spent the afternoon trying to work through it. Riddles were hard for her. Thomas said they were hard for him too, but that he had memorized some from a book. "We both know you're the bright one," he said, and Cargie smiled at her husband's pride over her.

She ate her lunch at the counter between customers. Some of the customers were discombobulated to come face-to-face with a no-nonsense colored woman instead of the proprietor. "Where's Mr. Cole?" they demanded.

"Mr. Cole has gone out, but I'll help you."

One woman squinted with suspicion. "I don't understand," she said. "Mr. Cole is *always* here. *Always!*" The woman's tone was so accusatory that Cargie suspected she thought Bill Cole was hog-tied in the back room.

"Mr. Cole will be back by one," Cargie offered.

"Well, *who* are *you?*"

"I'm Cargie Barre."

"Well!" the woman huffed, but she gave Cargie her name and paid Cargie's outstretched palm for her laundry.

Cargie thought some of the ladies were either dim-witted or block-headed, but she did not know which. Even after days had gone into weeks, they still cried, "For heaven's sake! You again?"

Eventually, most of the lunchtime crowd grew accustomed to Cargie, and some of them even took to calling her Miss Cargie. The ones who could not make peace with her switched their times to pick up their garments when Mr. Cole was in.

Every afternoon, Cargie and Mr. Cole reconciled the receipts with the money taken in. Mr. Cole dragged a chair into Cargie's office and set a grease-stained paper sack of Spanish peanuts on the desk between them. They washed the peanuts down with soft drinks—Orange Crush for Cargie and Coca-Cola for Mr. Cole. The drinks were ice cold from the watercooler in the cleaning hall.

Every Monday through Saturday morning, the iceman plunked a block of ice into a large ceramic water pot that squatted on an iron stand in the cleaning hall to cool the water for the workers. No one complained when the boss dropped a couple of soft drinks in to chill. In fact, it wasn't long before the swimming bottles multiplied, and Mr. Cole had to take care to fish out his and Cargie's and leave the Nehi Grapes, Dr. Peppers, and R.C. Colas to their rightful owners.

Cargie and Mr. Cole munched peanuts, drank their cold drinks, and reconciled the previous day's money and receipts. Cargie tallied the receipts, and Mr. Cole counted the money. One day, Mr. Cole asked Cargie if she wanted to tally the money rather than the tickets. "Just to switch things up," he said.

"No sir. You have your job, and I have mine. Best stick to them."

Cargie's long, slender fingers flew on the Standard adding machine, and the keys clacked like a tiny machine gun. Yards of skinny white paper squirted onto the desk and fell to the floor. Her aim on the keys was unerring, so when the cash and receipts did not reconcile, which was almost every day, the mistake was always Mr. Cole's. In Cargie's estimation he was susceptible to distractions.

If the money came to more than the receipts, Mr. Cole wanted to put the extra cash in his pocket. Likewise, if the money came up short, he was happy to reach into that same pocket and make up the difference. Cargie would have none of it.

"Can't we just write up a dummy receipt?" he said one day when there was an overage.

"Mr. Cole! We can't run a business that way!"

Cargie used a red pencil to document the errors in her ledger, each tiny notation an indictment against Mr. Cole's business acumen. They both knew the mistakes were his and had not occurred during Cargie's lunchtime watch at the counter. Mr. Cole worked hard to avoid Cargie's red marks, and over time, the occasions when the receipts and the cash did not match grew fewer and farther between, and the errors became less severe.

"Why, Mrs. Barre," Mr. Cole said one day, "I would not be surprised if you insist on using that red pencil just to make me pay more attention."

"Go on now," Cargie said.

He shook out a handful of red-skinned peanuts. "Yes ma'am. I do believe you are intent on getting my goat."

"Well, sir, you know what they say about that."

"What's that?"

Cargie paused and looked up, her hand hovering over the adding machine's keys. "If you don't want somebody to get your goat, don't let them know where it's tied."

Mr. Cole was the only white man Cargie had ever spent any time with, and she had come to know him quite a bit better than he knew. When she cleaned out the old desk, she found a slim leather-bound book pushed to the back of the top drawer. It wasn't a New Testament, as she first supposed, but a diary. Every page was filled with Mr. Cole's tight longhand, the same script he used to write receipts. On the inside cover, he had written, *Property of Pvt. William Cole.*

Cargie felt a quick pang reading that. She had not been permitted to keep her name when she married. She had been Cargie Pittman for twenty-two years, until suddenly—in the space of one day—she was supposed to become a person named Cargie Barre, as if who she was before amounted to nothing. To make matters worse, she could not share this sentiment with anyone, not even her own mother, who would have scolded her for being contrary.

Cargie read the first entry in the diary before she thought about whether or not Mr. Cole wanted to share his private ruminations with his bookkeeper.

7 February 1918, Hoboken, New Jersey
Well, I decided to keep a diary. They said we can't write about our location after we get to France, but I reckon it's okay to say I'm in Hoboken today. Somebody said Hoboken is an Indian name, but nobody can tell me what it means. The dock where our ship—the Martha Washington—*is moored is right across the river from New York City. I can see the skyscrapers over there from where I'm sitting in a café. The coffee here isn't anything to write home about.*

My company—the 125th Infantry—got to Camp Merritt two weeks ago, after six days on the train coming up from Camp MacArthur. Boy! Is it cold up here! I haven't been warm since we left Texas.

We're shipping out tonight and some of the boys are feeling low because we got word that a German U-boat sank the SS Tuscania *two days ago. The* Tuscania *was on its way to France—same as we'll be tonight. Rumor is hundreds are dead. Hope that's not true. Hearing that news sure made the war real.*

I'm writing this second part in my bunk with a flashlight. It's late and we're headed out to open water. There's nothing to see up on deck, and it's cold as all get out up there.

Seemed like everybody in New Jersey was at the dock to see us off, and we waved to them from the ship's deck like we knew them all. A bunch of crazy Wisconsin boys pulled off their shirts. There they were, bare-chested, whooping and hollering about how balmy it is in Jersey. Not even a chill in the air, they said. They sang fight songs and went on until a sergeant came along and made them put their shirts on.

Most of them were pretty lit. They came into the café this afternoon with Wally Shegitz—his buddies call him Walleye after a fish they have up North. Wally and I got to be friends back at Camp MacArthur, and he hollered for me to join them at the bar. They said they were having their last drinks on American soil. Wally said I had to have one for tradition, even if it was just a beer. I chose a whiskey because it's smaller. First whiskey I ever drank. Burned like fire.

Cargie had to know what happened after Private Cole reached France, so she put the diary back where she found it, rather than giving it to Mr. Cole, as she should have. The more journal entries Cargie read, the less she thought about Mr. Cole being white. At least, she ceased thinking of him the way she thought about other whites, in whose presence she'd been taught to feign humility, indeed humiliation, lest they think she was "uppity" and make trouble.

Hennie Filbert had been right. Mr. Cole was not that kind of white. In many ways, Bill Cole reminded her of Thomas. He was steady and even-tempered, as was Thomas. He was a cut-up too, same as her husband. They both delighted in teasing Cargie, but she fancied herself much better at hiding her goats than they were. The truth was that Bill Cole could've been green, blue, yellow, or even purple, and she would've felt the same about him.

She just plain liked him.

Chapter Twenty-One

Thomas thought Cargie's mother, Mrs. Rebecca Pittman, was as tiny as a banty hen and just as busy. She scratched like a chicken to get to the bottom of things. The day they brought her home from the train station to help with the soon-to-be-born baby, Thomas knew he was in for it. Mrs. Pittman's sharp black eyes looked him over good.

"So," she said. "You is the man that married my Cargie."

"Yes ma'am."

"Uh-huh. Well. I cain't hardly get a look at you, between all that black beard and that old hat."

Thomas took off his hat.

"I cain't say that's much better," she said.

The first night Mrs. Pittman spent in their spare bedroom, Thomas and Cargie lay in bed talking about her in low voices. Only a thin wall separated their bedroom from hers. "Mama thinks you're handsome," Cargie whispered.

"She does?" Thomas smiled in the darkness. "I reckon I see now where you got your smarts."

Cargie pushed his shoulder. "Go on now, you old vain thing. She asked me if something's wrong with you."

"What?"

"Shhh! She'll hear us."

"What did you say?"

"I told her nothing's wrong with you other than you aggravate me nearly to death every day of my life."

"Tell me what you really said."

Cargie lay flat on her back and ran her hand over the mound of her belly. "Have you ever seen anything more ridiculous?" she said. "Just look at that." She took Thomas's hand and placed it on her nightgown. "Feel that? She's kicking up her heels tonight. Mama says I'm carrying high and it's a girl, most likely."

Thomas felt the little creature bumping around in there. He could hardly believe they'd made a living thing, and he tried to imagine how the child looked, swimming around like a mermaid inside Cargie. He hoped the baby had good color. Cargie's skin was dark, except where it was stretched around her full womb. There, ragged caramel-colored marks emanated from her belly button like rings from a pebble thrown in water. Stretch marks, she called them. It stuck in Thomas's head that the baby might be similarly marked. He said nothing about this, but he prayed silently that the child would be a deep, rich brown, like a mallard drake's breast.

"What did you say to your mother about me?" Thomas insisted.

"I said there wasn't anything wrong with you and she only had that idea because you married me."

"*Cargie!*"

"Well?"

"She didn't mean it that way."

"Sure she did."

They lay side by side in silence for a while. Then Cargie said, "She asked me if you're a good man."

"Lord God. What'd you say to that?"

"I told her I didn't know, but you're good to me."

Thomas found Cargie's hand and laced his fingers with hers.

"Are you a good man, Thomas?"

He sighed. "No. Ain't anybody good except God."

Cargie turned to face him, her features hidden in shadow.

"Don't say ain't," she said.

"Don't tell me what to do, woman."

Thomas went for Cargie's ribs to tickle her, but she arched sideways and got hold of a tuft of armpit hair and yanked. He jumped so hard the headboard banged against the wall. "Cargie, that hurts! *Let go!*" He swatted at her arm, but she twisted so that he had a hard time getting in a lick.

"Hush up, now! Settle down!" Cargie hissed. "She'll think we're up to something in here!"

She let go, and Thomas fell back, massaging his injured armpit. "I think you brought the blood."

"Oh hush. Don't be ridiculous. I'm about to be turned inside out, and you're going on about a little armpit fur."

"Go to sleep, then. You got to make us some money before you're laid up with that baby."

She shoved him one more time and rolled over, and Thomas spooned to her back.

The next morning, Thomas walked Cargie to the corner of Jewella and Hollywood to catch the streetcar for town. A few of their neighbors waited there too. Thomas held back and pulled Cargie's arm. "Don't leave me alone with your mother," he whispered.

Cargie laughed. "I do kinda hate it, but you're all over Mooretown every day. Don't go home. Stay out 'til I get back."

"I can't just leave her alone at the house."

"Sure you can. She'll keep herself busy."

"That's what I'm afraid of," said Thomas.

The streetcar arrived and they moved toward the corner. "Go on now and have yourself a good day," Cargie said. She grasped the side rail with one hand and the bottom of her stomach with the other, as if helping to hoist herself up into the car. Thomas handed up her lunch pail, and she gave him a little wave before turning to find a seat at the back.

He considered taking Cargie's advice, but he found himself at the house again, climbing the back steps, and opening the screen door. There sat Mrs. Pittman, drinking coffee and looking over the newspaper at the kitchen table.

"Good morning," he said cheerfully.

"How are you today, sir?"

"Very well. Can I fix you some breakfast?"

"I fried me a egg. Cain't remember the last time anybody cooked me breakfast. Reckon I was a little girl."

"Then you're overdue. I'll fix you a big breakfast in the morning. How's that sound?" Thomas poured himself a cup of coffee from the percolator on the stove. "More coffee?"

"Yes sir."

He filled her cup.

"I'll just sit up here and let you cook for me like I's the Queen of Sheba," Mrs. Pittman said.

Thomas sat at the table and watched her doctor her coffee with milk and sugar.

"Don't mind me none," she said. "Just go on about your business."

"Reckon I will." Thomas blew across his hot coffee. "When I'm a mind to."

"Uh-huh."

Thomas was sure he did not want Mrs. Pittman running loose around the neighborhood, stoking God-knows-what gossipy fires that already smoldered about Cargie and him. "Looks like it's gonna be a mighty pretty day," he said. "How about I show you around this morning?"

She eyed him. "That's right nice of you, Thomas."

"You're gonna find out I'm a pretty nice fella."

"Uh-huh."

"Uh-*huh!*" he said.

She pursed her lips. "Well. I best spruce up if'n we's going out to meet folks."

"Yes ma'am."

Thomas rose and took their cups to the sink. Mrs. Pittman was a handful, but he'd put her on a short leash, if that's the way it had to be.

Thomas took Mrs. Pittman to the school first, even though she would not have any business there. The principal was also their pastor, so it was easy to make a case for the visit. Thomas introduced Cargie's mother to Pastor Euell and the two teachers, Mrs. McComb and Miss Simmons, who could not say enough good things about Thomas's tutoring. While they talked, a couple of his regular customers ran to him and hung on like baby possums. He slipped each one a candy from his pocket.

"Mr. Barre is a godsend," Pastor Euell said. "We're blessed indeed to have him. And Cargie too, of course."

They said their goodbyes and walked to the market on Henry Street. Mr. Crockett, the grocer, came out from behind the meat cooler to shake Mrs. Pittman's hand. "Pleased to meet you, ma'am, mighty pleased. Mr. and Mrs. Barre are top drawer, just top drawer. Why, just last week Mr. Barre fixed my electric refrigeration unit." Mr. Crockett led Mrs. Pittman to a metal door at the back of the store. "Look here, Mrs. Pittman." He opened the door, and cold air rushed out.

"Oh my," she said.

"You see what I mean? Mr. Barre fixed it up right. It would've cost me a pretty penny to have the manufacturer send a repairman, and I probably would've lost everything before he got here."

Mr. Crockett led them to the meat counter. "Look here, Mr. Barre, I got some fine pork chops this morning. Just look at that!" He lifted one of the chops on a square of butcher paper. "Make y'all a fine supper tonight."

"It's beautiful," said Mrs. Pittman.

"Very well!" he exclaimed. "One apiece for the ladies and two for Mr. Barre. Are y'all headed home? Should I hold them?"

"Hold them, if you don't mind," said Thomas. "I'm taking my mother-in-law to the café for lunch."

"Yes sir. They'll be waiting for you."

Thomas was surprised the ground did not open up right then and there and swallow him whole for showing off. He could almost hear Cargie say, "You vain thing!"

When they were walking to the café, Mrs. Pittman said, "I underestimated you, Thomas Barre."

"Uh-huh," Thomas said.

She stopped in the middle of the sidewalk, and Thomas stopped too.

"Why did you marry Cargie?"

"Cargie's different from other women," he said.

"Yes sir, she is. That's the very reason I's asking."

"I love Cargie, Mrs. Pittman. She's my friend."

"Your *friend?*"

"Yes'm."

"Uh-huh," Mrs. Pittman said, and she began walking again.

On their way home, laden with free groceries—"Your money's no good here," Mr. Crockett had said—Thomas led Mrs. Pittman past a two-story house on a large corner lot. Its tall white columns looked particularly majestic in the modest neighborhood.

"You say it's all colored around here?" Mrs. Pittman asked.

"Yes'm."

"I ain't ever knowed any black folk to live in such a house."

"Plenty of black folks around here have big houses, even mansions."

"I declare."

"Yes'm."

On the deep front porch, an ample young woman lounged in a rocking chair, a glass of iced lemonade in one hand and a cigar in the other. She braced herself against a white column with one foot. Her bare legs sprawled, and the hem of her cotton dress was tucked carelessly between them. She was barefoot and great with child.

"That's the new Mrs. Murphy—Lydie," Thomas whispered. "I'll give you the lowdown later."

"Afternoon!" Lydie called. "It's hot as hell up in there." She waived the cigar toward the house behind her. "Y'all want some lemonade?"

Thomas touched the brim of his hat. "Afternoon, Mrs. Murphy. No, thank you, ma'am. We have groceries to get home. How are you feeling today?"

"Got the sweats. Can't sleep. Fart like a mule. Feel like I'm gonna blow a gasket. But other than that, I'm fine and dandy." She tapped the cigar's ashes onto the porch. "How about you, Mr. Barre? How you doin'?"

"Mighty fine. This is my mother-in-law, Mrs. Pittman."

"Oh God. Mother-in-laws are the worst!" Lydie pulled on the stogy until the end flared, then took it out of her mouth, threw her head back, and launched a vertical plume of white smoke that rivaled the columns on the house.

"For heaven's sake!" cried Mrs. Pittman.

A guffaw honked out of Thomas before he could stop it.

"We best get along." Thomas said. "You have yourself a good day now, Mrs. Murphy, hear?"

Lydie smiled. "I'll do the best I can."

When they were out of Lydie's earshot, Thomas said, "Mr. Murphy's rich. You can see that. He owns three buildings on the Avenue—that's Texas Avenue—and he has an office in the Calanthean Temple. The Temple has music and dancing on the roof every weekend. Lydie was working in one of the buildings, and she started going to the dances. Next thing you know, Old Man Murphy's married to her, and she's getting big with his baby." Thomas paused. "Or somebody's baby—who knows? Lydie's been parked in this house for months, and Murphy stays in an apartment in one of his buildings. It's a mess."

"Well, I never. . . ."

"Oh, well, I don't reckon it's proper for me to tell you such things."

"No sir. It ought not be spoken about, but it's right out here for all the world to see, ain't it? That girl! Sprawled across that front porch like a hound dog full of puppies!"

"Yes'm. Lydie is Mr. Murphy's fifth, or maybe sixth, wife. He gets around."

"I's amongst the Canaanites," said Mrs. Pittman.

"We try to keep godly," Thomas said, "best we can."

Chapter Twenty-Two

"Cargie's getting close," Mrs. Pittman announced at supper about two weeks into her visit.

Thomas looked at Cargie.

"She knows," Cargie said.

"How close?" Thomas asked.

"Week or two at the most, I'd say."

That night, Thomas was shaken awake from deep sleep. He shot up in bed and cried, "Cargie? *Cargie!*"

"What's going on?" Cargie mumbled, half-asleep.

Mrs. Pittman was in their bedroom. "The maid from up at the Murphy place is in the kitchen. The Murphy girl's going, and there ain't nobody to catch the baby."

"Oh," Thomas said. "Oh. Lemme get some clothes on."

"Oh, Lord," said Cargie.

Thomas patted her. "Just stay here and sleep. It's barely past one. Will you be okay?"

"Go on now. I'm fine."

Thomas dressed quickly and carried his boots to the kitchen, where Mrs. Pittman and Lydie's maid waited. Mrs. Pittman had a satchel slung over her shoulder.

"I'm Thomas," he said.

"Mavis."

Thomas sat at the table and laced up his boots. He stood. "Okay. Let's go."

Thomas heard Lydie Murphy a block away. She was screaming bloody murder and cursing John Murphy in language so colorful it was nearly art. They hustled up the house's broad front steps and through the two leaded-glass doors, which stood wide open.

"I'm supposed to go to Mercy Hospital and get the twilight sleep!" Lydie yelled. "Where the hell is that worthless bastard?"

"I'll get some water boiling," Mavis said. "Towels is upstairs."

"You wait here," Mrs. Pittman told Thomas. "I'll holler for you if I need you." She flew up the staircase like a squirrel up a tree.

"*You!*" Lydie screamed when Mrs. Pittman opened the bedroom door, "Get the hell out of my house and find somebody to take me to the hospital!"

Mrs. Pittman said there wasn't time, and she shut the bedroom door behind her.

Thomas closed the front doors and sat at the dining room table. He stood again and paced in the foyer. Mavis came through with a big steaming pot, which he carried to the top of the stairs for her. He descended the stairs again and sat on the bottom step.

He put his head in his hands and listened to Lydie's labor. Every time a birth pain hit, she screamed as if she were being drawn and quartered. Between the screams, she cursed John Murphy and Mrs. Pittman and Mavis and demanded painkillers. There were clatters and bangs every now and again, as if Lydie had gotten hold of something and thrown it. She was sturdy, but the pains wore her down when they bunched into one another, and the cursing and carrying on slowed down.

"Breathe!" Mrs. Pittman hollered. "Push, girl!"

Lydie panted so hard that Thomas heard her downstairs. He thanked God for Cargie, who would sooner die than carry on so.

A baby cried, and Thomas jumped up and ran to the top of the stairs. The women's voices were muffled behind the door. The baby hiccupped and mewed, and Thomas laid his palm on the door.

Mrs. Pittman opened the door, and Thomas gave her a start, standing there with his hand up. She held the child, bundled in a blanket. "Don't worry," Mrs. Pittman said. "It won't be nothin' like that with Cargie."

"I know. What is it?"

"It's a boy. Mr. Murphy gots a son. Wanted to give you a look before I try and get her to nurse him."

Thomas looked into the folds of the blanket. The child was as red as a beet from the ordeal. Even worse, he had a jagged purple mark down his forehead from scalp to brow. "What happened?"

"Nothin'. He's doin' fine. He's big. A ten pounder, I'd say."

Thomas pointed to the mark. "There. What happened to him there?"

"Ain't you never seen a stork bite?" Mrs. Pittman took her forefinger and thumb and laid them over the baby's head like a bird's beak grasping it. "See? Stork bite."

"Will it go away?"

"More'n likely. Lots of babies is born with a mark. Ain't that right, little fella?" she cooed at the child. "What kinda mean old stork bites a little baby anyway? Hmm? Say." She petted the baby's furred scalp with her finger.

Thomas touched the child's forehead. He hoped the imperfection faded soon. This boy was going to have a hard enough go of it with Lydie Murphy for a mother. He didn't need any extra burdens.

Cargie's mother carried the birthmarked baby back into the bedroom, and Thomas stood in the open doorway.

"He's ready for his breakfast," Mrs. Pittman said.

"Gimme," Lydie said. "Give him to me." Her voice was as rough as nettles.

"Go on to your mama, now, Mr. John Murphy, Jr."

"Don't you call him that!" screamed Lydie. "I ain't namin' my baby after that son of a bitch!"

"Miz Murphy! It's his son!"

"You just shut the hell up. You don't know nothin'." The women and the baby were silent for a moment, and Thomas turned to leave. Before he walked away, he heard Lydie say, "This is Rudy. I'm naming him after my twin brother. He's kind and good and gentle as a lamb."

Thomas first suspected Lydie was kind and good and gentle when little Becca, named Rebecca after Cargie's mother, arrived to much less fanfare than Rudy. Lydie agreed to nurse Cargie's baby alongside her own so Cargie could go back to work. "Got two big tits," she told Mavis and Mrs. Pittman in Thomas's presence, "No sense wasting one."

"I declare, girl," said Cargie's mother. "Ain't you got no shame?"

Lydie did not reply, but she winked at Thomas.

Becca and Rudy thrived, even though Lydie nursed them while eating onions and peppers, crawfish and boudin, and pouring Tabasco pepper sauce all over everything. Mavis and Mrs. Pittman tried desperately to steer the nursing mother away from the spicy foods she loved. "For the babies' sake," they said.

"All that mess is gonna gripe them babies' bellies," said Mavis. "Done raised enough chil'ren to know about such things."

"Yes, indeed," agreed Cargie's mother.

But Rudy and Becca seemed to take to the spices as much as Lydie. Even after they were grown, neither of them met a pepper they did not like.

The older women contended with Lydie over the babies sleeping with her. Lydie wanted them close by so she could nurse them without getting up.

"You'll roll over on top of them," said Mavis.

"And wake up with one of them babies as dead as a doornail," added Mrs. Pittman.

But Lydie continued doing exactly as she pleased.

Thomas met Cargie at the Hollywood streetcar stop every evening, and they walked together to Lydie Murphy's house so Cargie could spend a few hours with her daughter. Becca came home on Sundays and was carried back and forth for feedings. "It feels like Becca belongs to everybody except me," Cargie lamented.

When Mrs. Pittman returned to Dallas to care for her white family, Lydie hired Mavis's granddaughter—barely more than a child herself—to tend the children six days a week so Mavis could go about her housework. Thomas paid the girl's wage, which earned Becca a place in the Murphy house after she stopped nursing. Thomas would've preferred to care for his daughter himself—he liked carting her around town and showing her off—but Becca was fussy if she missed a day with Rudy.

As far as Thomas knew, John Murphy never saw the son who presumably was his. When Rudy was barely a month old, Mr. Murphy took three loads of buckshot in the chest and face. The husband who shot him was so incensed that he reloaded his single-shot .12 gauge twice. The assailant attempted a defense of temporary insanity, but the jury convicted him on the reloads. The judge sentenced him to twenty years hard labor in the state penitentiary at Angola.

The funeral was closed casket, and Lydie was the only wife standing graveside when John Murphy went into the ground. She took it all: the mansion, the property on Texas Avenue, and the money. Lydie emptied the bank account and sold everything except the house, as if the lawyer might change his mind. The Widow Murphy—barely twenty years old—settled down to nest in tranquil celibacy. There were no more Saturday nights on the Avenue and no gentlemen callers.

Chapter Twenty-Three

1930

"Keep 'em coming," Thomas said a little too brightly when Cargie told him she was pregnant again.

"I've got to change my method," Cargie muttered.

Thomas and Cargie sat at the kitchen table, and Little Becca hung on her father's leg, receiving bits of green bean from his fingers. "Look at that baby go after those beans!" he said.

"See if she'll take a pea."

Thomas picked a purple-hull pea off his plate and placed it inside Becca's lower lip. The child worked her mouth, fist to lips, salivating profusely. "Looky there," he said.

"Give her a bit of cornbread."

Thomas pinched the bread.

"Too big," Cargie said quickly. "She might choke. About half of that."

"Lemme put a little butter on it," Thomas said. "There, child." The baby opened her little round mouth for the cornbread and gummed it vigorously.

"She's on her way," Cargie said. "She'll be eating your fried steak next week."

"Did I see you bring in a new book?" Thomas said.

"Yes sir. Picked it up on my way home."

Cargie rose and went into the dining room to retrieve the book from the buffet, where she always set her purse and whatever else she brought in from the workday. She handed the book to her husband, and he examined the creamy cover with a simple sketch of a rabbit.

"*The Velveteen Rabbit*. Is it good?"

"Supposed to be real good, from what the store clerk said."

"I don't reckon Becca would know the difference if you read to her from the *Shreveport Journal*," he said.

"Maybe not, but she wouldn't be fed." Cargie lifted her daughter to her hip and smelled her hair. "I'll just wipe her up tonight. Don't believe she needs a bath."

After Cargie left the room, Thomas called after her, "I best get moving on building your mama a house."

"Here we go," said Cargie.

Thomas had surprised Cargie by corresponding with her mother after she went back to her white family in Dallas. He addressed Mrs. Pittman as Pretty Mama in his letters. Cargie thought her mother would bristle at his familiarity, but she did not. In fact, she went as far as signing her letters back to him with the pet name.

Cargie had bought the vacant lot behind their house against the day they needed more room, and Thomas said he wanted to build a small house on it. In each letter to his mother-in-law, Thomas invited her to move to Mooretown, and he promised the house would be hers.

"I gots responsibilities here," she wrote back at first. But the day came when Mrs. Pittman wrote, "I's comin'. Be there before the baby."

Mr. Cole told Cargie that his banker friend, Mr. Walter Addington, said that many banks had gone under and many more were hanging on by a thread. Mr. Cole said that Mr. Addington had offered to deposit Cargie's money in First City Bank, where he was president. "First City has the new army airfield business," Mr. Cole said. "The government won't let it go under."

Cargie was alarmed, to say the least. She took off early that very day and paid a visit to her own banker on Texas Avenue, whom she had never met. Cargie was ushered into his office as soon as she told the teller who she was. Mr. Frank Reynolds—so said the brass nameplate—shut the door behind her and invited Cargie to sit.

Cargie did not sit. "I've come to draw out my money," she said.

"Mrs. Barre, please have a seat."

Cargie obliged, but she did not remove her coat or her hat.

Mr. Reynolds sat behind his desk. He was as round as Humpty Dumpty in a pinstriped waistcoat with a gold pocket watch chain draped across one side. "You need not worry about the security of your deposits," he said. "The bank is doing fine, and I don't see any reason for that to change in the foreseeable future."

"I hear a lot of banks are going under," Cargie said.

"That's a fact." Mr. Reynolds took a cigarette from a box on his desk and offered her one. When she declined, he asked, "Do you mind?"

"No sir."

"Mrs. Barre, do you know how a bank works?"

Cargie thought about her education on banking and discovered it was sketchy. "No sir, I do not. Not specifically."

He lit the cigarette and leaned back. "When you bring your deposit in here each week, Mrs. Barre, we don't just drop it in a box with your name on it back there in the safe."

"Well, of course not."

Mr. Reynolds leaned forward and looked her squarely in the eye. "Or any other version of that notion. The money you bring in is loaned to someone else. Maybe to a fella who wants to build a new house but doesn't have the cash, so he takes out a mortgage. Or maybe we loan it to a business, like the York Hotel, because they need to get some new kitchen equipment and don't have the capital on hand. The money that's actually inside these walls on any given day is a fraction of the amount people have deposited with us." He stopped talking and dragged on his cigarette.

"I see. Yes. Of course."

"Now, it's my job as the president to decide how much money that should be. On hand, that is, on any given day. With the help of the board, of course." He pulled a monogrammed handkerchief from his breast pocket and wiped the spittle that had accumulated in the deep corners of his mouth.

"I'm a conservative man, Mrs. Barre—our history makes us pessimists—but there isn't a banker in this city, or this nation for that matter, who is conservative enough to survive a run on his bank. No one keeps that kind of cash on hand. Couldn't stay in business if you did."

He stamped out his cigarette. "Would you mind taking a walk with me, Mrs. Barre?"

He rose and took his hat and coat from a rack in the corner, and they exited the office through a back door that opened onto a narrow alley between the bank and the next building. When they reached Texas Avenue, Cargie put a hand above her eyes to shield them from the glaring winter sun. They turned right and strolled toward the Calanthean Temple, where she and Thomas occasionally used to go to listen to music on the rooftop.

Mr. Reynolds said, "All the businesses on the Avenue—the people who work in them and the people who use their services—depend on one another." He glanced sideways at Cargie. "Have you ever seen anybody stack cards, Mrs. Barre?"

"No sir."

"It's a sight to behold. Two cards are balanced against each other." He angled his pudgy hands, fingertips to fingertips. "Then two more and a card is placed across the top, like a sawhorse. They make a bottom row like that, then another on top of it, and so on and so forth. The whole affair is delicately balanced, and the taller it is, the less it takes to bring it down." Mr. Reynolds stopped walking. They were across the street from the Antioch Baptist Church. They stood in silence a moment, admiring the red brick, the white trim, and the bell tower.

"Confidence is what holds an economy up," Mr. Reynolds said. "You can't see it, but it's there, as real as the air we breathe. When that confidence shifts toward fear, it can bring an economy down as suddenly as a puff of air brings down a house of cards. That's what's happening in our country right now. Shall we walk back, Mrs. Barre?"

"Yes sir."

They retraced their steps toward the bank. Their long shadows slid ahead of them, appearing much more similar than their persons. "The U.S. economy may continue downward," the banker said. "So a group of us who have a stake in the continued prosperity of the businesses on the Avenue have been strategizing how best to meet the . . . well . . . the threat."

"How long do you expect this to go on?"

Mr. Reynolds shrugged. "There's no way to know. We are in uncharted waters. Do you know what insurance is, Mrs. Barre?"

"I've heard of it. Don't have any myself."

"You might be surprised to find you do. Insurance can take many forms." He stopped and pointed to a vacant storefront. "A new oil and gas company is moving in there. Caddo Parish sits on one of the biggest oil fields in the country and folks will use oil and gas, no matter how bad times get. The bank holds that building, and we are working with the company's founders to ensure their success. It's one of the Avenue's insurance policies, a very important one."

He motioned for them to continue walking. "Another important insurance policy we have is people like you." They turned into the alley leading to Mr. Reynolds office. He opened the door. "After you, Mrs. Barre," he said.

When they were inside, he shrugged off his coat and hung it and his hat on the rack. "Please, have a seat." Mr. Reynolds waited for Cargie to sit and then settled in his chair and leaned back. "Do you know how many individuals make a deposit the size of yours every week, week in and week out?"

"No sir."

"A handful. Do you know how many of them are women?" He held up his index finger. "Only one. You." He lit another cigarette and dropped the match in the ashtray. "Do you think there is one employee out there who hasn't noticed you, Mrs. Barre?"

Cargie flushed. "I don't know about that."

"Let me assure you, there is not. There isn't a single person in this bank who wouldn't notice if you closed your account this afternoon and carried your money out the door. Not one."

"Well—"

"Every single employee would think you know something he doesn't. Every one of them would spread the word that Cargie Barre, who has made a deposit every week, for years, has taken it all out. And every one of them would believe that he should be the next in line." Mr. Reynolds paused. "Then every last one of them would spread the word to his friends and neighbors as fast as he could."

Cargie frowned. "Excuse me, Mr. Reynolds, but it's my money."

"Yes, it is. And you are perfectly within your rights to withdraw it, no questions asked." Mr. Reynolds stamped out his unfinished cigarette and leaned forward, folding his short fat arms on the desk. A gold nugget ring adorned his pinky. "But perhaps there's more at stake than your money. You seem to be a thoughtful woman, Mrs. Barre. Think about the impact of your actions this afternoon."

Cargie tucked her chin. The idea that anyone would pay the least bit of attention to anything she did or did not do was not only ridiculous, it was troubling. "I see your point, Mr. Reynolds," she said. "But I still have concerns."

"Welcome to the club, Mrs. Barre. We are all worried."

Cargie stood, and Mr. Reynolds scrambled to his feet.

"Good day to you, sir," she said.

"Good day, Mrs. Barre. It was a pleasure meeting you."

Chapter Twenty-Four

Cargie hurried home to tell Thomas about her meeting with the banker. "If you'd seen the look on Mr. Reynolds's face when he thought I might pull that money out," she said. "I tell you, Thomas, it was bone-chilling. All this stock market business, it touches everything. Everything, Thomas! It's a lot worse than we thought. I can tell you that right now."

"Steady, Carge." Thomas put his arm around her as they sat side by side on the couch in the living room, a location Cargie had chosen because of the gravity of her news.

Cargie pulled at her fingers, cracking her knuckles, a habit she had broken except in her most agitated moments. "Mr. Reynolds said folks are watching me, Thomas. And if I take my money out, they'll do the same. He said I could bring the whole bank down! Me! Why, that's the most disturbing thing of all."

"This isn't like you," Thomas said.

"I'm scared! I feel like the world could come crashing down around our ears. Bad things can happen suddenly, when it seems like life is going along fine and will keep going along as it always has. I shudder to think about an uncertain future for Becca." Cargie patted her belly. "For this next little one too."

How could she tell Thomas about the terrible things she'd read in Mr. Cole's diary? Starvation. Disease. Dead fathers and mothers and children. Ruined farms and villages. Plundered businesses. Horrors that befell regular folks who were minding their own business and trying to get along.

Thomas took her hands in his and held them tightly. "Cargie, listen to me. I'm not going to say things won't get hard. I've been listening to the radio. It's serious. But getting all worked up, fretting and worrying, it won't help. Let's try and put a handle on it. Make some plans for the what-ifs."

Cargie *would* feel better if they could answer a few what-ifs. What if Mr. Cole lost his business or had to let her go? What if the bank went under, and everything they had saved was lost? What if food got scarce? "I'm still thinking about drawing out the money," she said, "or at least part of it. We have to think about the future of these babies."

"Come here. I wanna show you something."

Thomas led her into the bedroom. He knelt beside the bed, reached up under the mattress and lifted it. Stacks of cash were arranged in neat rows on the bed's muslin-covered slat-board frame. Some of the banknotes were the new small type, and others were the larger currency Cargie used to bring home. She knelt beside Thomas and picked up a stack. It was money she had put in the dresser drawer every week. Money that was intended to be used to run the household.

Thomas let the mattress down and sat on the bed, and Cargie sat beside him.

"You know how I work things," he said. "I can get more out of a dollar than anybody. Or get by without it altogether. I like living that way. I guess it's a challenge. I used some of the money you brought home, but this was extra. I'm not saying we won't need it, but we haven't needed it yet."

"How much is it?"

"I dunno. Haven't counted it."

"It's insurance," Cargie said.

"Yes'm. I reckon you could call it insurance."

"I left Mr. Reynolds feeling like we needed some insurance, and here it is." She patted the bed. "Been rolling around on it every night." She bumped shoulders with her husband.

Becca, who had been talking gibberish to herself in the other room, began to cry for someone to fetch her out of the crib.

"What do you want to do with it?" Thomas asked.

Cargie stood. "Let's keep it right here close."

"I've been talking to them down at the lumberyard. It'll take some money to get going on your mama's house."

"Maybe I'll take a little out of the bank for that. I can talk it up that you're building a house." Cargie realized at that moment that she had decided to leave her money in the bank. She had more peace about leaving it than taking it. Pastor Euell said if you don't know what to do, follow your peace. "You sure we're doing the right thing, talking Mama into moving over here?" she asked.

"I reckon it's her decision."

"I love my mama, but having her in the backyard . . . I don't know, Thomas . . ."

Thomas pulled Cargie close, his knees on either side of her. He put his arms around her waist. "How're we gonna raise a passel of babies without some help?" he said.

Cargie pulled back. "A passel? Go on now. Don't start."

He stood and hugged her tightly.

"I love you, Thomas Barre."

"I love you, too, honey. We're gonna be fine. I got a good feeling about us."

"You're always looking on the bright side."

"Yes'm. You know who brightened up when I mentioned your mama was coming back to stay?"

"Lydie Murphy?"

"Oh, Lord, no! Pastor Euell."

Cargie thought about it. "I can see that." Maybe Mama wouldn't be in the backyard after all, at least not for long.

The next morning Cargie told Mr. Cole she had decided to deposit fifteen dollars a week in the First City Bank and leave the rest of it going to her own bank, if Mr. Addington was agreeable.

"I'm sure that'll be no trouble at all," Mr. Cole said. "I'll talk to him."

While Mr. Cole was busy with customers, Cargie took his diary from the back of the drawer, where she had kept it all this time. She had planned to return it to him and feign just having discovered it, but that had not happened. Instead she read the diary a second time, cover to cover, amazed at what she'd missed the first go-around.

It seemed that every day Cargie found herself desiring to read again a certain passage that came to mind. Even though she knew every word by heart, she told herself she needed to read exactly what Private Cole had written about something a French waiter said in the café. Or how he had described some tanks—a whole line of them—rolling into a village. Or the thing he'd said about the smell of No Man's Land. Cargie could not give up the diary. She could not let go of France, the soldiers, the war, maybe never to see them again. So she kept them all close at hand and prayed her betrayal would not be discovered. She opened the book and read the entry that was on her mind.

12 October 1918, Outskirts of R-

We spent all day getting to our positions for the big advance tomorrow. The 125th is support again, but most of the guys take it in stride. Seems like no matter where they tell us to start, we end up in front, mixing it up. It's getting cold, and I dread winter, wondering if I'll survive it. I don't have the thick blood of the Wisconsin boys.

Wally tells me not to sweat it. He says I have intuition, and a man can get everything else he needs with intuition. Wally and my Wisconsin buddies all call me the Cajun. I suppose they think everybody from Louisiana is a Cajun. They've never met a real one. They all think I have some kind of sixth sense about things. I reckon it's Mama and Daddy praying more than anything that's helping me find my way.

Today, a little after 1300, about a dozen of us doughboys, two officers, the chaplain, and a few Frenchmen were taking a break against a stone wall that was still standing from a bombed-out barn. We heard an aeroplane coming from the north behind us, and we jumped to our feet, at the ready. Pretty soon a scout plane crested the hill. He was flying low, intending to strafe us. The French guys who were with us scrambled to set up their machine gun.

The plane's gunner didn't hit anything except the stone wall on his first pass, but they swung around and came at us again from the south. We took cover, everybody except a big Greek from Detroit we call Crazy Connie—short for Constantine. Crazy Connie stepped out from behind the wall and started firing with his Springfield.

That pilot didn't account for American bravery! Ho! Connie's rounds hit the propeller, and the engine gave about three hard knocks and seized up. That was it for Fritz! The plane came down like a brick, and we ran toward the crash.

The pilot and the gunner might've been able to land and run away if the wheels hadn't caught in barbed wire the Germans themselves had laid down. That wicked stuff is everywhere. As it was, the plane cartwheeled. You could tell right away the gunner in front was crushed, but the pilot was alive and struggling to pull himself free of the wreckage.

A couple of guys wanted to put a bullet in his head right then and there, but the officers said to try and get him out so they could question him. We started cutting wires and pulling at him, him screaming, "Nein! Nein!"

Both of his legs were busted up, so we laid him on the grass. He was panting and repeating "Christian!" like he thought that would save him. Chaplain Davitt knelt on the ground and talked to him, but I couldn't hear what he was saying. I thought old Fritz was losing too much blood, and the officers had better hurry if they wanted to ask him anything.

Some farmers had been pitching hay nearby, and they were standing there with us. The sight of that German uniform must've set one of them off because he jumped forward and pushed his pitchfork into the pilot's gut so hard the prongs went right through him into the ground. The pilot screamed, and the farmer leaned on the pitchfork and yelled, "Mon Bayonet!" He pulled a photograph out of his pocket and put it in the pilot's face. "Mes fils! Mes fils!"

I asked one of the Frenchman what the farmer was saying and he said, "My sons! My sons!"

It was pandemonium. The farmer was red in the face, crying, spit flying, holding the photograph under the dying German's nose. The officers were trying to pull him off, and the chaplain was trying to give Fritz last rites. I imagine the farmer's photograph was the last thing that poor German saw in this world. I hope he really was a Christian. It was a grisly way to go.

The infantry guys don't have much good to say about the pilots because they're never down in the muck with us. The flyers put on airs too, no doubt about it. This one, though, he died like a doughboy.

Cargie closed the diary and held it to her breast, her heart thumping.

The war ended a month after the incident with the farmer, and eventually the army returned Private William Cole to Louisiana. Cargie opened the diary again and turned the pages until she reached the very last one. The final entry was years removed from the others, which had ended with Armistice.

11 February 1923, Shreveport
The war is over, but reconciliation is hard to come by.

Chapter Twenty-Five

Mae Compton's beauty was a charm. Wherever she turned she prospered. When Mae was in full bloom, people compared her to the actress Claudette Colbert. Mae did not think it was vain to believe they were right. She could see the resemblance herself in her large eyes and high cheeks, and in the symmetry of her features. Mae's fair complexion—she avoided the sun with vampirish dread—was framed by dark, natural curls. To heck with flat marcel waves. Buster liked her hair just fine.

Mae's mother and father decided she could attend Centenary College in Shreveport, as she desired. Mae insisted on moving to Shreveport at the beginning of summer to help Uncle Bill at the dry cleaners and Aunt Vida with the house, even though it meant leaving Buster behind in Whitesboro. "I know Buster," Mae said. "Once he gets a job, he'll be working all the time anyway. Besides, it's the least I can do in return for Uncle Bill and Aunt Vida putting me up."

Mae was the only student of her graduating class of eleven who aspired to go away to college. Buster did not see any reason for Mae to leave Whitesboro. Gainesville—barely fifteen miles away—had elevated its academic standing by opening a junior college on the top floor of the high school. As far as Buster was concerned, Mae could go to school there. He nagged relentlessly and chidingly, saying she would regret moving to Shreveport.

"It's pure foolishness," Buster said.

"What's foolish about it?" Mae asked.

"What's *not* foolish about it?" Buster shot back. "It's a big waste of money, for one thing. Your daddy could buy us a house with the kind of dough Centenary costs."

"*A house!* What do *we* need with a house?"

She had him there. Graduation was days away, and Buster had not yet proposed. Mae knew he was waiting until he was sure he had work. Buster was like that—he liked to be sure about things. Just the same, she did not like everyone, especially him, assuming she would say yes. Even though she never imagined saying no.

"C'mon, honey. Be reasonable." Buster tickled her, as he often did when he wanted to get her off a subject he didn't like.

"Don't!" Mae pushed his hands away. She was pleased he wanted her to stay, but she was aggravated that what he wanted was more important than what she wanted.

"Oh, baby, don't be that way."

"I don't want to go to stupid old Gainesville Junior College. It's not even a real college. I want to go to Centenary. I *am* going to Centenary. Daddy's already paid the tuition." This was a lie, but Buster didn't know.

Mae couldn't tell Buster her real dreams, which had less to do with sitting in classrooms than getting out of Whitesboro for a while. That revelation would only hurt his feelings. Buster didn't know Mae's dreams pulsed to the rhythm of railcars. She had ridden trains all her life, all over Texas and Louisiana, to Fort Worth, Texarkana, Shreveport, Alexandria, and New Orleans. Buster had never been with Mae when conductors tipped their hats and greeted her by name, took her bags, and showed her to the best seat. When they asked after the well-being of her sister, her mother, and her father, the Road Master.

Mae imagined herself working for the railroad in a big job like her father's. She imagined a future of travel that ranged farther and farther, until she bumped up against one coast or the other, one border or the other. She would come home from her journeys enveloped in the very air of the cities she had visited—spiced delicacies and French perfumes—aromas she never caught a whiff of in a one-horse town like Whitesboro.

Mae would have a fedora of her own—brown or black, she hadn't decided—banded with a crimson silk ribbon. She would sweep it off as she rushed through the door to greet her future children, her voluminous curls exploding from their forced confinement. In her valise, she would bring exotic treats that were not to be had around here. When they were old enough, Mae's children would ride the train as she had done, and their lives would spill out into the world.

But Mae couldn't get a job with the Texas Pacific Railway. She had no way to qualify, and her father wouldn't lift a finger to set her up with a railroad job out of town, completely on her own. No way. But going to Shreveport to attend Centenary, that was an idea she could sell.

On Decoration Day—the eve of Mae's departure—Buster proposed in the sanctuary of the Academy. *The Academy!* That old-time circuit preacher depot, whose walls now waited out the long silences between occasional sing-alongs and family reunions. Buster liked grand, sweeping gestures and an audience. When he led her down the aisle of the deserted little church, took both her hands in his, and knelt in front of the pulpit, Mae knew he was unsure what her answer would be.

He bent his face toward the old plank floor for a long time and then looked up. Without a trace of a smile, he asked, "Miss Mae Compton, will you marry me?"

She looked at him solemnly, her Buster Bear all shaved and trimmed. His dark hair was slicked down and smelled clean. His meaty hands held hers as if they were bone china rather than flesh the same as his, as if they were as fragile as his pride.

"Mr. Buster Meade . . ." She paused for effect. "Yes. Yes sir, I will."

"You will?"

"Well of course, silly. Don't be a dope."

He whooped then, swept her up, and spun her around. He set her down, fished in his pants pocket, and brought out a ring. "My mother's ring," he said. He slipped the delicate band with its tiny, solitary diamond onto her finger. "She wanted you to have it."

"Oh Buster, it's beautiful. I didn't expect a ring." Mae really hadn't, not in these times.

He picked her up again and carried her down the steps, shouting, "We're gettin' married!" at the top of his lungs.

There it was—Buster's big finish.

When Mae arrived in Shreveport, she realized immediately how little she knew her aunt and uncle. Her exposure to them had been limited to brief visits, during which they never exchanged more than banal pleasantries. Mae soon discovered Aunt Vida was the silliest woman she had ever met, and that was saying something.

Vida had two tiny Pomeranians, Puffy and Fluffy. What the names lacked in originality they made up for in dead-on descriptiveness. The creatures, no larger than rats, were crowded with dense white undercoats and silken apricot topcoats more luxurious than the expensive puff in Mae's dusting powder. On hot afternoons, the Poms lay on their backs, legs splayed, on the kitchen linoleum under an electric fan. They panted desperately while Vida hovered over them and showered their bellies with cool water from a Coca-Cola bottle corked with a tin sprinkle head. Mae's mother had one just like it she used for ironing, but Aunt Vida did not iron. She sent everything—*absolutely everything!*—to the store with Uncle Bill to be laundered or dry cleaned and pressed.

"Aunt Vida!" Mae said. "Why don't you shave the poor things?"

"It embarrasses them," answered Vida. "They cain't hardly hold up their heads without their fur. I just cain't do 'em that way."

What a dope, thought Mae. She put her hands on her hips. The Pomeranians cocked their heads, their sharp little ears flat against the floor. They regarded Mae with quick black eyes, as if she were something the cat had dragged in.

Vida took Mae shopping, but they only went to musty little dress shops where the old clerks made over them. The dresses were sized too large for Mae, and she didn't want them anyway. They were yesterday's fashion. She was dying to go to Rubenstein's and Selber Brothers, but it would only be frustrating to go with her aunt.

Mae was mad with boredom by the end of the first week. She began getting up early to go to the store with Uncle Bill. It was boring there too, but at least she could read her magazines without listening to Aunt Vida prattle and Fluffy and Puffy pant their little lungs out. Besides, the dry cleaners was only a few blocks from Centenary, where she could wander around the deserted campus and imagine how classes would be in the fall.

Mae wrote to all her friends and cousins to please, please, *please!* come and visit, but everyone had made their summer plans already. Her best friend, Sissy Gaines, was the very busiest of all getting ready for her own wedding at the end of June, but Sissy wrote back and said she would make time to come. Three days was all she could spare, but she would be there.

Mae came out of the bedroom, Sissy's letter in hand. "Aunt Vida! I need to make a long-distance call."

She followed her aunt's voice and found her yapping on the telephone. Whoever was on the other end wasn't getting a word in edgewise. Vida usually talked in first or second gear, taking her time about it. But if the other person tried to jump onboard and make it a two-way conversation, Vida upshifted, talking faster and louder until they gave up and she left them reeling in a cloud of chatter. "Vida was vaccinated with a Victrola needle," Mae's mother had said more than once, along with a lot of other things Mae should have paid more attention to.

Vida broke down and let Mae take her Cadillac LaSalle to the train station to pick up Sissy, only because there wasn't a choice. She was tied up hosting her bridge game, which wasn't as big a coincidence as she believed, and it would have been too difficult for the girls to manage Sissy's luggage on the streetcar. Sissy had brought extra suitcases for all the shopping she planned to do.

"I have to hear everything about the wedding plans—*simply everything!*" Mae said as soon as Sissy stepped onto the train platform.

"Oh my goodness, you can't *believe* how much there is to do to get ready," Sissy said, hugging her. "But, first things first. Buster is *beside* himself. He's working overtime every weekend, so I only ever see him at church, but it's just so sad! He mopes around like a lost puppy. He pleaded with me to try and talk you into coming home."

"I know, I know. It's so hard. His letters are pitiful."

"I don't think I could do it. I mean, I couldn't be away from Joe for this long."

"It's very hard."

They walked to the car in awkward silence.

"Well," Sissy said finally, "your sense of adventure is one of the things we all love."

Mae smiled, relieved. It would be a good visit after all.

The girls drove to the house to drop off Sissy's things and freshen up. The bridge club was going full tilt in the front parlor. Vida would not let Mae take the LaSalle downtown, so they caught the streetcar to Selber Brothers for a late lunch in the café. Sissy said the shopping in Shreveport gave Chicago a run for its money.

When Sissy and Mae finally went home, Uncle Bill and Aunt Vida were in the kitchen, cleaning up after supper.

"Can we help?" Sissy asked.

"Oh no, we've got it," said Uncle Bill.

"You can dry these dishes," Aunt Vida said. "I've been washing and drying dishes all afternoon because of bridge club."

Mae helped Uncle Bill arrange plates and bowls of leftovers in the icebox, and Sissy dried the dishes and carried them to the cupboard, where she came upon Fluffy and Puffy, stretched out with their bellies against the cool linoleum, their electric fan humming. "Oh, look at the puppies!" Sissy cried. "They are just precious!" She cooed and sweet-talked the little goblins until they softened up and permitted her to scratch their tiny heads.

"Will you look at that?" Uncle Bill said. "Those two snap at everybody."

"No, they don't," said Aunt Vida.

"Seems like they do," said Uncle Bill.

"They're discriminating, is all. They're good judges of character." Aunt Vida gave a nod of approval and finality.

"Well, they're darling," said Sissy. To the dogs she said, "You better watch out or I'm going to take you home with me! Yes, I am. *Yes, I am!*" Puffy and Fluffy rolled over and presented their lovely pink bellies, and Mae rolled her eyes. Sissy sure could lay it on, and Aunt Vida was lapping it up.

The girls finished the evening by trying on all the clothes and shoes they bought—mostly the clothes and shoes Sissy bought. They sampled each other's makeup, cleansing creams, and moisturizers. Mae was messy—she always had been—and she had spent a long time the night before cleaning jar lids and wiping screw tops to make her concoctions presentable.

When the time came to hang the new clothes in the closet, Sissy saw Uncle Bill's clothes pushed to the side. "Well, that's inconvenient," she said. "Is your aunt taking up the whole closet in their bedroom?"

"I'm pretty sure Uncle Bill was sleeping in here until I came." Mae said.

"Why would he do that?"

Mae lowered her voice. "When I got here Aunt Vida told me to lock the door every night before I went to bed because Uncle Bill sleepwalks. I asked her if he just got up and walked around, or what? She said he has nightmares from the war, and they make him do things."

"What things?"

"Aunt Vida said the nightmares make him think he's still fighting the Germans. She said he fights her sometimes because he thinks he's still over there."

"Your uncle is as gentle as a kitten."

"I remember Mama and Daddy talking about Uncle Bill having shell shock. I know I heard them say that before, so—"

"What does that even mean?"

"I don't know . . . exactly."

"C'mon." Sissy took Mae's hand and pulled her into the hallway outside Aunt Vida's bedroom door. Sissy put her hand on the doorknob.

"Don't!" Mae whispered. "What are you doing?"

Sissy put her finger to her lips and turned the knob until the latch clicked and the door opened slightly. Vida's snoring did not miss a beat, but one of the Poms growled. Sissy gently pulled the door closed and let the latch click softly. "Why isn't *her* door locked?" she whispered.

The girls tiptoed back to their bedroom.

"I'm treating you and Vida to lunch tomorrow," Sissy said, "We're gonna get to the bottom of this before I leave."

Before they went to sleep, Mae took the skeleton key and locked their bedroom door.

Just in case.

Vida ruffled her feathers like a fat hen, she was so full of herself driving the girls to lunch in her LaSalle. She really put on a show for Sissy, who had told Vida she simply must repay her hospitality by buying her lunch at the Washington Youree Hotel. Vida rubbernecked all through the meal, on the lookout for anyone she knew who might recognize her with a class act like Sissy Gaines, of the Gainesville Gaineses.

Sissy chatted about nothing and everything through the salad course, then got down to business when the entrees were served. "I couldn't help noticing a uniform in the closet of the bedroom where we're staying," Sissy said. "Was Mr. Cole in the army?"

"I wish he'd get rid of that old thing," Vida said. "It's an awful reminder for him, what with everything he went through."

"Oh?"

"Well, he was in the very worst of it, really. In France. He was a hero over there." Vida shook her head sadly. "Of course, I didn't meet Bill until after the war, and I had no idea. If I had . . . well . . . you cain't go back. What do they say? Hindsight is twenty-twenty. I had other suitors, lots of them. But I love my husband, and that's that."

"Oh, my goodness," said Sissy. "Has it been just terrible?"

Vida pursed her lips. She leaned toward the girls and lowered her voice, even though Mae was certain she was not going to say one thing she had not said before to everyone she knew. "Sissy, there have been times I feared for my life."

"No!"

"One night—Oh Mae, I don't want you to feel different about your Uncle Bill. Maybe I shouldn't say anything more."

"Don't worry, Aunt Vida. I love Uncle Bill."

"Well then, one night I woke up with his hands around my throat—my throat! And him calling me by a German name. Let me tell you something, you cain't know fear until you wake up from a dead sleep in the clutches of a soldier who's gone out of his mind. Altogether out of his mind!"

"What German name?" asked Sissy.

"What?"

Mae smiled.

"There are scads of Germans where I live," Sissy said. "I just wondered if it's a name I know."

"Oh, well, the whole business was so *awful* that I tried to forget. It was German, though, is all I'm saying."

"Oh, I understand. Does it still happen?"

"Well, it would if I didn't lock my door every night of my life. And I told Mae to do the same, didn't I, Mae?"

"Yes, Aunt Vida."

"You poor thing," said Sissy. She reached across the table and took Vida's hand. "I wish there was something we could do."

"So do I, dear, but we all have our crosses to bear."

"Yes we do." Sissy glanced at Mae. "Yes ma'am, we surely do."

They got home midafternoon. Vida lay down for her nap, and the girls took off for downtown again, where they planned to see *Anna Christie* at the Strand Theater. "What did you think of Aunt Vida's story?" Mae asked as they walked to the streetcar stop.

"I think your aunt doesn't want to sleep with her husband."

"Poor Uncle Bill. He deserves better."

"Yes ma'am. She's something. If the truth were known, your uncle probably doesn't want to sleep with her either."

Every night after that, for as long as Mae stayed with Uncle Bill and Aunt Vida, she tiptoed down the hall to check her aunt's door. Never once was it locked.

Chapter Twenty-Six

Jackson Carthage Addington knew the Fates were smiling on him again when he walked into Cole's Dry Cleaning and Laundry, where he was supposed to work off a gambling debt he had acquired in New Orleans, a debt his father had paid. Jax's best friend, Hollister, had introduced him to a speakeasy called Dante's on Ursulines Avenue. Not that Jax cared one iota for drinking. His weak stomach couldn't stand up to it. But Dante's—so named for the Italian gangster who owned it—had style in spades.

The speakeasy had a roulette table that was so beautiful it looked as if it belonged in Monte Carlo. A croupier named Henri with a French accent and a black tuxedo spun the wheel, and Jax felt like a million bucks every time he laid down a bet. He hung around the roulette all night, hoping for a glimpse of the speakeasy's elusive owner.

A friendly blonde in a tight red dress—she said her name was Teresa—snuggled up close to Jax and tucked her arm inside his. The odds were as friendly as the blonde, and Jax watched his stacks of chips sprout like weeds after a rain. Every time his number came in, the crowd who had gathered around the table clapped and Henri said, "*Félicitations, monsieur.*"

When Jax had amassed a small fortune—hundreds of dollars—he handed Henri two twenty-dollar chips for a tip.

"Merci!" said Henri.

Jax straightened his back. His chest swelled with pride and generosity. "Henri," he said, "tell the bartender the next round is on me. Everybody in the house."

The spectators around the table murmured approvingly.

"What'll you have, doll?" Jax asked Teresa.

"Absinthe."

"Isn't that stuff illegal?"

Teresa laughed. "It's Prohibition, honey. Everything's illegal."

Jax laughed too. "Ain't it the truth? Absinthe for the lady."

Eventually, the roulette wheel became less friendly, and the chips in front of Jax dwindled. They were too few to cover the bar tab before he noticed. "Got a lucky number for me?" he asked Teresa.

"Eleven," she said without hesitation, and Jax slid the remaining chips onto eleven.

"Good luck, sir," Henri said. He spun the wheel, and the ball landed on thirty-six.

"Sorry, doll," Jax said. "I would've taken you to Arnaud's if the luck had held."

"That's okay, Jaxy. Maybe next time." She kissed his cheek and disappeared into the crowd.

Jax made his way toward the bar, where Hollister was drinking rye whiskey. Jax smiled at the bartender as if he hadn't a care in the world. Then he turned his face away and spoke into Hollister's ear, "I bought a round for the house, but I lost everything. I got nothing to cover the bar tab."

Hollister grinned and clapped Jax on the back. "My man!" he said. Then into Jax's ear he said, "That's not good, Jax. Not in this place."

Jax laughed as if Hollister had just told him a good one. To the bartender, he said, "Hey mister, gotta take a leak. Toilets back there?"

The man nodded.

"That makes two of us," Hollister said. "Watch my drink?"

The unsmiling bartender nodded again.

"You got anything on you?" Jax asked when they were away from the bar.

"A couple of bucks, but we still gotta fill up at the all-night station to get back to Shreveport."

"Let's get out of here," Jax said.

They pushed through the crowd. Hollister looked worried, and Jax's nerves churned the acid in his stomach. He pulled a flask from his pocket and swigged Pepto-Bismol. They reached the rear hall, where Jax had seen an arched doorway. He opened it, and they slipped through to a dark, quiet courtyard.

"There," Hollister said, pointing to an iron gate, beyond which was the street.

A very large man in a dark suit and tie stepped out of the shadows in front of them. "Sorry, gentlemen," he said. "Private party." Jax looked across the courtyard and saw a man and a woman seated at a small table. Their cocktail glasses shimmered in the light of a hurricane lamp.

"We were just leaving," Hollister said.

"Through the back door?" asked the large man.

Jax clutched his middle. "Some dame in there took a bath in cheap perfume. I got a weak stomach, man. I had to get out of there pronto." He belched loudly.

The man who had been seated at the table with the woman stood. "Is there a problem, Rolando?" he asked. His voice was barely audible across the courtyard.

"Not sure, Boss," Rolando said. "These guys were trying to slip out the back."

The man crossed the courtyard to join them in the circle of light from the doorway. He was a slight man, no taller than Jax but not as gaunt. He wore a white linen suit and white straw fedora, a black tie and slim black loafers. He was an ugly man, with a beak of a nose and small black eyes. Constellations of pocks marred his cheeks. He smelled good, though. Whatever fragrance he wore made him smell like a man ought to smell, like a man might smell in Paradise. Fresh. Earthy. Powerful.

"Mr. Dante?" Jax said.

Dante cocked his head to one side. "Go inside, Rolando," he said. "Find out if these gentlemen have reason to leave through the back door."

Rolando left, and Jax and Hollister looked toward the iron gate that led to the street.

"There's a man out there," Dante said. "He isn't a nice man."

They stood in silence until Rolando returned. "Unpaid bar tab, Boss," he said.

"How much."

"A hundred bucks, give or take."

"How much exactly?" said Dante.

"One eighteen. That one," Roland motioned toward Jax, "bought a round for the house."

"Generous," said Dante.

"Your roulette was generous," said Jax. "Then it wasn't."

"Ah, temperamental beast. What shall we do with these two, Rolando?"

"I'm good for it," Jax said quickly.

"Good for it?" Dante raised his chin. "When did you become good for it?"

"My old man's a banker. In Shreveport. First City Bank. He's the president."

"What is your name?"

"Jackson Addington. My old man is Walter Addington."

Dante turned to Hollister. "Is this true?"

"It's true," said Hollister, his face grim.

"Very well, son of Walter Addington," said Dante. "You have one week, then you are a dead man. The debt doubles every day." Dante paused. "On the other hand, maybe I should do Walter Addington and Louisiana a favor and take my payment tonight."

"I swear I'll pay. All of it. The juice too."

Dante sighed. "Yes, you will. Afterward, you will not return to Vieux Carré. I will go to mass tonight. I will light a candle and say a prayer for Mr. Walter Addington, whose son brings him shame instead of respect."

Then he spat on Jax and walked away.

On the fourth morning after Dante, Jax worked up the nerve to come clean to his father. Walter Addington listened in silence to his only son, then went into his study and got on the telephone. Jax couldn't hear who he called or what he said. Finally, his father emerged and took his hat from the rack. "Tell your mother I've gone to New Orleans," he said. "And tell her why."

When suppertime came and went without his father's return, Jax told his mother that he had gone to New Orleans to meet with an investor.

Walter Addington finally returned late that evening. His shoulders were slumped, and his mouth was set in a frown that looked hours old. Jax met him in the foyer. "What happened?" he asked.

"I paid the man. That's what."

"Anything else?"

"He suggested I keep my money. He said he would liberate me— liberate, that's the word he used—from you, the son who brings me shame. He seemed surprised I didn't take him up on it."

Walter Addington shook his head, hung his hat on the rack, and crossed the foyer to the bottom of the stairs. He looked up the stairs and back at Jax. "You're getting a job, Jackson. For once in your life, you're going to take some responsibility for your actions, if it's the last thing I do."

Indentured servitude notwithstanding, the scenery in Cole's Dry Cleaners was just fine with Jax. Behind the counter, leaning over a movie magazine, was the most beautiful girl he had ever seen in person, maybe even in the movies. Her face was a lot prettier than Greta Garbo's mug looking up from the slick page of the magazine.

"Can I help you?" she asked.

"Have you seen it?"

"Seen what?"

"*Anna Christie*. At the Strand."

"I saw it the first week." She closed the magazine.

Jax smiled, but not too big. He wasn't much to look at, but he compensated for it with sharp wit and high-grade charm. "I thought it was aces," he said. "'Gimme a whiskey, and don't be stingy, baby.'"

"What? Oh . . . the movie. Can I help you? Do you need to pick up some clothes or something?"

Jax saw he was in danger of making a poor first impression. "Excuse my manners." He extended his hand. "Jax Addington."

She permitted him to give her hand a shake. "I'm Mae."

"Pleased to meet you, Miss Mae. Um, is Mr. Cole around?"

"Uncle Bill? Sure. He's in the office there. Wait here. I'll get him for you."

Jax watched the skirt of Mae's yellow summer dress twirl when she wheeled around to call her uncle.

That's the girl for me, he thought. *She's got class. I could do anything with a girl like Mae in my corner.*

Chapter Twenty-Seven

Jax went into a mild panic when Mae disappeared the middle of June. His heart was set on the girl, even though she ignored him. When he couldn't stand wondering where she was one more minute, he commented to Mr. Cole that the place was awfully dull without Miss Mae around. "She seems like a nice kid," Jax said, feigning interest in the classified ads.

"I'll be glad when she gets back," said Mr. Cole. "It's too quiet around here."

Jax turned the page of the newspaper. "She's coming back?"

"Oh, sure. Mae starts classes at Centenary in September. She's just gone home for her friend's wedding."

Jax's heart swelled, but he tried not to let it show on his face. "You know, Mr. Cole," he said, "some of the dry cleaners around town run advertisements in the newspaper. You ever think about doing that?"

"Reckon I mostly rely on word of mouth."

Jax pointed to a competitor's advertisement. "I got a buddy down at the *Journal* who does typesetting," Jax said. "He could probably get us a discount on an ad."

"That might be all right," said Mr. Cole.

"He might even print us some coupons. Ten percent off, or something like that, and I could take them door to door. Spread the word. I'm a pretty good salesman."

"Ten percent?"

"Could bring in a lot of new business," Jax said. "Folks appreciate a bargain, especially with times as tough as they are."

By the end of the week, Jax was canvassing neighborhoods in his best seersucker suit. He introduced himself as Mr. Cole's general manager, which he thought made the business seem larger than it was. His routine was to knock on the door, then stand on the sidewalk at the bottom of the steps. He didn't want the housewives, most of whom were home alone, to feel threatened. When the lady of the house opened the door, Jax gave his spiel about Mr. Cole, a veteran of the Great War, all-around good guy, and the best dry cleaner in town. Then he delivered a coupon into her outstretched palm as if it was a first-class ticket to all her dreams coming true.

The ladies often invited Jax inside for glasses of lemonade, iced tea, or Coca-Cola, which he always accepted. He unloaded the beverages he consumed into beds of azaleas and roses and cannas, and his prospects were none the wiser.

Jax returned to the dry cleaners before the afternoon heat set in, shucked his coat and tie, and read the newspaper. He took in some of the new business he'd drummed up too, even though Mr. Cole's bookkeeper, Cargie Barre, complained about Jax's ticket writing. She said he missed items and didn't write down the tally. Jax thought Cargie Barre was as persnickety as an old granny and twice as bossy.

Mr. Cole threw some good will Jax's way by bragging about him to Walter Addington, and Jax wasted no time trading on it. The old man had seized Jax's car after the incident in New Orleans, and Jax did not intend for Mae to come back to Shreveport and find him dragging around on streetcars. He needed his wheels. One night over supper, Jax said, "I've been burning up the tracks getting new business for Mr. Cole."

"So I heard," said his father.

"Yes sir," said Jax. "We're getting new customers every day.

"Sounds like you're doing all the good," said his mother.

"Bill Cole is a heck of a guy," Jax said. "Feels great to be helping a fella like that." He paused while their plates were cleared and dessert was served. "Say, Daddy, I was wondering if I could keep a few dollars of my pay for a new summer suit. I need to look sharp on my rounds."

"That's reasonable," said his father.

"Yes sir. My suits are taking a beating on the crowded streetcars in this heat."

"Oh Walter," said his mother, "shouldn't Jax have his Cadillac? He's working so hard. You said so yourself."

"The streetcars run all over town. I expect they can get him everywhere he needs to go."

The next day, Jax told his mother he had gotten sick to his stomach on the streetcar and had not been able to get the conductor to stop in time. It was a lie, but Jax reasoned it could have been true. He felt like death warmed over in the hot, crowded streetcars. "I vomited on a lady who was going downtown to shop," Jax said. "It was just awful, Mama. I was so embarrassed."

"Oh, Jaxy, honey . . ." His mother set her mouth. "Don't you worry. I'll get your car back. Let me handle your father."

"Thank you, Mama," Jax said, and he meant it. Nobody could work the old man like his mother.

Soon Jax was strutting a white linen suit, a white straw fedora with a black band, and summer oxfords of white canvas and black leather. He wore expensive cologne—very manly, though not quite as virile as Dante's. Jax had possession of his powder blue Cadillac Sixteen convertible too. He felt like a million bucks driving around town with the top down.

On the first day of July, Jax rolled to the curb in front of the dry cleaners and saw Mae at the counter with Cargie Barre. It was noontime, when Mr. Cole met Jax's father for lunch at the Youree Hotel. "Well, look at you," Mae said when Jax came through the open door in his new suit.

Jax swept off his sunglasses and his hat. "Miss Mae! Welcome back."

"That's quite a car you're driving."

"My ride has been released from purgatory, and so have I."

Mae cocked her head. "I imagine a lot of girls around here are happy about that."

Cargie coughed and cleared her throat.

"I don't see them beating down the door," Jax said.

"They will," said Mae. "Just give them a chance."

"That'll be the day."

Mae smiled. A warm, friendly smile.

Cargie pulled the morning's tickets off their spike and looked through them. Jax waited for her to carry them into her office and close the door behind her, as she did on every other day. But Cargie didn't budge.

"Say, are y'all going to the big Fourth of July celebration Friday night?" he asked Mae.

"Uncle Bill hasn't mentioned it."

"It's at the airfield. I got a buddy keeps an airplane out there."

"An airplane," Mae said, as if she didn't believe him.

"Ned Turner. Heck of a pilot. He'll take you up if you want."

"I've never been up in an airplane," Mae said.

"We'll be out there all evening," said Jax.

"Aunt Vida isn't keen on being outside."

"Well . . . hmm," Jax said. "The boys and I can swing by your uncle's place and pick you up if you want. It's no trouble at all."

"I guess that would be alright," Mae said slowly.

"Seven okay?"

"Sure," Mae said. "Seven o'clock will be fine."

On Friday afternoon, July 4th, Jax left work early and drove to the Shreveport Airfield. The hangar in which Ned kept his Curtis Jenny was a cavernous building with fifteen-foot doors at each end. Jax opened the doors and turned on a big electric fan to pull a breeze through the overheated hangar. No one was around to help him, so he rolled up his sleeves and swept the concrete floor. Then he wiped off a few chairs and a small wooden table at which Mae could sit. He found an old washtub the mechanics and pilots used to ice down beer, and he set it near the open door. Hollister was in charge of bringing ice and Cokes. "No hooch," Jax had told him.

Jax even went as far as scrubbing to a brilliant shine the dingy, stain-streaked sink and toilet in the tiny bathroom. From the looks of them, they hadn't been cleaned since the hangar was built. Doing these menial, unpleasant tasks on Mae's behalf convinced Jax that his love was true.

He was wringing wet by the time he finished. He drove home to bathe and change clothes. Hanging in his closet were new pleated khaki slacks and a powder-blue long-sleeved shirt that matched the Sixteen's paint perfectly. Jax never wore short sleeves—his arms were too skinny. His man at Selber Brothers put the ensemble together, and it looked absolutely aces. Jax's mother had paid for the new clothes, angel that she was.

Jax's dear mother was funding flying lessons in Ned's Curtis Jenny too. His father was in the dark about the lessons because he would've viewed them as a worthless and undeserved indulgence. "Who knows, Jaxy?" she had said as she opened her purse. "You might run your own airline someday."

The first time Ned took Jax flying was on a clear day, and Jax could see everything at once—the river, the city, the forests and farmland. He understood then and there that he was born for the air.

Flying the Jenny was easy—she *wanted* to fly. Getting off the ground wasn't hard either, once Jax got the hang of it. But putting the airplane down again was a skill that eluded him, even after dozens of attempts. Every time the Jenny's wheels touched the dirt, she bucked as if he'd laid spurs to her. Ned called the airplane's stiff-legged bouncing oscillations, and he put the blame on Jax. "You gotta ease back on the stick. Like this." Under Ned's hand, the Jenny obediently kissed the ground. Every time.

Oscillations weren't the only tricks Jenny had up her sleeve. Given a chance, she spun around swiftly and without warning, swapping ends so fast Jax did not have time to do anything but hang on. Only Ned's quick footwork on the rudder pedals kept them from tipping over and dragging a wing. "That's what we call a ground loop," Ned said. "Try to stay away from ground loops."

Jax could tell Ned was losing confidence in him. Ned's hands were never far from the stick, and his feet were always fighting Jax's on the rudder pedals. Jax was getting worried Ned would never trust him enough to let him fly solo, and he would never get a chance to take Mae for a ride.

Jax pulled up to the Cole house at seven o'clock sharp. He jumped out of the car and walked on a cloud to the front door. Mr. Cole answered the door and invited him into the front parlor. "Mae's still getting ready," he said and motioned for Jax to sit on the couch. Jax had just taken a load off when Vida Cole walked in.

"Hello, Jackson," she said coolly.

Jax stood. "Evening, Mrs. Cole." She sat, and he sat again too.

"Well," Mr. Cole said, "I hear the city's worked up quite a fireworks show tonight."

"Daddy said they hired a couple of Greek guys, brothers," Jax said. "They make the fireworks by hand."

"Should be quite a show. It's tinder dry out there, though."

"Yes sir. They'll have the fire trucks standing by. Heard they're gonna hose down the grass beforehand too."

"That's good. Real good," said Mr. Cole.

"So," said Mrs. Cole, "what time should we expect Mae home?"

"We won't be too late," said Jax. "It'll be dark by nine-thirty or so, and I doubt the fireworks'll go more than an hour. Maybe around eleven?"

"You know she's engaged. To a *nice* boy in Whitesboro."

"*Vida!*"

Mrs. Cole ignored her husband. She ran her palms across her lap, smoothing and straightening the skirt of her cotton dress. "I'm just pointing out the obvious fact that Mae is not available. I should think Jackson is getting to the age to be looking for a girl who is."

"Jax, I apologize. . . ."

"No sir. Mrs. Cole is right. My own mama cautioned me not to be taken with a girl who's engaged to be married." This was a lie, but Jax needed to put the kibosh on Vida Cole. "I told Mama that I intend to behave as a perfect gentleman. I'm not interested in Miss Mae or her fiancé having any complaint with me. The truth is I'm not in a position to be looking for a wife just now. I need to secure my future first."

"I should think so," she said.

"I just thought she'd enjoy getting out of the house," Jax said.

"She's out of the house plenty," said Mrs. Cole.

Jax turned to Mae's uncle. "Mr. Cole, did you know Ned Turner has gotten himself an airplane? A Curtis Jenny. Army surplus. Reckon you saw plenty of 'em in the Great War."

"Yes sir, a few. Well, good for him. Is she in pretty good shape?"

"Just like new. Ned's a heckuva mechanic."

"How about that. Can he fly her?"

"Like an ace." Jax did not mention that Ned was teaching him to fly. Mr. Cole would tell the old man, sure as hell.

Mae walked into the parlor. She was a vision in a pretty summer dress. It had blue checks all over and a wide white collar that lay across her shoulders, leaving bare the tops of her arms. Jax stood immediately. "Where are the others?" she asked.

"They'll meet us at the hangar," Jax said. He moved toward the door. "After you, Miss Mae. Mr. Cole, come out and see the Jenny if you can."

"I might wander out there for a little while after supper."

Jax looked at Vida, who had not bothered to get up. "Mrs. Cole, always a pleasure."

"You remember what I told you, Jackson," she said.

"Yes'm."

When they were outside, Mae asked, "What was that about? What did Aunt Vida say to you?"

"I don't think your aunt likes me as much as your uncle does."

"Don't worry about it." Mae paused as if she was about to confide something, then she said, "She's funny that way sometimes."

Jax opened the passenger door. "Let's go watch some fireworks."

"You're gonna have to put the top up. The wind will muss my hair."

"Sure thing." Jax raised the top up as quickly as he could, happy that, for once, the belligerent mechanism cooperated.

Chapter Twenty-Eight

Jax eased the Sixteen into the hangar and parked. Ned's airplane sat at the other end, next to the little table on which now sat a radio. The radio was on, and the Mississippi Sheiks keened "Sitting on Top of the World."

It was hot as the devil inside the hangar, even with the fan running full bore, and Jax wondered what he had been thinking to bring Mae here. What girl in her right mind wanted to spend an evening sweltering in a metal building that smelled like a bucket of oil? She was probably the first woman who had set foot inside the filthy hangar, with its oily rags and engine parts scattered all around. Spiderwebs and dead bugs, grime and dust were everywhere, in places Jax had not thought to clean.

Ned was right there to open Mae's door as soon as the Sixteen stopped rolling. Ned was the best friend a guy could have, but his pants were too short, his eyeglasses were smudged, and big sweat rings circled the underarms of his thin dress shirt, the only kind of shirt Ned ever wore. "I'm Ned Turner," he said, grasping Mae's hand. "Wanna go flying?"

God Almighty, Jax thought. *At least let her get out of the car.*

Ned pulled Mae to the airplane, and there was Hollister, pouring a tow sack of ice over soft drinks in the washtub. He threw the sack over the ice and turned to greet Mae. He was as tall and blond as a Viking.

"This good-for-nothing loafer is Hollister Caine," Ned said.

Hollister smiled, showing his big, white teeth. He wiped his palm on his pants leg and shook Mae's hand. "Pleased to meet you. Sorry, cold hands."

"Warm heart," quipped Mae, smiling just as brightly.

"My soul," said Hollister, putting both hands over his heart. He and Mae laughed, and Jax saw her give Hollister the once-over when he turned away.

"This is Jenny," Ned said. He rested his hand protectively, possessively, on the leather-wrapped curve of the cockpit.

"She's beautiful, Ned."

Ned beamed. "Ready to go up?"

"Sure. I'd love to."

Ned reached into the front seat and got out a leather helmet and goggles. Mae put her hand to her hair. "Oh, no. I can't put those on."

"It's windy up there. Seventy, eighty miles an hour, at least."

"I don't care. I can't wear that."

"Wait," Jax said. "Wait here. I have something." He went to the Sixteen and opened the glovebox. Inside, wrapped in tissue paper, was a sleek, white Hermes silk scarf he had ordered all the way from London, the same style as the flying aces wore in the Great War. Jax had been saving it for his first solo flight. He carried the scarf to Mae.

"Is this yours?" she asked as she unfolded the tissue paper.

"I want you to have it."

She touched the scarf and looked up at Jax. "Are you learning to fly?"

"Yeah, but don't say anything to your uncle. I don't want my mama to know. She's a worrier."

Mae held the scarf toward him. "I can't. You're saving this. It's special."

"Go ahead." He touched her hand. "Take it. It's your first flight, and I hope you have many more." He meant it too.

Mae accepted the scarf and pressed her lips together. Jax thought for a minute she might cry, but she did not. She handed the tissue paper back to him and unfolded the scarf. While the three young men watched, Mae lifted her shoulder length brunette curls and in one liquid motion wrapped the scarf into a perfect turban. When she dropped her arms, she had been transformed into an Arabian princess.

"My God," said Ned.

Hollister pulled a flask from his pants pocket, unscrewed the top, and held it out to Mae. "To a thousand and one Arabian nights," he said.

Mae accepted the flask and lifted it to her rosy lips, sipped the whiskey, then whistled, as clear and strong as a flute.

"Smooth, huh?" said Hollister.

Mae touched the back of her hand to her mouth. "It must be."

Jax felt he was losing ground, despite his gift of the scarf, but he could not think of any way to draw Mae's attention back to him without looking desperate and pathetic.

Ned placed a wooden box beside the airplane and held Mae's hand as she climbed into the front cockpit. She chastely wrapped the hem of her dress around her legs and lifted in one foot and then the other. She accepted the goggles, and Ned climbed in behind her. Jax and Hollister pulled the airplane out of the hangar, and Jax went to the front and put his hands on the wooden propeller.

"Mags off!" he barked.

"Mags off. Check!" returned Ned.

Jax pulled the big wooden propeller through several revolutions, then yelled, "Contact!"

"Contact. *Clear!*" yelled Ned.

Jax pulled hard on the end of one blade and quickly hopped aside. The engine issued noisy coughs, then caught with a throaty roar.

Jax gave a salute, and Mae mouthed, "Thank you," as they passed.

Jax's spirit soared.

He and Hollister watched the Jenny take to the air. Ned circled the airfield a couple of times then turned north, disappearing beyond the pines. Jax paced around the hangar, fidgeting with the radio, breaking up the ice, anything he could think of to calm his nerves.

"You're sick, my man," Hollister said.

"What's this?" Jax asked, holding up a bottle. "Tonic water?"

"Ned brought it."

"Gin too?"

"A little."

"Y'all take it easy, okay? I can't take her home all lit up."

"Sure, Jax. For sure. Whatever you say."

Ned and Mae returned an hour later. The sun was low, and the fireworks crew were making preparation for the show. People had gathered in small groups around the airfield. Ned put the Jenny down in front of the hangar and quickly rolled to a stop.

"Ned could fly that thing downtown for dinner and park it on Market Street," Hollister said.

Ned cut the engine, and Jax placed the steps beside the plane. "What'd you think?" he asked Mae.

"It was like a dream. It's too much to talk about."

"Did you find some cool air?"

"Oh yes! Have you felt that?"

"Yes, I have. It's aces."

Mr. Cole arrived at the hangar, and Ned showed him the Jenny, nose to tail. He bragged on Mae, saying she took to flying like a natural and should learn how. Mr. Cole hugged his niece. "Wouldn't that be something? And wouldn't your mama just skin me alive?"

"Well," Mae said. "I don't know if I could learn, but that sure was fun."

"I'm proud of you, honey. You're a brave girl."

Mr. Cole hung around for the beginning of the fireworks show, then he left, saying he was ready to turn in. When Mr. Cole had driven away, Ned opened a bottle of tonic water and poured some out. He replaced it with gin and handed the bottle to Mae, who hesitated to take it.

"What is it?"

"It's gin and tonic," said Jax. "You don't have to drink it. We have Coca-Cola." He reached into the washtub.

Ned pointed to the bottle's label. "See this? It has quinine in it. Now quinine is taken for malaria. This is nothing but good old malaria medicine."

"You don't need the hooch," said Jax. "Tonic water is still malaria medicine without gin."

"This ain't hooch," said Ned. "It's Bombay. Got it from Royce."

"Sounds terribly exotic," Mae said and took the bottle.

Jax did not put up any more objections. Mae was a grown woman, engaged to be married. She could answer for herself to Vida Cole if it came to it.

"Speaking of Royce," Hollister said, "he's supposed to be here tonight."

"He's probably over there with the colored folks," said Jax.

"We oughta go over and see what they have to eat," Hollister said. "I didn't have any supper."

"We could do that. That okay with you, Mae?"

"Sure, I could eat a bite."

Mae had almost finished the gin and tonic, and Ned made her a fresh drink. They walked across the airfield to where a crowd was gathered around picnic tables loaded with pots and platters. In front of the tables, torches had been stuck in the ground around a patch of hard-packed dirt, making a dance floor of sorts. Firelight illuminated the dancers' sweating faces as they bobbed and weaved to a quick melody played on guitar, banjo, and harmonica. The fireworks were in full swing overhead, lighting the night sky, but no one paid them any mind.

"That dance is called the Big Apple," Jax told Mae as they approached. Mae's eyes shone, and Jax thought it was from the gin. They reached the tables, and Jax saw Royce's mother, Beulah, talking with two other women. "Mama B!" he called.

"Jackson Addington! Get your skinny ass over here!" She met them halfway and gave Jax a crushing hug. "Where you been keepin' yourself, son?"

"I ran into some trouble in the Quarter."

"I heard a little bit about that."

"Yes'm, but it's all blown over now. I'm back in business."

"Royce'll be glad to hear it." She patted Jax's flat belly. "I got fresh cornbread over there, and cold buttermilk on ice."

"That sounds real good, Mama B. Just what the doctor ordered."

Beulah said hello to Ned and Hollister, hugging each of them in turn. Then she folded her thick arms under her bosom and regarded Mae. "Honey, what in God's green earth is a pretty thing like you doing tied up with this bunch? Does your mama know you're out here?"

"No ma'am."

"Well, I'm your mama tonight, darlin'. Now, y'all come on over here and get some food."

They grazed the tables and watched the dancers. Mae ate a few oysters and a piece of Beulah's cornbread. She finished her gin and tonic, and someone handed her a cold beer.

"Is it okay?" she asked Ned.

"Liquor to beer, you're in the clear," Ned said.

Mae's eyes were never off the dancers, and her foot tapped to the beat. As couples wore down and fell out of the whirling ring, others moved in and took their places.

"Do you like to dance?" Jax asked.

"Sure do."

"Well, let's get out there." Jax took the beer from her hand and set it on the table.

Just then, Hollister came out of nowhere and said, "My man, isn't that Black Olive over there?"

"Who's Black Olive?" asked Mae.

"Nobody. Let's go," said Jax.

"Over there." Hollister motioned toward Cargie Barre and a man Jax assumed was Cargie's husband. He was even taller than Cargie and wore a thick black beard and a gray trilby hat. A little girl perched on his shoulders with her arms wrapped around the crown of the hat. They stood near the parked trucks and cars, watching the fireworks.

"That's Cargie Barre," Mae said. She looked at Jax.

"Okay, okay," Jax said. "She gripes about my tickets all the time, like it wasn't me who brought in all the new business in the first place. Anyway, I got mad about it one day and told this knucklehead that she looks like a black Olive Oyl. I mighta called her Black Olive." Jax laughed, hoping Mae would think it was funny.

"Oh, Jax. That's so mean," Mae said.

Jax felt his countenance fall. He managed a sheepish smile and said, "I was having a bad day."

Cargie and her husband had walked to a truck, and he opened the passenger door for her. "I've never seen her husband or her little girl before," Mae said. "I never imagined Cargie doing anything except scribbling in those boring old ledgers."

Jax extended his hand. "Dance?"

He led Mae to the makeshift dance floor. Mae kicked off her shoes, took his hand, and followed him into the circle, where Jax immediately lost her among the dancers. He tried to follow her white turban as it dipped and bobbed, but he could never quite catch up. He danced as long as he could then retired to the sidelines. Mae never slowed down.

The musicians carried the dancers into the Lindy Hop. Jax stepped in to get his partner back, but he was cut off by Royce, who grabbed Mae's hand and pulled her away. Royce, though tall and thickly muscled, was light on his feet and unerring in rhythm. He improvised, and Mae followed his moves as if she knew them already. They moved with such vigor that clouds of stirred dust hid their shuttling, rolling feet.

The other dancers drifted to the edges, where they stood between the torches, watching and clapping in time to the music. Royce pulled Mae toward him, bent forward, and rolled her across his back. They fell apart again, arms outstretched, connected by their fingertips. Then they both dipped low and wagged their knees. The crowd went wild, whooping and hollering.

"You go, girl!"

"Cut a rug, Royce!"

Beulah came alongside Jax and slipped her arm around his waist. "We gotta put some meat on you, Jaxy. What you been eatin'?"

"Not much."

They both watched Mae and Royce. "They have to play out soon," said Jax.

"Royce won't quit before she does, and I gotta feelin' she won't quit before Royce."

Jax laughed then. "I gotta feelin' you're right, Mama B."

Beulah squeezed him. "Be careful what you wish for, baby boy."

The musicians stopped playing, which was the only thing that stopped Royce and Mae before they collapsed. Folks brought them folding chairs and cold beers. They fell into the chairs and held the bottles to their foreheads while they caught their breath. Mae had tied her turban so securely that it had not moved on her head. Sweat ran down her face and neck.

Royce said, "Lady Sheik, you're one helluva dancer."

"You too, mister."

"You gotta name?"

"I'm Mae."

"Royce."

He pulled a white handkerchief from his pocket and held it out to her. "Go ahead and take it. It's clean."

Mae took it and dabbed at her face and neck. "That was crazy," she said.

The women carried the empty platters and pots to their vehicles, and the men loaded the tables and chairs.

"Anybody know what time it is?" Jax asked.

Royce consulted his pocket watch. "Getting on toward midnight. About time we moved this party to Bistineau."

"Lake Bistineau?" Mae asked. "Over in Bossier?"

"Yes'm, that's the place," Royce said. "Come along with us."

Jax knew the juke joint on the lake would be hopping all night, and Hollister and Royce would be there until the bitter, whiskey-soaked end. It was no place for Mae. "Miss Mae," Jax said. "We better get you home."

Mae nodded. "Maybe next time, Royce."

"Yes'm. Anytime. Jax, why don't you drop by the house Sunday afternoon?"

"I'll be there."

Someone had set Mae's shoes beside her chair. Jax knelt in front of her and lifted one foot after the other onto his pants leg, wiping her soles with his palm and gently slipping them into her tee-strapped sandals. She permitted Jax to take her hand and help her up from the chair. "C'mon," he said. "I'll walk you to the hangar." He didn't dare leave to get the Sixteen for fear Mae would disappear before he returned to fetch her.

"What's at Lake Bistineau?" she asked as the two of them walked across the deserted airfield.

"A juke joint. Do you know what a juke joint is?"

Mae shook her head. She leaned heavily on his arm with a fresh bottle of beer dangling from one hand.

"We'll go over there sometime," he said. "Just not tonight."

The radio broadcast static through the open door of the dark hangar. Jax led Mae to the Sixteen and opened the passenger door. He held her hand as she slid into the seat.

"Put the top down, will you?" she asked.

"Sure thing."

Jax backed the convertible out of the hangar and got out to close up. Mae waited in the car, eyes closed, holding her bottle of beer to her forehead. She did not open her eyes again until he pulled to the curb in front of her uncle's house. The stop roused her, and she sat up.

"Thank you, Jax."

"Yes'm." He got out and opened her door. "Just leave the beer. I'll take care of it." She handed him the bottle and let him take her hand to help her out.

"Oh, your scarf," she said. "I can wash it and bring it to you Monday."

"It's yours, Lady Sheik. Remember? A souvenir of your flight."

She smiled. "Thanks. Thank you."

Jax walked her up the steps to the porch, and Mae opened the screen door. "See you Monday?" she said.

"Yes'm"

Mae gave him a little wave before going inside. He hoped that damned Vida Cole was asleep.

Jax got in the car and sat a while, thinking about the evening. He reached for the half-emptied bottle of beer and took a swill. It tasted good, like he imagined Mae would've tasted if he'd been able to kiss her goodnight. He started the Sixteen and pulled away. The streets of Shreveport were empty all the way to the Traffic Street Bridge, where Jax slowed and threw the empty bottle as hard as he could. It hit one of the bridge's iron beams and shattered. He shrugged and pressed the accelerator. The Sixteen roared across the Red River into Bossier, where Jax would pick up the highway to Lake Bistineau.

Chapter Twenty-Nine

Little Becca was just shy of her second birthday when her sister Adele came knocking at the door to enter the world. Thomas was worried. Everything about Becca's infancy had been easy. She followed the Murphy boy into the world, took hold of his hand, and never let go. But little Adele was going to be on her own, without another baby to grab on to. "I have not found a wet nurse," he wrote to Cargie's mother, "and it doesn't look like I will."

He had scoured Mooretown, bringing his daytime lady friends into his confidence so they could hunt for mothers-to-be and mothers with infants, a subject too indelicate for Thomas to ask around about himself.

"Don't worry none," Mrs. Pittman wrote back. "We gots options. Be there before August." Thomas had halfway expected Cargie's mother to write something along the line of, "Hasn't my daughter got bookkeeping out of her system yet?" But Rebecca Pittman knew Cargie as well as he did, and she seemed to have accepted her daughter's choices.

Bill Cole and Cargie were planning to open a second, larger Cole's Dry Cleaning and Laundry across the river in Bossier City in anticipation of all the new business from the army airfield. Downtown Bossier businesses were failing every month because of the Depression, and Mr. Cole had asked Cargie to give up a Sunday afternoon or two to scout locations. "The army won't even break ground until next year, but he's chomping at the bit to buy something," Cargie told Thomas.

"Why's he in such a rush?" Thomas asked.

"He's afraid prices'll go up when the army starts building."

Cargie sat on the bed and bent sideways past her belly to lace up her everyday shoes. She straightened suddenly and said, "Whew. Got to come up for air."

Thomas knelt and laced her shoes for her.

"Thank you, honey," Cargie laid her palm on his close-cropped head. "You're getting some gray up there, Mr. Barre."

"It's all these cares and worries I'm toting around."

"Go on now."

Thomas got to his feet then grasped Cargie's hand and pulled her up.

They won't," Cargie said.

"Who won't?"

"Prices. They won't go up. Not for a while."

"How do you know?"

"Speculators are scarce as hen's teeth. They all ran off with their tails between their legs."

Thomas and Becca walked Cargie to the streetcar stop, where she caught a car to the dry cleaners. Afterward, Thomas carried Becca to Lydie's house to spend the afternoon with Rudy.

On the way home, Thomas passed the Bishop place. Roshe Bishop sat on the front porch with a younger man. During the week, while Roshe worked at the refinery, Thomas did many small jobs around the house for Gertie Bishop, who returned the favor by giving him vegetables and herbs from her garden. According to Gertie, Roshe worked every hour of overtime he could lay hold of, and he was always too tired to tend to things around the house that needed fixing.

Thomas stopped and said, "Afternoon, Mr. Bishop."

"It surely is," said Roshe.

Thomas looked at the other man and touched the brim of his hat. "Thomas Barre."

The young man dipped his chin but did not offer a name. "This here's my baby brother," Roshe said. "He over from Mississippi lookin' for work."

"Is the refinery hiring?"

"No sir."

"Glass factory?"

Roshe shook his head and spat off the side of the porch. "Ain't no place hirin', seem like."

"Hard times everywhere," said Thomas.

"I reckon that's right."

"Been working on a little house for my mother-in-law."

"I seen it."

"Could use a hand. Somebody can handle a hammer and saw."

The brother looked up, interested. "How much it pay?" he asked.

"I reckon a hard worker would be worth, oh, I don't know, a couple of dollars a day. One dollar for half a day, such as today."

"You workin' on Sunday?" Roshe asked.

"Reckon it ain't right, but I'm kinda under the gun."

"I done give the Lord enough days of rest," said the young man. "Don't reckon he's got a right to begrudge me workin' a Sunday or two." He stood and stepped over the sprawled legs of his brother.

"Alrighty then," said Thomas. "What's your name, son?"

"Elijah," the boy said.

Thomas tipped his hat to Roshe and said, "Enjoy your afternoon, sir."

"I'll come along directly and see what's what," said Roshe.

That evening over a supper of leftover potato salad and ham sandwiches, Thomas told Cargie that Elijah had worked like a mule. "A young fella like that ought to have work," he said.

Cargie fed Becca pinches of ham dipped in tomato catsup. Becca loved catsup, and Thomas had more than once caught her trying to climb onto the table and get the bottle. "I'll ask Mr. Reynolds if anybody's hiring when I go to the bank on Friday," Cargie said. "He knows every business on the Avenue."

By the following weekend, Elijah had a job as a derrick man with the new oil company, the one whose office Mr. Reynolds had shown to Cargie. Thomas lost his helper, but he gained a friend in Roshe. "Gonna round up the fellas and help you build your house," Roshe said.

"I'll feed 'em all the barbeque they can eat. Their families too," said Thomas.

The following Sunday after church, a dozen Mooretown men showed up with their hammers and saws and their wives and children. The women brought side dishes.

"This could be the start of something new," Thomas told Cargie.

Cargie frowned at the crowd in her backyard. "We'll see how the work goes after their bellies are full," she said.

But as soon as dinner was eaten, the men jumped up and went to work, and they did not let up until it was too dark to see. By then, the framed walls were covered with shiplap and the house was capped with a fine tin roof.

Thomas was cleaning the barbeque pit after everyone had gone home. He heard a noise, and he peered into the darkness beyond the dim yellow light thrown out by the porch lamp. Standing near the corner of the house was the biggest dog he had ever seen, so utterly starved that Thomas did not see how it was alive. The huge head hung low, and the mangy hide clung to its skeleton as if the skin were ready to shed in ribbons like drying velvet coming off a buck's antlers. "Mercy," he said aloud.

He went inside to get his old pistol and put an end to the animal's misery. But instead of getting the gun, he found himself at the stove scrambling eggs in bacon grease. He emptied the eggs onto an old platter and carried it outside. The dog had reared up onto the barbeque pit and was licking the grill, but it shuffled away at the sound of the screen door. Thomas stepped off the porch and placed the platter on the grass. Then he sat down on the step to wait.

The dog paced back and forth just beyond the light, energized by the smell of food.

"Come. Eat," Thomas said softly.

The dog lifted its head.

"Come on now. You got nothing to lose."

The animal worked up courage in fits and starts, stepping into the light, turning back, stepping in again. Slowly, painfully slowly, it made its way to the platter. Thomas watched it nibble tentatively and then take great bites. The eggs were not enough to sate the dog, but that would have to come with time. In Thomas's estimation, it was enough for a first meal.

"You may be dead already," he told the dog. "But I'm willing to give it a try if you are." The dog sat and looked toward him, but it did not meet his eye. It ran its tongue around its mouth.

"Who are you talking to?" Cargie said from behind the screen door.

He pointed toward the dog. "Near starved," he said.

"Did you feed him?"

"Yes'm."

"Reckon you got yourself a dog."

Thomas was not sure if his wife approved or if she saw dogs as threats, as many folks did, especially an animal as enormous as this one. Would Cargie worry about Becca playing in the yard with it around? Thomas had not thought this through. He should have gotten the gun. "I was gonna shoot it—put it out of its misery," he said. "But next thing I knew, I was scrambling eggs. What do you think? Bad idea?"

"Let's give him a chance. Everybody ought to have a chance, even a half-dead dog. I'll get an old blanket to put down there beside the porch."

"Thank you, honey. I'll find a clean bucket and put out some water."

"You're a good man, Thomas."

When Thomas saw the dog in full light the next morning, he was certain it would not survive. It curled in a tight, frowsy ring on the blanket Cargie had put down beside the porch and did not move when Thomas opened the screen door and walked out into the warm sunshine. But when he said, "Good morning," the dog's head came up, and its tail thumped hopefully.

A week passed before the skittish stray allowed Thomas to touch him. Thomas discovered the dog was male when he greased the animal's dry, patchy hide with Crisco while the dog stood patiently. When Thomas had finished, he took the animal's face in both his hands and looked steadily into the yellow eyes. The dog shifted his gaze back and forth, avoiding eye contact.

"You are Lazarus," Thomas said. The dog tried to pull back, but Thomas held fast. "What say you, Lazarus?" he said. "Can I trust you around my baby girl?" The dog pulled harder, but he did not growl or try to bite. Satisfied, Thomas released him, and Lazarus backed away and shook his head. "Don't worry, big fella," Thomas said. "You're doing fine."

Chapter Thirty

By September, the Centenary football team practiced on the field every day, and Mae often walked from Uncle Bill's store to the campus, where she sat in the empty grandstand and watched the afternoon drills. The boys, outfitted in their numbered jerseys and leather helmets, charged back and forth with gusto, despite the sweltering heat.

Mae had never been to a college football game, but watching those practices made her look forward to the Gents battling it out against Hendrix on the Saturday after the fall term began. Uncle Bill had already bought their tickets and an extra ticket for Mae's father, who planned to take the train to Shreveport Friday afternoon if he could get away.

Buster wanted to come—badly—but his stubbornness wouldn't let him. He told Mae that missing a day and a half of work to watch a football game was foolish. He emphasized "foolish" so pointedly that Mae was sure he was punishing her for her own foolishness. She had not made even one trip home to see him since Sissy's wedding. She could have, and she should have. Mae had no good reason for not taking the train home every weekend and spending Sunday with her fiancé. Why, then, had she not?

Buster loved football. Mae had endured many afternoons of boredom while Buster and her father were glued to the radio, hanging on the announcer's rapid blow-by-blow. Big moves on the field either stood them on their feet with shouts of victory or pushed them, groaning, deep into their chairs. They participated in the games with the happy enthusiasm men reserved for their activities with one another. In these fraternal moments, Buster was animated and all in. Football uncapped his emotional fount in ways Mae never could. When the game was over, Buster again became the person he was with Mae. Levelheaded. Protective. Patronizing.

Oftentimes after a game, Mae engaged Buster in activities she knew he hated, such as making him drive her to Miss Viola's Dress

Shop in Gainesville, where Mae tried on everything Miss Viola had, sometimes more than once. She asked Buster's opinion about one dress, then another, and then the first again, until he was in agony. This she did simply to be mean, as payback for Buster being so much happier listening to a football game than he ever was doing anything with her.

If Mae could have articulated her most extraordinary recollection of the Fourth of July celebration at the airfield—the magical memory that warmed her as thoroughly as a bottle of malaria medicine—it would have been the camaraderie with which Hollister, Ned, and Jax welcomed her. They had opened the sweet communion of their fellowship to her as if she were their equal. Their generosity was as utterly intoxicating as flying in an airplane, or her first taste of gin, or dancing with a handsome black man.

Nevertheless, sitting in the grandstand watching the college boys train, Mae felt a pang for Buster, squeezed as he was into the narrow path of his own sensibilities. Buster would never attend college, even though he was a promising athlete—big *and* fast. It never would have occurred to him to try to make his way onto a college gridiron because he believed his lot in life—husband, father, breadwinner— left no room for chasing foolish dreams. Not that he would have permitted himself to dream them in the first place. Buster participated in the games via radio on Saturday afternoons because that was all he had. Deep down, Mae knew that Buster believed he had given her every other day of his week, even though she had not asked for them.

A dark-haired young woman made her way up the bleachers. Mae recognized the summer dress she wore. Mae had seen it during her last shopping trip to Selber Brothers and fallen in love with it instantly, but it had been a little too pricey to justify to her father. The girl's wide-brimmed hat hid her face as she took the steps in ivory Mary Jane shoes without a scuffmark on them. She carried a matching pocketbook under her arm. When she reached Mae's row, she looked up and smiled.

Her black hair was bobbed. Her eyes were dark brown, and her eyelashes were longer and thicker than the best mascara could bring off. The girl's skin, though fair enough, carried smoky undertones, as if her forbears had spent their days in the sun and passed to her its absorbed radiance.

"Hi," Mae said.

"Hi. Mind if I sit with you?"

Mae moved her pocketbook into her lap, and the girl sat beside her. "Miriam Landau," she said.

"I'm Mae Compton."

Miriam pointed to the field. "Coach is working them hard. That's my twin brother, there. Number forty-nine. Micah, but everybody calls him Mike."

"I've been watching number forty-nine. He's fast. I haven't seen anybody catch him."

"Only his girlfriend."

They both laughed.

Miriam glanced at Mae's hand. "So you're engaged? Is your fiancé on the team?"

Mae held out her left hand and looked at the ring. "No. I mean, yes, I'm engaged, but he's back home in Whitesboro."

"I don't know it," said Miriam.

"Whitesboro, Texas. It's a little-bitty town up by the Oklahoma border."

"Are you coming to school here?"

"Yes ma'am."

"Wow. That's brave."

"It feels a little too brave right now. Buster—my fiancé—isn't happy with me."

"Most girls start college and *then* get engaged. Well, truthfully, a lot of girls come to school to find a husband. Not me. Not you, obviously, but a lot of girls. So. Wow. What's your major?"

"Commerce."

"Even braver. I'm music. Junior year."

"What instrument?"

"Piano. And voice. I think of my voice as an instrument. I'm very serious about music. No time to try and catch a husband. He'll have to catch me."

"That's the spirit." Mae was genuinely impressed and thought that she and Miriam might become great friends.

They watched the boys run laps. Coach ran behind the team, barking at stragglers like a sheepdog keeping his herd together. The *Shreveport Journal* had run a story about Centenary's head coach, who in less than a decade had transformed the Gents into a winning team the town could brag about. A photograph accompanied the story, in which Coach Homer Norton wore a stylish woolen sweater and looked like an ivy leaguer. As far as Mae was concerned, Coach was as dashing and sophisticated as a movie star.

"Have you met anyone yet?" asked Miriam.

"Not here. Not at the school, I mean. There's a guy who works at my uncle's dry cleaning store, and I've met a couple of his friends."

"What's his name?"

"Jax Addington."

"I know Jax. We went to school together. We were in the same class."

"Really? What about Hollister Caine? And Ned Turner?"

Miriam laughed. "Oh my goodness, what a small world! Yes, we were all in the class of twenty-eight. Well, except Ned. He should have been, but he jumped ahead of us and graduated in twenty-seven. I heard he went to a school up north—Massachusetts, I think—that has a big aeronautical program. Ned's a genius, really."

"He took me flying in his airplane."

"He's back from college already? And he has an airplane? I wonder what he's doing."

"I don't know. We didn't talk about it. He's a sweet guy, though."

"Always was."

"What about Hollister? What was he like in school?"

"Well, you can probably imagine."

"Lady-killer," Mae said, and they both laughed.

"Yes ma'am. I had a crush on Hollister Caine all the way through school, but we never went out. I would have if he had asked, but I was shy, and I don't think he noticed me. The girls—you know, the more forward girls—they swarmed him like ants.

"Hollister was the starting quarterback for the Highlanders—our football team—but he was sweet too. Hollister never came off like he thought he was a big shot or anything like that. Centenary and Louisiana State offered him athletic scholarships, and he chose State. He was a great player, really a natural athlete. Everybody loved Hollister."

"I guess he's just home for the summer," said Mae.

"Well . . . no . . . not exactly." Miriam opened her pocketbook and took out a lacey handkerchief. She dabbed her perspiring temple. "I haven't seen Hollister since graduation, so I don't know this firsthand, but a mutual friend told me that Hollister was back home working for his father. His family owns the hardware store on Line Avenue."

"Why would he give up college to come back home?"

"I don't think he had a choice. Hollister liked to have a good time. He was always flirting with the razor's edge, if you know what I mean." Miriam placed her hand on Mae's arm. "I was told he was drinking a lot—too much—and got kicked off the team. He and his father were always crossways, so he wouldn't have had a way to stay without his scholarship."

"Oh gosh. That's so sad."

"Mr. Caine—Hollister's father—is a hard man. He was always hateful to Hollister, or at least it seemed that way to me from the things people said."

They sat in silence. The boys on the field collected their gear and trudged toward the locker-room entrance.

"What about Jax?" Mae asked.

Miriam stretched her legs out straight, feet together, and propped the heels of her Mary Janes on the bleacher in front of them. "Jax missed a lot of school, so I didn't see very much of him." She circled her hand over her middle. "He had this stomach thing, a nervous stomach or something like that, and it caused him to be absent most of the time."

"He's pretty thin."

"He always was."

"Did he graduate?"

"Oh, yes, of course. He walked with us. I heard he had private tutors and all that to help him keep up. I never heard what happened to him after graduation, so I'm glad to know he's out and about. You said he works for your uncle?"

"Cole's Dry Cleaning. Over on Prospect."

"That's who we use."

"Those boys—Jax, Hollister, Ned—they're kind of a mismatched trio."

"Yes ma'am. I don't remember them ever hanging around together in school. I wonder what brought them together."

"No telling," Mae said.

Miriam tucked her handkerchief back in her pocketbook. "Well, I better get going. I told Micah he could use my car tonight. His is on the fritz. Will you be staying in the dormitory?"

"No, with my aunt and uncle."

"Well, how about I pick you up for registration? It's hard to know what to do until you've done it. We always try to help the freshmen girls."

"I would love that. I've been a little nervous about it."

"It's a madhouse, all right, but we'll get you through it. We have a lot to talk about. There are two sororities on campus. I'm in Zeta Tau Alpha. The other one, Chi Omega, just started last year. I can introduce you to the girls in both groups. You'll want to meet everybody before you pledge. That is, if you think you'll want to pledge."

"Of course I do," Mae said.

Miriam stood. "I'm so glad we met. I'll call you in a few days. Is your uncle in the book?"

"Yes. Or you can call the cleaners. I help out there a lot."

"If you want to take a tour of the women's dormitory before registration, just let me know. I'm an assistant, so I have a key. If you're interested, that is."

"I wish I'd thought about staying on campus. It didn't occur to me with Uncle Bill and Aunt Vida living so close."

"I understand. My home is near the college too. Actually, though, you have to live on campus for two or three terms—I can't remember which—to qualify for a degree, so it's something to think about. What with study groups and all the activities, it's just easier to live in the dorm. Besides, we have a lot of fun."

"I don't want to miss a minute," Mae said.

"Nor should you," said Miriam. "Well, toodeloo."

"Bye-bye."

Jax was younger than Mae had imagined. He was only twenty or twenty-one at the most, yet his brown hair was thinning and already shot through with gray. Mae was glad she had been kind to Jax. After the Fourth of July celebration, she had even gone as far as accepting an invitation to take a ride in that big convertible he was so proud of. She permitted him to buy her a Coca-Cola, and she kept the conversation going, chatting about anything she could think of to avoid awkward silences.

Mae did not tell Miriam that she had ridden around Shreveport and Bossier with Jax, and even out to Lake Bistineau to get a look at that old juke joint. Mae was engaged to be married, after all. Miriam might've thought she was flighty or unfeeling for running around town with a single man—even a harmless boy like Jax—while her unhappy fiancé was two hundred and fifty miles away. Mae loved Buster, and she was faithful to him. There was absolutely no point in letting her new friend get the wrong idea about the kind of girl she was.

Chapter Thirty-One

Jax ran bootleg for Royce to line his own pockets while he handed his father every single paycheck from Cole's Dry Cleaning and Laundry. Jax could've quit Mr. Cole and paid his father in full but keeping his foot in the door at Cole's Cleaners kept his foot in the door of Mae Compton's life. After the Fourth of July celebration, Jax had watched Mae hang around her uncle's business, which meant she had free time—time she could've used to go home and be with her fiancé. But she did not. Most girls did not let their boyfriends out of their sight if they could help it.

Jax had finally worked up the nerve to invite Mae out for a ride in the Sixteen, and to his surprise and delight, she accepted. He bought her a Coke, and she asked him to drive her out to Lake Bistineau to see the juke joint, which he was happy to do. He wheeled the Sixteen off the highway and up a dirt road that ended at the tree-choked lakeshore, where a weathered building squatted under the pines. No windows. No sign. A long plank deck jutted low over the swampy water on pilings that were blackened with age and moss. Electric lightbulbs were strung between posts along each side of the deck, and a few tables and chairs were scattered around.

Mae eyed the building, absently tapping her bottom lip with the straw that stuck out of her bottle of Coca-Cola.

After a minute, Jax said, "It's kind of a dump."

"I'd like to see it when it's hopping," she said. Jax did not offer to take her, having seen how easily she was swept away from him before.

The next big move in Jax's plan had been to take Mae flying, just the two of them, but he had failed to meet Ned's expectations in the Jenny. By summer's end, Ned was dodging Jax to avoid their flying lessons. To make matters worse, after Mae started classes in September, Jax only saw her a couple of days a week when she walked from the campus to the cleaners to study. She sat at the counter with her nose buried in her books until Mr. Cole closed the store and drove her home. She had no interest in chatting with Jax, much less taking a ride with him.

Jax was dead in the water. He had just about resigned himself to quit Cole's Dry Cleaning and move on to other girls when a miracle came his way. The fella who owned the hangar where Ned kept the Jenny bought a Monoprep, an apple red, sporty two-seater with a docile personality. Ned's landlord was happy to let Jax fly his airplane for a fee, as long as Ned was satisfied with his handling of her. The little monoplane was a kitten compared with the squirrely Jenny. In no time at all, Jax handled the Prep better than her owner, at least according to Ned, who seemed eager to put any possibility of Jax flying his dear Jenny behind him.

Whereas the Jenny had tandem seats, one in front of the other, the Prep carried pilot and passenger side by side, shoulders touching. It was easy to have a conversation, even with the engine and wind roaring. The airplane's windshield was connected to the wing overhead, thus enclosing the cockpit, so Mae's hair would not be mussed.

At the owner's request, Ned had installed a manifold on top of the engine, under the cowling, and connected it with tubing to a small opening near the bottom of the firewall. One twist of a valve and engine-warmed air folded around the occupants' feet and legs for cozy winter flying.

Jax took the Monoprep on scouting trips, looking for the most exciting scenery with which he could impress Mae, and getting more and more comfortable with the airplane. One Saturday morning, he flew to Baton Rouge to check out the Louisiana State campus. He landed and taxied to a fuel pump in front of a large hangar, and the attendant ran out to meet him.

The attendant wore dark slacks, a starched white shirt, and a leather flight jacket. His black hair was close-cropped on the sides and long on the top. A sheaf, board straight, hung over his army-issue sunglasses. He swept the hair back—a gesture he must've made a thousand times a day—as he came around to Jax's side of the Prep and opened the door.

"Morning, sir! Beautiful bird. Top her off?"

"Sure. Thanks."

Jax got out and stretched his legs, while the attendant fueled the plane.

"Where you out of, mister?" he asked. His speech was quick and clipped, as if he were rushing to get out what he wanted to say before he was cut off.

"Flew down from Shreveport."

"Need a ride anywhere?"

"Yeah, I'd like to have a look around town," Jax said.

"Be happy to take you anywhere you want. Got a brand spanking new Packard limousine out back."

"A limousine, huh."

"Yes sir. We get plenty of VIPs through here, and the big wigs like to go in style."

"Nothing wrong with that."

"Facilities are inside the hangar. Ice cold pop and fresh coffee too. Make yourself at home, and I'll bring the Packard around."

By the time Jax had used the facilities, the attendant had pulled the limousine to the hangar door. Jax got into the rear seat, which was plush and spacious. "This isn't bad," he said. "I'm Jax, by the way. Jax Addington."

"Billy Dean Simmons." Billy Dean flew down the blacktop highway toward town, the Packard floating on its suspension.

"I wanna bring a college girl down here soon," Jax said.

Billy grinned at Jax in the rearview mirror, showing a gap where an upper tooth was missing.

"So where would you take a girl around here?" Jax asked. "I thought she might like to see the Louisiana State campus."

"Yeah, sure. That'd be all right. Ever seen the State House on the riverfront?"

"Never been here."

"I'll swing by. Then we can head over to the campus if you want."

The Louisiana State House sat on a bluff overlooking the river, as majestic as a castle in a fairy tale. The façade boasted the biggest stained-glass window Jax had ever seen, bar none. Billy parked the Packard in front, and they got out and climbed the steps. Billy opened one of the tall wooden doors for Jax. "After you, sir."

Jax walked inside to a massive winding staircase. It wrapped around a center column that rose from a black and white checkered floor to the capitol dome. The dome, made entirely of stained glass, spread like an enchanted parasol, its countless shards of color set afire by the sunlight.

"A girl could feel like Cinderella in here," said Billy. He took off his sunglasses, and Jax saw that he was just a kid, probably no older than sixteen or seventeen.

"This is the place, my man," Jax said.

"There's a mom-and-pop Cajun café across the street. Good gumbo. Best oyster loaf in town."

"I'm sold."

They drove back to the airport, and Billy parked the Packard beside the Prep. "She took ten gallons," he said. "A buck even."

"How much for the trip into town?"

"On the house, friend. The Capitol's happy to have your business." Billy smiled, but not so wide that the gap in his teeth showed again. He took a pouch of tobacco and papers from his pocket and rolled a cigarette with one hand. Jax had never seen it done half as quick. Billy lit the smoke and picked a thread of loose tobacco from his lower lip.

"You here every Saturday?" Jax asked.

"Every Saturday and Sunday, rain or shine. I'm it on the weekends."

Jax reached into the Prep and pulled a bottle from behind the seat. He handed it to Billy.

The boy studied the label. "Canadian Club. Fellas around here would give an arm for this. We mostly just get rum down here."

"How much is an arm?" Jax asked.

Billy laughed. "I dunno. Six, seven bucks. Maybe more. Most of these guys are flush."

"If you can get eight, I'll come back tomorrow with a few cases. I'll pay you ten percent for being the middleman."

"No kidding?"

"I'm dead serious."

Billy stripped the ember and tobacco from the butt of the cigarette and tossed them away. He rolled the paper into a tiny tight ball and put it in his pocket. Then he stuck out his hand. "You got a deal, Mr. Addington."

Jax shook on it. "Where are you from anyway?" he asked. "You don't sound like a Louisiana boy."

"Oklahoma Panhandle."

"Never been there."

"No reason to go. They call it No Man's Land. I call it the Land of Dried Up Dreams.

"Sounds like a good place to have in your rearview mirror."

"You got it right. Hopped a freight out of there the day after my mama died. I was fourteen."

"What about your daddy?"

"Dirt poor and handy with a strap. I thought he was hard-boiled at the time. He was hard enough, I guess, but the old man couldn't hold a candle to the railroad bulls. Saw the bulls beat a man to a pulp one time. You ever heard that saying? Beat to a pulp? It's real." Billy tucked the whiskey under one arm and rolled another cigarette and lit it.

"What happened?"

"Tramps had a camp in the woods outside Durant, Oklahoma. Bulls charged us one night whilst we slept. Everybody scattered 'cept a broke-down fella called Danny Boy. Old Danny Boy was too slow, and the bastards caught him. Beat him to a pulp. A bloody pulp, I tell you."

Jax wished Billy would stop repeating himself so he could stop imagining it.

"Danny was a hero in the war. Had a Medal of Honor. Saw it myself."

"What'd y'all do?"

"Moved camp."

Billy drew down the cigarette in a couple of long drags. He stripped it as he had the previous one and tucked the balled paper in his pocket, adding it to whatever collection he had in there. He laid his hand on the Prep. "Gonna learn to fly these things. Gonna borry a bird, fly back home, and snatch away my kid brother." He swept his palm down like an airplane dipping to the ground. "Gonna come outta nowhere like a chicken hawk." He dropped his hand and laughed. "That'll be a sight for the old man."

"Yes, indeedy."

"I'll be here tomorrow. Come on back. And thanks for the bottle." Billy looked at the label again. "Hey, wait a minute. What kind of game you running? You trying to get me killed?"

"What?"

Billy pointed to the label. "W-H-I-S-K-Y. That ain't how you spell whiskey. Do I look stupid?" His hand balled into a fist.

"Calm down, my man. That's how the Canadians spell it. Same with the Scots. Go to a library and check it out."

Billy studied the label, skeptical.

"Open it," Jax urged. "The proof's in the pudding."

Billy opened the bottle, unclenched his jaw, and took a sip.

"If your customers know what's what, they won't buy Canadian or Scotch unless it's spelled like that. Otherwise, it's hooch for sure."

"It's pretty good."

"Pretty good? It's top drawer."

Billy took another pull and rolled it around in his mouth before swallowing. "I'm still gonna check it out, though," he said as he screwed the cap back on.

"You should. You absolutely should. Then meet me here tomorrow."

"Okay. Yeah. Sure."

All the way back to Shreveport, Jax calculated the possible profits from the Baton Rouge connection. His mind returned again and again to one inescapable conclusion: He was going to need a bigger airplane.

Chapter Thirty-Two

Mae sat on her bed in Aunt Vida's house looking at Buster's letters heaped in a pile in front of her. During her first weeks in Shreveport, she had waited breathlessly for his letters, running to the front hall to retrieve the mail as soon as the postman dropped it through the slot. Her separation from Buster had been raw then. Painful.

For years, she had been the better half of Buster and Mae, the stars of the Whitesboro High School Royalty Revue. One day, she would no longer be Mae Compton. She would become Mrs. Buster Meade. It had all been decided forever. Actually, it was never decided. It simply was.

At the beginning of summer, Buster's letters had been poetic, urgently and plaintively declaring his love with words he never used when they talked. Mae was the woman of his dreams. The light of his life. His princess. He could not breathe without her. Without her he was only half a man. She had not known he had it in him.

He wrote to her every day, faithfully, despite working long hours six days a week. He signed his letters, "Please come home. Your loving Buster Bear." But the plea accompanying Buster's sign-off eventually bled into the preceding paragraphs. "Must you stay in Shreveport, my love, my darling? Wouldn't it be better for us to be together? Think about it, will you?"

As more weeks went by, Buster lost all patience with indulging Mae's whim. His letters began and ended with piteous wheedling or angry browbeating, depending—Mae suspected—on how his day had gone. The dried ink of his tight, angular pen spun off the page in brittle, accusing strands that made her feel as guilty as sin and choked the joy out of her afternoons. By the time summer's heat began to slack off, so had Mae's interest in what her fiancé had written. Some days, she found herself refolding his letter before she had finished reading it. Stuffing it back into the envelope without bothering to take care for the corners.

Mae had not gone home since Sissy's wedding, an unkindness that made her feel like a heel and gutted the devoted platitudes she penned in her own letters. Everything she had been doing—all the fun she had not written about—made her feel even worse. Lies of omission piled up between Buster and her in a big, stinking heap. She had not written to her fiancé about flying in an airplane on the Fourth of July, or dancing with a black man, or drinking gin until she was tipsy. Nor did she mention any of these adventures in their brief Sunday afternoon telephone calls.

Mae had not written a single word about Registration Day and the excitement of six hundred bright and privileged scholars bringing their glory to the Centenary campus. She had not told Buster about her new friends, Miriam and Micah Landau. Buster would have been jealous, and he would have told Sissy, making sure she felt as jilted as he. Mae did not recount the thrills of the Saturday football games he refused to attend. She left that to her father, who had managed to make it to two home games, even though he was much busier than Buster.

Mae did not write and tell Buster about the weekend the Landau family invited her to go with them to watch Micah run against the Aggies at Texas A&M. Miriam's father, who had hardly said a word during the drive to Texas, hooted and hollered until he was hoarse. Even Mrs. Landau, who was the picture of decorum, stood up and whooped when Micah scored a touchdown. After the game, they ate supper at a fancy restaurant, and everyone drank red wine with the meal, even Mae, as if it were nothing at all.

"I thought alcohol was illegal," Mae whispered to Miriam after the waiter poured her a glass the color of rubies.

"Daddy brought it. No one cares if you bring your own."

They spent the night in the modern LaSalle Hotel in Bryan, and Mae and Miriam shared a room and stayed up late talking about everything they loved and hated about Centenary. On Sunday morning, they ate breakfast in the hotel's sunny dining room before driving back to Shreveport, and for the first time in Mae's memory, she missed church when she was as fit as a fiddle.

But she did not write to Buster about any of it, and eventually she realized she was only writing the same thing over and over again—a paragraph or two.

"Miss you so."

"Life is so dull without you."

"Wish you were here."

While she penned, "Wish you were here," Mae had the sudden and unsettling thought that she most certainly did not wish for Buster to come to Shreveport, where he could lay his heavy, protective arm across her shoulders and put a stop to all her running around.

Mae surprised herself one day when she passed the Centenary office—where the assistants mimeographed copies of lessons for the students—and the thought occurred to her that she could mimeograph a letter and save herself a week's worth of coming up with something to say.

Buster became irritable during their brief Sunday afternoon long-distance telephone calls. Mae always did the calling—it was she who was away—and she paid Aunt Vida from her allowance every month when the bill came. Most Sundays Mae spent more time waiting for the operator to set up the circuit to Whitesboro than actually talking to Buster. When they finally were connected, he gave clipped, one-word responses that made him sound even farther away than the scratchy connection.

"Don't you want to talk?" Mae asked.

"It's long distance, Mae. It costs a fortune. Wouldn't cost a dime for you to come home."

"Try and be patient, B-Bear, it's only a couple of weeks 'til I'm home for Thanksgiving."

"Well, I'll see you then, I guess."

"I love you."

"Most fellas wouldn't put up with this, Mae. I hope you know that."

"We agreed about me coming to school."

"No, I never agreed."

Mae hesitated.

"I'll see you in a couple of weeks," Buster said. "Bye."

"Bye, honey," Mae said, but he had already hung up.

Buster did not write any letters after that, and Mae did not try to call the following Sunday.

She was as nervous as a cat the afternoon before Thanksgiving when the train pulled into the tiny Whitesboro depot, and she saw Buster standing beside her father. Buster wore dark slacks, a gray vest, and shirtsleeves. He looked grown up. And thin.

Her father wore a suit and tie. He took her valise and hugged her tightly as soon as her foot touched the platform, smelling—as he always did—of Aqua Velva. "Got somebody here who wants to see you," Her daddy stepped aside. "Do you know this guy?"

Mae looked up at Buster and smiled sheepishly.

"You sure are a sight for sore eyes, Mae Pearl Compton," Buster said. He opened his arms. "Come here, you."

"I'm sorry, honey," she whispered when she hugged him because he was crying.

"Maypearl!" cried Vic when Mae opened the screen door into the kitchen, "It's been *for-ever!*" Mae's younger sister, Victoria, had run Mae's first and middle names into a single word ever since she could talk.

"Look at you! We're gonna have to put a brick on your head."

"I'm the tallest girl on the basketball team now," Vic said proudly.

"Oh my."

"I *like* it. I *want* to be tall. And I'll marry me a big tall man, and we'll have a passel of tall kids. I *like* tall people!"

Mae laughed. "Well, I don't guess I can call you Little Bit anymore.

"Sure you can."

"All right, honey. Where's Mama?"

"She's out back cutting collards. She wanted to get a frost on them, but Daddy says it's not gonna get cold enough."

"Let me get out of these travel clothes, and I'll help." Mae squeezed her sister. "It's *so* good to see you. My goodness, it's nice to be home."

Mae went to her room by way of the living room, where Buster and her father had settled in to read the newspaper. Her daddy looked up from the paper and said, "Sure feels good having my college coed home."

Mae bent and kissed him on the cheek. "I love you, Daddy."

Buster put down his newspaper and winked at her. He sprawled on the couch, as he had always done. Mae's house was his home away from home and seeing him here with her family felt as comfortable and right as slipping her feet into a pair of well-worn shoes. Everything fit. Everything made sense. And there weren't any questions looking for answers.

Buster hung around until Mae was finished helping her mother. Then the two of them went for a drive in his truck. It had been five months, but when she climbed in and sat close to him on the bench seat, it seemed as if she hadn't been gone at all. The truck smelled of engine oil and vinyl and Buster. Most of all it smelled like the past and the future.

Buster drove through Whitesboro and stopped in front of a shotgun cottage at the edge of town. The narrow, deep house was set back from the street, and in the waning light Mae could see that it was in good repair and freshly painted. A blue flower box was attached below the single window beside the front door. The yard was clipped and free of rubbish.

"Fella at work owns the place," said Buster, "but he's willing to sell. Says it's been hard to keep it rented since the Crash. Wanna have a look?"

"Okay."

Buster came around and opened her door. He held her hand as they walked up the sidewalk and climbed the two steps to the front porch. He opened the door, and they walked into the living room. It was plain and square. Buster walked across the room to another doorway, his dress shoes tapping in the hollow space, and Mae walked past him into a second room just like the first. She did not stop but went directly through the third doorway, which led to a kitchen the same size as the other two rooms.

On the back wall was a wide farm sink—its white enamel lightly stained—set in a tiled counter. An electric icebox hummed in the quiet of the empty house. Mae walked across the room and looked out the window over the sink. Autumn had been dry, and the unfenced backyard was mostly bare dirt, with patches of brown grass here and there. She turned around and looked at the open door to a bathroom that had been sectioned off from the kitchen. She could see a sink, a toilet, and a claw-footed bathtub.

"It's not the Taj Mahal," Buster said, "but it's not bad. The company's already given me a raise, and the boss says I ought not to have any trouble making foreman if I keep my nose clean."

"Your friend has taken really good care of it."

"Well, like I said, it's no mansion, but I've saved enough money to buy it."

"Gosh, honey." Mae looked around. "Wow."

Buster walked across the kitchen and stood beside her at the sink. They both looked out the window. "I can picture us washing the dishes together," he said. "Well, you wash, and I'll dry. Think you could be happy here for a while, at least until we can afford something bigger? Maybe we can build our own house in a couple of years. We could buy a few acres out in the country, and you could design our dream house." He squeezed Mae. "What do you think?"

"It's not that I don't like it. It's just that maybe we should wait until I get out of school. It's such a long time, and who knows what we can afford by then."

"About that. It's too long, Mae. Four years is just too long." Buster folded his arms across his chest.

Mae bumped against him playfully. "It's not so long when you think about our whole lives."

"Well, it's too long for me."

Mae could see that no amount of wheedling would move him. She was to come home, marry him, and get on with it. That was all there was to it. "Let me finish out the school year," she said. "Daddy's already paid for it."

"Then you'll come home?"

"I'll come home when school's out." Mae did not say aloud the rest of the sentence that ran through her mind, ". . . for the summer anyway."

"Okay." Buster unfolded his arms and pulled her close. "Now we're getting somewhere." He lifted her face and kissed her. They necked for a little while, then Mae pulled back.

"I better get home. Mama will be wondering."

"She knows you're with me."

"Yes, but still." Mae backed up, away from his reaching arms. "I need to help her finish getting the food ready. I still think you should wait on this house."

"Just leave that to me, babe. And don't worry about anything. I'll take good care of us."

It was late that evening when Buster finally drove home, and Mae knew he would be back early the next morning to see her. To sit at the kitchen table and watch her fry bacon and three eggs sunny-side-up in the grease. To watch her pull two slices of crisped bread from the toaster and smooth butter on them. To have her set the plate of food in front of him and pour his coffee, as if she were already his wife.

Mae walked into the kitchen after kissing Buster goodnight on the front porch and found her mother sitting at the Formica table drinking her Ceylon tea. "Have some tea, honey?" she said.

"Yes'm. Don't get up. I'll fire the kettle." Mae made her tea and poured a little more scalding water into her mother's cup. Her mother bobbed the infuser in the hot water to get the last of the flavor. "Buster took me to a house he wants to buy. For us."

"He told your daddy and me about it."

"It's a little soon. I'm just starting school."

"He won't wait for you to graduate, Mae. You know that."

"I got him to agree to wait until summer. I'm really enjoying Centenary, and I don't want to leave. I've made some friends, and I like most of my classes. Some of the classes are hard. Really hard. One class is just a bunch of facts and figures and formulations about the cotton business. I'm bored to tears in there, really. But I like Centenary, and I like Shreveport. A lot."

"Listening to you makes me wonder if you can be happy in Whitesboro."

"I think about that sometimes too." The truth was that Mae thought about it constantly. What she would really like to do is get a job, maybe a secretarial position, and work in one of the tall buildings in downtown Shreveport. For the first time in her life, the dream of being on her own seemed to be within reach.

"You need to know something," her mother said. "We haven't said anything to Vic, so you're going to have to keep it to yourself."

"What is it?"

"Your daddy's being promoted."

"Oh, Mama, that's wonderful!"

"Well, yes, it is. We're very happy, but it means a move. He's going to Fort Worth after Christmas to find us a house, and Vic and I will move there when school lets out in May. This house," her mother looked around the kitchen, "is the only home your sister has known."

"She'll be happy. Vic loves an adventure."

"You're right. I'm not worried about her."

After a moment Mae said, "I can't imagine living in Whitesboro without y'all around."

"No, daughter, I didn't think you could."

Chapter Thirty-Three

A week after Thanksgiving, on a Friday afternoon, Mae showed up at the dry cleaners for the first time in a fortnight. Jax said hello and asked if she had a good Thanksgiving as she pulled out her textbook and thumbed through the pages.

"Sure, it was fine," she said.

"That's nice."

Mae did not look up again to invite conversation.

Jax hung around, trying to look busy. The afternoon's tickets were on a shelf under the big cash register, so he picked them up and began sorting through them. He leaned against the counter while he looked through the slips of paper, pretending to tally the afternoon's business in his head. He happened to glance up and see Cargie Barre through the half-open door to the little office, where she holed up all the time like a troll in a cave. She stared at him as if she had caught him dead to rights with his hand in the till. He glared back, but Cargie did not even have the good sense to look away.

"What?" he mouthed.

Cargie got up from her desk and came out of the office, never breaking eye contact with him. She parked herself in front of him and stuck out her hand, palm up. Cargie had recently given birth and returned to her Olive Oylness. She was taller than Jax by a couple of inches, and even more so with him slouched against the counter. He stood up straight and glanced toward Mae to see if she was watching, but she was focused on her studies. Mr. Cole was in the cleaning hall.

Jax had the urge to punch Cargie Barre right in that homely puss of hers, she was so damned uppity. She and Bill Cole carried on as if neither of them realized she was only a bookkeeper and colored to boot. She had a superior air about her too, like she thought she was better than Jax. He glanced at Mae again, who had looked up and was watching the face-off. Watching Cargie with her outstretched palm. Looking at the wrinkled tickets in Jax's clenched fist. Jax stuck out the tickets, just a little bit, so Cargie had to reach for them. She snatched them and went back into the little office and shut the door behind her. Jax turned to Mae and smiled. But she had already put her attention on her textbook again.

Before Mr. Cole closed up and drove Mae home, Jax nonchalantly mentioned he was flying down to Baton Rough the following day.

"With Ned?" Mae asked.

"No, I'm flying on my own these days—a nifty little red coupe. Say, maybe you'd like to ride along and see the Louisiana State campus."

A pause.

"That is, if your Saturday plans are flexible. It's a real pretty flight."

"Sure," she said finally. "Why not?"

"Pick you up at nine?"

"Okay."

Jax grabbed his hat and said goodbye before Mae had a chance to think about it and change her mind.

Jax dreaded facing Vida Cole again, so he was thrilled when Mae came out the front door the minute he pulled to the curb. He jumped out of the Sixteen and opened the door for her.

"Let's go," she said.

"Sure thing."

He wasted no time pulling away and driving to the airfield, where the Monoprep sat in front of the hangar like a proud winter cardinal, Jax having wrestled it out early that morning before he picked Mae up.

"It's so pretty," she said.

"She's a dream to fly. You'll love her."

The morning was chilly, and Jax opened the heater valve as soon as the engine had warmed.

"Oh my," Mae said. "That's nice."

"It's about a two-hour flight," Jax told her when they were cruising a thousand feet or so above the river.

Mae leaned over and looked at the gauges in front of Jax. The smell of her hair was intoxicating. "How fast are we going?" she asked.

Jax pointed to the airspeed. "Eighty miles an hour, but we ought to have a tailwind, so more like ninety-five or a hundred across the ground."

"Fast."

"Yes'm. Very." Jax liked her leaning into him. "This is the altimeter," he said. "It tells how far above the ground we are. See, we're at a thousand feet."

"Uh-huh."

"And this is the engine tachometer. It tells how many revolutions per minute—RPMs—the engine is turning—same as in the Sixteen." Mae nodded and turned away to look out her side at the river. Jax took the hint and shut his piehole. All this talk about the gauges was boring—he was boring himself to tears.

Jax had chosen to take her by way of Natchitoches, an old French town with double-gallery houses like the ones in Vieux Carré. When they reached Natchitoches, he descended and circled the center of town. "I hear there's a good restaurant downtown," he said. "A French family serves food as good as anything you can get in the Quarter."

"Ooh, I feel a little queasy," Mae said.

Jax stopped circling right away and turned southeast toward Baton Rouge. "Happens to everybody," he said. "Here, you take the stick. Flying will take your mind off feeling sick."

Mae tentatively took hold of the stick on her side. "What do I need to do?"

"Just keep the wings level."

Mae seemed fine with her attention divided between looking outside and feeling as if she were flying the airplane, which was actually flying itself. "Next stop, Baton Rouge," Jax said brightly.

Mae spent the rest of the flight watching the Louisiana landscape pass under the wings of the Prep, and Jax pretended the silence between them was the comfortable sort shared by couples in love.

Billy Dean met them in front of the hangar. The morning was warming quickly, and he was in shirtsleeves. On the front pocket of his starched white shirt was a black outline of Louisiana with Baton Rouge written across it in gold cursive. He opened Mae's door as soon as the Prep stopped rolling. "Welcome to the Capitol, miss."

"Thank you."

He took her hand and helped her out of the airplane. "Just inside the hangar, over there, are the facilities. Fresh coffee and ice-cold pop too. You just make yourself at home, Miss . . . ?"

"Compton."

"Miss Compton. Please make yourself comfortable." Billy turned to Jax and said, "I'll take care of the bird, Mr. Addington, and bring the limo around."

"He knows you." Mae said as she and Jax walked to the hangar.

"I've been making some deliveries for a little side business I run."

"What do you deliver?"

"Oh, medicine mostly. Sometimes doctors and druggists need supplies in a rush."

"Not malaria medicine, I hope!" Mae said and laughed.

"Lord, no!" Jax laughed too. It was the truth. He never went near a bottle of tonic water if he could help it.

Billy drove the Packard limousine around and opened the rear door for Mae. She climbed into the backseat, and Jax saw her run her palm over the plush upholstery. He settled in beside her, but not too close.

Billy took a different route from the one he had driven with Jax. He drove west to the river before turning south toward town, giving them a pretty view of the Mississippi all the way to downtown Baton Rouge. Mae's eyes widened when she saw the State House. "My goodness," she said. "It looks like a castle."

"Right out of a fairy tale."

"I'll say."

Billy parked at the base of the steps leading up to the building, got out, and opened the rear door.

"Come back in a couple of hours," Jax told him.

"Yes sir, Mr. Addington. I'll be here."

As soon as they walked into the spacious rotunda, Mae looked up at the magnificent dome and twirled around unselfconsciously. "It's enchanted!" she cried. She ran up the steps. "I could get married here! Can you imagine how beautiful it would be?"

Jax gazed at her leaning over the banister. The light coming through the stained-glass dome radiated around her thick, curly hair, and she looked like a saint illuminated by a colorful heaven. "Instead of a church?" he called.

"Sure, why not?"

The rotunda amplified their voices, as if they were speaking on stage. As if they were actors in a play.

"It's just that most girls want to get married in a church."

"I'm not most girls."

He grinned. "No ma'am. You sure aren't."

When they had seen enough of the State House, they walked across the street to the little café Billy Dean had recommended. They ordered oyster loaves and ate them over butcher paper with remoulade sauce dripping from buttery grilled French bread.

"I met someone at Centenary who went to school with you," Mae said. "The Landau twins, Miriam and Micah. Do you remember them?"

Jax held up a finger while he finished chewing. He wiped his mouth. "This is messy. Yeah, I remember Micah really well. He played football with Hollister. Micah's old man is a big shot with Gulf Oil. I think his mama had family money too, best I remember. They're rich, you know. Rich Jews."

"I didn't realize. I thought they were Methodists or Baptists, like the rest of us."

"I don't mean anything bad by that. Just that they're Jews and they're rich. The Jews own half of Shreveport. I know some people don't like them much, but you can't fault folks for making good." Jax took a small bite and chewed it thoroughly. He was likely to pay for the greasy sandwich if he did not eat slowly. He was likely to pay anyway, and he couldn't afford stomach cramps or worse during the flight home. He reached into his front pants pocket and felt for his flask of Pepto-Bismol. "I kinda remember Micah had a sister," he said. "But I didn't remember her name. Miriam, you say?"

"That's right. Miriam said she was shy in school. She's really serious about her music."

"Micah was a blue streak on the field."

"He still is. Say, you should come to a game next fall, if you're not working on Saturdays. It'll be Micah's senior year."

"I'd like that."

"Do you like working for my uncle?" Mae asked.

"Mr. Cole? Sure. He's a prince. Heckuva guy."

"Isn't he really good friends with your father?"

"Oh yeah, they're pals. That's how I got the job."

"Do you think you'll stay on at my uncle's? I mean, in the future?"

"Oh, I don't know. Cargie may run me off."

"Oh, don't be mean. She's a sweetheart. Her baby was a little girl. Her second little girl. Did you know that?"

"No. I didn't know what she had."

"This is a *lot* of food," Mae said of the oyster loaf. "Kind of a mess to eat, but it's delicious."

"Let me get you a fork." Jax jumped up and got two forks from the counter. He returned to the table and handed one to Mae. He opened the French bread and stabbed a fried oyster.

"Cargie named her baby Adele," Mae said. "Isn't that pretty? I think it's an old English name."

"Yeah, it's nice. Cargie's okay. She's just not too crazy about me."

"That's what you said about Aunt Vida."

"It's true too, isn't it?"

"Well, you can't count her. My aunt doesn't like anybody."

Jax laughed. "Careful now, she might be listening."

"Isn't that the truth? Not to speak ill, but she does like to know everybody's business."

"She's kinda known for that."

"She has opinions about everybody too."

Jax decided it was time to take the high road. "I guess she's entitled. Like they say, opinions are like noses. Everybody's got one. But as far as staying at Mr. Cole's, I doubt I'll be there too much longer. I'm really a sales guy. That's where I've done your uncle the most good. I have a few other irons in the fire, so we'll see."

"I didn't mean to pry. I was just curious."

"Hey, I'm an open book. Ask me anything you want to know."

"Well, I was kind of wondering how you and Hollister and Ned got to be such good friends. Did y'all run together in high school?"

Jax's gut signaled it was time to stop eating. He put down his fork. "No, not really. We just sort of fell in together afterward."

"I see. Well, you guys seem thick as thieves. I had a lot of fun on the Fourth of July."

"Everybody enjoyed the heck out of you, Mae. You were the belle of the ball." Jax winked. "Lady Sheik."

"That's me!" Mae beamed more brightly than he ever remembered seeing before.

Billy Dean was waiting at the curb when they walked out of the café. When they got back to the airport, Mae went into the hangar and Billy handed Jax a wad of cash as soon as she was out of sight.

"Did you get the case in the back of the Prep?" Jax asked.

"Yeah. I can sell it as fast as you bring it."

"I'll be back tomorrow with a regular load."

"I'll be here," said Billy.

They had a headwind going back to Shreveport, and Jax felt as if they were barely crawling along, even with the throttle wide open. By the time they reached Natchitoches, the land below them was dark, but they could still see the sun sitting on the horizon. Jax pointed to the lights of Natchitoches shining in the darkness below them and said, "Look down there."

"It's already nighttime down there," Mae said.

"But we can still see the sun." Jax was worried Mae had become impatient with the long trip home. She'd hardly said a word the entire time. "Are you comfortable, Mae?" he asked. "Are you warm enough?"

"Don't worry about me. I'm fine."

When they reached Shreveport, Jax set the Prep down smoothly, using the city lights reflecting off the river to judge their height above the darkened airfield. After landing, he taxied into the hangar through the open door, rather than pulling the Prep in by hand. There was no need for Mae to watch him try and wrestle the airplane inside. He shut the engine down.

"It doesn't get old, does it?" Mae said before she got out.

"What doesn't get old?"

"Flying. I don't believe I'll ever get tired of looking at the world from up there."

"Me either. Flying is absolutely aces. I was thinking about taking a trip to Marshall, Texas, next weekend. It's a short hop—less than an hour—and there's a big pottery factory there. Might be fun to see it."

"I know about Marshall Pottery. Mama has some flowerpots from there."

"Wanna fly over there next Saturday if the weather's good? Maybe have lunch and look around?"

"Sure. Sounds fun."

"Alrighty then. I don't know about you but I could use a good night's sleep after the day we've had. I'll drive you home."

"Thanks, Jax. That was the most fun I've had since the Fourth of July."

Jax imagined himself on the gridiron with a Hail Mary spinning toward him. He leapt impossibly high—a yard of air between his cleats and the turf. He felt the ball touch the sweet spot in the center of his chest, and he wrapped his mighty hands around it. He landed lightly and looked across a playing field on which no man was his equal. Then he ran, agile as a cat, all the way to the end zone. The band struck up "Happy Days Are Here Again" and Mae broke away from the sideline and ran to him. She wrapped her arms around Jax and kissed him as if she would never let go.

The crowd went wild.

Chapter Thirty-Four

Mae bought a diary after Jax flew her to Baton Rouge. It locked with a tiny metal key, and she kept it in the suitcase she had pushed to the rear of her closet at Aunt Vida's. She locked the suitcase too, so private were the thoughts she recorded in the diary's pages. During the long flight home from Baton Rouge, wrapped in the low roar of the airplane's engine and the wind rushing past, Mae gave desire its head and permitted her thoughts to gallop unrestrained. *What if I don't marry Buster? What might become of me then?*

She wrote everything in her new diary that she had not written in her letters to Buster, beginning with her arrival in Shreveport the year before. She even wrote about the dreams that carried her to Shreveport in the first place. The words poured from her heart through her hand in a torrent she hardly recognized as her own thoughts. She struggled afterward to read what she had written, so rushed was her cursive.

She and Jax flew to Marshall before Christmas, scooting so low over flat cotton fields that Mae felt as if she could have reached out the side of the airplane and picked a boll herself. They surprised one old farmer who dragged a pick sack between the dried stalks, gleaning leftover lint from the harvested plants. He looked up so suddenly when the Prep roared over that his hat slid off the back of his head. When Mae looked back, he was still watching them, and she wondered if he was awestruck or annoyed. Mae wrote everything about the Marshall trip in her diary, but there was no point in writing about it to Buster. The trip to Marshall was only a drop in a river that was sweeping her away.

Mae went home for Christmas. By then, Vic knew they were moving to Fort Worth. So did Buster. He promised Mae they would ride the train to Fort Worth at least once a month using her free passes. "I won't have you homesick for your mama and daddy," he said. He wanted to go to the little shotgun house again and talk about how they might furnish it. He had not bought it yet. Thank God. Mae didn't want to see the house again. She made excuses until Buster finally said, "Why don't you like the house, Mae?"

Mae hated the shotgun house and its three rooms lined up one after another. First this. Then that. Then the other. Plodding along. She did not want to settle for a life in that house. In the back of her mind was the idea that the house was only the first concession in a long line of compromises that would eventually become a lifetime of settling.

"Maybe we can do better," she said.

"It's all we can afford right now, honey. You need to be reasonable."

"Let's wait a bit."

"Well, we have to figure something out pretty quick."

"I can stay with Sissy and Joe for a little while if I need to."

"You won't need to if we're married."

"How are we going to have time to plan a wedding with Mama and Daddy in the middle of moving to Fort Worth?"

"When do you want to get married then?" Buster snapped. "When we're eighty?"

Mae laughed out loud, then she saw how hard Buster's eyes were. "Well, of course not, B-Bear," she said quickly. But all the while, Mae could not help thinking, *Maybe not when we're eighty. Maybe not ever.*

Chapter Thirty-Five

1931

Jax often spent Sunday afternoons with Mama B and Royce. Royce stayed with his mother at her house in Bossier City, even though he owned a house on Loggy Bayou below Lake Bistineau. Royce had a wife and four children there too. The wife threw Royce out when the children were young, saying she would not have her babies grieving for their daddy when his sins came home to roost and he landed in the penitentiary at Angola or face down in Loggy Bayou with a bullet in his head.

Royce was welcome to come home every Friday for an afternoon liaison while the children were in school, as long as he brought money for the coming week, which he did faithfully and without complaint.

Jax drove to Mama B's house on the Sunday after New Year's, when the sun had commenced its dive toward the pines. There was a police blockade on the Shreveport-bound side of the Traffic Street Bridge. The lawmen were searching every automobile, delaying motorists in a line that stretched half a mile. This was a lousy break—it would keep Jax from bringing a load of bootleg back to Shreveport, but he was already across the bridge, so he drove on to Mama B's to see what was cooking. Royce's Lincoln Continental was in the driveway. Royce drove a Lincoln because everyone else drove Cadillacs.

It had been years since Jax had knocked on Mama B's door before going in. He swung the door wide open and was about to shout, "Mama B!" when he came nose to nose with a .38 special. Jax said, "Whoa!" and raised his hands.

"Who the hell is this?" squealed the gunman in a high-pitched Irish brogue. Freckles speckled the man's red face, and his hair bristled like snags of copper wire rooted in his scalp. Jax looked from the gunman to Royce, who stood behind him.

"Put the gun down, Red, for God's sake," barked Royce. "This is Jax. He's family."

"He ain't *my* family," cried Red. "Ain't yours either from the look of him."

Royce stepped forward and laid his palm across the .38 and gently lowered the weapon. "Jax is with us. You'll aggravate me if you shoot him."

Red lowered the gun but held it at his side a moment before sliding it into the holster under his left arm. "Well, hell, Royce, if you say so." The Irishman stuck his hand toward Jax. "Red Malone."

Jax shook the man's hand, his palm sweating. "Jax Addington."

"The bread pudding's about to come outta the oven," Mama B said as she came around the corner from the kitchen. She stopped short. "Jackson! I figured you done forgot about us today." She ushered Jax to the kitchen and pushed him into a chair at the enameled table. "You had your dinner yet?"

"Yes'm, ate with the family."

"Well how about some coffee and bread pudding?"

"Thank you, Mama B. That sounds real fine."

Royce came into the kitchen followed by Red Malone. They sat at the table with Jax.

"I didn't see a car," Jax said.

"It's in the shed around back," said Royce. He dug a lighter out of the deep front pocket of his high drape pants and laid it on the table. He flipped it over so the Jack Daniels Old No 7 engraving was face-up.

"There's a police blockade on the Traffic Street Bridge going toward Shreveport," Jax said.

Red Malone had turned his chair around and straddled it with his arms folded over the back.

"That Delia's no damned good," said Mama B to no one in particular.

"No need to rehash it," Royce said. "What's done is done."

"Every judge and jury in Bossier go to Delia's," observed Jax.

Red looked up quickly but said nothing.

Royce reached into his shirt pocket for his Lucky Strikes and shook one out of the dark green pack. He opened the back door, letting in fresh air and bands of sunlight, and cocked his head as he lit the cigarette. The three men sat in silence while he smoked and Mama B served them bread pudding, which they ate between sips of scalding coffee. Afterward, they sat some more, and Royce smoked some more, and Mama B cleaned the kitchen.

"Where you from, Red?" Jax asked, finally.

"New York. And Hot Springs of late," Red answered glumly. "Royce, I need to call the missus if I can't get outta here tonight."

Royce said, "Telephone's in the parlor but it's a party line. Don't recommend using it."

Jax swirled the loose grounds in the bottom of his cup and said, "I have an idea to get you out of here, Red. How do you feel about airplanes?"

A couple of hours after leaving Mama B's, Jax flew to her neighborhood in the Monoprep. He set the little red airplane down on the unnamed dirt road in front of her house, which dead ended at the edge of a vast and fallow cotton field. On the far side of the field, work crews had already begun grading the land to transform the former plantation into an army airfield. Mama B, Royce, and Red came out of the house, and Jax opened the passenger door but he did not cut the engine.

Red ran to the plane and climbed in next to Jax. "You got the number I gave you?" Red asked Royce.

"Got it right here." Royce patted his shirt pocket.

"Give us about half an hour before you call," Jax said.

Royce nodded.

Red said, "You go over to Delia's and get Boolie outta there. Drive her up to Hot Springs in my car, will you?"

"Red, you know I can't go driving a white woman to Hot Springs."

Red grinned and elbowed Jax. "Who said she was white?"

Royce did not smile. "What if she doesn't want to?"

"Tell her I love her. Tell her I'll get her away from that damned whorehouse and set her up in an apartment in Hot Springs. Got it all figured out."

"I'll call you when things cool down," Royce said. "Y'all best get going." He backed away from the airplane.

"Tell Boolie everything I said," Red shouted as Jax pulled away.

Mama B and Royce stood in the yard, and Jax waved to them as he taxied to the end of the road to give the Prep plenty of room. He spun the airplane around on the mains with the tail skid scraping the dirt. A neighbor's face showed in a gap in the curtains of her front window for a minute before she backed into the shadows.

Jax opened the throttle, and the Prep accelerated. He raised the tail skid enough to clear the dirt but kept the propeller high above the rutted road. As soon as the airplane lifted from the ground, Jax eased the stick forward. The Prep rode a frictionless cushion of air a foot or so above the road, and the airspeed needle wound to eighty miles per hour. They sailed to the end of the road and over the cotton field, the wheels inches above last year's broken stalks. Then Jax pulled the stick back and to the left, and the Prep made a dramatic climbing turn, rocketing out of the twilight shadows into slanting sunlight.

"Hot damn!" exclaimed Red.

"Ever been up before?"

"Hell no!"

Jax leveled off a thousand feet above the ground and turned the airplane north. Below them, the eastbound lane of Shed Road, leaving Bossier City, was clogged with automobiles. Jax pointed and said, "Another roadblock."

"Go over there. I wanna see."

Jax turned the airplane toward the flashing lights of the police blockade.

"You see any state guys?" Red asked. "Or G-men?"

"I only saw local boys."

Jax put the police under the right wing, and Red hung over the door and hurled expletives and insults at what he called those coonass cops until they fell away behind the airplane's tail.

"Circle around again," he told Jax.

Jax banked steeply and brought them back around to circle the checkpoint. Red shouted and cursed some more, but his voice was torn apart and swept away by the wind. Jax rolled out on a northerly heading and reached under the panel to open the valve for the heated air.

"Snug as a bug in a rug," Red said. He turned up his jacket collar and settled into his seat. The warm air and drone of the engine put him out like a light.

A full moon shone through the windshield. Jax unfolded an Arkansas highway map he'd found with Ned's gear and held it up to the moonlight, but he could not read it. He fished in the pocket beside the seat for a red filament flashlight the owner kept there and was grateful when his fingers found it. Jax had not driven, much less flown, into Arkansas before, and he wished desperately for one of the modern direction finders Ned talked about all the time. The device homed in on a radio beacon and led you straight to it.

Jax scanned the darkness below and saw the twinkling lights of a town. South of the town flashed the green and white beacon of an airfield. Jax studied the map. They were passing Magnolia, Arkansas. An hour went by, and Jax searched for Hot Springs among the lights that flickered in and out of view. The earth seemed closer than it had in Louisiana, even though the altimeter reading had not changed. Jax pulled out the map again and shined the red light on it, searching for landmarks that would lead them to the landing field.

There was a sudden rush of movement in his peripheral vision, followed by a scrape. The Prep bumped in the glass-smooth air, and Jax looked left and saw pine boughs speeding by just beneath the left wheel. Something—a branch?—twirled in the wheel's spinning spokes. "What the hell?" he said aloud. The next second, Jax's blood went cold in its courses. He jammed the throttle in and pulled back on the stick. The Prep lurched.

Red woke up. "What the hell?" he cried.

The airplane buffeted, and Jax was sure they were dragging treetops. Red's head swiveled from side to side. The right wing dropped, and through his panic, Jax realized he was stalling the airplane. He lowered the nose, and the buffeting stopped.

Jax collected himself. He willed himself to stop shaking. They were still flying. Below them—far below—moonlit pools of water shone among shadows. Wisps of white steam rose here and there like mystified cobras, and vapors clung to the treetops like disembodied spirits.

Jax looked ahead and to the left and right until he was satisfied that everything was beneath them. They were climbing through twenty-six hundred feet. He leveled off and swung the airplane around to the left. Hot Springs came into view amid the massive dark shadows of mountains.

Red said, "What the hell was all that ruckus?"

"That bump? Oh nothing. We hit a patch of rough air back there. It happens. The map shows the airfield is southwest of town."

Red was still blinking. "Yeah," he said.

Jax banked toward the southwest. When they cleared the mountains, he pulled the power and descended rapidly over the lights.

"That's Grand Avenue," Red said, pointing to a wide boulevard lined with streetlights. "Just follow Grand west and we should see the landing field." Red lifted himself in the seat and craned to see over the nose. "There! Right there," he said, pointing. A half dozen automobiles, parked side by side, shined their headlights across a field. "That's my boys! Right on time."

Jax circled the field, losing altitude. He straightened out and put the airplane down at a speed so slow the Prep stopped almost as soon as the wheels touched the ground. To Jax's relief the left wheel rolled smoothly, undamaged. The pine branch that had been caught in the spokes had worked itself free and was gone.

"That was great!" shouted Red as his men ran toward the Monoprep. "What a getaway!"

"It's the only way to go."

"You can say that again." Red slapped Jax on the back. "I owe you one, Jaxy. Now, shut her down. You're spending the night."

The next morning, Red said he was taking Jax to breakfast at the Venetian Dining Room in the Arlington Hotel, but his wife objected. "It's business, my love," Red told her. Ms. Malone was a large-bosomed, red-faced woman who cooked all the time, given the stench in the house, which had almost overwhelmed Jax when he stepped through the door the night before.

"Go along, then," she said. "But you gotta come back, lad, and let me put some meat on those bones."

"Yes ma'am," Jax said, but he determined then and there he would avoid Mrs. Malone's cooking like death itself.

The Arlington Hotel towered over a downtown the likes of which Jax had never seen or imagined. Beautiful bathhouses and restaurants and gambling houses, right out in the open, lined Central Avenue going up to the hotel. Red said the Arlington was where all the bosses stayed when they came to town, and Jax had no reason to doubt him.

The Venetian Dining Room was a high-ceilinged hall, bright with morning sunlight pouring through its tall windows. The creamy arched ceiling was supported by two rows of gilded columns, each with a vase of fresh flowers on a pedestal in front of it. The maître d'hôtel seated them at a white-clothed table set with the hotel's signature crystal and china.

"This is aces," Jax said.

"It ain't bad," agreed Red.

All Jax could think about while Red prattled about new ways to make money was bringing Mae to Hot Springs for a weekend at the Arlington and watching her eat breakfast in this room. Jax didn't know how he would possibly manage to get Mae to come to Hot Springs for a whole weekend, but his mind was whirling.

"We can always use a visionary guy like you in the organization," Red said.

"The organization?"

"The fella I work for, outta New York."

"Can I ask you a question?" Jax said.

"Ask me anything," Red said. "You're with me now."

"Why are you here instead of New York?"

Red pushed his empty plate forward and leaned toward Jax with his elbows on the white tablecloth. "Got a little too hot in New York because of some business that went bad. G-men were all over me."

"What if they find out you're here?"

"Feds can't touch me here. Local boys won't give 'em the time of day." Red leaned back. "So what would you think about working directly for me?"

Jax almost said, "And cut Royce out?" but he thought better of it. Instead, he said, "Royce and I got a pretty good system now. Better not upset the apple cart."

"Okay," Red said. "But let's me and you keep in touch."

Chapter Thirty-Six

Jax had been saving his bootleg money to buy Mae a house. He had his eye on a red brick bungalow with white trim, only two blocks from the Centenary campus. The house stood on a sweeping corner lot. It had two roomy bedrooms and a large living room with a picture window that faced Alexander Avenue. The kitchen was spacious, and there was even a sunroom across the rear of the house with tall windows that caught the morning light. He called the owner to ask about the price, and like every other piece of property since the crash, it was dirt cheap.

Jax planned to present the house and a diamond engagement ring to Mae when he proposed, down on one knee. Red had given the ring to Jax in Hot Springs. No charge. "You're in luck, Jaxy," Red said when Jax told him about the girl he planned to marry. "I got a beautiful ring that fell off the back of a truck. It's yours if you want it."

Jax was about to make an offer on the house on Alexander Avenue when Ned told him about a Cessna Model AW that had come up for sale in Longview, Texas. "Engine's got 125 horsepower," Ned said. "Ought to be plenty of power and speed for your runs. Let's take the Monoprep over to Longview and have a look at her."

The Cessna was a beautiful bird, barely two years old, with a powerful radial engine just waiting to carry dozens of crates of Canadian Club to Billy Dean's customers in Baton Rouge. Even more important, the Cessna had a rear seat to accommodate two extra passengers. The minute Jax saw the cabin's side panels, inlaid with polished walnut, and the red upholstery with white stitching that still smelled like new leather, he had a revelation. He saw himself flying Mae and two other people—her girlfriends? another couple? did it matter as long as Mae went?—to Hot Springs.

"She'll carry anything you can fit in there," said the man who owned the airplane.

"She better," Jax said.

Ned looked at every nook and cranny of the engine. He read the maintenance logs cover to cover. He asked the owner a lot of questions about who had done what maintenance and when, to see if the owner's answers matched the logs. Afterward, the owner let Ned and Jax take the Cessna for a test flight. Jax was surprised at how heavy the controls felt and how stable she was.

"The bigger they are, the easier they are to handle," Ned said.

After they landed and were taxiing to the ramp, Jax asked Ned what he thought. "She's in perfect shape," Ned said. "And the price is a steal."

Jax counted thirty five C-notes—all the money for Mae's house—into the owner's outstretched hand. The old coot squared the stack of bills and said, "That airplane woulda cost you twice as much when she rolled off the line."

"Yeah, well, times change," said Jax.

Ned flew the Cessna back to Shreveport, and Jax flew the Prep. Jax didn't even mind when Ned outran him and was soon out of sight. During the flight home, Jax calculated how long it would take him to save enough money again to buy the house, but even the best case was too long. Then an idea came to him suddenly—as his best ideas always did—and he knew how he could have his cake and eat it too.

Ned flew right seat with Jax until he could handle the Cessna on his own. Then Ned showed him how to compute weight and balance, a series of complicated mathematical computations that Jax had no patience for. "Listen to me, Jax," Ned said. "What that old guy said isn't true. You can't just fill the airplane with cargo. You'll kill yourself if you overload this bird. Or worse, if you load too far aft, she'll go nose up on takeoff, and you are done, my friend. You will not be able to recover. Understand?"

"Sure," Jax said.

"I'm not fooling around," said Ned.

"I got it."

Ned oversaw Jax's weight and balance computations and flew the first run to Baton Rouge with him. During their takeoff roll, Jax was shocked at how long the Cessna bumped across the turf, tail up, and still she wouldn't fly. "Patience," Ned said when Jax tried to coax the wheels off prematurely. Ned pushed the stick forward and let the Cessna continue to build speed. When the sluggish airplane finally lifted from the earth, the controls were so heavy that Jax wondered how he'd land the thing again. But he managed well enough when they got to Baton Rouge, and Ned signed him off.

Jax made a few more whiskey-laden runs to Baton Rouge alone, after which he felt he was ready to fly Mae to Hot Springs. One night at the juke joint on Bistineau, Jax told Hollister about his plan to take Mae away for the weekend, just to see what Hollister thought his chances were.

"She won't go," Hollister said. "She's not that kind of girl."

"Maybe she will if it isn't just me and her. If it's a group thing, you know? A bunch of friends."

"Maybe."

"She could invite a couple of her girlfriends," Jax said.

"My man," Hollister said. "Do what you want, but what do you think those girls will do the minute you get to Hot Springs?"

"Disappear?"

"If I know girls." Hollister refilled his glass from a bottle of Templeton on the table. He took a drink, smiled and said, "You want some help with this project of yours?"

"I dunno."

"I could come along and bring a date."

"Who would you bring?"

"I'll ask Rita."

"Rita? Can't you do better than that?"

Rita was Delia's daughter, a hardened professional at the ripe age of fifteen. Rita was dirty, surly, and skinny. She was too young and too old at the same time.

Hollister shrugged and said, "No strings."

Chapter Thirty-Seven

A cold snap settled in after Mae returned to school from Christmas break, and it felt as if it would go on forever. She dragged to and from her classes with the weight of Whitesboro on her shoulders. Then one dreary afternoon in late February, Jax invited her to fly to Hot Springs with him, Hollister, and a girl named Rita.

"We're going up Saturday morning and coming back Sunday afternoon," Jax said. "And we're staying at the Arlington Hotel. Have you heard of it?"

"Of course I've heard of the Arlington," Mae said.

"Have you been there?" Jax asked.

"No, haven't had the chance yet."

"Well, it's absolutely aces. Hollister and I can bunk together, and you and Rita can share a room, if that's okay."

"Now, who is Rita?"

"She's a girl Hollister knows. I met her a couple of times. Real nice girl from Bossier. You'll love the Arlington Hotel. The rooms have hot mineral water that comes right out of a tap. The bathhouses are something to see too, but they say the Arlington has the best mineral treatments. It's top drawer."

"How will we all fit in the airplane?"

"I got a new bird that can carry all of us. Can't wait to show her to you."

Mae hesitated. It was one thing to make a day trip with Jax, but it was altogether another to go off with him for the weekend. Mae didn't want people to get the wrong idea about the kind of girl she was. "Are Rita and Hollister dating?" she asked.

"Nah, they're just friends. Like us."

"I guess I could go . . . maybe. If—"

"It'll be aces," Jax said. "We'll paint the town red."

Mae told Miriam she was going home to Whitesboro for the weekend. Miriam was her best friend these days and her confidant in most matters, but she was awfully old-fashioned about some things.

Mae would not have mentioned she was leaving town at all, except that she didn't want Miriam dropping by the dry cleaners looking for her. Or telephoning Aunt Vida. For one thing, Aunt Vida would talk Miriam's ear off. For another, Mae had told Aunt Vida she was going to Hot Springs with her school chums, which was so close to the truth that it was hardly a lie at all.

On Saturday morning, Mae rode to work with Uncle Bill and walked from there to the Centenary campus, where Jax was waiting in his Sixteen in an alley behind the Administration Building. He took her valise and set it in the backseat, then opened the car door for her.

"Where are Hollister and Rita?" Mae asked.

"They'll meet us at the airfield."

As far as Mae was concerned, trains were the most glamorous way to travel. Except maybe for steamships, but Mae had never been on a ship. She held to this opinion, even after flying with Ned in the Jenny and with Jax in the Monoprep. But Jax's new Cessna was so beautiful that it changed Mae's mind the minute she saw it. The Cessna was fire engine red, and *big*. The hefty engine had a ring of cylinders that stuck out like wheel cogs behind the propeller and made the airplane seem almost as substantial as a locomotive.

Jax opened the Cessna's door and stowed Mae's valise behind the rear seat. "Climb on in," he said. "It's a little chilly out here just standing around." Mae climbed into the rear seat, which was as fancy as a railcar, with inlaid wood panels and plush leather seats.

A red coupe raced past Mae's window, kicking up dust as it skidded into the hangar. A few minutes later, Jax opened the airplane door, and Hollister heaved two bags behind Mae's seat. "Good morning, Lady Sheik," Hollister said.

Mae smiled and was about to answer when a pale, thin girl plopped onto the seat beside her. She wore a flapper dress that not only was out of style and too large, it was a poor choice for daytime. Her eyes were heavily kohled, and she reeked of stale cigarette smoke under heavy, floral perfume. She gave Mae a hard look and said, "Take a powder, sister."

"Excuse me?"

"Hollister's mine."

Jax got in and scooted across to the left seat, and Hollister climbed in beside him. Jax started the big engine and taxied away from the hangar, while Rita hung on the back of Hollister's seat, giggling and whispering in his ear. "Sit down and buckle up," Jax said.

Rita ignored Jax, until Hollister said, "Be a sport, honey, and do what he says."

She sat back and sullenly latched the seatbelt across her lap loosely, so that she could still reach around the front seat to poke and tickle Hollister.

Chapter Thirty-Eight

Jax lifted off the airfield into a bright winter day. The air was so clear that it seemed as if they could see all the way to Canada and Mexico, to the Pacific and Atlantic Oceans, if they could only climb high enough. Jax said as much to the others.

"How high would we have to climb?" Mae asked.

"I dunno. I'll have to ask Ned."

They reached Hot Springs, and Jax circled the tallest mountain. "There's a lookout point there at the top," he said, pointing. "We'll go up to it after lunch if y'all want."

"Sure," said Hollister.

"Sounds like fun," said Mae.

Rita said nothing. She was sullen because Jax had forbidden her smoking in the airplane. She'd lit a Lucky Strike as soon as they were airborne, and there had been quite a row before she finally stomped it under her shoe.

After the hotel's limousine picked them up at the airfield, after they checked into their posh rooms, and after a lunch of Monte Cristo sandwiches on the hotel veranda, Jax hired a car to drive them up the mountain to the summit. They climbed the lookout tower's winding staircase all the way to the top, and Jax felt like he was sitting on top of the world.

Rita paced back and forth on the tower's platform, chain-smoking and tossing the burning butts off the side onto the rocks and brush below. "That's a good way to start a fire and burn the whole place down," Jax said when he could not stand it anymore.

Rita looked straight at him and flicked her lit cigarette off the mountain, even though it was only half-smoked. Hollister walked over to her and whispered something. She refused to look at Jax after that, but at least she began grinding her cigarette butts under her heel. Jax did not care if she ignored him, but he wondered who the hell she thought was treating her to this little holiday.

Rita declined the mineral water treatments that Jax had scheduled for the girls before dinner. She went off with Hollister instead, leaving Mae to enjoy the ministrations of the Arlington Hotel alone. Jax suspected that was fine with Mae, since the two women had hardly spoken to each other the entire trip. Jax also suspected that Hollister sprang for another room because his valise mysteriously disappeared from theirs.

On Saturday evening, the four of them had supper at the hotel, then went to the Southern Club for drinks. Jax picked the Southern Club because that's where all the wealthy tourists—gangsters, actors, baseball players, and businessmen—drank and gambled. Jax hoped Mae would get a glimpse of someone—anyone—who was famous. After they were seated and ordered drinks, Jax leaned toward Mae and said, "Al Capone comes here all the time."

"Are you teasing me?"

"No ma'am. See that empty table on the mezzanine? That's where Capone plays poker with his buddies when he's in town. He comes here a lot during the winter, so we just might see him." Capone did, in fact, play poker at the Southern Club when he was in town. Red Malone had told him so, and Jax was pleased as Punch when Mae started watching the club's entrance.

Jax and Mae nursed gin and tonics, while Hollister and Rita downed whiskeys as fast as the waiter could bring them. When it was time to call it a night, Hollister stood, swayed in place, then staggered toward the coat check. Rita was just as drunk and almost fell down as soon as she got out of the chair. "We're gonna take a stroll," Hollister slurred as he helped Rita into her coat.

"Suit yourself," Jax said.

Mae and Jax stopped outside the club and watched Hollister and Rita lean into each other and weave their way up Central Avenue. "How far do you think they'll get?" Mae asked.

"As far as the next barstool."

Mae did not laugh as Jax expected. She was soft on Hollister, and Jax could see that even running with that little whore Rita wasn't enough to put Mae off him. "Shall we?" Jax asked, and he ushered Mae across the street to the Arlington.

Hollister and Rita were bleary-eyed when they all met in the lobby for brunch early Sunday afternoon. Rita still wore the dress she'd had on the day before. Hollister had at least showered and shaved. He was still or already drunk, but not so impaired that he staggered or slurred. Hollister was a bootlegger's dream. His capacity for whiskey was Olympian.

"It stinks in here," Rita said. An unlit cigarette bobbed between her thin lips, which were stained such a deep crimson that they appeared almost black. Her earrings—too large for daytime— stretched her earlobes into pendants.

Jax wanted to say, "You stink," but he didn't for Hollister's sake. Instead, he said, "You mean the bacon? It smells pretty good to me. Let's eat."

The afternoon sunlight slanted through the windows in the Venetian Dining Room, and a guy in a tuxedo played classical music on a long grand piano. The maître d'hôtel instructed the host to seat them next to a window overlooking the gardens. Jax had found the maître d'hôtel early that morning and tipped him generously for the best table. As soon as they were all seated, a young man in a white waistcoat poured iced water into crystal glasses at each of their places, and a waiter passed out menus and offered coffee, tea, champagne, and cocktails.

Before the waiter returned, the captain rolled a cart to the table with a dark green bottle tilted in an ice bucket. He held up the bottle. "Dom Pérignon, nineteen twenty-six. A gift from a secret admirer for the beautiful lady and her party." He set a champagne coupe in front of Mae, uncorked the bottle, and poured. "I hope you approve, miss."

Mae looked confused, but she raised the shallow glass to her lips and sipped. "It's delicious," she said.

"Excellent," the captain said and poured for the rest of them.

Jax looked around for Mae's secret admirer and found him at a table tucked in the corner farthest from the door and half-hidden by a tall potted palm. He was a heavy-set man, round-faced with a receding hairline, and he worked a fat cigar between thick lips. He wore a starched white shirt and dark tie, and his suit coat was folded neatly over the back of the chair next to him. A man in a hat and overcoat, despite the warm room, stood against the wall behind the table. His coat bulged on one side as if he were lopsidedly fat.

"Mae, look over there," Jax said. "Corner table."

Mae put her hand on Jax's sleeve. "Is that . . . ?"

"Yes ma'am. In the flesh."

The gangster looked up from his newspaper and made eye contact with Mae. He removed the cigar from his mouth, smiled affably, and lifted his coffee cup in salute. Then he turned his attention back to his newspaper.

"That oughta blow your wig," Hollister said.

"I really didn't believe all that stuff you said last night," said Mae.

"To tell you the truth, I hardly believed it myself. All I can say is, Al Capone has very good taste."

"Here, here," said Hollister and raised his glass.

Rita said nothing, and she refused to touch the champagne.

When time came to fly home later that afternoon, Mae and Rita waited in the backseat of the heated hotel limousine while Jax and Hollister readied the Cessna.

Jax pulled back a tarp behind the rear seat that covered cases of Canadian Club that Red's men had loaded under cover of darkness the night before. "Would you look at this?" he said to Hollister. "They loaded more than I told them."

Hollister elbowed past Jax and looked. "You keep saying this airplane will hold anything you can fit in it," he said. "Just pile the bags on top." Hollister pried up the lid on a crate and pulled out a bottle. "For the trip home," he said.

"Help me move a few of these forward," Jax said. "We'll put the bags in the very back. They're lighter." Hollister rearranged the crates, stacking them to the roof behind the rear seat, then they covered the crates with the tarp and stowed the overnight bags aft. Jax opted not to top off the fuel, which he reasoned would lighten the load enough to be safe. "Go get the girls," he told Hollister. "Let's get out of here."

"What's all this?" Mae asked when she climbed inside.

"Medical supplies," Jax said. He winked and added, "Sometimes I gotta mix a little business with pleasure."

The wind was dead calm. Jax taxied to the farthest boundary of the airfield and held the brakes while he poured the coals to the big radial engine. When he released the brakes, the Cessna lurched forward, and Jax had to jerk the stick back to keep her from nosing over on the neglected turf. He eased the stick forward slowly when the airplane had built some speed. The tail skid came up and they bounced across the airfield on the main wheels.

"This is taking a while," Hollister said.

Jax did not respond. He eased the stick back some more and felt the mains lift off, but they quickly settled on the ground again. Jax looked from the windshield to the side window to the windshield again while the wheels skipped along the turf and the airplane quickly approached the end of the airfield. He felt bile rise from his stomach and the stick became wet from his sweating palm. He belched loudly and eased the stick back very slowly, very gently. Finally, the Cessna's weight transferred from the wheels to the wings and they gained a few inches of altitude.

"We gonna clear that fence?" asked Hollister.

"Yeah. Sure." Jax continued to pull back on the stick, then stopped when the Cessna's stall warning horn chirped.

They cleared the fence.

They were fast approaching the river and the trees along each bank. To their left was Grand Avenue with its two-story houses. Beyond the houses were the mountains. The terrain to the south rose just as rapidly. Jax headed toward the river while the Cessna clawed for altitude.

"We gonna clear those trees?" asked Hollister.

Jax glanced at him but said nothing. Hollister opened the Canadian Club and took a long pull.

They cleared the trees. Barely.

"My man!" Hollister said. He turned around and said, "You girls okay?"

"What the hell was all that?" said Rita.

"You okay, Mae?" Jax asked.

"I saw my whole life go by just then."

"What?" Jax turned around to look into Mae's face.

Mae waved her hand. "Just watch where you're going. Don't worry about me."

"Yeah, watch it," said Rita.

Jax turned and looked forward. "I'm sorry about that," he called toward the backseat. "But we're good now. We're fine." To Hollister he said, "Absolutely aces."

"Definitely deuces, but at least I'm awake," Hollister said. He took another pull of whiskey and handed the bottle to the backseat. "Here, girls," he said. "Take the edge off."

Jax followed the river until the Cessna put a thousand feet of air between them and Arkansas, then he turned south for home. "I told you this bird'll handle anything we can cram in," he said to Hollister.

Hollister laughed. "But not well, my man. Not well at all." He turned toward the backseat. "Ladies, how about passing that bottle back up here?"

Chapter Thirty-Nine

Hot Springs was too much for Mae to write about in her diary. She could not bear to reduce to mere words all the thoughts and emotions that town aroused, so she only made a brief entry, *Feb 21-22, 1931, Hot Springs, Arkansas. All of my yesterdays and tomorrows passed before me.*

Between the pages of her diary, Mae placed an envelope she had found in her hotel room after Sunday brunch. "Miss Mae Compton" was printed in neat, masculine letters on the envelope. Inside was a single page of hotel stationery on which "Room 442. Anytime. Al" was written in looping cursive.

How had he learned her name?

The Friday after Hot Springs, Mae walked to the dry cleaners and spread her homework on the counter as she always did. But she was too distracted to study, so she daydreamed about hostessing luncheons for her sorority sisters—anywhere but Aunt Vida's—and taking dictation in one of the tall office buildings downtown. Fantasizing about having a job drove Mae into her textbook, even though she wasn't in the mood.

She was just finishing when Jax pulled up in his big convertible and came into the store. The afternoon was cool and cloudy, and Jax wore a leather jacket over his shirt and tie and high drape pants.

"Hi, Mae," he said.

"Hi, Jax."

"Would you mind taking a short ride? There's something I want to show you."

"Uncle Bill will be closing soon," Mae said.

"It won't take long. I promise."

Mae did not want to go, but she felt obligated to at least give Jax a few minutes after he had given her a whole weekend in Hot Springs. "Sure," she said, closing her book. "That'll be fine."

Jax drove Mae to a red brick house with white trim on a corner lot two blocks from Centenary College.

"What's this?" she asked.

"Just come inside with me."

Mae followed Jax up the steps to the porch and watched him open the front door with a key that he pulled from his pocket. They walked into a living room with a picture window. From there, Jax led Mae through the vacant rooms, as Buster had led her through the tiny shotgun cottage in Whitesboro. They stopped in the sunroom, where the windows gave a view of the deep backyard, which was carpeted from flower bed to flower bed with dormant St. Augustine grass.

"Whose house is this?" Mae asked.

"It's yours."

"What?"

Suddenly, dramatically, Jax dropped to one knee and said, "This house is empty. It's waiting for you." He pulled a ring—a big diamond ring—from his pocket and took Mae's hand. Before she could pull her hand away, he slid the diamond up against the modest band that had belonged to Buster's mother. "It's waiting for us," he said. Then Jax pressed a key into Mae's palm, closed her fingers around it, said, "Just think about it."

"Jax, no—" Mae pulled the ring off her finger.

"Keep it for now," Jax said as he struggled to his feet. "And the key. At least until you've thought it over."

"I better walk back to the dry cleaners," Mae said.

"I understand."

Jax didn't show up at the dry cleaners the following week or the week after that, and Mae asked her uncle what had become of him. "Jax is spending a lot of time in Bossier City," Uncle Bill said. "He's a good salesman, and I asked him to take care of the nuts and bolts of the cleaning contract for the new airfield. There wasn't much for him to do around here anyway."

Mae waited for Jax to contact her, so she could return his ring and the key to the house. When three weeks had gone by without any word from him, she found herself walking to Alexander Avenue after class, instead of to her uncle's dry cleaners. She let herself in and walked through the house, stopping to examine each room as she had not had time to do with Jax. Then Mae sat on the polished hardwood floor in the living room and imagined how she would furnish the house if it were hers.

A few days later, Mae took the streetcar downtown. She went to every department store and browsed their furniture, imagining the pieces she liked the best in the house on Alexander Avenue. The following week Mae returned to the house and sat in the same spot in the living room. She imagined all her sorority sisters there with her, sitting on the couch Mae had seen at Selber Brothers and on the settee and chairs she had seen at Rubenstein's. She imagined them chatting as they balanced plates of canapés and cups of tea on their knees or set them on the sweet occasional tables she had seen in the window of a furniture store on Market Street.

Mae imagined that after she graduated—or sooner if she decided to get a job downtown instead of returning to Centenary after summer break—she could hostess luncheons for the Junior Service League ladies. Miriam's mother was an officer, and Miriam planned to join the league as soon as she graduated. Mae was certain Miriam would write her a letter of recommendation, even if she didn't finish school.

The house was humble compared to the mansions on Highland Avenue, but Mae knew she could make it as quaint and elegant as a country cottage. She wrote page after page in her diary about the house and the furniture she'd picked out. She wrote about the diamond ring Jax had given her too. The diamond was a fine stone and a full carat in weight. So said a jeweler when Mae took it to one of the shops downtown. She went ahead and had the ring sized—what was the harm? After that, whenever Mae walked to the house on Alexander Avenue, when she went inside and closed the door behind her, she took off Buster's ring and put Jax's on in its place. Over and over, she wondered what kind of man bought a house and a diamond ring then said, think about it. And what kind of a man disappeared for weeks afterward instead of pressing her for an answer?

Mae's dreams about living in the house wrapped around her like the warming weather until she believed she would move in and begin decorating as soon as the semester ended. When she remembered the house came with Jax, she felt her face pinch the same way it had when she was a child and her mother gave her a spoonful of cod liver oil. "Ew, it's nasty!" Mae had cried with her thumb and forefinger clamping her nostrils closed.

Her mother had only smiled and said, "Oh, honey, it's not as bad as all that, and it's over anyway. Now, go outside and play."

Chapter Forty

During the weeks in which Jax did not see Mae at all, he was anxious every minute and drank bottle after bottle of Pepto-Bismol to sooth his raging gut. One day, when he couldn't stand it anymore, Jax stopped at the house on Alexander Avenue instead of just driving by. He parked, got out, and walked around to the backyard. He inspected the lawn, which he had hired a man to mow and trim every week. The neighbor from across the street, who was always outside working in her flower beds, came around the side of the house, still holding her pruning shears in her gloved hand.

"Good morning," she said.

"Morning," said Jax.

The woman removed her glove and extended her hand. "Ada Tidwell," she said.

"Pleased to meet you, Mrs. Tidwell," Jax said and shook her hand.

"This house has been sold," Mrs. Tidwell said.

"So I heard."

"There's a young woman comes and goes here pretty often. She has a key."

"Have you spoken with her?" Jax asked.

"No sir. She's in and out too fast. Is she moving in?"

"She hasn't said," Jax replied.

"Well, what's her name?"

"Mrs. Addington," Jax said. "Mrs. Jackson Addington."

Jax expected Mae to make her choice as soon as the school term ended, so the last week of the semester, he finally confided to his dear mother that he had asked a girl to marry him. "Well, who is she?" his mother asked.

"It's a surprise."

"A surprise? Oh, honey, don't be ridiculous. Bring her to supper."

"I will. Just as soon as she says yes. *If* she says yes, that is."

"At least tell me her name. Do we know her family?"

"Patience, Mama, patience. I can tell you that she's beautiful and sweet and smart."

"Well for heaven's sake! I want to meet her."

Jax dared not drop any hints about who the girl was. His mother saw Mae at church every Sunday and undoubtedly knew she was engaged to be married. "She wants to get married in the State House in Baton Rouge," Jax said.

"Oh Jaxy, that would be lovely!"

"Don't say anything to Daddy yet."

"Why not?"

"What if she says no? I don't want to tell anybody—except you—until she says yes. Then, believe me, I'll shout it from the housetops."

"Your father can make arrangements for the State House."

"Not yet, Mama! I mean it, not a word." Jax's stomach rolled, and he belched. "Excuse me, Mama, but you have to promise. Not one word."

She patted Jax's hand. "Don't get in a tizzy, honey. I promise. Not one word."

On the first Monday in June, Jax went to the dry cleaners. He knew Mae would be there because every Monday afternoon since he had proposed, Jax had parked up the street and watched her walk from the campus to her uncle's business.

"Jackson!" Bill Cole said when Jax walked through the door. "It's good to see you, son."

"Likewise, Mr. Cole." Jax removed his new fedora and said, "Hello, Miss Mae."

"It's been ages, Jax," Mae said.

"Yes ma'am. Seems like forever."

"Well, you're just in time to take me out for a Coca-Cola. These examinations are murder. I sure could use a break."

"It'll be my pleasure," said Jax. He opened the car door for Mae, and they drove to the market up the street in awkward silence. He parked and went inside, while Mae waited in the car. He bought her a cold bottle of Coke and put a soda straw in it, the way she liked it.

"Let's drive out to Lake Bistineau," Mae said when Jax returned to the car. "I want to see that juke joint again."

Twenty minutes later, Jax wheeled the Sixteen into the packed dirt clearing beside the juke joint. He cut the engine and set the brake and willed his churning stomach to settle down. He should have taken a swig of Pepto while he was in the market, but he had been too focused on Mae to think about it.

"Will you bring me here if I marry you?" Mae asked.

Jax gripped the steering wheel. "Yes ma'am," he said. "And anywhere else you want to go."

"Then I guess I better marry you."

"You mean it? You're saying yes?" Jax looked down at Buster's ring. "Do you still have the ring I gave you?"

"Of course, silly."

"Okay . . . well . . . that's good." Jax resisted an impulse to thank Mae. He reached around her shoulder and hugged her awkwardly. His mouth was too sour to kiss her, and he hoped she wouldn't think it was strange that he didn't. "Well, heck," Jax said. "I guess we have some planning to do. My father can help us get the State House in Baton Rouge, and—"

"Oh, no," Mae said. "We can't go to the State House. We have to elope."

"But when we were in Baton Rouge, you said you wanted to get married in the State House."

"Yes, but that was—anyway, now I want to elope. And you can't tell anybody ahead of time either."

"Sneak off to Baton Rouge?"

"No, silly. To Hot Springs."

Jax was confused, but he was not about to let the logistics dampen his jubilation. He could roll with the punches. "Hot Springs it is. Is this weekend too soon?"

"Let's go up Wednesday," she said, "and get it done."

For a second, Jax's mind played a trick, and he thought Mae said, ". . . and get it over with." But she hadn't said that at all.

On the drive back to Shreveport, Jax told Mae he wanted Hollister to stand up for him.

"That's fine, but I hope he doesn't bring Rita."

"I'll tell him Rita's not invited. Would you like to ask Miriam, or somebody else? Maybe your friend from back home? We could fly over to Texas and pick her up."

Mae was quiet. She stared out the side window.

"Mae?"

"No. I guess not," she said, finally.

Jax dropped Mae off at the dry cleaners. Then he found Hollister and told him the news.

"Congratulations, my man," Hollister said with genuine enthusiasm.

"Will you come with us? Stand up for me?"

"Wouldn't miss it. Mae doesn't mind?"

"No, but she doesn't want Rita to come."

Hollister lit a cigarette. He had recently taken up smoking, a habit that surprised Jax because Hollister had always said tobacco dragged a man down. "Don't worry about Rita," he said.

"Why not?"

Hollister drew deeply and the ember of his cigarette flared, as if it would burst into flame. He blew the smoke sideways. "Because she's gone."

Before Jax telegraphed the Arlington Hotel to reserve the bridal suite and a room for Hollister, he sent a message to Red Malone that he was getting married at the county courthouse on Wednesday afternoon. Jax wanted to make sure the gangster met his beautiful new bride.

Chapter Forty-One

Mae sat on the concrete steps of the front porch of the house on Alexandria Avenue with her book satchel beside her. It was a mild and sunny Tuesday, the eve of her wedding day, and she had that very morning successfully completed her freshman year of college. Tomorrow morning, she would put her satchel away for the summer, if not forever.

The lawn was emerald green and recently clipped, and the cannas had unfurled in the shaded flower beds along the front of the house. Mae watched the neighbor who lived across the street, a woman of middle age, prune her rose bushes. The woman hadn't noticed her yet.

Mae unbuckled the satchel and took out a pen and her stationery, her good stationery with her name embossed in gold leaf across the top. Mae had carried the stationery and a stamped envelope addressed to Buster around in her satchel ever since she decided to say yes to Jax. Now she could no longer put it off. A letter had to be mailed.

The neighbor looked up and saw Mae. She waved and removed her gloves, laying them on the ground with her shears. Mae wished she had gone inside to write her letter, but it was too late now to escape gracefully. Then the neighbor's telephone rang, and she hurried into the house to answer it. Mae stopped twirling her pen and laid the nib to the paper.

Dearest Buster,
By the time you read this I'll have eloped with a man from Shreveport. I can't explain how this happened, except to say I probably never was the girl everybody thought I was. I hope you can forgive me someday.
I'm sorry.
Mae

Mae slipped Buster's mother's ring from her finger, folded the letter around it, and put it in the envelope, taking care for the corners. She licked the flap to seal it. She took Jax's diamond ring from her pocketbook and put it on her finger. Then she got up, brushed the back of her skirt, and walked down the street to put her letter in the campus mailbox.

Chapter Forty-Two

Early Wednesday morning, Jax picked Mae up at the campus. He found her sitting on a bench with her valise beside her. She wore a green skirt and floral blouse that he had not seen before, and she was crying. She did not give him a chance to get out of the car and carry her valise or even open the door for her. She dropped the bag in the backseat, opened the door herself, and got in.

"Mae, what's wrong? Why are you crying?"

She waved her handkerchief dismissively. "Every girl cries on her wedding day," she said. "I have to call my mother after the ceremony. I'll call collect."

"Okay."

"What's wrong with her?" Hollister whispered to Jax as they were pulling the big Cessna out of the hangar.

"She says it's nothing, just wedding day jitters."

Mae cried in the backseat of the Cessna all the way to Hot Springs and in the backseat of the Arlington Hotel limousine all the way to the courthouse. She and Jax rode together in the back of the limousine, huddled against their respective doors, and Hollister rode in front with the driver.

The justice of the peace pulled Jax aside and echoed Mae's claim that girls cry on their wedding day. "There's more bawlin' and squallin' in here ever' week than you can shake a stick at, believe you me," he said. The JP's secretary, who was witnessing the marriage along with Hollister, put her arm around Mae and told her to be brave, that she was starting a new life and everything would be fine.

Mae managed to sob her way through a vow to love, honor, and obey Jackson Carthage Addington, and Jax vowed to love, honor, and cherish Mae Pearl Compton.

"Do you have a ring?" asked the JP.

Jax fished a gold band from his shirt pocket and put it on Mae's finger, next to the diamond engagement ring, and the JP pronounced them man and wife. He said Jax could kiss the bride, but Jax only got in a peck before Mae turned her head and asked if she could use a telephone to make a collect call to her mother.

"You can use the justice's office right in here, honey," said the secretary, leading Mae by the hand. "It's real private."

"Thank you, ma'am," Mae said and disappeared behind a door with frosted glass.

"I'll wait outside," Hollister said.

"I'll come with you," Jax said quickly. As soon as they walked outside, Jax spotted Red Malone in the parking lot, leaning against the limousine.

"So you went through with it," Red called. "Your goose is cooked now, lad."

Jax and Hollister went to him, and Red hugged Jax. Then he nodded toward Hollister and said, "Who's this?"

"He's with me," said Jax. "My best man."

Hollister stuck out his hand. "Hollister Caine."

Red shook Hollister's hand. "Red Malone. Glad to know you, Hollister. The missus is having a reception for the bride and groom at our house. Nothing fancy, but we want to celebrate with you and—say, where's the bride?"

"Calling her mother. She'll be out in a minute."

"Wedding day's rough on a girl."

"Rough on everybody," Jax said. They stood around for half an hour, with Jax checking his wristwatch every minute or so. Finally, he went back inside and asked the secretary if Mae was still on the telephone.

"Yes sir. Be patient. You have her for the rest of your lives, but right now she needs her mama."

Jax waited in the courthouse lobby until Mae finally came out of the office, red-eyed and shiny-faced. She was still pretty, even after crying all day, and Jax crooked his arm. Mae smiled weakly and put her hand through it. Jax stopped before opening the courthouse door and said, "A fella I do business with is outside. His wife is putting on a reception for us at their house. Is that okay?"

"Who are they?"

"His name is Red Malone. He's a businessman here in town. I get the medical supplies I told you about from him."

"That's awfully nice of them, but I need to fix my face. Go get my valise and bring it to me."

"You look fine."

"No. I look awful. Go on now. I'm going to the ladies' room. Give the valise to Mrs. Davis."

"Who's that?"

"The secretary, silly. Now go. Shoo."

Jax felt a weight lift. Worry had been lying across his shoulders like a yoke all morning. Even though all his efforts to win Mae had come to fruition—they were married!—Jax did not feel as if he had won her at all until this very minute, when Mae spoke to him as a wife speaks to her husband. He suddenly felt buoyant. He hurried to get Mae's valise and tell Red they would take the limousine to his house as soon as Mae fixed her face.

"You remember where the house is," Red said. "Pratt Street, a block south of Olive."

"I remember. We'll be along directly."

"I'll ride with you, Red," Hollister said. "If you don't mind."

"Good idea," said Red and Jax at the same time.

"Wow," Mae said when the limousine stopped in front of the Malone house. Cars were parked in the yard and up and down the street. "Looks like a lot of people are here."

"Shall I wait for you, sir?" asked the driver.

"We'll be a while," Jax said. "Can we telephone the hotel when we're ready to leave?"

"Certainly, sir. I'll take the luggage. It'll be waiting for you in your rooms. And on behalf of the Arlington Hotel, congratulations, Mr. and Mrs. Addington."

Mae and Jax heard voices as soon as they got out of the limousine. Jax led the way up the steps to the deep front porch, which was overhung by a gallery on the second story. He knocked several times but no one answered, so he tried the doorknob and found it unlocked. The door opened to an empty parlor.

"Everybody must be out back," he said.

"Maybe we shouldn't go through the house," Mae said.

"Yeah. You're right. Let's walk around the outside."

"Ho! The man and wife!" shouted Red as soon as Jax and Mae came around the side of the house. Everyone cheered as if they had known the bride and groom all their lives. As if they had been rooting for them all along. Mrs. Malone immediately whisked Mae away to the food-laden tables and the women congregating there.

"Don't worry, she's in good hands," Red said as Jax watched them go. "C'mon and have a pint. You gotta long night ahead of you."

Several casks stood on sawhorses under a spreading live oak, and Red drew a pint of Guinness from one and shoved it into Jax's hand, sloshing the ecru froth all over Jax's new wingtip brogues. "No worries today, Jaxy. Have 'em shined at the hotel on me. Come. Eat."

Jax shook the foam from his hand and followed Red to the tables, not because he was hungry, but because Mae was there. He sipped the thick, creamy ale, then drank deeply, feeling the Guinness coat his stomach better than Pepto-Bismol ever had.

"Mrs. Malone!" hollered Red. "Is there anything for a man to eat?"

"For a man, aye, Mr. Malone. But nary more'n a crust of bread for an old goat!" Red's wife grasped her husband's chin in her hand and stuffed a hunk of bread into his mouth. The women laughed and Mrs. Malone said, "That's how you tamp the rowdy in your husband." Red made a show of yelling and swiping at his wife's backside, the coarse bread crumbling from his mouth.

Mae giggled. She held a glass of whiskey, which she sipped between nibbles of bread. "It's soda bread, Jax." She motioned to a platter of crusty round loaves. "Try it. It's really good."

Mrs. Malone pointed to a bowl that held a slithering mess of meat, carrots, potatoes, and something green. "Lamb stew!" she said. "Lamb, not mutton. I made it myself in honor of the bride."

"Thank you," Mae said. "It looks delicious."

"Black pudding and white pudding!" cried Mrs. Malone, pointing to a platter on which rounds of firm black gristle were piled beside pale, gelatinous rounds of similar size. "And my famous potatoes and kale." Green slime floated amid lumps of boiled potatoes like seaweed.

Jax watched Mae's face as Mrs. Malone worked her way down the table, showing off her robust Irish delicacies. Mae's eyes widened, seemingly in delight. She smiled and winked at Jax every time he caught her eye. If it were possible, Jax fell even more deeply in love with her.

Suddenly, the backyard erupted with shouts. Jax looked up and saw two priests, one of whom wore a long black robe with a red sash. Four musicians carrying instruments under their arms followed. "Now it's a celebration!" hollered Red. "Drink! Eat! Then we dance." Red motioned for the men to draw glasses of whiskey for the priests and musicians, who accepted them readily. Clergymen who drank were nothing new to Jax. He routinely ran whiskey to several churches in Shreveport and Bossier, always in the dead of night, where he oftentimes was met at the back door by the pastor or priest himself.

Jax took advantage of the distraction to stand beside Mae. She smelled like a freshly bloomed rose. He leaned toward her and whispered in her ear—that lovely ear nestled in soft, dark curls, "The Catholics aren't like us Baptists when it comes to drinking and dancing. They don't mind it a bit."

"Well, my goodness. That's convenient." Mae said and giggled. She was making good progress on her own glass of Old Bushmills.

Jax stopped counting after his third pint. When the sun got low, some of the men strung electric lights through the low branches of the oak tree, and the guests danced their Irish folk dances under it. The musicians played quick music on banjo and fiddle, penny whistle and concertina. Mae got right in the middle of it and so did Jax, forgetting all about his lack of rhythm. He stomped and spun and twirled Mae around like he knew what he was doing. No one— not even Mae—seemed to mind that he was out of time to the music.

At the end of the evening, the musicians slowed it all down and played mournful, lilting melodies. The songs were beautiful, and some of the older men, ruddy and tough, blubbered over missing the old country.

Red and Mrs. Malone had retired to rocking chairs on the back porch, from which they watched the party wind down. "Get your bride, Jaxy," Red called, "and your friend. We'll have a toast."

Jax found Hollister deep in his cups, playing a gambling game with a few of the younger men. Hollister bowed out of the game and staggered to the porch with Mae and Jax. Red unscrewed the top of a Mason jar, raised the clear liquid toward the nighttime sky, and said, "To the bride and groom! The sweet shine of the New World. May your mornings bring joy and your evenings bring peace." He took a swig and handed the jar to Jax.

Jax sipped the moonshine. It was smooth, the smoothest he had ever tasted. He handed the jar to Mae, who took a sip and passed the jar to Hollister.

"Sweet," Hollister said after he took a deep pull.

"It's Possum Kingdom shine," Red said. "The hillbillies north of here make it from the springs."

"Can I get some?"

"I'll send a couple of jars with you."

After the toast, Jax went in the house to call the hotel to send a car. Red followed him inside. "No business on your wedding day, Jaxy," Red said. "But I'll meet you for breakfast at the hotel in the morning. Got a proposition for you."

"Thanks, Red. Thanks for everything."

"Congratulations, son," Red said. "Mae's a peach. Couldn't a happened to a nicer guy."

Chapter Forty-Three

Jax hoped Mae didn't think it was strange when he invited Hollister into their suite for a nightcap, but he was as nervous as a cat about being alone with his new bride. Hollister followed them into the sitting room with a jar of moonshine tucked in each elbow.

"I need to freshen up," Mae said and disappeared into the bedroom, closing the door behind her.

"We need to eat something," said Hollister. "We're all pretty lit."

"Yeah. Did you eat any of that Irish slop at Red's house?"

"Lord, no."

"Me either," said Jax.

"Good whiskey, though, and a helluva romp."

"Yes sir. Helluva good time was had by all."

The bridal suite came with a celebratory basket for the newlyweds, and Hollister rummaged through it. "We have champagne, chocolate, caviar from Russia." He held the flat tin toward Jax.

"What else?"

"Soda crackers."

"Gimme some of those."

"Here you go, champ." Hollister pitched a cellophane-wrapped tube of crackers to Jax. "Let's see. More crackers. Grapes and strawberries. Couple of apples. Oranges. This is real nice, Jax. There's a brick of cheese from Wisconsin."

"Slice that for the crackers." Jax fished in his pocket for his knife and tossed it to Hollister.

Hollister lifted a bottle of Canadian Club from the bottom of the basket and held it up. "Feels like home now," he said, and they both laughed.

By the time Mae came out of the bedroom—still in her day dress and looking peaked—Hollister had cut up an apple and the cheese and opened the tin of caviar. He spread the brown paper the moonshine had been wrapped in on a low table in front of the couch and arranged the food on it.

"That looks good," Mae said. "I could use a little bite."

"We all could," said Hollister.

Mae sat on the couch, and Jax sat beside her. Hollister pulled a wingback to the table and set the jars of moonshine in front of him. They ate, only speaking to say how good this or that was. The color came back into Mae's face. "What time is it?" she asked.

"Who knows?" answered Hollister.

Jax squinted at his wristwatch, a Rolex Oyster with a stitched leather band. He had bought it with the first profits from the lucrative Baton Rouge run, and he planned to buy Mae a matching one if she wanted it. "It's a quarter to two," Jax said when he had finished admiring his watch.

"Oh golly," Mae said. She leaned her head back and closed her eyes.

"How about that nightcap?" said Hollister. He unscrewed the top of the Mason jar.

Jax groaned. "Not for me."

Mae pushed herself up. "Sure, why not."

Jax watched them drink. He had fantasized nonstop about taking Mae on their wedding night, fantasies in which Jax himself was transformed into a virile, bare-chested rake, à la Douglas Fairbanks in *Thief of Bagdad*. Fairbanks had been Jax's first and most enduring infatuation. He first saw the actor in *The Mark of Zorro* on his tenth birthday. Jax's mother indulged him by taking him to a matinee, even though it was a weekday and he was home from school with a stomachache. After the movie, Jax had commandeered an old walking cane from the umbrella stand and spent the rest of the evening marking every wall, door, and stick of furniture with an imaginary Z.

Never once in all of Jax's fantasies and visions about Mae had he appeared as the sickly runt that he was. He did not think there was enough moonshine in the entire Possum Kingdom to get Mae past her first glimpse of the scrawny weakling she had married.

Mae and Hollister swayed in wider and wider circles each time they passed the jar across the coffee table. When their outstretched hands could no longer synchronize to make contact, Jax grabbed the sloshing jar. Hollister's eyes fluttered, and Jax picked the half-burned Lucky Strike from his friend's mouth and stubbed it out in the ashtray. Mae sat with her eyes closed, her chin propped on her palms and her elbows propped on her knees. Jax touched her arm and said, "Come along, Lady Sheik."

"Hmm?"

"Time for beddy-bye."

She looked up at him with unfocused eyes. "Is it time?"

"Yes, dear."

"Okay . . . okay . . . I can . . ."

"Here we go. Upsy-daisy." Jax pulled on Mae's arm until she was standing. She leaned against him heavily.

"I can . . . I promise," she mumbled.

Jax walked Mae into the bedroom and closed the door behind them. He sat her on the bed, holding her so she wouldn't tump over and fall to the floor. He opened her valise and took out her silk honeymoon negligee. It was dusty pink with black lace roses around the neckline. "Mae, this is beautiful," he said.

"Huh?"

"Okay, Lady Sheik, let's get you ready for bed." Mae was so out of it that Jax could have done anything he wanted. What he did was undress his bride tentatively, respectfully, and then he slipped the negligee over her head. Mae obliged his requests that she lift an arm here or put a hand through there. Jax eased her back onto the pillows and lifted her delicate feet with their polished red toenails onto the bed. He leaned over her and kissed her rosy cheek. She did not smell quite as fresh and nice as she had earlier in the day, but she was still the sweetest girl around. "Good night, my love," he said.

Jax took his own valise and an extra blanket from the closet, then he closed the bedroom door behind him. Hollister had slid off the chair and lay on the floor between it and the coffee table. Jax fished the room key from Hollister's pocket, then unlaced and removed Hollister's oxfords. He put a pillow from the couch under Hollister's head and unfolded the blanket and covered him with it. Then Jax picked up his valise and opened the door to the hallway. He paused and looked back inside. "Okay then," he said. "I'll leave you two to sleep it off. Don't do anything I wouldn't do."

The hallway was dimly lit and dead quiet. Jax opened the door to Hollister's room and went inside. He undressed to his shorts and bare feet, went into the spacious bathroom, and turned on the hot mineral water spigot on the bathtub. While the tub filled, Jax hopped back and forth across the tiled bathroom floor, trying to recall the steps of the Irish jig. Eventually, he tired and stepped out of his underwear into the steaming water. He relaxed, closed his eyes, and loosed his imagination.

He was the Thief of Baghdad, running as swiftly as a jackal across the desert sand. He darted stealthily between towering palms illuminated by a bright crescent moon that was as sharp as a sickle. He climbed a rose-covered trellis on a torch-lit marble palace and stole in through a window. He passed from room to room, gliding silently through a thousand veils so smooth they slid across his arms and shoulders like water. In the heart of the palace, he found the Lady Sheik, waiting for him.

The next morning, Jax met Red in the Venetian Dining Room. Red laughed at the sight of him and asked, "Up all night?"

Jax grinned. "Thanks for the party, Red. We had a helluva time." He sat down and motioned for the waiter to pour coffee.

"You're family now," Red said.

"So, what's cooking?"

"I keep thinking about that dry-cleaning business in Bossier that you told me about."

Jax put his coffee down. "You mean the army contract I'm working for Bill Cole."

Red leaned forward, shirt-sleeved forearms on the table, and said, "See, that's the thing. I think that contract oughta be *your* business."

Jax's stomach seized, and he turned his head and belched. "Excuse me. I don't know anything about dry cleaning, Red. I'm a sales guy."

"No, I know. You won't have to do a thing. Just be the front man. I gotta guy to run the laundry."

"Why do you want to get into the laundry business?"

"Here's the thing, it ain't for cleanin' clothes. It's for cleanin' cash."

"I don't follow."

"The G-men got a new scheme," Red said. "They're going after guys for not payin' income tax. It's trumped up, right? But it's gettin' serious. They indicted Capone a couple of months ago. Word on the street is there's more indictments comin'."

"So you take the cash from . . . well . . . whatever . . . and say it came from a business?"

"A legit business that takes in a lot of cash. Like a laundry."

"But you could do that right here in Hot Springs, where you can keep an eye on things."

"Yeah, yeah, we could. We will. But we can run a big operation in Bossier under the cover of that army contract. Lots of cash. Besides, I want to throw the opportunity your way. Get you outta runnin' bootleg all hours of the day and night." Red punched Jax's arm playfully. "You're a married man now, Jaxy. It's time to settle down and put down some roots. You got a wife to keep happy." Red winked. "And to keep an eye on."

"It's just that Bill Cole is Mae's uncle."

"Yeah, I get it. Hell, we're all family men. She'll be mad for a while, but she'll get over it. She'll have her man home every night, and you can buy her lots of pretties with all the dough. Don't worry. Your new bride'll be just fine. Now, what's the name of that army guy you been workin'?"

Jax could see this was going to happen whether he liked it or not. Whether he was part of it or not. Red only bothered to bring him in as a friendly courtesy. "Lavender. Captain John Lavender," Jax said. "He's at Delia's every Thursday night."

Red leaned back, reached into his pants pocket and pulled out a money clip stuffed with bills. He unfolded a five-spot and laid it on the table. "Have a hot breakfast on me, Jaxy." He stood and shouldered on his suit coat. Straightened his tie. Then he leaned over and kissed Jax on the forehead. "Don't worry about a thing, son. I'll take it from here."

Chapter Forty-Four

Mae woke up midmorning with a piercing headache that only began to let up after she took half a dozen aspirin tablets. She was certain that she and Jax had not consummated their marriage. The moonshine had finished the job Old Bushmills started, and Mae suspected her new husband had been put off by his walleyed bride. Jax left her to herself—alone in the suite—all afternoon, where she lay around trying to prepare herself to bear, stone cold sober, whatever the night would bring.

That evening, she and Jax dined in the Arlington Hotel's grand ballroom, just the two of them. Hollister was elsewhere, finding his own entertainment. Jax's mood was buoyant. He seemed as chipper and satisfied as a man with ten concubines.

"Where will we stay when we get back to Shreveport?" Mae asked. "We don't have any furniture yet."

"I booked a suite at the Washington Youree. We can stay there until the house is ready."

"For how long?"

"As long as we want."

"Well, I need to get my things from Aunt Vida's house," Mae said.

"Want me to drive you?" Jax asked. "Or you can take my car. We need to get you some wheels, my dear."

"I just dread going over there. You know how Aunt Vida is. She's liable to give me an earful, even though not one bit of this is any of her business anyway."

Jax wiped his mouth. "We could have the Youree send someone to pack up your things and bring them to the hotel, if you want."

"Would they do that?"

"Sure. They'll do anything for a price."

"Well, gosh, that sure would be nice. I know I have to face her sometime, but I'm just not ready."

"Consider it done."

"Do you think we could have a cocktail on the veranda after supper?"

"Whatever you want, my dear. It's a beautiful evening."

Mae had two cocktails while the day cooled down and they watched people stroll up and down Central Avenue. Later that night, she dutifully slipped into her dusty pink nightgown and waited in bed with the door closed but unlocked. But Jax never opened it. The following morning, Mae dressed and packed her things. She found Jax downstairs in the Venetian Room, drinking milk and reading the newspaper. He beamed when he caught sight of her. He rose quickly to pull out a chair.

"The usual?" he asked.

"Sure."

Jax motioned to the waiter and gave him Mae's order, a single sunny-side-up egg, grits, extra-crispy bacon, and dry toast. He ordered oatmeal for himself, and the waiter poured fresh coffee for Mae. "Well, my bride, we need to round up that no good friend of mine so we can go home. Have you seen him?"

"No. Not since night before last."

"Not to worry. He'll show up eventually. He always does." Jax grinned, showing all his dingy little teeth.

The Washington Youree Hotel was so swanky that the very idea of living there made Mae feel as if she were dreaming, but the double staircases and indoor fountain in the marbled lobby were as real as could be. Mae sat on a red velvet loveseat, feigning bored sophistication, while Jax checked them in. When he had finished, Jax escorted her to the elevator, where two bellmen waited with their luggage. They rode to the top floor, and the bellman opened a door at the end of the long hallway.

"After you, my dear," Jax said.

Mae walked into a high-ceilinged sitting room with tall windows. Fresh daisies were arranged in a crystal vase on a table in front of the window. There were two bedrooms, their doors standing open on either side of the sitting room. "This one gets the morning sun." Jax pointed to the bedroom on the left and told the bellman to put Mae's valise in it.

The bellman deposited Jax's valise in the other bedroom and asked, "Will there be anything else, Mr. Addington?"

Mae had only seen her father tip with change, but Jax peeled off several dollar bills and said, "A bottle of Bombay. Bring up some ice and tonic water too. And see if Andrew has any Guinness down there. Tell Andrew I'll . . ." Jax lowered his voice, and Mae could not hear the rest of what he said.

"Who is Andrew?" she asked when the bellmen left.

"Fella I know that oversees the restaurant in the hotel. Are you hungry?"

"A little bit."

"Would you like to rest a while, then freshen up and get a bite downstairs? I want to take you car shopping this afternoon if you're up to it."

"Are you sure, Jax? All this money . . ."

"It's nothing—a few dead presidents. Don't worry about it. I need to go out, but I'll be back in, say, an hour or two."

"All right."

"Don't forget the bellman's coming back. He'll let himself in if you're in the bath or resting."

"Okay."

Jax kissed Mae on the cheek, a quick dry peck. "I'll see you later, honey. We'll get you some smart wheels—whatever you want."

"Thank you, Jax."

"I must be the luckiest guy in the world."

When Jax left, Mae sat on the couch in her new home away from home. She did not know if her new husband was the luckiest guy in the world or not, but he certainly was the oddest.

The salesman at Red River Motor Company rushed to greet Jax enthusiastically. "Let me introduce you to my bride," Jax said proudly.

The salesman shook Mae's hand. "Pleasure to make your acquaintance, Mrs. Addington. Name's Ralph Cooper, but folks call me Coop." He winked at Jax and said, "You old dog." Mae started to give her Christian name, but Coop had already turned his full attention to Jax. "It's about time you switched to a Chevy, my friend. You been driving that big Caddy around for—how long now? Two, three years?"

"Lord, Coop, not even. The Sixteen's just fine. We're here to get something for the missus."

"Oh, well, in that case, we got in a brand spanking new Sport Roadster that might be just the ticket." Ignoring Mae entirely, Coop led Jax to a butter yellow two-seat convertible. The black top was down to show off a black cloth interior.

Jax stuck his hands in his pockets and walked around the car slowly. "I like the wire wheels," he said.

"Those are brand new this year. She has six cylinders under the hood. Blows the Fords right off the road."

"Mae?" Jax asked.

"Can I talk to you a minute?" Mae asked. "Outside?"

"Sure. Sure. Give us a minute, Coop."

Mae walked outside, and Jax followed. "I know it's only a Chevrolet," Jax said when Mae stopped and turned to face him, "but I can get a really good deal from Coop. It's just so you have something to drive around town for now. I'll get you into a Caddy later. Or a Lincoln. Whatever you want. I promise."

"It's not that. I just . . . I can get by without a car, especially while we're at the Youree. I can walk or ride the streetcar."

"Oh, no, that won't do at all. No wife of mine is slugging around on the streetcar. I won't have it."

"Well, it's a lot of money, is all."

"You're gonna have to stop worrying about money, Mae." Jax grasped her arm lightly. "We're just getting started. Now, do you like this little breezer, or should we keep looking?"

"I like it. It's pretty."

"Okay. Cool your heels and let me go work Coop."

On their first Sunday as man and wife, Jax drove Mae to First Baptist, where Jax's parents and Mae's aunt and uncle attended, and where Mae had gone to church since she moved to town. Jax's parents, Walter and Lucinda Addington, to whom Uncle Bill had introduced Mae ages ago, were bound to know she had been engaged, as did everyone else at First Baptist. Mae dreaded the sideways glances and whispering gossip she expected to ripple through the congregation when she and Jax came through the door. Mae would be lucky if there was anyone—right down to the mice in the belfry—who did not know that she had jilted her fiancé to marry Jackson Carthage Addington.

Mae had not known Jax's full name until she stood in the JP's office in Hot Springs vowing to commit her entire being to him for the rest of her life. That middle name had popped its head up and startled Mae. Not because Jax had a middle name—most everyone did—but because she had not even wondered what it was. In that moment, the name "Carthage" had flashed by her like a warning sign.

"Ooh, I have butterflies," Mae said as they walked up the steps together. They were late and everyone was already inside. The pipe organ bellowed behind the heavy wooden doors.

"Hey, I'm in the same boat. I haven't darkened the door here in over a year."

"But you weren't *engaged*!" Mae snapped. She was suddenly irritated that he thought they were in the same situation.

"Hell's bells, Mae. If it comes up, tell 'em Buster cheated on you."

"Jax!"

"Sorry. Heck. Tell 'em anything you want. They don't know the difference."

"Let's just go inside and get it over with."

Jax opened the door, unmuffling the righteous, booming pipes of the organ. Not one person glanced their way as they slid into a pew at the back of the sanctuary. Mae should have remembered that First Baptist people were too well mannered to gawk and gossip, at least until they were in the privacy of their own homes.

After church, Walter and Lucinda Addington seemed stunned to silence by Mae's presence at their Sunday dinner table. They were through the salad course and well into a fine plate of roasted hen and cornbread dressing before Jax's mother ventured to make small talk. "Mae," she said. "Jax tells me your father has taken a promotion in Fort Worth. Will y'all be visiting there soon?"

"Maybe later this summer. Mama and my sister are still in Whitesboro. They stayed until school was out, so they're still packing up for the move."

"I see."

They returned to the clink of sterling forks against bone china.

Mae lived like a princess in the Washington Youree Hotel, entirely cocooned from the real world. Jax was often elsewhere when she woke up from a night's sleep on feather pillows and Egyptian cotton, and his bedroom door was always open when Mae ventured into the sitting room.

The first morning that Mae woke to an empty suite, she went into Jax's bedroom to investigate. She looked through all the drawers of the bureau and the nightstand. In the nightstand was a dog-eared novel by Dashiell Hammett, *The Glass Key*. Mae read the first page. She could have settled in and read the whole book if she hadn't been worried about Jax catching her in his room. She put it back, thinking she should pick up a novel to while away her idle hours. She rummaged through Jax's closet and found a box from the drugstore on the top shelf. She stood on her tiptoes, reached inside and pulled out a bottle of Pepto-Bismol. There were many more bottles in the box. She went into the bathroom and opened the medicine cabinet. Besides the shaving cream and razor and toothpaste was a bottle of French cologne, which Mae sniffed. It was nice enough, but Jax wore too much of it. A little less would have been nicer.

Mae usually ate breakfast and read the newspaper in the sitting room. Afterward, she often went to Uncle Bill's to help out or simply knocked around town until midafternoon when Jax returned. If a new motion picture was playing, they went to see it. Jax's favorite theater was the Strand, with its wide Magnascope screen. Oftentimes in the evenings, they strolled the sidewalks and window-shopped.

Jax changed his routine from time to time. On those mornings, Mae found his bedroom door closed when she went into the sitting room, and she knew he was sleeping in. He usually emerged in the early afternoon, fully dressed and ready to eat a late lunch and spend time with his wife. On Saturdays, he was gone all day, and he always left a note on the table beside the vase of fresh flowers. The note read that he missed her terribly and hoped she had a good day, or some version thereof.

Every evening, Mae retired alone to her bedroom, wondering why Jax made no advances beyond chaste kisses on her cheek. He had not kissed her on the lips since the wedding. Much less wanted to neck. Much less gone to bed together. Mae wondered if her new husband had another woman, a mistress or even a prostitute, which no wife worth her salt would tolerate. But every time they were out and about of an afternoon, when Jax crooked his arm and Mae rested her hand on that chicken wing of his, she was grateful he had no interest and she did not care why.

During their first couple of weeks at the Youree, Jax took Mae to all the department stores and introduced her as Mrs. Jackson Carthage Addington to the headmen. Some of them already knew Jax. All of them grasped Mae's hand gently and bobbed their heads politely. "Mrs. Addington is to have anything she wants. I'm good for it," Jax told each and every one of them. Mae heard him say it over and over, until she believed it right along with the store managers.

"Take your time shopping for the house," Jax told her after they made the rounds. "There's no rush at all."

"Shouldn't we pick out the furniture together?"

"Oh, sure. But you're the boss. Get what you like."

"Shouldn't I let you know before I buy something?"

"Surprise me. Say, how does a drive sound this evening? It's a nice night and only an hour down to Natchitoches. We could have supper at that little Frenchy place and stroll along the river."

"Sure," said Mae. "That would be aces."

Chapter Forty-Five

At their fourth Sunday dinner with the Addington's, during the salad course, Jax's father suddenly asked, "Are you two still at the Youree?"

"Yep," said Jax.

"Well, how in the world—" Walter Addington stopped abruptly. He shook his head but said nothing more the rest of the meal. After dessert, he told Jax he wanted a word with him in the study.

"Sure," Jax said. "No problem."

Mae followed Jax's mother into the parlor. "Go ahead and bring our coffee," Mrs. Addington told the servant. "No need to wait for the men."

After a few minutes in the parlor with Mrs. Addington, Mae said, "My goodness, I need to powder my nose."

"Of course, dear. You know where it is."

"Yes ma'am."

In the front foyer, Mae turned left toward the study, instead of a right toward the powder room. She heard Jax and his father talking inside. Mr. Addington said something about ". . . throwing money all over town . . ." Jax responded, but Mae could not make out what he said.

"Does that girl have any idea?" asked Mr. Addington.

"Just stop right there!" Jax hollered. Then something, something, in a low voice.

Mr. Addington said, "I'm not going to . . ." something. Mae moved closer to the door.

"This time, it's not your concern," said Jax.

"It's my name, and I will not permit you to drag it through the dirt any longer. I mean it, Jackson. I've had enough of your shenanigans. You are my only son, but you are the sorriest excuse for a man—"

"Go to hell!"

Mae heard footsteps and she scuttled away quickly, rounding the corner into the powder room just as she heard the study door open and slam. She closed the powder room door, her heart pounding. She was panicked over what would become of them—of her house!—if Jax's father cut him off.

Jax called to her from the foyer. "Mae, get your things. We're leaving."

She checked her face in the mirror and relaxed her expression. She opened the door. Jax stood by the front door with his hands stuffed in his pockets. "What's going on?" she asked.

"Get your things and tell Mama goodbye. We're leaving."

"Well . . . okay . . . just give me a minute."

"I'll be in the car." Jax opened the door and went outside.

Mae went into the parlor and told Mrs. Addington they had to leave. Mrs. Addington patted her hand. "Don't worry, dear. I'll see you next week."

Mae wanted to say goodbye to Jax's father, but the study door was closed.

During the drive back to the hotel, Jax said nothing. His hands clenched the steering wheel, white-knuckled.

"Is everything okay?" Mae ventured.

Jax looked straight ahead. "Yeah. Sure."

"You seem angry. Did something happen with your father?"

Jax glanced her way. "My old man's a pain in the neck. But there's nothing to worry about. Nothing whatsoever."

They had a light supper and cocktails on the hotel rooftop that night. Sunday nights were quiet, and there were only a few couples dining. A man in a white jacket played the latest hit songs on a baby grand piano. Jax motioned for the waiter to bring him another Guinness and Mae another gin and tonic.

"This is the life," Jax said after the waiter brought their drinks. They listened to another song, and Jax said, "What if we stayed here instead of moving into the house?"

"What?"

"I mean live here, at the Youree. We could be footloose and fancy free. We could travel. See Chicago, New York, L.A. We could even travel abroad."

"What would we do with the house on Alexander Avenue?"

Jax sipped his Guinness and said, "I'd sell it."

"Gosh."

"I'm serious. What do you think?"

"Where would the money come from? Enough money to live this way all the time?"

"Let me worry about the money."

"I don't know," Mae said slowly. "I need to think about it."

"Take all the time you want. There's no rush at all."

This had become Jax's answer to everything, but instead of putting Mae at ease, it unsettled her. Every single time he said it.

The day after the semester ended, while Mae was in Hot Springs marrying Jax, her best friend, Miriam, had boarded a train bound for New York City. From there Miriam had sailed to Europe, where she stayed with cousins in France. She sent a postcard to Mae at Aunt Vida's house, which Uncle Bill brought to the store and gave to her. God bless him.

> Dearest Mae,
> I hope you are enjoying summer break. My piano is improving by the day. We took an excursion to the coast to see Nice. It was so beautiful. See you when I get back.
> Best,
> Miriam

The postcard was a photograph of a long beach with a promenade running its length. Palm trees towered over the boardwalk like frondy umbrellas, and people strolled in their shade. A building with a veranda all around it stood on pilings over the water. It was topped with an ornate dome and spires and looked very exotic.

"I believe that's a casino," Uncle Bill said.

"My goodness," said Mae.

Mae kept the postcard in her purse and took it out from time to time to look at the photograph. She thought about what Jax had said and tried to imagine what it would be like to travel all the way to France and be one of the people strolling on the promenade.

Mae felt as if she had shopped for furniture for the house on Alexander Avenue forever, but she had yet to make a single purchase. She was always thinking the store's next shipment might contain a couch or loveseat or end table that she liked even better than those she had seen. As much as Mae had wanted the house—enough to marry Jax!—she actually gave serious thought to Jax's proposition to live at the Youree and travel. But she did not give him an answer.

Mae dashed off a note asking Miriam to call her at the Youree as soon as she returned to Shreveport. "Ask for Suite 601," Mae wrote. "I'll explain everything when I see you." She mailed the note to Miriam's house, where it would be waiting for her. When Miriam returned from Europe, she telephoned the suite.

"We must have lunch together *immediately*." Mae said. "Can I pick you up at noon?"

"I'll see you then," said Miriam, who sounded very, very tired.

Mae picked Miriam up and drove to a corner delicatessen on the outskirts of town. Jax had taken Mae there once, and the place served delicious muffuletta sandwiches. More importantly, Mae knew there was absolutely no chance that she and Miriam would see anyone they knew. During the drive, Mae kept Miriam busy talking about her trip to France. Miriam didn't ask a single question about Mae's new yellow convertible or why she was staying at the Youree. She didn't even ask about the fat diamond on Mae's hand, although Mae caught her glancing at it more than once.

"This is off the beaten path," Miriam said when they parked in front of the delicatessen, which was on the wrong side of the railroad tracks and flanked by weathered shotgun houses.

"Wait 'til you taste the sandwiches. Trust me, you'll want to come back."

They went inside and ordered at the counter, then sat down at one of the enameled tables. "The suspense is killing me," Miriam said. "Did you and Buster get married?"

"Buster took up with another girl," Mae blurted. She teared up at the terrible lie.

"Mae! No!" Miriam cried.

What else could Mae have possibly said? That Buster wanted her to move back to Whitesboro and live in a crummy little shotgun house that was almost as bad as the ones around the delicatessen? That he wanted her to be satisfied, *completely*, with being Mrs. Buster Meade and nothing more?

Miriam reached across the table, and Mae took her friend's hand.

"Oh, Mae, I'm so sorry."

Mae nodded and brushed a tear from her cheek.

"So, honey, tell me, whose ring is this?"

Mae burst into tears she could not control. She was mortified with embarrassment.

"Honey, please," Miriam said. "Do we need to leave?"

Mae shook her head. She pulled some napkins from the tin dispenser on the table. "No," she said, dabbing her eyes. "I'll get hold of myself." The lady working the counter brought their sandwiches to the table. She did not linger or ask if they needed anything. "My heart was broken," Mae said.

"I have no doubt," said Miriam.

Mae paused. It was everything she could do to say the next words. "Jax was so kind. I guess he just swept me off my feet."

"Jax?" Miriam's eyebrows furrowed. "Jackson Addington?"

"I know, I know," Mae said. "I can hardly believe it myself. I hope I haven't made a horrible mistake."

"Do you love him?"

The lie had been told, and now Mae could be truthful, mostly. "I don't know, Miriam. I feel as if I walked through a looking glass. Everything is topsy-turvy. Nothing seems real."

"I guess so. Where are you living?"

"At the Youree."

Miriam's eyes widened.

"I know. Jax has been spending money like a drunken sailor. We're staying in a *huge* suite on the top floor, and Jax bought me that brand-new convertible. He told me to buy everything I want for myself and the house—oh, goodness! He bought me a *house*, Miriam! On Alexander Avenue, near Centenary."

"My word!"

"Jax and his father had a terrible row last Sunday, and I was afraid Mr. Addington would cut him off. I don't know what'll happen to us if he does. But Jax isn't worried at all, and he hasn't slowed down one bit. He's still spending money like crazy. I honestly wonder if his mother is paying for all of this."

Miriam picked up a potato chip. "Lucinda Addington came from old Baton Rouge money, so that's entirely possible."

"I don't think Jax can do any wrong in her sight." Mae looked at her sandwich. "I'm sorry, honey. I don't think I can eat a thing."

"We'll get them to wrap these up," Miriam said. "They look delicious, but I've lost my appetite too."

"I'm so sorry," Mae said. "Some lunch date I am."

"Don't be ridiculous. You needed to get all this out. So, when do you move into the house?"

"I don't know. The other night, Jax asked me if I would like to keep living at the Youree and travel. He's talking about seeing the world, Miriam."

"That would cost a fortune."

"I know, but he seems to think he can afford it. It's tempting, you know?" Mae took Miriam's postcard from her purse and laid it on the table. "I can't imagine what it would be like to visit a place like Nice."

"It is beautiful."

"But I love the house too. I love to think about furnishing it and having all the girls over for luncheons."

"Do you think you'll go back to school?

"I don't know. I've always wanted to work in an office. I'm good at dictation and typing. Of course, I can't work if we're traveling."

"You have a lot to think about, my dear," said Miriam.

Chapter Forty-Six

The army airfield's base commander showed up at the dry cleaners during the afternoon lull. Cargie was recording the morning's receipts and her office door was open, and Bill Cole was at the counter when the front door jingled and the colonel walked in.

"Afternoon, Horace," Mr. Cole said. "I'm surprised to see you here."

"May I speak with you in private, Bill?" the colonel said.

"Sure. Just a minute." Mr. Cole stepped into the doorway of Cargie's office, his back to the colonel. "Mrs. Barre, Colonel Hickman and I are going to step out back for a few minutes." Mr. Cole nodded toward the open window and mouthed, "Please listen." Then he opened the counter flap and led Colonel Hickman out the back door.

Cargie got up and turned off the fan. Soon she heard the men's shoes crunch on the gravel of the alley. They stopped under her high window.

"Here. This is good," Mr. Cole said.

"The most important thing is that this is completely reversible," began Colonel Hickman. "I felt you should hear the facts directly from me because Jackson has been negotiating on your behalf. I probably need to tell Walter too, as a courtesy."

"What's going on?" Mr. Cole asked.

"The officer I tasked to negotiate with Jackson—a Captain John Lavender—is being court-martialed. He became involved in illegal activities in Bossier City—prostitution and distributing contraband."

"Contraband?"

"Whiskey. Captain Lavender has been supplying whiskey to some of the officers and enlisted men on base. In any case, certain individuals—associates of Jackson—used these activities as leverage to extort Lavender into signing a service contract for the airfield's dry-cleaning business. All of it."

"With who?"

"Addington's Dry Cleaning and Laundry. Apparently, Jackson has secured a building in downtown Bossier and put out a shingle."

After a brief pause, Mr. Cole asked, "Who are these associates?"

"That's ambiguous. Lavender was reluctant to give details. They thoroughly intimidated him. I did get out of him that he was kidnapped from a brothel and taken to an empty warehouse in Bossier where his options were laid out for him, apparently quite rigorously. He was roughed up pretty badly."

"Good Lord."

"These men are professionals. Jackson may be in over his head."

"Lord, Horace. My niece married Jax a couple of months ago."

"I'm sorry to hear that, Bill. He's mixed up with some pretty shady fellows."

"Yes sir. Sounds like it."

"Lavender has not demonstrated the sort of mettle the army expects from its officers. I have no qualms about abrogating the contract he signed. The full authority of the United States Army is behind me to honor our verbal agreement."

The men were silent a moment. Then Mr. Cole said, "I'm just wondering what might happen to Jackson if he doesn't get that contract. He might be next."

Colonel Hickman said, "That's entirely possible."

"I'm just thinking about Mae."

"I understand."

"Let's leave it," said Mr. Cole. "I'm not ready to risk putting Mae's new husband in danger."

"I imagine he's already in danger."

"Probably. Still, giving that contract to me isn't worth the risk that it'll make matters worse. Let him have it."

"If you're sure. . . ."

"Yes. I feel that's the thing to do at this point."

"All right. But you shall have the officers' business, and guests of the airfield. I insist."

"Very well. Thank you, Horace."

Colonel Hickman said, "I'd like your opinion about whether or not I should take this to Walter."

"I'll tell him," Mr. Cole said quickly. "Seems like I ought to be the one."

"Thank you, Bill."

Cargie turned on her fan and sat down. She was still going over the conversation in her mind when Bill Cole opened the door a while later, carrying their cold drinks and Spanish peanuts. "Did you get all that?" he asked.

"I certainly did."

"I tell you, Cargie, I'm worried about Mae and what she's gotten herself into."

Since their Sunday afternoon trips to Bossier City, Bill Cole had begun calling his bookkeeper by her Christian name. In private. This pleased Cargie, but she had not been able to bring herself to return the familiarity. "It's not my place to say anything," Cargie said.

"Go ahead and speak your mind," Mr. Cole said. "I'd like to hear your opinion."

"Well, Mr. Walter Addington is a fine man, and I know he's a good friend to you."

"He is that."

"But that boy of his is nothing but trouble, front to finish."

Cargie handed Bill the cash box. He opened it and took out a stack of bills to count. Cargie went to the file drawer and took out a fresh roll of paper for the adding machine. Bill Cole separated the bills by denomination, and Cargie tallied the receipts with staccato clacks.

"I suppose there is a somewhat insincere quality about Jackson," Bill said. "I've always tried to look past that, for Walter's sake."

Cargie refrained from telling her friend that he never should have trusted Jax to negotiate the contract in the first place.

After a moment, Mr. Cole added, "I sure never expected Mae to get caught up with him. I would never have agreed to let him work here if I'd thought—"

"No sir," Cargie interrupted. "There was no way to see *that* coming."

"I believe you are correct on that count. But still, it's hard not to feel a little bit responsible."

Cargie stopped punching the keys. "Don't you take that on. It's not your burden to bear."

After a pause, Mr. Cole said, "I know you're right. I'll leave it."

Cargie added the last few receipts and advanced the tape. She tore it off and wrapped it around the tickets, as was her habit. "Thirty-six dollars and fourteen cents."

"To the penny."

"Why, Mr. Cole, I believe you're getting the hang of this."

He laughed and held up his Coca-Cola. Cargie clinked her bottle of Orange Crush against it.

"We're a good team, Mrs. Barre."

"Yes sir. The best."

Just then, the bell on the front door jingled, and Mae called, "Uncle Bill? Are you here?"

"Oh, Lordy," said Cargie.

"I suppose there's no time like the present," Mr. Cole said.

"Would you like me to watch the counter? You could talk with her in here."

Mr. Cole thought a moment. "Maybe it's best if I just close up for a little while. I'd hate for a customer to overhear if she's, well, crying or whatnot."

"Very well." Cargie put the receipts in the file drawer and collected her purse and hat. "I'll see you bright and early in the morning."

"I'll let you know how it goes."

Cargie opened the door as Mae was about to knock. "Good afternoon, Miss Mae," she said.

"Hi, Cargie. Hi, Uncle Bill. I just dropped by to visit for a little while. Is there anything you need me to do?"

"I'm just heading out," Cargie said. "Thomas is expecting me home early today, so I best run along." Cargie said goodbye and hurried out the door.

Cargie rode the streetcar to the Strand Theater to see *The Public Enemy* and get her mind off the afternoon's developments, even though the Strand was a white movie house and going to picture shows there violated Cargie's policy of not giving her hard-earned money to white businesses. The Strand's owners were happy enough to take her quarter at the box office, the same as if *she* were white too. But after that, Cargie was expected to enter an alley so narrow she had to squeeze between the wall and the steep iron staircase that climbed the theater's three-story wall. She was expected to climb the rickety steps while they rattled and squeaked in protest—feeling for all the world as if they were about to come off the wall—and take her seat in the upper balcony. Where the white folks wouldn't have to look at her.

Cargie did all this to watch *The Public Enemy*, and it wasn't the first time she'd done it either. The first time had been to see *All Quiet on the Western Front.* Cargie had happened across the novel by the same name in the library on Texas Avenue. The book was written by a former German soldier who, like Bill Cole, had endured the trenches of the Western Front. Private Cole's diary was plenty disturbing, but Cargie was shocked at how much brutality he had left out. Mr. Erich Maria Remarque—despite having a lady's name—had not been shy about letting folks who read his novel in on every grisly detail about the trenches and No Man's Land, the prisoners of war, and the poor civilians and even animals who were brutalized in the wanton conflict. Even though the book was fiction, it was just as real as Private Cole's diary. Cargie had to stop reading several times, so intense and vivid were the scenes. Yet she was captivated and kept going back until she finished.

When the moving picture based on the novel came out, Cargie wanted to see it. Badly. But it did not play at the colored theaters. So—after wrestling with and subduing her convictions on the sidewalk in front of the box office—she crossed her personal picket line for the first time in her life and gave her quarter to the Strand.

All Quiet on the Western Front had kicked off Cargie's closeted literary and cinematic life, which she lived within the brackets of what she had come to think of as her white life. Cargie's white life began each morning when she said goodbye to Thomas and their children and boarded the streetcar, and it ended when her family met her at the corner each evening. Sometimes, when Cargie laid her head on the pillow next to Thomas's, she wondered how it was possible that he could not hear and see all the people and action going on inside her noggin.

When Cargie pushed her quarter under the box office glass to see *The Public Enemy,* crossing a picket line was the farthest thing from her mind. The top balcony of the Strand was a good place for her to have a minute to herself before she went home. She needed to get used to the idea that the business expansion she and Bill Cole had planned for so long was not going to happen. She was angry—very angry—about it. She was furious with Jackson Addington. Cargie had known that boy was no-count the first time she laid eyes on him, and he had done nothing but prove her right at every turn. Jax was the worst kind of troublemaker, the kind who never admits the truth to anyone, least of all himself.

Chapter Forty-Seven

When Mae left her uncle, she drove directly across the Traffic Street Bridge to Bossier City. She wheeled her little yellow convertible all over downtown until she finally found Jax's business, a two-story building that took up half a city block. The brick exterior had a fresh coat of white paint and foot-tall black letters proclaiming, "J. Addington's Dry Cleaning and Laundry." The slogan beneath the business's name promised, "Cleaner Than New."

Five white trucks with the cleaner's name and slogan painted on their sides sat in a row beside the building, and Jax's Sixteen was parked in front with several other cars. Mae considered marching right through the front door to see what was happening in there. She imagined confronting Jax in front of his employees, but that would only make her look like a fool for not knowing what her husband was up to in the first place. Better to have it out with him privately back at the hotel.

Mae was about to drive away when she saw Red Malone come out the front door with one of the men who had been at her wedding reception in Hot Springs. She ducked down and peeked over the dashboard to watch them. They got into a car and pulled out of the parking lot. After they drove away, Mae sat up. She had seen enough to know that everything Uncle Bill had said was true. She drove to the Youree and went directly to their suite, where she made a gin and tonic to calm her nerves while she waited for Jax. The gin helped so much that she made another, stiffer, drink as soon as she finished the first.

Jax came in at his usual time. "Hello, doll," he said cheerily. "Wanna go upstairs for cocktails? Looks like you got a head start."

"We need to talk, Jax."

Mae told her husband everything Colonel Hickman had said to Bill Cole. She did not mention driving to Bossier to see the dry cleaners for herself because she wanted to see if Jax would try to deny the whole thing.

Jax collapsed onto the couch and clutched his midsection. "Oooh! My gut!" he cried. He rolled around for a minute and finally stilled, slouching against the armrest. "I *told* Red you'd be upset if he opened a dry cleaners in Bossier. I *told* him your uncle was planning to get the army business. I just *knew* you'd be mad as a wet hen."

"Red? For heaven's sake, Jax! I saw the place myself. It's *Addington's* Dry Cleaners. It's *your* business. Unless you married Red too."

"For crying out loud! Don't talk crazy. I knew you wouldn't understand." Jax tugged his flask from the front pocket of his high drape pants and up-ended it, pouring Pepto-Bismol down his throat. Then he rocked back and forth with his arms folded across his stomach.

"Understand what? That you stole Uncle Bill's contract? You were supposed to be talking to the army on his behalf, Jax, not yours. What have you done?"

"Nothing. I haven't done anything. That's what I keep trying to tell you. It's Red's business."

"You expect me to believe J. Addington's Dry Cleaning and Laundry belongs to Red Malone?"

"Yes, that's what I'm saying. Red's a businessman. Dry cleaning is what he does. He just asked to use my name because of Daddy's reputation around here. Red thought it would give him an edge breaking into a new city. Oh, I shouldn't've let him. I knew better. But it just didn't seem to matter, and he offered to pay me every month for using the name. It seemed like a good deal at the time. But now I can see it was a stupid idea.

"I haven't talked to that army guy since, well, I can't *remember* the last time—it's been so long. I didn't know a thing about Red going after that contract until it was already done. By then, it was too late to do anything about it.

"I'll tell you whose fault all this is. Cargie Barre's, that's who. If Mr. Cole hadn't listened to her he would've already bought a building and been ready to go. She kept dragging her feet, 'It's not time. It's not time,' she said. 'The prices are still going down.' And now look what happened. Penny wise and pound foolish, that's Cargie. This is all *her* fault."

"Well I don't know about that," Mae said.

"It's true! Mr. Cole should've been set up in Bossier months ago, and we wouldn't even be having this conversation. He was ready too. He had a warehouse picked out and everything. If he hadn't listened to that darned Cargie, your uncle would be in business with the army right now, and Red Malone would be out of luck."

"Jax, Uncle Bill said some men beat up Captain Lavender. He said they're criminals and they . . . well . . . they blackmailed the Captain into giving the army business to you. Could those men have been Red and the others who were at the reception?"

"What? Red, a criminal?" Jax got to his feet and paced, still holding his stomach with both hands. Mae watched him go back and forth. Finally, he stopped in front of her. "You went to Red's house and met his family and friends. You ate their food and drank their whiskey."

Mae looked down.

"Red and his wife were the only ones who made a big deal about us getting married. Hell, Mae, Red's a family man. All he cares about is providing for his family. I can't believe what these guys are saying. I'll tell you who's coming up with all this. That low-down skunk Lavender, that's who. That guy probably gave the farm to Red, and now he's in trouble for it and making excuses."

"Well, he was beaten up. Colonel Hickman told Uncle Bill."

"I don't doubt it for a minute." Jax sat on the couch next to Mae. "Lavender spends his free time at . . . well . . . he's all the time hanging around an infamous house of ill repute over there in Bossier. Infamous, I tell you. Lavender's carrying on with a married woman too. It's no wonder some guy beat him up. The wonder is nobody put a bullet in him."

Jax reached for Mae's hand. For once, his hand was warm, but his palm was as sweaty as always. "Mae, what in the world would I do with a dry-cleaning business? I don't know the first thing about it. You know that. Besides, I've got my hands full with my medical supply distribution business. It's really taking off since I got that Cessna."

Mae could not stand to look Jax in the face. She stared at his pale, thin hand clutching hers. Short ashen bristles darkened his knuckles. "I saw your car there, Jax. I drove over to Bossier and found the building. I saw Red too."

"Well, see? Red's there all the time. I stopped by to say hello this afternoon. Why didn't you come in? Red thinks the world of you. He talks about you all the time."

"Well, I . . ."

"I guess you were thinking a lot of terrible things this afternoon, weren't you? Oh, darling, I just hate all these lies and half-truths flying around."

Mae did not believe him. Suddenly, she did not believe one single word Jax was saying now or had ever said. "I think it's a good time to go and visit my family in Fort Worth," she said.

"That's a great idea, honey. If you want me to go with you, I'll try to work it out, but it's not very good timing for me, business-wise."

"No, I should go alone. It'll be good for me to spend some time with my folks. See their new house and all."

"Well, dear, that would be aces. It really would." Jax patted her hand. "The main thing is that everything is good between you and me. We're a team now. We gotta stick together. Now, how about we get some fresh air. I'll see who's playing on the roof tonight. I'm thirsty as all get out."

Mae did not think she could bear to listen to one more word out of her husband's mouth. "I'm sorry, Jax. All this ruckus gave me a terrible headache. I think I'll lie down for a little while."

"Whatever you say, doll. Take as long as you need. I'll be right here."

Chapter Forty-Eight

Back in June, immediately after Mae had made her vows to Jax in the JP's office in Hot Springs, she had called her mother to tell her where she was and what she had done.

"Are you in love with him?" her mother asked.

"No ma'am."

Mae's mother was quiet for a long time, despite the long-distance charges.

"Mama?"

"Mae, darling, we women are passengers. We don't get to decide where the tracks and trains go, but we *do* get to choose which train we board. If you want to be happy, you must always be looking ahead. A woman can't afford surprises. She has to know what's around the next bend. Now, honey, you looked ahead to your life with Buster, and it wasn't what you wanted."

This was the heart of the matter. Mae's emotions swelled at the thought of Buster. At the thought of home. Had she done the wrong thing leaving him? "Mama, I'm afraid."

"I know, honey."

"Everything's out of control, and I feel so confused."

"Are you?"

Mae nodded as if her mother could see.

"Has what you want changed?"

Mae thought about this and realized she had not changed one iota. She still wanted all the same things she always had. "No ma'am," she said.

"Look ahead to your life with this man, the same way you looked ahead to your life with Buster. Only you know if this train is going your way. If it isn't, don't board. Leave that JP's office and be on your way."

Mae was silent.

"And, Mae, don't lie to yourself. If you don't love Jax now, you never will. But no matter what happens, you always have a home to come back to if you need to. Your daddy and I will welcome you with open arms. Nothing can ever change that."

"I love you, Mama."

"I love you too, dear."

"Give Daddy my love."

"I will, honey. Go on now."

Mae had sat in the JP's office for a long time after she hung up the telephone. She concluded that her mother was right—she'd probably never love Jackson Addington. She wasn't sure she had ever loved Buster, for that matter. But in that moment, Mae truly believed that Jax's train was going her way.

Mae was just as certain now that she had been a fool. She had boarded a runaway train and had no idea what waited for her around the next curve. She decided to drive to Fort Worth that evening rather than spend another night in the hotel suite with her lying husband. Mae didn't bother to check the train schedule—she would keep the convertible in her possession. Just in case.

Mae stuffed her suitcase and overnight valise with everything she could fit in them. She called for the bellman to fetch her luggage and have her car brought around. Jax's bedroom door was closed, and the bellman's knock and the shuffle of luggage did not bring him out. Mae dashed off a note and left it in the spot beside the flower vase where Jax always left his.

> My dear husband,
> I decided to go on to Fort Worth. The sooner I leave the
> sooner I'll be home again.
> Mae

Her parents' new home on Fairmount Avenue sat on a corner lot and had a wraparound porch. It was larger and more beautiful than the house in Whitesboro, and Mae felt a thrill, seeing all of her parents' hard work come to fruition. She parked in the driveway and lugged her suitcase and valise up the steps. Her mother greeted her at the door, having waited up for her, as Mae knew she would. The kitchen was brightly lit, and the teakettle was waiting on the stove.

Mae told her mother everything that had happened, beginning with Red Malone's whiskey-soaked wedding reception. When she got to the part about some men beating up an army captain and making him sign a contract with J. Addington's Dry Cleaning, her mother set down her teacup. The thing her mother said next and the way in which she said it made Mae's blood run cold. "Get yourself together, Mae. And leave him."

Mae didn't realize how tense she had been until she felt the anxiety drain out of her after a few days of nestling in the safety of her family. Her father's promotion meant he was home for supper every evening. After supper, the four of them—Mae, her parents, and her younger sister, Victoria—sat on the front porch drinking Coke floats from frosted glasses and watching the neighbors stroll the sidewalks. Mae and Vic worked their ladder-back rockers like children, vigorously pumping against the porch rail with their bare feet. Their parents chatted with the neighbors who took time away from their evening constitutionals to visit on the porch a while.

"So how's your summer going?" Mae asked her sister.

"It's a little boring," Vic said. "But maybe things'll pick up. I've got my eye on a tall drink of water at church. Dewey Daggett. He's a looker. Basketball player too. He lives over on College Avenue. I ride my bike by his house sometimes."

Victoria licked the ice cream from the back of her spoon and let the spoon fall into the empty glass with a clatter. She rounded her lips and loosed a long, deep burp that any street tough would have envied. "Dewey treats me like I'm his kid sister or something, even though I'm just a couple of years younger. He's seventeen going on thirty and a Wisenheimer too. To tell you the truth, Maypearl, I don't know why I'm bothering with him." Vic rocked violently with a disgusted look on her face that suddenly turned to a smile. "But he's just so *cute*."

Mae laughed. "What do the boys around here do with themselves on Saturday nights?"

"Oh, they hang out at the hamburger joint up on Magnolia—Rockyfellers—or they drive around the neighborhood. They drive by girls' houses too. Junior and senior girls. I hear the girls giggling about it at church. But they never drive by here."

"Maybe we can do something about that."

Vic stopped rocking and planted her feet on the porch. "Like what?"

"Shush. I have an idea. Just wait 'til Mama and Daddy go to bed."

Later, in Vic's bedroom, Mae held the hand mirror up to her little sister, who had been transformed from a gangling fifteen-year-old into a beautiful young woman.

"Maypearl! I look like a movie star!"

"I'm not finished." Mae coiled Vic's long braid and secured it with bobby pins. Then she took her own floral chiffon scarf and tied it into a turban around Vic's head. "Stand up," Mae commanded. Victoria hopped to her feet, and Mae took her sister's floppy shirttail and tied it at the waist of her shorts. Mae took a step back and put her hands on her hips. "He won't think you're a kid now. C'mon, let's go find this Dewey Hot Shot Daggett."

The two girls crept down the stairs and out the front door, easing it closed behind them. Vic ran to the convertible ahead of Mae and jumped over the door into the passenger seat.

"Move over, kiddo. Tonight you're driving," Mae said.

"Really?"

"Daddy says you drive as good as he does."

Vic scooted over and started the car. Mae put the top down, and Vic backed out of the driveway as soon as Mae was in the car. They drove to College Avenue and pulled to the curb across the street from Dewey's house. The front windows were open, and a man was sitting inside, listening to a radio. "That's Dewey's daddy," Vic said. "He's a deacon."

"Do you think Dewey's home?"

"He's probably out running around."

"Let's drive by that hamburger joint."

Vic drove south to the Piggly Wiggly and made a U-turn, then she drove north on College Avenue. "There they are!" she cried as they approached the schoolyard. "I'd know that bunch anywhere."

Mae grabbed Vic's arm. "Turn left! Quick! Before they see us." Vic made a hard left. The tires and the sisters squealed. "Stop the car," Mae said. "Here, behind the church." Vic pulled to the curb, and Mae opened her door and got out.

"Where are you going?"

"I'm going to sneak around to the front of the church and watch. You take the car and drive past them. Then come around again and stop and see where it goes."

"You mean it? By myself?"

"Yes, by yourself. Go on now, before I change my mind."

Vic drove away, and Mae sneaked around the side of the church. She stood behind a tall, thin cedar at the corner. The boys were talking and laughing in the schoolyard across the street. There were four of them under the streetlamp on the corner. They all wore dungarees and white tee shirts. "I ain't got no reason to climb it. Ain't nothing at the top," one of the boys said.

"Hell's bells, Jimmy. If everybody thought like you, we'd still be wearing knee pants and stockings and speaking the King's English," said a boy with thick black hair who was a head taller than the others. Mae was certain he was Dewey Daggett.

The yellow convertible rounded the corner. Vic looked like she was thirty years old.

"Who's that coming?" said Jimmy.

"Ain't a cop," said another boy.

Vic stopped at the corner, and all four boys stared at her. "Aren't you boys a little old to be playing in the schoolyard?" she said.

"Do we know you?" asked the tall one.

"I don't know. Do you?"

"Oh, Lord," whispered Mae. "C'mon, little sister."

The boys stood, awkward and quiet. They watched Vic but stole glances at one another too. "Do you live around here?" Dewey asked.

"Don't you recognize me?"

"You look kinda familiar . . . I guess."

"I'm Victoria Compton, silly. I go to church with y'all."

The boys, led by Dewey, approached the car. "You look different," Dewey said. "Is this your car?"

"It's my sister's. So, what are y'all up to?"

"Dewey's trying to talk me into climbing that flagpole," said Jimmy.

"Well, if I were you, I'd tell Dewey to climb it himself," Vic said. This brought laughter from the boys, who elbowed one another and agreed that Dewey should do the climbing since he was the one shooting off his mouth about it. "I think whoever climbs that pole ought to tie my scarf at the top to show he was there," Vic said. "Like those explorers do when they plant a flag."

"There you go," Mae whispered.

"Gimme the scarf," Jimmy said and stuck out his hand.

"Wait a minute," said Dewey. "I thought y'all said I should climb it." He held out his hand, and Vic unwound the scarf and handed it to him.

"Be right back, boys." Dewey trotted to the flagpole and looked up. Then he draped the scarf around his neck, spit on his palms, and rubbed them together. "Here goes nothing," he called to the group.

Vic got out of the convertible and leaned against it, watching the man of her dreams shinny up the wooden flagpole, alternately pulling and pushing himself until he reached the top. With one hand, he looped the scarf below the finial and made a wide, dramatic sweep with his arm. Then he shinnied down again.

The next morning, Mae supervised Vic while she applied mascara and lipstick before church. She did not permit her little sister to wear as much as the night before, which would have brought on a hissy fit from their mother. "I'm going to leave this makeup with you," Mae said. "Nobody's open today, and I have more at the Youree."

"Oh Maypearl!" Vic wrapped her arms around Mae's neck and hugged her. "What would I do without a sister like you?"

The Compton family strolled together the few blocks from the house on Fairmont to the Baptist church. When they reached the corner where the De Zavala School flagpole stood, Vic elbowed Mae and pointed up. The colorful chiffon scarf furled and unfurled in the breeze. "Flag's still flying," she said.

During the long drive back to Shreveport, Mae made up her mind that she would move out of the Youree and into her house on Alexander Avenue, even if it meant sleeping on the floor. She would buy all the furniture she wanted on Jax's accounts. No more putting off purchases in case something better came along. She would get everything she could lay her hands on before she and Jax split. Then, at least, she would have something to show for the marriage.

Chapter Forty-Nine

Mae was a nineteen-year-old grass widow when she answered an advertisement for a stenographer-typist position at a downtown law firm. She had not seen her husband since she'd left the Youree— mere days after she returned from Fort Worth. "I'll wrap things up here and come along as soon as I can," Jax had said.

"Take your time, darling," Mae responded. "There's no rush at all."

When Mae left their suite, Jax's things were scattered all over his bedroom, as if he had no intention of ever leaving. The very next thing Mae did was breeze through every department store downtown and buy furniture on Jax's accounts—a whole houseful. She bought a Murphy bed for the spare bedroom, just in case Jax ever showed up.

Stenography had been Mae's strong suit at Centenary. Only one professor had spoken fast enough to outrun her, and he was from Massachusetts and therefore did not count. Mae was a fast typist too—sixty-five words a minute all day long without a single mistake. She could even kick it up to seventy-five in a pinch. The morning of her interview, Mae marched into the Slattery Building, boarded the elevator, and told the attendant, "Carter, Rose, and Peabody, please."

"Yes ma'am. Fifteenth floor." The attendant slid the door closed and they took the long ride up to Mae's future.

Five other girls, Mae's competition for the position, waited in the reception area. She nodded to them and took a seat. Within an hour, they were all writing for their lives, or at least for their livelihood. Mae bit her lower lip and scribbled shorthand as the Dictaphone machine went on and on about the problems with some gas lease or other and their possible solutions. The recording was as boring as her cotton market class at Centenary, but at least she only had to copy the words and not worry about what they meant.

After they took dictation, the girls were charged with typing their notes. The lady running the show, Mrs. Mitchell, told them their work would be compared with a perfect transcription of the recording. Afterward, they all waited in the reception area while their work was examined. Mae was certain she had done a good job, but she could not help worrying that her best might not be good enough.

Finally, Mrs. Mitchell opened the door to her office.

"Mrs. Addington?"

"Good luck," one of the girls said.

"You too," said Mae. She got up and went into Mrs. Mitchell's office.

"Please have a seat, Mrs. Addington," Mrs. Mitchell said. She closed the door and sat behind her big desk. "Your accuracy is excellent. It says here you studied commerce for a year at Centenary. Is that right?"

"Yes ma'am."

"I telephoned Centenary, and they said your grades were above average. Why only one year? Why aren't you continuing your education?"

Mae was surprised by the question, and she sensed her answer was important. "Well . . . I never really intended to earn a degree. I've always wanted to work in an office, and I thought Centenary was a good place to learn the skills I needed."

"I see. Well . . . hmm . . ." Mrs. Mitchell ran her finger across the application. "How long have you been married?"

"Since June."

"But you didn't leave school *because* you married?"

"Well, of course not. Jax, my husband, encouraged me to stay in school. But as I said, I've always wanted to work."

"What about children?"

"Excuse me?"

"When do you and your husband plan to start a family?"

Mae felt very irritated at Mrs. Mitchell for poking around in her private life, but she had to admit that a woman who might turn up pregnant at any time would not be worth the trouble to train. "Unfortunately, my husband and I won't be able to have children," Mae said with a perfectly straight face. "I'm afraid it will just be the two of us."

"Oh, Mrs. Addington. I'm so sorry! I wouldn't have—please forgive these personal questions."

"Well, they're very disturbing. I had no idea what to expect, but—"

"We have a unique position coming open," Mrs. Mitchell interrupted. "We haven't advertised it yet, but I think you might be perfect for it. It pays more than the job you applied for. Are you interested?"

"Yes, of course."

"Mr. Carter's secretary is moving out west in a few months. To Arizona. Anyway, Miss Camille has been with Mr. Carter since the firm started. Going on forty years now. I suppose he believed she would be with him forever. But she's having some health problems, and her doctor says—well, anyway, Miss Camille can never be replaced, and I think we've all just pretended she isn't really leaving." Mrs. Mitchell took a folder from her desk drawer and put Mae's application and test results in it. "And here you come, a serious woman with a college education. Married and settled, it seems. I'm just wondering. . . ."

"My goodness."

"Well, there would be a lot to learn before Miss Camille leaves. And Mr. Carter will have to sit down with you first, before we even *consider* you for the position."

"Of course."

"Do you have time to wait for me to speak with him?"

"Certainly."

Mae waited in the reception area where she had started the process that morning. After a while, Miss Camille, who seemed too old and decrepit to travel to Bossier City, much less Arizona, approached Mae and introduced herself. She sat beside Mae and asked about her family and her time in Shreveport. She chatted casually, as if they were seatmates on a train.

Finally, Mrs. Mitchell emerged from the private offices and said, "Mr. Carter will see you now."

"He doesn't bark or bite," said Miss Camille.

Mae smiled.

Mr. Carter appeared startled when the door to his office opened. His spectacles rode the end of his nose above a great white mustache, and thin wisps of white hair moved about his head in a breeze of electric static. He stood and hesitated, not appearing to know what was expected of him.

"This is Mrs. Addington," Mrs. Mitchell said.

"Yes. How do you do, Mrs. Addington?" Mr. Carter said. He had the deepest Southern drawl Mae had ever heard.

"Very well, thank you, Mr. Carter."

"Um, well . . ." Mr. Carter looked at Mrs. Mitchell.

"Miss Camille will take care of everything," Mrs. Mitchell said.

He brightened. "Perfect. Thank you, ma'am." Mrs. Mitchell nodded to Mae and opened the door, indicating her interview was over. "Oh, one more thing before you go, Mrs. Addington," Mr. Carter said.

"Yes sir?"

"Are you any relation to Walter Addington over at First City Bank?"

"He's my father-in-law."

"Well, how about that? Please give Walter my regards."

"Yes sir, I will."

Mrs. Mitchell walked Mae to the elevator and said, "Welcome aboard. Please be here at nine tomorrow."

"Yes ma'am."

"Come see me first and I'll show you the ropes."

The next day a small desk was placed in Miss Camille's office, which one entered to seek passage into the inner sanctum where Mr. Carter conducted his lawyering. Mae was to learn, through instruction and osmosis, everything Miss Camille did to ensure Mr. Carter's continued success, and thereby, the continued success of his gas, oil, and property clients. Mae was determined to be a quick study and get Miss Camille on her way to breathing desert air as soon as possible. She had her sights set on Miss Camille's big oak desk and the prestige it promised, not to mention the twenty-five-cent raise she would earn when she assumed the full range of her duties.

But within her first week, Mae discovered there was a knotty problem Mrs. Mitchell neglected to mention during orientation: Mr. Harry Peabody, the junior partner in the firm. Mr. Peabody showed up at Mae's desk the first time Miss Camille trundled down the hall and left her alone, as if he had been waiting around the corner, twisting his pencil-thin mustache with gleeful anticipation. He leaned over Mae's shoulder—as if to read the correspondence she was typing—and stuck his hawkish nose deep into her curls.

Mae stopped typing and ducked. "May I help you with something?" she said.

Mr. Peabody grinned and said, "Harry Peabody. Partner in the firm. I like to be a pal to the new girls, especially the ones who smell as fresh as you do."

"I'm sure you do," Mae muttered. Just then Miss Camille came back and saved her, but Mae was worried about the next time, not to mention after Miss Camille left and she was on her own. How would she push him off and keep her job?

"So, tell me about Mr. Peabody," Mae asked during the morning coffee break. Three times a day, the secretaries and stenographers and clerks escaped their desks and file cabinets for a few minutes respite in a ladies-only breakroom, where they enjoyed morning and afternoon coffee, lunch at noon, and an all-day smorgasbord of office gossip.

"You mean Harry the Hands?" said Martha, who was Mr. Peabody's secretary.

"More like Harry the Snout. He just stuck his nose in my hair."

"Well, that's a new trick."

"Foreplay," said Barb. Barb was Mr. Rose's secretary, and the office rumor was that they were lovers and had been for years. Barb chain-smoked, wore false eyelashes, and smudged her eyelids with kohl.

"Yeah, that's it," said Martha. "Hands isn't used to married women, and he's working up his nerve to go in for the Big Feel." Martha blinked rapidly behind her thick-lensed eyeglasses. "Men don't make passes at girls who wear glasses. Buy yourself some specs, Mae."

"I don't think eyeglasses will be enough to keep him off Mae," Barb said.

When Mae returned to her office, she looked up "foreplay" in the big dictionary behind Miss Camille's desk. The definition made her blush and she turned the page quickly.

Mae fretted through the next couple of days, wondering what she would do when Mr. Peabody showed up again. Miss Camille would be leaving soon, and Mae knew it was just a matter of time until Hands cornered her alone. One morning, she almost jumped out of her skin when she looked up from her typing and found him standing in front of her desk. Miss Camille was nowhere in sight.

"Good morning, Mrs. Addington," Mr. Peabody said stiffly. "Um, is Mr. Carter in his office?"

"Yes."

"Okay. Well. I'll just poke my head in."

"All right."

"Oh, and by the way, um, well, about the other day, um, I hope you know that was all in good fun."

"Pardon?"

"Oh, well, um, if I came across as *forward*, you see." Mae could hardly believe her ears. Was he *apologizing*? "Anyway, no harm done, right?" he asked hopefully.

Mae looked at him steadily, but she said nothing. She had no idea how he had managed to get himself on the hook, but she wasn't about to let him off.

Peabody glanced toward Mr. Carter's office, and then looked at his wristwatch. "Oh, geez, look at the time. I better get on to my next meeting. I'll catch up with Mr. Carter later. Well, I'm glad we got a chance to clear up any misunderstanding about the other day. So, have a lovely afternoon, Mrs. Addington, and please let me know if you need anything. Anything at all."

Mae could hardly wait until lunchtime to tell Martha and Barb about the turn of events.

"The word's out on you," Martha said. "It's all over the office."

"What word?"

"About your husband," said Barb.

"Jackson?"

"That's right." Barb tapped her cigarette against the ashtray. Barb did not eat during lunch. Instead she smoked and drank coffee that she spiked from a flask she kept in her purse. "They found out your hubby's a gangster."

Mae started to object.

"You can't hide anything around here," Martha said around a mouthful of sandwich. "But don't worry. We're still friends."

Barb lit a second cigarette from the butt of the first. "We're just now friends," she corrected.

Miss Camille took off for Arizona as soon as Mae had her bearings. She left Mae her big oak desk and her title of Moat Dragon, which was what everyone at the firm called the three executive secretaries who guarded the partners. Mae could not decide if the moniker was a complaint or a compliment, but she supposed that depended on the day.

Chapter Fifty

Mae's tummy fluttered at the thought of hosting a luncheon for her best friend, Miriam, and Miriam's mother, Mrs. Landau, who was a charter member of the Shreveport Junior Service League. Mrs. Landau was a powerful woman, and it was she who would carry the day on Mae's acceptance to the league.

Mae agonized over the menu, even though they would hardly eat a bite in one another's presence. She finally settled on a cold luncheon to ward off the August heat. She used a juice glass to cut little rounds of white bread that she spread with a savory blend of cream cheese, mayonnaise, and herbs. She had wrangled the recipe from the Youree's head chef. Mae added paper-thin slices of cucumber and put the clever little sandwiches in the icebox to chill. She prepared a spicy tomato-based soup with diced cucumbers and green peppers, to be served cold. The soup, another Youree kitchen invention, tasted like summer. She planned to serve it in her new Art Deco bowls, which she chilled in the freezer.

The cucumbers, tomatoes, and peppers came from Mae's nosey neighbor across the street, Ada Tidwell, whom Mae had seen the afternoon she wrote her final letter to Buster. Mrs. Tidwell knocked on Mae's door almost every evening with some gift or other from her prolific garden. "Now, Mrs. Addington," Mrs. Tidwell said as she handed Mae a bowl of vegetables. "Where *has* that husband of yours been keeping himself? I never see him."

"He was here last night, Mrs. Tidwell," Mae responded without missing a beat. "Didn't you see his car?"

"Oh, well, I'm the world's worst for noticing who's coming and going. My nose is always in the flower bed or the garden. You know that, Mrs. Addington."

When Mae had prepared everything as well as she possibly could for the luncheon, she waited in her living room and watched out the big front window for Miriam and her mother. She was surprised when Miriam drove up alone, and she went outside to meet her.

"Hi, sweetie," Miriam said as she got out of the car.

Mae resisted a very strong desire to ask Miriam where her mother was, which would have seemed ambitious and indelicate. Instead, she invited her friend inside and offered a crystal tumbler of iced tea with a perfect lemon wedge perched on the rim.

"The house is just lovely," said Miriam.

"I'll give you the royal tour," Mae said.

The women spent the better part of an hour drifting from room to room, talking about this and that. When they were finished, Mae invited Miriam back to the living room to wait. They sat on the couch beside each other. Eventually, Mae asked casually, "What time should we expect your mother?"

"Oh, Mae, I'm so sorry. She isn't coming."

Mae was shocked that Mrs. Landau had not bothered to send a note to cancel. Despite her disappointment and annoyance, Mae put on her best cheery face. "Well, my goodness, Miriam, that's no trouble. I'm sure she's very busy. All kinds of things come up unexpectedly. I'll meet with your mother another time."

"Oh gosh, Mae. This is so hard."

"What, honey? What's hard?"

"She isn't coming for lunch. Ever. Neither are the other ladies in the league."

"What—I don't understand."

Miriam stood. She carried her iced tea and her purse to the kitchen, and Mae followed her. "What's going on, Miriam?"

Miriam set her glass on the counter. She took a handkerchief from her purse and dabbed her eyes. "It really doesn't have anything at all to do with *you*. All the ladies in the league love you, just like the girls in the sorority. So does Mama. She thinks the world of you, truly, but . . ."

"But what? For heaven's *sake*, Miriam, spit it out."

"They won't let you join the league, Mae."

Mae sat down on her new bar stool, one of three that had wooden legs, metal footrests that circled the legs, and deep cushions of creamy leather. "I don't understand," she said slowly.

"It's because of Jackson."

"What about him?"

"Did you know he's a bootlegger?"

Mae almost laughed out loud. She almost said, "A bootlegger! Why Jax hardly touches the stuff." Then Miriam's words fell into place like a missing puzzle piece, and a perfectly reasonable picture emerged where there had been only murky, nagging denial before.

"Jax told me he delivers medical supplies," she said.

"Well, that's what they call it. Some of the whiskey is even marked, 'For Medicinal Use Only.'"

"How do they know?"

Miriam looked down.

"How do the ladies in the league know that Jax runs bootleg? I'm his wife, and I didn't know."

"Some of their husbands are customers."

"I see. So . . . well . . . gosh, Miriam. I guess it's okay for your husband to *buy* whiskey, but it's not okay for him to *sell* it?"

"It's just that the league is working on its application to the National Association and being accepted is *really* important to them. Maybe if they were already accepted, the leadership wouldn't be so particular."

"You mean about having the wife of a bootlegger on their membership roll?"

"Oh, Mae."

"What if I get a divorce?"

"Well . . ."

"I've been thinking about divorcing Jax anyway."

"Well, gosh, Mae," Miriam said with a pained look. "Then you'd be *divorced*."

Chapter Fifty-One

Mae parked under the carport of her red brick house, and for a brief moment, she missed living at the Washington Youree. It would've been nice to have a mouthwatering supper brought to her by a liveried waiter in the hotel's fancy dining room. She would've enjoyed cocktails on the rooftop too, even if she had to drink them with Jax.

Jax had taken dancing lessons while they lived at the Youree—Mae was certain of it. On Saturday nights, he had tried out this or that new move while he pulled and pushed her around the moonlit rooftop dance floor. He looked at his feet a lot and often lost the beat, but despite his halting rhythm, Mae felt closest to Jax when they danced.

Mae sensed her husband's silent yearning when she tried to follow him across the floor, with the band playing and some crooner leaning into the microphone. She might have kissed Jax in one of those boozy, woozy moments, and in doing so she might have ignited a spark that transformed whatever they were doing into a marriage. But something had always shattered the enchantment—Jax belched, or stumbled, or muttered to himself—and Mae had to turn her face away.

"This is your dream, kid," she said aloud as she pulled a bowl of tuna salad from the icebox and a loaf of bread from the pantry. She made a sandwich and ate it standing at the kitchen counter, staring out the window at nothing.

After supper, Mae took a cool bath, put on her robe, and poured a Coca-Cola over ice. She turned on the radio and settled on the couch to read a movie magazine and wait for Guy Lombardo's program. The announcer said they had a special guest who was making his radio debut, a solo singer named Bing Crosby. Mae smiled, thinking Bing went right to the top of the list of silly names musicians made up for themselves.

An hour later, Mae woke up and realized she had slept through the program. She stood and stretched and turned off the radio. Then she went to the living room's picture window to close the drapes before going to bed and discovered Hollister's red Ford coupe parked at the curb. She hurried out the front door and down the sidewalk.

Hollister was lying across the front seat, out cold. Mae opened the door, and her hand flew to her nose at the overpowering stench of whiskey, stale tobacco smoke, sweat, and filth. Mae leaned inside and pushed his shoulder. "Hollister?" She pushed him harder. "*Hollister!* Wake up. What are you doing?"

He roused and wiped the drool from his mouth with the back of his hand. "Uh?"

"C'mon. Come inside." Mae tugged at him until he was more or less sitting up. He threatened to roll out of the car, and she pushed against his shoulder to keep him upright.

"Mae, you smell really good," he slurred.

"Better than you, my dear."

"Sorry . . . been on a bender."

"Okay, big guy. Let's get you inside. I can't carry you. You're gonna have to walk. Think you can do that?"

"Sure. Sure. No problem."

"Let's go."

Mae pulled, and Hollister staggered to his feet, swaying dramatically. When he had stabilized, Mae slung his arm across her shoulders, slowly walked him into the house, and sat him down on the couch. She left him there and went into the spare bedroom to pull down the Murphy bed and get a pillow from the top shelf of the closet. Hollister would have to clean up before lying down on her fresh linens. That was all there was to it. Mae went back to the living room and found him sound asleep again, his chin resting on his chest. She shook him awake.

"You need to clean up, Hollister. You'll sleep better."

He ran his palms down the front of his shirt. "Whaddaya mean?"

"Think if I run some water you can get yourself in and out of the tub?"

"Uh-huh. Sure."

"Okay, be right back."

Mae ran a warm bubble bath. She laid two fresh towels on the hamper beside the bathtub and went back to the living room to fetch him. She held out her hand and said, "C'mon." Hollister took Mae's hand and, with much effort, pushed himself up. He permitted her to lead him to the bathroom, steadying himself with one hand against the wall.

"Go in there and undress," Mae said. "You can hand your clothes out to me." He stood in the open doorway, not moving. "And don't lock the door. Just in case."

Hollister gazed at the bathtub. "What will I wear if you take my clothes?"

"Just wrap one of those towels around you. The bedroom's right there." Mae pointed to the door. "Go in there and get in the bed when you're done."

He nodded but did not move.

"You okay? You need anything?"

"No'm. I'm fine."

"Don't forget to hand your clothes out to me. Everything."

She gave him a small push, and he walked into the bathroom and closed the door behind him. He bumped around while Mae waited outside. She heard him use the toilet. He ran water in the sink for a long time. Then it got quiet, so she knocked on the door. "Hollister?"

He opened the door, bleary-eyed and still fully clothed.

"Get undressed and hand me your clothes. Then get in the bathtub and wash up."

"Okay," he said and closed the door again. He shuffled around, moving from one side of the bathroom to the other. The hamper scraped across the floor. Eventually, he opened the door enough to push out his shoes, followed by lumps of clothing. He shut the door again.

Mae carried the clothes to the tiny laundry room off the carport and pulled the string hanging from a bare overhead bulb. She filled the copper bowl of her new electric washing machine with hot water and loaded Hollister's clothes, poured in a full cup of Oxydol, and turned on the agitator. By the time Mae had washed Hollister's clothes and wrung them out, she found the bathroom door open and the bedroom door closed. She expected a mess, but he had managed to clean up after himself.

Mae hung Hollister's clothes in the sunroom. She turned on the fan so his shirt and trousers would be dry enough to iron before she went to work in the morning, then she went to the kitchen to make herself a cup of hot tea and check the icebox and the pantry for milk, eggs, and bread. It was after midnight before Mae got into bed. She could hardly sleep, and she did not hear a peep from the spare bedroom.

Chapter Fifty-Two

Mae rose early the next morning. She wanted to open the door and peek in to make sure Hollister was still there, but she didn't dare. Besides, his Ford was at the curb and his clothes were in the sunroom, stiff and dry. He had not gone anywhere.

Mae dressed quickly, ironed Hollister's shirt and trousers, and hung them neatly on hangers on the bathroom door. She folded his underwear and socks and laid them on the hamper with a fresh towel. Before she left for work, she dashed off a note and left it on the kitchen counter.

> Hollister,
> Fix yourself some breakfast. Stick around today and rest. I'll cook supper for you when I get home.
> Mae

Mae was busy all day taking dictation, typing, and filing, yet the hour hand crawled around the clock in slow motion. It seemed as if six o'clock would never come, and when it finally did, she rushed out the door, eager to stop at the market and get home.

She was heartsick when she turned onto Alexander Avenue and saw her front curb empty. She felt like crying. She carried the groceries into the kitchen and tossed the beautiful New York strips—the best steaks City Market had to offer—into the freezer. Her note from the morning lay on the counter. Had he not even read it? She picked it up and was about to toss it in the wastebasket when she realized it wasn't her note at all. Hollister had written,

> Mae,
> Thank you for last night. Running an errand, but I'll be back for supper.
> Hollister
> P.S. I told the neighbor I'm your brother.

Mae laughed out loud. She read the note again and clasped it to her throat. He was coming back! She looked at the kitchen clock, which seemed far more energized than the one at work. The hands stood at a quarter to seven.

Mae pulled the steaks out of the freezer and laid them on the counter. She would pan sear the tender strips to medium rare with butter and serve them with fluffy baked potatoes loaded with butter, sour cream, and chives. She had bought everything to make a Caesar salad too, and she planned to toss it tableside, the way they did at the Youree.

She had just put the potatoes in the oven when she heard a knock at the front door. She opened it to Hollister, wearing a starched shirt tucked into pressed khaki trousers. His face was freshly shaved, his hair was freshly trimmed, and he smelled like a man who knew how to wear cologne. He carried a large paper bag, and bottles clinked inside it when he walked through the door.

"Hello brother," Mae said. "Hope you're hungry." Hollister let go of one of his million-dollar smiles, and Mae realized how lonely she had been to see his face.

"I brought supplies," he said. He carried the bag to the kitchen and pulled out bottles of tonic water, Bombay gin, and Templeton rye. "How about a little malaria medicine?"

"Sure." Mae felt flushed and nervous and very, very happy.

Hollister pulled half a dozen limes from the sack and corralled them on the counter. "Do you like limes? A little lime does wonders for a gin and tonic."

"Yes. Sounds refreshing."

Hollister seemed to know where everything was. He folded the paper sack and put it in the narrow pantry with the others Mae had saved. He popped ice cubes from the tray in the freezer, took her paring knife from a drawer and sliced limes into perfect sections, and assembled her drink with the finesse of a professional bartender. He handed it to her and poured himself a generous glass of rye, straight up. He held up his glass.

"What are we toasting?" Mae asked.

"The best of times, and the worst of times."

She hesitated.

"Just the best of times then," he said quickly and touched his glass to hers. "So, little sister, tell me about our childhood in Texas."

Mae laughed. She took the iron skillet from a cabinet and set it on the stove, then went back to separating and washing Romaine leaves. "Daddy works for the railroad. He and Mama were living in Texarkana when I was born. I guess you were born there too, brother, since you're a couple of years older."

"Sure miss the old home place."

"No, you don't. It was a section house, and we were awfully glad to get out of there. I was in the fourth grade when we moved to Whitesboro. That's where our little sister, Victoria, was born. Vic is fifteen going on thirty. She's something, that one. You'd like Vic." Mae suddenly remembered Rita—how young she was—and she blushed. She put the back of her hand to her cheek. "I think that gin went to my head."

"I'll go a little lighter this time." Hollister took her empty glass and mixed another drink while Mae busied herself with the parmesan cheese and Caesar dressing. "So, tell me about you, Mr. Hollister Caine. Do you have brothers and sisters?"

"A brother, Allister. Five years older than me. He's named after the old man."

"Allister and Hollister?"

"Right. Like there weren't enough names to do better than that. Allister and my father run the hardware store. Caine's Hardware on Line Avenue. It was my grandfather's—he started it, oh, forty years ago."

"Do you work there too?"

"Lord, no. I liked to hang around there when my grandfather ran it. Not so much since my old man took over."

"I heard you played football at State."

"That's right."

"And you were the starting quarterback."

Hollister drained his glass and reached for the Templeton. "Did Jax tell you all that?"

"Oh, no. Jax and I never talked about you. Miriam Landau told me. She went to school with y'all."

"I knew Mike Landau. Didn't really know Miriam."

"Mike's playing for Centenary."

"Yeah, and they had a great season. Mike's a hell of an athlete."

"Do you miss it? Playing ball?"

"Oh, sure."

"Miriam said you were really good."

"I was pretty good. I liked it."

Mae stopped fussing with the salad dressing. "What happened at State, Hollister?"

He set his glass down and turned it slowly with his fingertips on the rim. "Everything just kinda got away from me, and I couldn't reel it back in."

Mae rubbed salt and pepper into the steaks. She put butter in the skillet and turned on the burner. After moment she said, "I'm sorry you didn't get to stay in school. It must've been fun, living on campus and all of that."

Hollister looked up. "I could've stayed, even if I wasn't playing. But I decided to come back to Shreveport."

"Oh? Miriam thought you had a football scholarship."

"I did, but I could've stayed in school without it."

"Well, it's good your father would have paid for school, with or without football," Mae said.

"I have a trust, Mae," Hollister said.

"A trust?"

"From my grandfather. I'm not rich or anything, but it's enough money to get by. The trust would've paid for me to stay at State, not my old man."

"Oh." Mae laid the steaks in the hot skillet. They sizzled and smoked.

"My father doesn't approve," Hollister said. "He thinks the trust lets me do as I please. Which it does. But Granddaddy set it up with the bank before he died, and nobody can change it. My brother gets money every month too, same as me."

"Wow. So you don't have to work?"

"Nope. I'm footloose and fancy free. Hungry too. Those steaks smell great."

"Almost done. Let's eat in the dining room."

"You can cook, girl," Hollister said after supper. "Want another drink?"

"Sure. I don't mind if you smoke."

"Nah. I'm tired of smelling like a dirty ashtray." Hollister carried their empty plates to the kitchen. Mae had never in her entire life seen Buster, or Jax, or her own daddy for that matter, pick up a plate from the supper table. He returned with the drinks and sat down again. "So, what's the deal with that husband of yours?"

"I haven't seen him in weeks. Not since I left the Youree and moved in here. For all I know, he's still at the hotel."

"He's staying in an apartment in Bossier, Mae. Near the dry cleaners."

"Oh. Well, that's good to know."

"What happened?"

"Nothing. Nothing ever happened. I don't know what's going on. You know, the people down at the law firm where I work think Jax is a gangster."

Hollister laughed.

"Is he?"

"Jax? Lord, no. But Red Malone and that bunch are. They're Irish mob. At least, I think they are."

"Bootleggers?"

"For sure. And a lot of other stuff. That's what the dry cleaning business is all about. They're laundering money from all their bootlegging and gambling. Probably prostitution too. Did you see that piece in the *Journal* about the government bringing Capone up on income tax evasion?"

Mae shook her head and said, "I still can't believe we saw him in Hot Springs."

"That was crazy. Now all those mob guys are scrambling to hide their money from the Feds."

"I can't believe Jax is tied up with them."

"He's up to his ears in it," Hollister said.

"Do you think he's trying to protect me?"

"I dunno. Maybe. Maybe he's just trying to keep his head above water."

The conversation lulled. Rita has been on Mae's mind ever since she mentioned Vic. Finally, she asked, "Do you still see Rita?"

"No."

Mae was about to change the subject when he added, "She left town with some schmuck."

"Oh."

"Supposedly, they went to St. Louis. Sounds like a cliché, doesn't it?"

"I'm sorry," Mae said.

"For what?"

"I thought . . ."

"No, that thing with Rita was just—I don't know what that was."

They sat in awkward silence, then Hollister said, "It's late. I should go."

"I'm sorry I brought all that up."

"Don't be."

Mae did not want him to go, but it was very late—almost one o'clock—and Mr. Carter would expect her to be alert in the morning. "This was so nice," she said. "Will you come back to see me?"

"If you want me to."

"I could use a friend, Hollister."

"Me too, Mae." He drank the rest of the whiskey in his glass. "Can I take you out tomorrow night?"

"I'd like that."

He stood and carried his glass to the kitchen, and Mae followed him. He turned on the faucet and put the stopper in the sink's drain. "Don't worry about the dishes. I'll let them soak tonight."

"So, do you want to go someplace nice tomorrow night? Or someplace a little bit naughty?"

"Naughty," Mae said without missing a beat. "What about the juke joint at Bistineau? I never got to go there."

"It burned down, but I know another place I think you'll like. Pick you up at seven-thirty?"

"I'll wear my dancing shoes."

"I'm counting on it."

Mae walked Hollister to the front door and stood on the porch until he pulled away. Then she walked out to the yard, the night quiet all around, and watched his taillights round the corner onto Wilkinson Street.

Chapter Fifty-Three

The Blue Goose Grocery and Market was a white frame double shotgun house in the same neighborhood as the delicatessen where Mae had taken Miriam to break the news that she had married Jackson Addington. The Blue Goose stood at the corner of two rutted dirt roads, just south of the railroad tracks, and it had a large blue goose painted on one wall. Hollister parked across the street, and music drifted from the market into the coupe's open windows.

Mae looked toward the back porch, where men and women were talking and laughing, many of them with bottles or glasses in their hands. A gang of children ran down the street past Hollister's window. "That's not your typical grocery store," Mae said.

"It's a speakeasy, Mae," Hollister said. "Is that okay?"

"Sure."

Hollister reached across Mae, opened the glovebox, and took out two enameled cups. He pulled a bottle of Templeton from under the seat and poured a little for Mae and a lot for himself.

"What are we drinking to?" Mae asked.

"The Shreveport Home Wreckers," Hollister said. He pointed to the market. "The guys playing tonight."

Mae held up her cup, and Hollister tapped it with his. "To the home wrecking blues," he said.

"Amen, brother."

They finished their drinks, and Hollister returned the cups to the glovebox and the Templeton to its hiding place under the seat. He got out and came around to open Mae's door. The sun was down, but the sky was still light above the treetops. A cool, dry breeze came across the railroad tracks and gave Mae a chill in her sleeveless dress. Hollister took her hand and led her across the street and up the back steps. The market's rear room was packed. They weaved between the slow dragging couples to an empty table against a wall. "Wait here," he said. "I'll be right back."

Mae watched the Home Wreckers, who weren't more than a dozen feet away. One of them sat in a straight-backed chair with a steel guitar across his knees. He wore a floppy hat that hid his face, but he looked up once and caught Mae's eye. He smiled and winked then put his head down again and worked the guitar's strings. He wore a broken bottle neck on the third finger of his left hand—where another man might have worn a wedding band—and he ran it up and down the frets, making the instrument whine and keen as if it were alive.

A second musician blew a long riff on a kazoo, then raised his voice and crooned,

> Tell me, baby, what's the matter now?
> Mmm, tell me, baby, what's the matter now?
> Are you tryin' to leave me?
> And you don't know how?

Hollister was back at the table, his hands filled with bunched newspapers, and two bottles of Coca-Cola dangling from his curled fingers. Mae took the bottles, and Hollister spread the newspapers on the table releasing the savory aromas of barbequed ribs and roasted corn on the cob. "Hungry?" he asked.

"Smells delicious." Mae sipped her Coke. "Oh," she said and put her hand to her mouth.

"It's spiked with rum. Do you like it?"

"I do."

They ate and watched the dancers and the Home Wreckers. When they had finished, Mae asked if there was a ladies' room.

"C'mon, I'll show you." Hollister gathered the newspapers. "Another Coke?"

Mae nodded, and Hollister showed her to the ladies' room, where a line of women waited. Mae took her place at the end, and a few of the girls smiled at her shyly. As far as she had seen, she was the only white girl in the place.

When Mae's turn came, she did her business and checked herself in the cloudy mirror under a dim bulb. She made sure there was no food between her teeth and applied fresh lipstick. She took a tissue from her clutch, folded it, and blotted her lips, adding a perfect impression to the others imprinted at odd angles on the paper. Mae snapped her pocketbook closed, opened the restroom door, smiled, and made her way back to her date. Hollister stood when she approached the table. "Would you like to dance?" he asked.

Mae extended her hand, and he led her onto the dance floor and took her in his arms. She pressed her body against his, following the rhythm of his hips. Hollister danced gracefully, intuitively, and slowly. The Home Wreckers paused, and in that brief fermata, Hollister raised Mae's chin and kissed her, and she discovered fire.

"Take me home," she said.

"Are you sure?"

"So sure."

Mae unwrapped for Hollister the treasure she had promised Buster as one promises a treat to a dog who behaves himself. The treasure Jax had left untouched, though he had every right to it. Hollister opened Mae's gift effortlessly, passionately. He was urgent, yet patient. Firm, yet mellow. But when he breached her virginity, she cried out in spite of herself.

"Mae?"

"Don't ask," she breathed. "And please, don't stop."

Afterward, Mae lay in Hollister's arms, her face against his chest. "I've gone and fallen in love with you," she said.

He squeezed her. "Marry me, Mae."

"I'm already married."

"Get a divorce. Or have it annulled." He paused, then said, "Jax is a weird little guy."

In a single summer, Mae had jilted her fiancé, married a man she did not love, and fallen for her husband's best friend. Adding a divorce, much less a second marriage, to that mix might be too much for Mae to hold her head up when she walked down the street. She had to preserve some dignity. "Would you mind terribly if we kept on like this?" she asked.

"Living in sin?"

She raised up and looked at him. He smiled, and she lay her head down again. "Divorcing Jax won't get me out of living in sin. Sometimes it feels like everything I think and do—everything I *want*—is a sin. Like I'm steeped in it."

"I know the feeling."

Mae closed her eyes. After a long silence, when she was almost asleep, Hollister said, "We'll keep on just as we are."

"Yes," Mae said. "Just as we are."

Mae and Hollister did not leave the house all weekend, and by Sunday afternoon they were down to soda crackers and Campbell's tomato soup, which they ate in the sunroom while reclining on the couch under a shared blanket. A hard rain had set in and it did not let up all day.

Hollister leaned over and set his empty bowl on the floor, then he laid his head in Mae's lap. She set her half-eaten soup on the occasional table and ran her fingers through his heavy, straight hair. It was variegated from blond on top to tawny undertones. He rolled over and slipped his arms around her. "This is whoopee weather," he said and laid his head against her breast.

"Shouldn't we use something, Hollister? I don't want to get pregnant."

"You won't."

"That's not what Mama said."

He laughed, then he raised up and looked at her. He had not shaved all weekend, and his chin and cheeks were thick with sepia stubble. "I had a vasectomy, Mae. When I was in Baton Rouge."

"What's that?"

"It's a surgery doctors do on men, so they can't get a girl pregnant."

Mae had never heard of such a thing. "Ever?" she asked.

"Well, I've heard people say it can be reversed, but, yeah, it's probably forever."

"Why did you do that?"

"There was a girl I went with at State. Her name was Melody. *Is* Melody. We went together for a long time. Melody got pregnant, Mae, but she didn't tell me because she didn't want to have a baby."

Mae had gone to school with a girl who got pregnant and was whisked away before she started showing. The family said she had gone out west to stay with a sick aunt. The girl returned the following year with a much-sobered disposition and no baby. Girls in Whitesboro went off to have their babies, but Mae knew that more sophisticated girls used other methods. "What did she do?" Mae asked.

"She took care of it."

"An abortion?"

"There was a doctor in town who was popular with the coeds. One night at a party, a friend let it slip that Melody had been to see him."

"Hollister, I'm so sorry."

"I could never decide which was worse," Hollister said. "That my kid never got a chance to see the light of day, or that he—she— might have grown up with me for an old man."

"Oh, Hollister."

"That sounded pathetic, didn't it? But I couldn't get that baby out of my head, so a couple of weeks later I went to see that bastard myself. I told him to fix me. He didn't want to, but I didn't give him a choice."

They sat in silence for a few minutes, then Hollister took Mae's hand. "Do you want children?"

"I used to think I did."

"And now?"

Mae leaned over and kissed him. "All I want right now is you."

Mae called her mother and told her that she and Jax had separated. Of course, Mae's mother was not surprised. If anything, she seemed to be relieved. "I don't want to go through a divorce right now," Mae said. She did not say that she needed to remain Mrs. Jackson Addington at the law firm because it made life so much easier.

"The main thing is that you're away from him," her mother said. "Just give it some time. A man like Jax won't take long to meet someone else, and then he'll come to you for a divorce."

"I hope so," Mae said.

"I'll break the news to your Daddy and Vic. They'll be fine with it. We all want you to be happy."

"I love you, Mama."

"I love you too, dear."

Vic wrote Mae a letter soon after. "I never even got to meet Jax," she whined. Then she went on to say that she had been on two dates with Dewey Daggett. He had asked her out on more, but their mother had said Victoria was too young to go steady. "Mama says I can only go out with Dewey once in a while. I have to date other boys too, not just him. The meanie."

Mae felt she was responsible for the new dating rules their mother had come up with. But when she thought about how quickly young girls fall for boys, she thought her mother's wisdom would work to Vic's advantage in the end. "Listen to Mama," Mae wrote back to her little sister, "and save yourself some heartache."

Mae did not make any attempt to locate Jax and ask him for a divorce. She didn't want to think about her summer marriage and the way she had permitted herself to be paraded all over Shreveport. She could hardly acknowledge it had happened, much less track Jax down and go through the to-do of divorcing him.

At Carter, Rose, and Peabody—particularly Peabody—Mae continued to be Mrs. Jackson Addington. She was Mrs. Addington to her neighbors on Alexander Avenue too, specifically Mrs. Tidwell, who asked from time to time just how long Mae's brother intended to stay with her.

Chapter Fifty-Four

Jax had not seen Mae in the flesh since she left the Washington Youree Hotel, but in his fantasies, their love affair thrived. Their escapades reached around the world, the specifics of which depended on the latest movie Jax had seen or novel he had read. Jax had even gone as far as writing down his ruminations. He collected them in a rolltop desk in his apartment up the street from the dry cleaners, where he had moved after Mae left the Youree.

One idle rainy afternoon, Jax pulled out some stationery he had lifted from the hotel and wrote a letter to Rudyard Kipling, whose stories enthralled Jax and provided him much fodder for his daydreams. In his letter, Jax described the adventurous and carefree life he enjoyed with his beautiful wife. He told Mr. Kipling that he and Mae planned to book passage to India in the autumn, and they hoped to visit some of the exotic locations the author used in his stories.

As Jax penned these words, the thought occurred to him that he really could go to India and see Kipling's muse firsthand. But then he thought about trying to transport enough Pepto-Bismol to get him through the trip, and he remembered that Mae would not actually be with him. Having his beautiful wife on his arm as he had at the Youree was, in a sense, the entire point.

This brought to mind a photograph Jax kept in a drawer in the rolltop desk. He took it out and studied it. In the picture, which was taken at evening time, he and Mae sat side by side at a white-clothed table on the Youree's rooftop. Jax wore a white summer suit, as he had almost every day that summer. Mae wore a chiffon evening dress and a gold necklace and earrings he had given her as a surprise. Her dark, curly hair fell to her bare shoulders.

They were listening to some singer—Jax couldn't recall who— and they looked relaxed and happy, even rich and beautiful. The Youree Hotel photographer had snapped the picture when they weren't looking, and they had been startled by the flash. The next day, the photographer tracked Jax down and gave him the picture. "You have a lovely wife," he said.

Jax reached into his pocket. "How much do I owe you?"

"It's on the house."

The photograph was the only one Jax had of himself in which he looked, if not handsome, at least like somebody. He wanted to put it in his letter to Kipling, but it was the only copy. Then Jax got an idea. He closed the desk and locked it, put on his suitcoat and slipped the photograph into his inside breast pocket. He drove to the Youree and found the photographer. It took the man a week to find the negative and make two dozen copies. By then, Jax had a blazing passion to write letters to famous people all over the world and include the photograph of him with his beautiful wife.

Jax used the Washington Youree Hotel as his return address, and he bribed the desk clerks, each according to his appetite, to keep him in hotel stationery and save his incoming correspondence. Along with the photograph, Jax slipped a trade card for J. Addington's Dry Cleaning and Laundry inside each letter.

Jax became so proficient at penning his fantasies that he decided to write a novel, but he abandoned his manuscript after he realized he was not willing to share his glory with anyone, not even a character of his own creation.

Many people wrote back. Their letters, bearing colorful postage, made their way from distant lands to the Youree Hotel. Month after month passed, and Jax's accounts of his marriage to Mae and their adventures together mushroomed into an epic love story that circled the globe. And he did not stop there.

Jax talked about his wife incessantly to his friends, constructing elaborate high jinks that he and Mae laughed their way through, all the while falling ever more deeply in love. Jax's experience had taught him that people were generally too well mannered to challenge a story, even one that was an obvious bald-faced lie. Only Hollister, his closest friend, narrowed his eyes as if he might take Jax to task. But in the end, Hollister only smiled and said, "Good for you, my man."

Chapter Fifty-Five

1933

Prohibition was ending, and Jax wracked his brain for weeks to come up with a last hurrah before he was out of business. The idea he'd been looking for came to him at a time he least expected, on a Sunday afternoon while he was having coffee in the parlor with his mother. She upended her Belleek cup to get the last sip before setting it back on the saucer, and Jax caught a glimpse of the mark on the bottom. "Mama, is that a different cup you have?" he asked.

His mother turned the cup over on her napkin. "My goodness, Jaxy, you have a good eye. Yes, it's one of the new ones. Your daddy ordered them to replace the ones that had gotten chipped or broken over the years."

The Belleek trademark—a hound, harp, and tower—had changed. To Jax's thinking, his mother's old china had become more valuable the minute it did. Everything was always changing, and people would pay good money to hold on to a little bit of how things used to be. Jax put down his cup and saucer and stood. "I gotta go, Mama, I gotta get back to Bossier."

"On Sunday, dear? I hope you're not working on the Lord's Day."

"Course not, Mama." Jax leaned over and kissed her cheek. "But I forgot I told Mae I'd bring her dry cleaning home with me this afternoon."

"I miss seeing Mae, honey," his mother said. "Looks like she'd take time to see *me*, or at least pick up the phone, even if she doesn't want to be around your daddy."

"I'm sorry, Mama. Mae's funny that way. But she loves you very, very much." Jax leaned down and kissed his mother's cheek. Then he hugged her and held her tightly, as he always had, and as he never had another woman.

Jax drove directly to the dry cleaners afterward and found Red Malone reading the *Shreveport Journal* in the manager's office. Red was the only one in the building. "Jaxy! What brings you by on a Sunday afternoon?"

Jax pitched his idea to make one final run of bootleg in memorial bottles that commemorated Prohibition. "We could charge an arm and leg, Red, and I think they'll pay. Everybody hates to say goodbye to the good times."

Red was so keen on the idea that he called Owney Madden himself, and Madden commissioned black ribbons with gold letters that would be affixed to every bottle that went out on the last runs before Prohibition ended.

Jax wrote Owney a letter on the Washington Youree stationery, and he slipped in the photograph of him and Mae before he sealed the envelope. "We hope to get to New York next year," Jax wrote, "and the Cotton Club will be at the top of our list of places to visit." He mailed it to Madden care of the Cotton Club in Harlem.

Owney never wrote back.

Jax made one last run to Baton Rouge in the Cessna before America finally ended her illicit love affair with booze. "What's all this?" Billy Dean asked when he saw the crates stacked in the back of the Cessna, "I won't be able to give it away by this time next week."

Jax pulled out a bottle and pointed to a thin black band that had been added below the Canadian Club label. Gilded script ran the length of the band. It read, "December 3, 1933. Thanks for a great run. Owney and the Gang."

"Top drawer," Billy said. "I can move as much of this as you can get. C'mon inside the hangar. There's somebody I want you to meet."

Jax followed Billy Dean into the hangar, to the limousine, which was parked against the back wall with its innards scattered all around it. A pair of legs, bent at the knees and terminating in heavy work boots, protruded from beneath the car's front grill. Billy kicked one of the boots, and a long, skinny boy slid out on a creeper. "This here's my brother, Harvey," Billy Dean said. "Kid's a natural grease monkey. Harvey, this is Mr. Addington."

Harvey hopped up and wiped his hand on his overalls. He was a skinnier, younger version of Billy Dean, and he looked just as world-weary as his older brother. Harvey shook Jax's hand firmly but did not speak.

Billy Dean said, "I flew up to Oklahoma and snatched him out from under the old man's nose, just like I said I would." He pointed to a Stinson, one of the half-dozen aircraft in the hangar. "In that bird right over there. She belongs to one of my customers. One of *our* customers. Yes sir, I done it, didn't I, Harve?"

Harvey nodded and grinned, showing mineral-stained teeth.

"Harvey here's takin' lessons. Already flies better'n his big brother."

"How do you like Louisiana, Harvey?" Jax asked.

The boy nodded.

"You like it?"

Harvey glanced at his brother.

"It's okay, Harve," Billy Dean said. "Mr. Addington's our friend."

"Yeth thir," Harvey said slowly. "I like any plathe that ain't got the old man in it."

Chapter Fifty-Six

1934

Cargie Barre was great with child and mad with summer heat. She had been surprised by her third pregnancy, even though at thirty years of age she was plenty ripe for childbearing. This pregnancy, like the others, was precipitated by carelessness. During the worst of the heat, Cargie spent a lot of quarters going to picture shows. The movie theaters had refrigerated air, and Cargie went when she did not think she could bear to sweat a minute longer.

She went no matter what was playing, even if she had seen the film half a dozen times. With one exception. She refused to see *Imitation of Life* a second time because the first time made her as mad as a wet hen. Cargie missed a lot of refrigerated afternoons during *Imitation of Life*'s two-week run at the Strand, until *The Thin Man* came along and knocked it off the Magnascope screen.

In the movie, white Beatrice was smart and resourceful, whereas black Delilah was as simple as a child. Poor Delilah only took a 20 percent interest in Aunt Delilah's Pancakes, the business that was built on her secret recipe. Delilah would have refused even that because she found her complete and absolute fulfillment in cooking and cleaning for her white lady. But sympathetic white lady Beatrice, benevolent genius that she was, said she would put the money in the bank for Delilah's daughter because her negress Delilah was just too simple to consider her own daughter's future.

Cargie was further infuriated by the oh-so-clear message that Delilah's daughter had betrayed her race by trying to pass as a white girl. Righteous Delilah justified Jim Crow by teaching her wayward daughter that one drop of black blood made one black, and such a person could never be truly white, no matter her appearance. Delilah seemed to believe that no matter how tempting the privileges of whiteness, the Godly thing to do was to bow one's head and accept the millstone the Lord had laid around one's neck by making one black.

After the movie, Cargie descended the narrow staircase into the alley and came around the front of the theater in time to hear a white woman comment, "Why, that was the most sympathetic picture about coloreds I ever saw."

"You have ever seen," Cargie muttered under her breath. "It was the most *fatuous* movie about colored people you . . . *have* . . . *ever* . . . *seen*." The white woman heard Cargie's voice, if not her words, and she smiled at her. Cargie turned her head as if she did not notice and walked away toward the streetcar stop.

The next morning, Cargie took Bill Cole's diary from the back of the desk drawer, where she had kept it all these years. She needed to feel her connection with her white friend. Cargie turned to her favorite passage.

3 August 1918
We were lolling around camp after breakfast this morning when we heard aeroplanes in the west, coming from behind our line. A few of the boys were keen to tally the planes they saw, and they had a contest going about who had seen the most different types. These fellas are walking Encyclopedia Britannicas when it comes to planes, and they were pretty disappointed this morning when a couple of Sopwith Camels came into view. We've seen scads of Royal Flying Corp Camels.

The Camels are fighters, and we always see them in squadrons, so it was kind of unusual that there were only two. When they got close, we saw that one was painted camouflage and armed with machine guns, as is customary. This plane had Thunder *painted on the side in black blocked letters. We had never seen a plane with a name painted on it.*

Now here's a marvel—they synchronize the machine guns to fire between the propeller blades when the engine is running. It sounds impossible, but it's true. The preacher back home says knowledge will cover the earth like water covers the sea the closer we get to the Lord's return. War will cover the earth too. Between this awful war—the whole world's fighting—and the things people know how to do these days, it seems like the end of time could be right around the corner.

The other Camel was very strange. It had no armament at all and was painted snow white with big RFC roundels on the undersides of the wings. Lightning *was painted in black cursive letters on the side.* Thunder *and* Lightning. *We didn't know what to think. One of the guys said the flyboy in* Lightning *sure was feeling lucky. We all agreed he was a sitting duck painted up like that with no machine guns.*

I expected the planes to pass us by, but when they came overhead, the camouflage one peeled off and the white Camel continued straight ahead and appeared to dive toward the earth, which brought a roar from all the fellas standing around. It seemed like the pilot almost kissed the ground before he pulled up, up, up, all the way over until he was upside down and coming back toward us. The engine went quiet for a second, and then that crazy aviator turned his plane right side up again and the motor roared to life.

One of the Britannicas hollered, "Immelmann Turn!" He said the aviators use the maneuver in combat to get the enemy off their tails and regain the advantage. He'd read up on it and he dipped and arced and twisted his hand to show us how it went.

The Immelmann was something to see, and the aviator didn't stop there. He rolled that Camel again and again, all the way across the tops of our heads. The plane was so low that I felt like I could almost reach up and grab a wingtip as it flopped by. That pilot was as mad as a hatter, but brave too. All the guys were jumping and shouting. It was quite a show, and we all felt good seeing it and suddenly very brave ourselves, like our side has something the other side doesn't. Right then I felt like there was no way we could lose the war. I think the other guys felt the same.

Let me tell you, we didn't know the half of it. The white aeroplane landed and parked next to its mate. The aviator pulled off his goggles and leather cap, and—big surprise!—the pilot was a girl! Well, the guys just went wild. She made a big show of fluffing out her long red hair and climbing down from the cockpit one long leg after the other. The officers were falling all over themselves to take her hand and help her down the steps they had set beside the plane.

She was a vision for sure. She had on a Royal Flying Corps shirt with the sleeves hemmed above the elbows of her creamy smooth arms. She wore her white aviator's scarf tied in a bow around her throat. Her shirt was tailored and tucked into trousers, and her trousers were tucked into little leather boots. She waved real big at us, and I felt like she'd flown all the way from England just to see me.

The pilot from the other plane came around to meet her. She hooked her arm in his and they headed our way. Ten-hut! We snapped to attention and then got the at-ease command. Every one of us tried to look as sharp as he could, dirty and battle worn as we were. I sneaked my hand up to smooth my cowlick, but it wasn't any use.

She shook the hand of every single soldier. When she stopped in front of me, her blue eyes and red lips and apple cheeks put me into a trance straightaway. She said her name was Adele and she thanked me for helping stop German tyranny. She asked my name, but I was dumbstruck and could not muster it. Then she put her hand out, and her fingernails were lacquered, with white tips that matched her scarf. Paris-style, the guys said later. When I touched her fingers, my heart was suddenly as desperate as a sun perch flopping on a creek bank. I grabbed her hand in both of mine and didn't let go. The other pilot—her escort—said, "Steady, private," and pushed my arms away. Adele smiled and showed me her perfect white teeth.

She moved on to the next doughboy, but her escort stayed put. They were both tall, but he was way over six feet. Taller than any of us, or so it seemed. He leaned toward me and said, "The queue for falling in love with Adele forms over there." Then he called me "brave lad," and I halfway expected him to tousle my hair. But at least he didn't laugh at my foolishness.

Adele had tea with the officers in their tent before she and her wingman flew away later that afternoon. We heard she's only sixteen, the daughter of an earl or some such. Everybody talked about how smart she is and how brave too, because the Camel is a handful and has killed a lot of men. All I can think about is, if I make it through this war, how will I ever find a girl like her back home?

Cargie tucked the diary into her desk drawer when she saw Bill Cole coming through the front door after a long lunch with Walter Addington. She wanted to call, "Did you find a girl like Adele? Is Mrs. Cole anything like her?" Instead she said, "Been dead as a doornail here, Bill."

Bill hung his hat on a peg beside the door. If he was surprised to hear her say his Christian name for the first time in their lives, he did not comment on it. "Walter sent you something," he said.

"What is it?"

He lifted the counter flap and came through. "Here you go." He handed her a very thick brown book.

"What in the world?" Cargie took the book and read the spine, "*Security Analysis*, Graham and Dodd."

"Walter says these men have come up with ideas for getting at a company's value and whether or not its securities are trading at a good price. He thought the book had your name written all over it." Tucked inside the back cover were a few folded pages. "Walter sent those too," Bill said. The first page was a handwritten note on First City Bank stationery.

Dear Mrs. Barre,
I hope the principles and techniques Messrs. Graham and Dodd put forth in their book will interest you. If so, these companies are a good place to start looking. They make up the Dow Industrial Average. The Average is the benchmark for American Industry. In other words, these should be some of the strongest companies in the country, but you will be the judge of that. The names and addresses listed are your contacts for their financial records.
Respectfully,
Walter Addington

Cargie laid the note aside, her conscience smarting from all the wicked thoughts she'd had about whites since seeing *Imitation of Life*. A body had to remember to take people as they came, individually, instead of lumping them all together in a bunch. She opened the book and began to read.

"The book looked a little dry to me," Bill said.

"Uh-huh," Cargie said without looking up.

"Well, I'll leave you to it then." Bill said. He left and closed the door behind him.

Mr. Graham and Mr. Dodd hooked Cargie in the Preface, where they laid out their intentions right up front. They were quick to say they had left some things out, such as judging the future prospects of an enterprise, not because it is not vitally important to do so, but because there simply wasn't anything to say on the subject.

Cargie respected a man who did not speak when there was nothing to be said. And so, for the first time since she had graduated college, Cargie believed she was about to sit at the feet of someone who knew more than she did, and to Cargie's thinking, that was saying something.

Chapter Fifty-Seven

1941

Everyone sitting around the Compton Thanksgiving table on Fairmount Avenue believed Mae and Hollister had been man and wife for years. They had shared holidays for a decade, and Hollister was a model son-in-law to Mae's parents and a good uncle to Vic and Dewey's two children, Dewey Junior and Bobbie. Mae and Hollister even wore matching gold wedding bands, inscribed inside with the phrase "For Good" though no one knew that but them.

The Nazi's were all anyone talked about that year. Herr Fuehrer was on a tear, striking Europe with sudden lightning squalls and striking terror in the red heart of the large but disheveled bear to Germany's east. The French were down. The English, despite suffering heavy bombardment, stood bravely in the gap against the Reich's wanton expansion, while America hung back and girded herself for war. Again.

Hollister and Dewey Senior pulled out their draft cards, slapped them on the table, and covered them with five-dollar bills. Mae looked at Vic, who winked, even though Mae saw in her sister's eyes the same gnawing dread she felt.

"Whatcha got, Dew?" Hollister asked.

Dewey slid his card out from under the five-dollar bill. "Thirteen-oh-four."

Hollister uncovered his. "Twenty-seventeen, my man. Pay up." Dewey scooted the bill toward Hollister, who picked up the money and put it in his wallet, along with his draft card. "We'll all go together if we wade into this thing," Hollister said.

"That's a fact," agreed Dewey.

Two weeks after Thanksgiving, on a Saturday night, Mae and Hollister went to the Calanthean Temple on Texas Avenue to Jitterbug to Cab Calloway. The entertainer swung his conked hair in time to the band's rhythm, and he danced wildly and tirelessly. No matter what song Cab was singing, the message was always the same, "The world's going to hell in a handbasket, but tonight we're alive!"

The next morning, Sunday, they slept in and ate a late breakfast before retiring to the sunroom to read the paper and drink coffee. When they grew sleepy again, they cuddled and dozed under a quilt on the generous sectional sofa Mae had purchased at Rubenstein's the year before. They were awakened around three o'clock by Mrs. Tidwell rapping on the sunroom window.

"Uh-oh," Hollister said. He pulled the quilt over his head.

"For heaven's sake!" Mae said. "What is she *doing?*"

"Mrs. Addington?" Mrs. Tidwell reached past the shrubs and rapped insistently on the glass. "Mrs. Addington! Are you in there? Turn on the radio right away. The Japs are coming and they're trying to kill us all!" Mrs. Tidwell disappeared and reappeared at the door. She jiggled the knob, trying to open it.

"*Mrs. Tidwell!*" Mae cried.

Mrs. Tidwell cupped her hand against the glass to block the afternoon glare and peered inside. "You need to turn on your radio right now!"

Mae sat up, keeping the quilt pulled up to her shoulders. "I will, Mrs. Tidwell. Thank you."

"Are you alone? Is your brother with you?"

"He's around here somewhere."

"Well . . . okay . . . as long as you're not alone. This is all very upsetting."

"Indeed," said Mae.

As soon as Mrs. Tidwell left, Hollister got up and turned on the radio.

"That's it," Mae said. "I have to put up some blinds."

News of the attack was on every station. "It's still happening," Hollister said. "Sounds like they're hitting Hawaii." He left the room and came back with the lovely globe Mae had found at Feibleman's. Hollister settled on the couch next to her and rested the globe on his lap. He spun it around to Hawaii, so tiny in the big Pacific Ocean. "Where did they say it was?" he asked.

"Pearl Harbor?"

"Yeah. I think that was it. Here's Honolulu. From what they're saying, it's close to there."

"It sounds so pretty, doesn't it?" Mae said. "Pearl Harbor."

"It sounds like Paradise. I don't see it on here."

"Well, it's on the map now. I'll go put on a fresh pot of coffee."

They listened to the radio in the sunroom until late that night. Mae's Sunday evening blues, which she felt at the end of every weekend, deepened into grim melancholy. "Not the navy, Hollister," she said suddenly.

"What?"

"Please don't join the navy. I can't stand the thought of you on a ship with those U-boats sneaking around. They give me the heebie-jeebies."

Hollister laughed.

"I mean it. I'm not kidding. I know you're going to volunteer. Just not the navy. Please."

"Okay. Not the navy." He pulled her close. "Even though I really, *really* like the ocean."

"It's not funny." Before Mae could stop herself, she began to cry. She did not want to talk or even think about it. She only wanted to cry.

"Marry me, Mae," Hollister said. "It's high time you got your divorce and married me. For real."

"I already feel like we're married. I've always felt that way."

"But we're not. If I don't come back, you won't get anything from the War Department. More importantly, you won't get anything from my trust."

"I don't care about any of that."

"Well, it's important to me."

Mae shrugged.

"Look here." Hollister sat up. In all these years, Mae had never seen him angry until this very minute. "I want to know you'll be taken care of."

"I want to know you'll come home."

"That's not up to me."

"It might be. You might go over there and be all brave and reckless if you think I'll be all right without you."

"I wouldn't do that, Mae."

"Good."

"So, you'll marry me?"

"Yes. Yes, I will. As soon as you get back home."

"Dammit, Mae."

"I didn't ask you not to go because I know you have to, but I need something to hold onto. Promise you'll come home and marry me."

"Mae . . . I can't promise."

"Yes you can. You just say it and mean it. You promise. And then you keep your promise. I *need* that."

Hollister sat on the edge of the couch with his forearms resting on his knees, staring down at his clasped hands. "Okay. All right. I promise." He looked up at Mae and smiled, as if the hardest part were already out of the way.

Chapter Fifty-Eight

1945

Mae was deadheading roses in the front yard on a Saturday morning in late June when Jax pulled to the curb in his ancient Cadillac Sixteen. It had been years since she'd seen him, but he did not seem much changed. Mae stopped pruning and stood with her gloved hands on her hips while Jax got out of the car and walked up the sidewalk. He wore a straw fedora and sunglasses and a white summer suit cut in the latest fashion. As he always had.

"The Sixteen looks like it just came off the line," she called.

Jax stopped, removed his sunglasses, and looked back toward the car. "She's still a beauty, isn't she?"

"Yes sir."

"You're not looking too bad yourself, Mrs. Addington."

"Thank you, Jax. I see you're holding your own too."

"War's been hard on everybody, but I've managed."

"Thank God it's over. Well, Europe anyway."

Jax looked down briefly, then he said, "Say, mind if I come in for a minute?"

"Sure. Of course. I should've asked already. C'mon. I'll fix you something cold to drink."

Mae opened the door and went in ahead of him. As far as she knew, Jax had not been inside the house since the day he proposed to her. Certainly, he had never seen it furnished. He walked into the living room and looked around. "It looks great, Mae."

"Please, have a seat. Want some iced tea or a Coke?"

"Anything cold. Surprise me."

Mae went to the kitchen and fixed two glasses of iced sweet tea. "I'm glad you came by," she said when she returned to the living room. "I need to talk to you about something." Jax was standing in front of the big picture window. When she handed him a glass, she saw tears in his eyes. "Jax, what is it?"

"It's Ned." He wiped his eye with the palm of his hand. "God Almighty. Crying like a little girl." He inhaled deeply. "Old Ned bought the farm, Mae. Over Tokyo."

"Oh, Jax." They sat on the couch. Side by side. "I'm so, so sorry, Jax. What happened?"

He pulled a handkerchief from his pocket and blew his nose noisily. "His B-29 took a hit during a bombing raid. The letter his wife got—did you ever meet his wife? Her name's Ruth."

"No. I heard he had married."

"Oh, Lord, they've got six, seven kids. She's a Catholic. Anyway, the letter said Ned stayed with the plane 'til the crew got out. He tried to parachute out, but it was too late."

"Gosh, Jax. All those children . . ."

"Yeah." He stuffed the handkerchief back into his breast pocket. "Never knew a nicer guy than Ned Turner. Man, he was smart. Guy was a genius. Anyway, I wanted to come by and tell you in person, since you knew him and all."

"I'll never forget that first flight," Mae said.

"Yup. First time up is pretty magical."

"It's just so awful that we're still fighting Japan, what with Germany surrendering and the troops in Europe coming home. Everybody says it's just a matter of time, but that almost makes it worse. To still be losing lives over there, that is."

"We're giving them what-for, though, and Ned was part of that."

"I suppose."

"So, what did you want to talk to me about?"

Mae hesitated. The timing was terrible, but she did not want to wait and have to track Jax down later. She had put off her divorce long enough, and now Hollister was coming home. "Jax, we never see each other anymore. Gosh, it's been, how long?"

He rubbed his pants leg. "Oh, I don't know. It seems like yesterday to me."

"Don't you think it's time we thought about moving on?"

He pointed to the gold band on Mae's left hand. "Is that Hollister's?"

"He'll be home by Christmas. How long have you known?"

"Oh, I've always known. I knew on the Fourth of July."

"Would you like your rings back?" Mae asked.

"No, no. They're yours. Just maybe don't sell 'em."

"Oh Jax, I wouldn't ever do that."

He smiled.

"I'd like to keep the house," Mae said.

"Oh, sure. Of course. Stay here forever."

"I mean transfer it to my name. I work for an attorney who handles that sort of thing."

"Oh . . . well . . ." Jax tugged at his collar and took a sip of tea.

"Is there a problem with that?"

"It's just that, when I got the house—I don't know if you remember—I got the house about the same time I bought that Cessna. You remember the Cessna, don't you?"

"Yes. Of course."

"Well, I had to get rid of her, oh gosh, ten, twelve years ago. She was a great airplane. Could carry anything you put in her. I made a lot of money with that airplane. Furnished this whole house." Jax looked around the room. "It really does look great, Mae. You have such a good eye for decorating."

"Jax, what does the Cessna have to do with the house?"

"See, I had to *choose* back then, and I really needed the airplane to make enough money for, well, for everything we wanted to do."

"But I'm here. I've been here for fourteen years." Mae's words summoned a sudden realization, and her hand flew to her mouth. "My God, Jax."

He managed a sheepish smile.

"Tell me you have not rented this place *all these years!*"

"Well . . ."

"How could you? Fourteen years!"

"I'm sorry, Mae."

"Who owns the house? Who do you send the check to every month?"

"Well, it was Old Man Purifoy for years and years. But he died a year or two ago, so now I send it to his son."

"Did you ever even *try* to buy it? When you had all that money?"

"Well, by then, we—"

"Never mind. Just never mind. I'm sorry about Ned, Jax. I really am. But you need to go."

"Well . . . okay." He stood. "Do you want me to take this to the kitchen?"

Mae reached for the glass. "Give it to me. And please, just go away."

Mae looked up Leonard Purifoy and pestered him to sell her the house. "I'm attached to the place for its sentimentality," Purifoy said when Mae showed up on his front doorstep. "What with it bein' Mama 'n Daddy's first place and all."

"There must be a price you can live with, especially knowing the house is going to someone who will care for it just as lovingly as your folks did."

Leonard Purifoy rubbed the gray stubble on his chin. He stood behind the screen door, not coming out on the porch or inviting Mae inside. He was shirtless, and his faded, paint-stained khaki britches threatened to slide right off his hips. "Cain't say as I could name a price right now. Reckon all them fellers comin' home from the war is gonna be gettin' hitched 'n lookin' to settle down somewheres. No tellin' what the place'll be worth then."

"So, you *would* sell it for the right price."

"Cain't rightly say," he drawled. "But you's welcome to stay 'til I make up my mind. Long as the rent's paid ever' month, that is."

Mae consulted Mr. Carter, who had continued his lawyering as if he intended to do so until the last trumpet sounded. "No legal instrument exits, Mrs. Addington," he said when he learned Jax had never signed a contract on the house. "I'm afraid you must appeal to Mr. Purifoy's sense of decency. If he has one."

Hollister finagled his way onto a cargo plane that was headed stateside and arrived home weeks before his repatriation was scheduled. He showed up on Mae's doorstep without warning, just as he had years before. Hollister, who had always been world-weary, did not seem much affected by the war, but on his first night home, Mae had found a jagged foot-long scar on his side. When she asked him what happened, he said a German had tried to gut him like a fish.

During the war, months sometimes passed with no word from Hollister. Then Mae would get ten or fifteen letters in the same delivery. His letters were vague about where they were and what they were doing. He wrote about the things the guys said and did. Often his letters were humorous and they had filled Mae with hope. At least until she read a newspaper or saw a newsreel at the movie theater.

Even though Hollister was alive and in her arms, his old wound disturbed Mae. She imagined him lying on the ground, bleeding, and his buddies lifting him and carrying him on a stretcher. She imagined him lying in a crowded makeshift hospital, trying to get well while bombs went off around him day and night. "Where did it happen?" she asked. "*When* did it happen?"

"Belgium. Forty-four. It was crazy, Mae. I had the strangest feeling the night I happened on this German, and we looked each other in the eye. We both knew only one of us was gonna walk away. I swear it felt like the whole war came down to the two of us." Hollister sat up and adjusted the pillows against his back. "It was kinda like football over there, you know? Bunch of guys thrown together. Trying to get something going. It wasn't a game, but it felt like one sometimes. There's always a key guy. The one guy the whole play hinges on. Take him out and the field just opens up." Hollister pointed to the scar. "The German was that guy."

"What did you do?"

"I blew his brains out, and we overran them."

Mae waited three days after Hollister came home before she told him she might not be able to keep the house.

"What did you offer the guy?"

"Everything I've saved, which is more than it's worth."

"Mind if I give it a go? The trust will buy the house, and you can keep your savings."

"Of course I don't mind, but I'm afraid Leonard Purifoy wants to keep the cow and sell the milk as long as he can."

"I'll talk to the bank tomorrow. We'll make him an offer he can't refuse.

"I don't know, honey. He seems like a pretty tough nut."

"I'll wear my uniform." Then Hollister smiled his million-dollar smile, and Mae knew she had her house.

Chapter Fifty-Nine

1949

Cargie and Thomas were forty-five and fifty-three, respectively. Becca and Rudy were married with a baby girl of their own. Adele was away at Cornell University studying architecture. Only Cassie was still at home, and she spent most of her time holed up in her bedroom. She emerged only when driven out by hunger or to commandeer the bathroom. Or to run out the front door to school or the houses of her friends.

The young ladies who visited Cassie were ushered from the front door into her bedroom immediately. When they ventured out to the kitchen for chips and Coca-Colas, always in tandem with their hostess, they passed through Cargie's and Thomas's presence in silence, with eyes cast down demurely. But they yelped and howled like hyenas behind Cassie's bedroom door.

Cargie and Thomas had begun to talk about the things they might do when Cassie left for college, things they had put off doing for years. They wanted to travel, not just in the United States, but abroad too, and they talked about which cities and countries they most wanted to see. Most of all, Cargie and Thomas looked forward to lazy Saturday mornings, reading the newspaper in bed with the whole house to themselves, as they had done when they began their married life. Then one day, Cargie came in from work and sat Thomas down on the couch.

"Uh-oh," Thomas said. "Bad news?"

"I'm pregnant," Cargie said. "Surely for the last time, unless we're to be like Sarah and Abraham."

Thomas took in a breath. "I thought . . ."

"I know," Cargie said. "So did I."

"Becca and Rudy's little one is gonna have an auntie who's younger than she is."

"Or uncle," Cargie said. "Seems to me you're due a son."

"Hmm," said Thomas. An ancient panic caught in his throat. He swallowed it, as he always had, and said, "As long as the baby's healthy, that's all that matters."

"All our plans out the window," Cargie said.

Thomas took his wife's hands in his. "Just on hold, honey. We'll get to 'em eventually."

Thomas and his mother-in-law's friendship had cooled as Cassie grew older and made fewer demands. Pretty Mama spent more time with her closest friend, Mavis, and with her other church friends. Not to mention Pastor Henry Euell, with whom Pretty Mama had supper at least one night a week. Thomas stayed busy cooking, helping the neighbors, and puttering around the house and yard. But when Thomas and Pretty Mama were thrown together to prepare for another baby, they remembered how much they enjoyed each other's company, and their friendship blossomed again.

One night, when Cargie was working late, Pretty Mama made the trip from her house across the backyard to keep Thomas company. She came through the back door into the kitchen without knocking. Thomas was reading in the living room and when he heard her, he got up and went into the kitchen. It was January and cold, and the old dog, Lazarus, was curled on a blanket beside the stove.

"Don't reckon I'll ever get used to a dog in the house," Pretty Mama said by way of a greeting.

"Good evening to you too," Thomas said. "The old boy's arthritic in his hind end, and the warmth does him good."

"All the same," she said and sat down at the kitchen table.

"Cargie's working late. She telephoned and said Mr. Cole will drive her home."

Pretty Mama shook her head but refrained from commenting.

"Would you like some coffee?" Thomas asked.

"It's mighty late, but I reckon so."

"I'll put on a pot." Thomas sat the percolator on the countertop and plugged it in. He took a sponge from the sink and rinsed it in hot water. He wiped a grease splatter from the tiled backsplash behind the stove.

"Cargie's hopin' for a boy," Pretty Mama said.

"Yes'm. She thinks I ought to have a son."

"And what do you say about that, sir?"

"I'll be happy as long as the baby's healthy," he said.

When the coffee was ready, Thomas poured two scalding cups and set one in front of Pretty Mama. He got the cream from the refrigerator, and they both added generous amounts of sugar and cream to their coffee, the way Thomas used to drink it all the time when he was young but never did now.

"Why don't you want a boy?" Pretty Mama asked.

"I never said I don't want a boy."

Pretty Mama set her cup down and eyed him.

"I didn't ever say that," he repeated.

"I watched you ever' time I put a daughter in your arms," Pretty Mama said. "And ever' time you was *relieved* to know the baby was a girl. I seen it on your face."

"Go on now," Thomas said.

"I know what I seen."

Thomas shrugged. "Raising girls is easier than raising boys," he said.

"By whose estimation?"

"By mine, I reckon."

"What do you know about raising boys?"

"I *was* a boy," he said.

"And here I thought you hatched out of a egg. Full growed," said Pretty Mama.

Thomas laughed.

"I's serious. Why don't you tell me about when you was a boy, seeing as I still don't know the first thing about you, even after you been married to my daughter more'n twenty years. Even after we done raised three girls together."

"I was a boy," Thomas said. "And then I was a man."

And without thinking about it any more than a man thinks when he dips an oar into the water or swings an axe to chop kindling, Thomas told his mother-in-law a very old story—a secret story that no two ears had ever heard—about a boy who became a man in one day. When he finished, he asked her what she thought about the tale.

"It answers lots of questions," she said.

At that moment Cargie came in from work, and Pretty Mama said her goodbyes and went out the back door and across the yard to her house. They never spoke of it again.

Chapter Sixty

1950

Jax sat in the backseat of his mother's car and watched her go up the sidewalk and knock at Mae's front door. He had not seen Mae since she told him to get out of her rented house five years before, and he was glad she had managed to hang onto it. Mae opened the door and Jax's mother went inside. Mae did not look toward the car before she closed the door, and Jax watched hopefully for her to open it again.

The morphine from the night before had worn off, and Jax's rotted gut made itself known. He'd refused his morning injection because he wanted to be clear-headed, to remember everything and reimagine it in the days to come. The front door opened, and Mae walked out, still buttoning her coat. She came down the sidewalk, opened the car door, and got in the backseat with Jax. "Thanks for coming out," he said.

Mae reached into her coat pocket and pulled out the silk Hermes scarf Jax had given her on the Fourth of July. It was yellowed with age and deeply creased from being folded for so long. "Remember this?" she asked.

"Boy, do I."

She lifted her hair and wound the scarf into a turban as deftly as she had on the Fourth of July twenty years before. Then she placed her hands in her lap. Jax smiled with all the old charm he could muster. "Lady Sheik," he said. He had nothing to lose now. "I have always loved you, Mae."

"I know."

Jax looked down at his bloodless hands and rolled them in the woolen blanket that lay across his lap. He was an invalid now, never without a blanket. "In my mind, we never separated. We went on together and had many adventures, all over the world."

Mae hesitated. "I hope we were happy," she said, finally.

"We were. Very. And rich too."

She laughed, and her laughter warmed him like summer sunshine. She leaned forward and hugged him more tightly than she ever had before, as tightly as his mother always hugged him. When she pulled back, Jax saw tears in her eyes. "You take care of yourself now, hear?" she said.

"Sure. Always."

Mae pulled the scarf from her head and shook out her hair. "And you keep this too. You never know when you might need it again." She winked and opened the door.

"Wait a minute. Here, before you go." Jax reached into his shirt pocket and took out a copy of the photograph of Mae and him sitting at the white-clothed table on the Youree's roof. Mae looked at the picture for a long time, and Jax thought she might be reliving all the fun they'd had that summer, as he had relived it so many times.

"Thank you, Jax."

"See you later, Mae."

She got out and hurried up the sidewalk. She was running by the time she reached the door.

Bill Cole came out of the dry cleaners and walked to the car. He opened the door and squatted on the sidewalk to bring himself to Jax's level. Jax thought the old guy was pretty limber to pull that off. Mr. Cole pulled his sweater closed at the neck and said, "It's cold as all get-out this morning."

The open door chilled Jax, despite the heavy blanket. His mother would've told Bill Cole to get in the car and close the door, but she was inside the dry cleaners, giving them time alone. "How's everything, Mr. Cole?"

"Very well, Jackson. We're still rocking along around here."

"Is Cargie still working for you?"

"Yes sir. Going on twenty-three years."

"Long time."

"Yes sir."

Both men looked down. Mr. Cole shifted his weight, then he put one knee on the sidewalk and leaned forward with his forearms resting on the other knee. After a moment he said, "Did you know I was with the expedition forces in the Great War?"

"I knew it," Jax said. "Don't guess we ever talked about it, though. Did you see a lot of action?"

"Yes sir. Quite a bit."

Jax felt like a madman was sweeping his gut with a flamethrower. He just had to hang on a little while longer. When his mother got back in the car, she would hand him a hypodermic needle. Jax had no problem pulling down his pants and sticking the needle into what was left of his buttock. No problem squeezing the plunger until sweet Vitamin M flowed through him like Possum Kingdom moonshine. He twisted the blanket in his hands.

"It troubled me for years," Mr. Cole was saying, "that I made it back home and so many fellas didn't. Most of them were better men than me. I just could not reconcile that."

"Makes me think about Ned Turner," said Jax. "Best friend a guy ever had."

"Yes sir, Ned had a lot going for him. No telling what he could've done with a long life."

"I really felt it. In here." Jax untangled one hand from the blanket and pointed to his chest. "They never found him, you know. Sometimes I imagine Ned's still over there, living in a paper house with a geisha girl."

Mr. Cole smiled. "That's a nice thought. For a long time after I came home, I thought I might do something special because I hadn't died in the war."

"Make a mark someway," Jax said.

"I guess so."

"Did you ever see anybody die?"

"Quite a few."

"Done a lot of things, but I never saw a man die."

"That's a blessing.

Jax pressed his lips together as the flamethrower made another pass.

Mr. Cole said, "A fella who knows he's dying usually needs to get a few things off his chest." He glanced down the street. Everyone was indoors because of the cold. "Even a fella who isn't a Catholic can feel a need to make a confession." Bill Cole waited a minute, but Jax said nothing. "Over there, at the frontline, we all followed a rule about that, even though nobody ever told it to us."

"What's that?"

"A fella's last words stayed on the battlefield. They didn't come back to camp without him."

"Good rule," said Jax.

"Well, that's how it was at the front."

Jax said, "I regret that Barksdale business."

"I appreciate that, Jackson."

Jax started to add that he never intended for it to happen, but what difference did that make now?

"You can leave that burden right here," said Mr. Cole. "No need to carry it with you when you leave."

"All right."

"No harm done. Everything worked out."

"Okay."

They sat in silence until they were sure neither of them had anything more to say. Then Mr. Cole made a move to get up. "Thank you for stopping by, Jax."

"Would you ask Cargie to come out here?"

"Yes sir." Mr. Cole took hold of the car and pulled himself to his feet with a grunt. He put out his hand. "It was good to see you, son."

Jax shook the man's hand. "You too, Mr. Cole."

Bill Cole shut the car door and went inside. Jax pulled the blanket higher on his chest and waited. It was a little while before Cargie Barre opened the dry cleaner's front door. It occurred to Jax that he had never seen her use that door. She always used the rear door because that's how things were done.

Cargie walked to the car and opened the door. She bent forward awkwardly. She was pregnant again, which surprised Jax. It seemed to him Cargie was getting on in years to be pushing out babies. This one was big and riding lower than the others, making Jax wonder if Cargie had worn out her undercarriage. Nevertheless, she sat on her heels as Mr. Cole had done. "Hey, Cargie," he said.

He thought she wasn't going to speak at all. Finally, she said, "Hey, yourself."

"Congratulations," he said.

"Thank you. This one's Mr. Johnny Come Lately."

"How do you know it's a boy?"

"Don't reckon I do for sure, but my patient husband is due a son."

"I used to call you Black Olive," Jax blurted. He had not intended to lead with this. He realized just then that he had not imagined what he would say to Cargie Barre at all.

Cargie's face was impassive. She was looking down her nose at him, as she always had. She had no sympathy, even now. "Why'd you call me that?" she asked.

Jax wondered if she was thinking about black olives and green olives and the fact that she had never looked like an olive of any sort, even when she was stuffed with a baby. "I thought you looked like Olive Oyl. Except black."

Cargie pursed her lips.

"You know, Olive Oyl and Popeye."

"I know who Olive Oyl is."

"Oh."

"I called you names too." Cargie pointed to her temple. "In here."

"I don't guess I'll ask what they were."

"No sir, I would not care to repeat them. But I reckon thinking them was just as bad as saying them out loud."

"We didn't get on very well, did we?"

"No sir. We did not."

"Well. Anyway. I told Mr. Cole I was sorry about the Barksdale business. Don't know if it mattered much to you, except that you and Mr. Cole are friends. I can see that now."

"We are. Real good friends."

"Well, like I said, y'all should've had the Barksdale business."

Jax thought her face softened a little. She seemed to really look at him for the first time.

"It seems like a good day to try and settle the books," Jax said.

"Consider us square," Cargie said without hesitation. She stuck out her hand, and Jax took it, surprised at how warm she was. They sat this way a moment, neither moving, and he looked down at their hands wrapped around each other, dark and pale. He pulled back, embarrassed at holding her hand too long, but Cargie held on a few seconds longer, then squeezed his before releasing it.

She struggled to her feet with one hand on the car and one under that monstrous belly. She gently closed the Caddy's door and walked to the dry cleaners, opened the door, and went inside. She did not look back. Jax pulled the blanket up to his neck. His mother came out and got in the car. She started the engine and turned the heater up.

"You okay, Jaxy?" she asked.

"Yes, Mama."

"Ready to go home?"

"Yes'm."

Jax's mother passed a hypodermic needle to the backseat, and Jax shot himself full of Vitamin M. The morphine wrapped him in warmth. A mirage of palm trees and a desert castle shimmered before his mind's eye. Jax closed his eyes and his vision cleared. The Lady Sheik stood in a moonlit window, her dark curls backlit by a thousand candles. She gazed out the window into the night, searching. Searching for him.

Chapter Sixty-One

When the early flowers—the jonquils, daffodils, and irises—had broken through the earth and bloomed, Cargie gave Thomas his one and only son. Thomas cried when Pretty Mama brought the baby out and placed him in his arms. "What are you gonna call him?" she asked. "Cargie's leavin' it to you."

Thomas shook his head.

"Why don't you call him David?"

Thomas smiled then, with tears running down his cheeks into his graying beard. "Like King David in the Bible?" he asked.

"Yes sir, just like King David. Turns out he was a good man, after all."

Chapter Sixty-Two

1957

On the morning Hurricane Audrey made landfall, Mae and Hollister were vacationing in Cameron, Louisiana, as they had done every summer for twenty-five years. Mae was awakened a little after three by a driving rain and discovered Hollister's side of the bed was empty. She went outside and saw him sitting in the car, smoking and listening to the radio. They were both smoking that year to keep their weight down, as the advertiser's slogan promised—*Reach for a Lucky Instead of a Sweet.* Mae rushed through the downpour and got in the passenger seat.

"What's going on?" she asked.

"Weather Bureau issued an update," Hollister said. "Hurricane's moving faster than they thought. It'll be here in a few hours."

"We should leave," Mae said.

"Now?"

"Yes. What are we waiting for?"

"The Primeaux. We have to warn them."

The cabin in which Mae and Hollister were staying—had stayed every June—belonged to Tud and Flo Primeaux. Tud was a shrimper, but he was an able carpenter too. He built the cabins himself, without the help of any man. Only his wife, who Tud was fond of saying worked from can 'til can't.

Mae had a soft spot for Florence Primeaux, especially since the war. During the years Hollister was in Europe, Mae made the drive to Cameron alone and stayed in their cabin. Without Hollister around, Mae paid more attention to Flo and Tud and their children. Each morning during those years, Flo sent Mae a hot breakfast by her eldest daughter, Charlotte, who was just achieving womanhood, and Mae gave Charlotte movie magazines. One morning, Mae gave the young woman a makeover, applying mascara, rouge, and lipstick. She discovered then that Charlotte was beautiful and showed her in a hand mirror. "Don't you ever forget this," Mae said.

Charlotte gazed at her reflection, then she handed the mirror back to Mae and said, "Gotta go. Mama got chores." But she stopped in the doorway, open to let the Gulf breeze in, and she turned to Mae and smiled.

During those solitary trips, Mae wrote to Hollister every day. She wrote about the sunrise and the beach birds catching their breakfast. She wrote about the dolphins that swam lazily down the shoreline and about a stingray she almost stepped on because it had buried itself in the sandy shallows. Mae liked to imagine what Hollister was doing while she trudged on alone. She imagined him seeking cover in bombed-out buildings—like the ones in the newsreels at the movie theater—with the sound of mortars exploding all around. She saw him opening her letters as he hunkered down, out of the enemy's sight. She pictured him smiling and escaping the awful war for just a few minutes.

She wrote about Flo's oyster gumbo and crawfish étouffée, and fresh-baked French bread, buttered and crusty. She wrote everything about the Friday night shrimp boil on the beach, even though she and the Primeaux were the only ones attending. Cameron's beach was quiet during those years, with so many men gone and their women working in the war effort. Tud was the only able-bodied man around, having refused to register for anything having to do with the United States government, especially conscription.

Before the war—when Tud and Flo's three children were young—Hollister had played with them endlessly. The kids were beach rats. Ankle-biters, Hollister called them. He built elaborate, moated castles with them, which the tide took every evening. He chased the children with sand crabs in his outstretched hands, their claws winding. He permitted the kids to bury him in the silty sand, so that only his ruddy, sunburned face showed amid an expanse of ecru.

The Primeaux children left Cameron one by one as soon as they were able. Tud cursed his children's faithlessness, but Mae believed Flo was happy for them, even though she never said a word in their defense.

The early morning of June 27, 1957, while Mae and Hollister sat in the car in the driving rain listening to the radio, everyone else on the coast was sleeping peacefully in the arms of their life-long experience and the prior evening's weather advisory. The Weather Bureau had predicted Hurricane Audrey would make landfall Thursday afternoon, giving everyone plenty of time to assess the situation at first light.

At half past four that morning, Mae stood with Hollister on the Primeaux's tiny front porch, soaked from the wind and rain, while Hollister knocked persistently. For the most part, Tud tried to refrain from showing his bad temper to paying guests, but awakened from sleep by Hollister's pounding, Tud, bleary-eyed and irritated, jerked the door open. "Why you don't sleep, mister?" he said. This Tud called Hollister—mister—despite the years.

"The Weather Bureau put out a new report," Hollister said. "Audrey'll make landfall this morning. We need to get out before the water closes the roads."

"Nah, nah, nah. We stayin' put. Done nailed up boards to save the wender glass. Audrey, she blow in, make a little mess and blow out. Just like you folks what rents them cabins."

"Audrey is unpredictable," argued Hollister. "Why take a chance? We can drive up to Lake Charles for a couple of hours—we'll buy you and Flo breakfast there—and drive back. We'll help you clean up too, after the storm." Hollister glanced at Mae.

"Of course we will," Mae said.

Flo stood behind her husband. Mae had watched this wiry scrap of femininity clean, cook, and corral children without complaint for twenty-five years. When Flo looked up at Tud, Mae thought she saw a plea in her eyes. If Flo could've found her tongue, Mae believed she would have said, "Please, husband, let's go. Just this once, let's be reasonable people instead of stubborn Cajuns."

Mae could not hold her own tongue. "For God's sake, man, say yes," she shouted above the wind. "Think about your wife, you stubborn old goat!"

"You daren't talk to him like that, missy!" cried Flo.

"You muzzle that 'un, mister," said Tud. "Before she git you in a heap a troubles." Then he slammed the door.

"I'm sorry," Mae said.

"Doesn't matter," said Hollister. "Guys like that go down with the ship, and they don't give a damn who they take with 'em. C'mon, let's get out of here."

When they got on the highway, the big tires of their Chrysler Imperial skidded and crunched and made the most God-awful sound. "What *is* that?" Hollister said. He leaned over the steering wheel and strained to see beyond the slapping windshield wipers. "Something's washing over the road."

"Slow down, honey. Stop the car."

Hollister stopped in the middle of the highway. Mae retrieved a flashlight from the glovebox and opened her door enough to shine the beam onto the road. The beam illuminated a tide of scurrying creatures, their pinchers high and threatening in their panic. "It's *blue crabs!* Millions of them."

She handed Hollister the flashlight. He opened his door and looked out. "Good Lord," he said.

"Let's go."

"Yeah." Hollister eased down on the gas pedal. "Slow. Slow," he said as if coaching himself. "The road's slick with them. We don't wanna end up in the ditch."

It took them two hours to drive from their cabin on the beach to the north side of Lake Charles, fifty miles inland. They kept the car's radio tuned to a Lake Charles station the entire trip. By the time they pulled into the parking lot of a diner, reports were coming in of a twelve-foot tidal swell, with twenty-foot waves riding on top of it.

Hollister had saved them.

Chapter Sixty-Three

1967

No one knew how old Rebecca Pittman was when she succumbed to a weakness in her heart that had nibbled at her vitality for years. At certain times, Thomas had noticed his mother-in-law taking a seat to hide her breathlessness, but he had never mentioned it. She would not have been happy if he'd made a fuss. One day, when Pretty Mama could no longer hold the malady at bay, she took to her bed and told Cargie to gather the family.

Cargie's mother had never seen a doctor in her life, so Cargie called on her own physician to make a house call. After he examined Mrs. Pittman, he told Cargie and Thomas that she only had a week or two to live, so ineffective was the echoing beat of her heart. The doctor wrote a prescription for a diuretic to slow the floodwater seeping into her lungs, and Thomas filled it at the Mooretown pharmacy.

Thomas spent hours beside his mother-in-law's bed. He read aloud to her when she was awake and silently to himself while she slept. He offered chicken broth and herbal tea and 7-Up and ginger ale, all of which she refused. "She's shutting down," the doctor said during his daily visit. He handed Thomas and Cargie a prescription for morphine and told them to give it to her if they thought she was in pain.

Cargie made her phone calls, and family members began to arrive from out of town. Adele came on Friday after work with plans to stay, and Becca and Rudy put her up in their spare bedroom. Cassandra's husband could not get away from work, but she packed up her boys—school was out for the summer—and came for the duration. Cassie moved into her old bedroom, and David welcomed Cassie's two sons, teenagers themselves, to stay with him in his room, which had been converted from the house's deep side porch. The boys slept on pallets and came and went with their uncle through the side door, only showing themselves at mealtimes. Lydie Murphy opened her mansion, which had half a dozen bedrooms, and Cargie's siblings and their families stayed there. Rebecca Pittman's only living sister, Caroline, insisted on staying in the little house Thomas had built, where she slept on a rollaway bed.

Cargie and Thomas had food brought in by the truckload, and they hired a housekeeping service to help out at Lydie's place. Cargie wanted Mavis, who was certainly too old herself to clean up after such a crowd, free to spend time with her dying friend. They all waited together, coming and going as necessary for work and other obligations, but for the most part camping out and keeping watch for the death angel. As her hospice progressed, Rebecca Pittman withdrew into herself. She closed her eyes and refused to speak, even though everyone believed she was awake.

"Expect a rally a day or so before the end," said the doctor. "That'll be your time to say goodbye." The rally came as predicted, and everyone who had wandered away on his or her own business was recalled. Thomas supervised the visitations, ushering the keeners out before they got the chance to tune everyone else up.

Rebecca Pittman smiled and squeezed hands and gave kisses. She permitted hugs and mouthed "Thank you," and "Bless you," and "Love you," as appropriate. Her strength waned late in the afternoon, and she lay panting. The time for diuretics had passed, and Thomas had nothing more to offer her except to hold her hand. Caroline sat across the bed from him and held her sister's other hand. Cargie was not there. Watching her mother pant for every breath was more than she could bear.

Thomas could hardly believe how quickly the years had gone by. He looked at all the photographs hanging above the straight-back chairs that lined the walls of the bedroom. Some were old and some were new, but all were pictures of people Rebecca Pittman loved. It seemed only a short time ago that Thomas was spreading plaster on these walls, hurrying to finish in time for it to dry and take a coat of paint before his mother-in-law arrived.

Pretty Mama worked her mouth in a whisper that was not quite a word.

"She's gettin' close," Caroline said.

Thomas nodded.

There again, the whisper. "I think she's trying to say something," Thomas said. He took one of the long cotton swabs from the drawer and swished it in a cup of iced water they kept on the nightstand. He ran the wet swab around the inside of her mouth. "Is that good, Pretty Mama?" he asked.

"David," she whispered.

"She's calling for your son," Caroline said.

"Looks that way," Thomas said. He turned to Cargie's nephew, who stood at the foot of the bed. "Ritchie, would you mind tracking down my son? Cargie too." Ritchie nodded and left the room. "Miss Caroline," Thomas said, "could I steal just a minute alone with your sister?"

"Of course you can. Guess you ain't said your goodbye, what with herding everybody in and out of here."

"No ma'am, I have not. Thank you."

Caroline got up and left the room, and Thomas closed and locked the door behind her. He knelt beside the bed and kissed his mother-in-law on the cheek. "I'm here, Pretty Mama," he said.

"Thomas?"

"Yes'm. It's just you and me."

Pretty Mama smiled and raised her hand to his face. He grasped it and guided her palm against his cheek. Her hand was icy cold and dry, and Thomas covered it with his own. Warming it, he hoped.

"Time's here, son," she said.

"I know."

"It's gonna be okay."

"Yes'm."

Rebecca Pittman mustered her strength and opened her eyes. They were the same quick black eyes that had always put Thomas on his heels. "I's talkin' about *your* time," she said. "Time to make peace with the past. You gots to tell Cargie."

"Tell her what, Pretty Mama?"

"Go on now. You know."

Thomas's mind raced. "After all these years? It would only hurt her. What's the use in that?"

Pretty Mama pulled her hand from his grasp and laid it against his chest.

"You got old sin," she said, "buried deep inside. You gots to confess it and get it out of you."

"Confess?"

Pretty Mama closed her eyes again. "It'll be okay," she whispered. "You'll see."

The doorknob jiggled, followed by a knock. Thomas stood. He unlocked the door and opened it to David and Cargie. The boy was as tall and thin as his father had been at seventeen, and he looked as if he would rather be anywhere else but here. Thomas pulled David close and held him, making eye contact with Cargie over the boy's shoulder.

Cargie moved past them to her mother's bedside. "She's gone," she said. Thomas continued to hug his son while he reached for Cargie's hand and held it tightly.

Chapter Sixty-Four

David was back in school and busy with football and everything else that goes along with senior year when Thomas finally worked up the nerve to sit his wife down in the living room after supper one night.

Cargie said, "You must have something serious to say, Mr. Barre, if we're in here."

"I do," Thomas said, "and I've worried myself sick wondering if you'll leave me over it."

"Go on now."

"You know about the Tatums," he said. "In East Texas."

"Did something happen? Is everybody okay?"

Thomas took Cargie's hands. He kissed each one and then held them. "Just let me talk," he said. "No questions until I get it all out."

Cargie pretended to turn a key over her closed mouth. She smiled and slid her warm hand between his again.

"On a Saturday morning," Thomas began. "A warm Indian summer day a long time ago, a boy went hunting and never went home again. His name was David Walker, and he was seventeen years old."

Thomas had kept a narrator's distance when he told his mother-in-law the story so many years before. He'd talked about David Walker as if he were another person, even though Pretty Mama knew better. But once Thomas got rolling, telling his story to Cargie, he became lost in the brightness and nearness of his memories, as if they were from a day or two ago, rather than half a century before.

He talked at length about the goodness of his mother and father and grandfather, as he would not have thought to do before he was torn from them. He described the white man, alive and in death, and once again he felt his hands grip the oar in fear and swing it without premeditation. Once again, his clothes were slick with Huck's blood. Once more, he looked through the eyeholes of a Klansman's hood and breathed the dead man's stench. He got all the way to burying the stolen treasure under the Mooringsport railroad trestle before he paused to catch his breath.

"Go on," Cargie said. "Keep talking."

"I stole a pirogue and paddled into the Caddo swamp," Thomas said. He told Cargie about building a hut out of switchgrass. About Old Gourd, the wood stork who was his only companion for weeks on end, and about the family of beavers who entertained him while he fished. He described Caddo in winter—a marble-floored cathedral of smooth black water and towering cypress.

He told her about leaving the swamp in which he'd felt so safe and comfortable. He told her about meeting a father and his sons and a worn-out mule pulling a stump from the stubborn ground. He described at length the grinding, unending labor of cotton farming. He told her about Big Sherman's optimism and Audie's intelligence. About Sherman's frustration and rage.

He told her about the one and only time another person had washed his feet and how profoundly humbling it had been. About Luke's precocious boldness and Zachary's thirst to learn everything there was to learn. Zach had graduated from Wiley College in the class before Cargie's. He became a journalist and a writer because that was the only profession that permitted him to explore all the things that interested him.

"He lives in Chicago," Thomas said.

"I know," said Cargie. "I've seen his letters."

Thomas told his wife about building a room for Audie and about Deet, who guided him every step of the way. He even told her about Joseph Baldwin III, who had unknowingly made a gift of the materials, and how Mr. Baldwin might even now be reaping a reward for his unintended generosity if Deet had anything to say about it. Then he stopped because Cargie had tears in her eyes. "Are you okay, honey?" he asked.

She pulled her hands from his and brushed her cheeks with her palms. "Why am I just now hearing all of this?" she said.

He did not know what to say.

"Your name is David Walker," Cargie said, as if she did not believe it.

"It *was* David Walker. A long time ago." He tried to meet her eye, but Cargie looked away.

"What about your parents? Are they still living?"

"No, Cargie, they passed. Years ago."

"Brothers and sisters?"

"Just me," Thomas said.

"Only you? Did you ever go back and tell your mama and daddy that you were okay?"

"I went back lots of times to check on them, but I didn't—I couldn't—"

"Since we moved here?" Cargie interrupted.

"Yes."

Cargie looked out the front window at the empty street.

I've been thinking," Thomas said, "that I should turn myself in. I need to confess."

"Confess? Confess to who?"

Thomas shrugged. "Your mother said—"

"What does Mama have to do with any of this?"

"She knew, Cargie. I told her years ago. We never talked about it again, but right before she died she said I need to confess. To get the sin out." The look on his wife's face made Thomas think she was about to slap him, and he jerked back a little, reflexively, before he saw that her hand wasn't moving.

Cargie got up then. She moved stiffly after sitting for so long. "Let me tell you one thing, and you can take this to the bank," she said. "You have four children, and every single one of them thinks you hung the moon. Your daughters are happy in their lives. Your son is in his senior year of high school, and you are not going to ruin it for him—for any of them—just to ease your guilty conscience. No sir! That'll happen over my dead body." Cargie poked Thomas in the chest with her long and surprisingly strong index finger. "Or yours," she said. Then she turned around before he could respond and walked out of the room.

Later that evening, Thomas knocked tentatively on their bedroom door. Cargie did not open it, so he knocked again. "Not tonight," she called from inside, and that night Thomas and his wife slept apart for the one and only time in their marriage.

Chapter Sixty-Five

Cargie suspected she knew the very night her husband told her mother about his past. She had worked late, going over a company's financials that arrived in the mail that day, and as usual, she lost track of the time. Bill Cole had waited patiently to drive her home, and they had talked the whole way to Mooretown about the company's strengths and weaknesses and whether or not they would invest in it.

Cargie had come in, worn out and toting David—*David!*—in her ballooning belly, and she'd found Thomas and her mother at the kitchen table. They were drinking coffee, even though it was after nine. Neither of them drank coffee that late anymore. There was something about them that night, something Cargie had not been able to put her finger on. Now she knew it was her husband's secret hanging silently between them in the yellow light. Thomas had tossed and turned all night, and she had scolded him for drinking coffee so late.

Cargie tossed and turned all night herself after Thomas told her. She turned his story over and over in her mind. It wasn't hard to believe a Klansman had assaulted him—that had been common—nor was it difficult to comprehend the fear he must have felt, for his own safety and the safety of his family. She understood completely why he had run away and hidden. But Cargie could not reconcile the man she had known for forty years—the man who had shown so much love and kindness to everyone, even the cast-off dogs who wandered into his yard—*that* man, with a man who had left his own mother and father to wonder what had become of their only child long after the danger had passed. Who had left them to wonder *for the rest of their lives!*

She had to get to the bottom of why. If she could.

"Who else knows about all of this?" Cargie asked Thomas the next morning. He had made her breakfast, as he did every morning, and he sat across the table from her, drinking coffee while she ate it.

"Nobody."

"Except Mama."

"Nobody living," Thomas said.

"Why her and not me?"

Thomas shook his head.

"Say," Cargie insisted.

"Because I should've *already* told you, Cargie. Before you married me, but I didn't. And then I couldn't. Maybe I shouldn't have told you now." He got up from the table and went to the stove, where he fussed with the greasy frying pan.

"Why *did* you tell me, husband?" She could not bring herself to call him Thomas. Or David. He turned around, and this time Cargie met his eye. "Looks to me like you were well on your way to taking this to your grave," she said.

"I was."

"If I had known *before* we married, I would've insisted you go to your parents and put an end to their wondering and worrying. Your grandfather too. Maybe him especially. I wish I *had* known."

"Gramps had already passed by then."

Cargie's eyes narrowed. "How do you know?"

Thomas sighed. "I read about it while I was working in the library at Wiley."

"When did your parents die?"

"Daddy died in forty-one, and Mama the year after."

"Lord, Thomas, they had three grandchildren by then! What would it have meant to your mama and daddy to be able to enjoy them? What would it have meant to our daughters to know their grandparents? I just can't . . . I can't understand this. There's no excuse."

Thomas turned around and faced the stove, his palms flat on the tile countertops on either side of it.

"Help me understand," Cargie said.

Thomas looked down. He shook his head. Then Cargie saw his shoulders buck and heard her husband sob for the first time in forty years. She had never seen more than a silent tear run down his cheek before. Certainly, she'd never heard him weep, as he was doing now over the stove. She felt pity then. She got up from the table and went to him, but he was lost in his grief and didn't seem to know she was there. She took him by the shoulders and made him turn around.

"Look at me, Thomas."

He would not look up.

"Come, sit down." Cargie led him at the table and he sat. With some effort, she knelt in front of him.

"This is a terrible thing you've done," she said. "And I'm not talking about that white man. I'm talking about your parents, Thomas. You should have gone to them when it was safe to do so. You should have told them, for their sakes."

"I couldn't," Thomas said. "You don't understand. I couldn't face them."

"Yes, I do understand. You didn't want to face them, but you could have."

Thomas shook his head.

"Yes," Cargie said. "You could have, and you should have. It was wrong of you not to. That's the sin Mama was talking about."

"No."

"Yes, Thomas. You stayed away because you were ashamed. You've been lying to yourself for a long, long time. You stayed away for you, not for them."

Thomas looked up at her then, and Cargie saw the truth in his eyes.

"My God," he said. "What have I done?"

"We'll get through this," Cargie said.

Chapter Sixty-Six

1968

As soon as David went off to college, Thomas was determined to turn himself in for his moldy crime, and nothing Cargie said could put him off that notion. He wanted to gather their children and tell them the truth before he and Cargie headed out, first for Mooringsport, then to the Miller County sheriff's office in Texarkana. He pestered Cargie about it for weeks, and he brought it up again on the eve of their departure.

"Let's just wait and see what happens," Cargie said.

"There's a real good chance I won't come home tomorrow night, Cargie."

She sat on the bed and patted it for Thomas to sit beside her. "You're gonna have to trust *me* this time," she said. "Do you trust me?"

"I trust you, but I think it's a mistake."

Cargie wasn't worried about Thomas going to jail because she had taken out insurance against it. She couldn't just sit by and watch her husband destroy himself and their family, so she had gotten the number of a high-profile civil rights attorney in New York City and telephoned his office. The man charged her a fortune, but in return he agreed to clear his schedule and wait by the phone on the day Thomas turned himself in. If Thomas ended up in handcuffs, Cargie would make the call, and that famous Yankee lawyer would hop on a private jet to Little Rock, where he would explain to the Arkansas governor himself what was about to happen when Thomas's story hit the front page of every major newspaper in the country.

"If those rednecks think Little Rock is a nightmare now, just wait 'til I'm finished with them," the attorney said. Cargie thought the lawyer was excited enough at the prospect of taking up Thomas's fight that he might have paid her for the privilege if she had been inclined to bargain.

*   *   *

Cargie crawled under the train trestle at Mooringsport because her husband was too large and too stiff to do it himself. Thomas followed her progress, walking alongside the trestle, hacking down the overgrown brush with a machete and occasionally dropping to one knee to see where she was. It crossed Cargie's mind that anyone who saw them would think they were crazy old coots.

"Lord have mercy . . . *humph!*" She pulled and pushed herself up the rising bank under the trestle, flat on her stomach and grateful for thick blue jeans and a denim jacket that saved her knees and elbows. She ducked her head as the space between the dirt and the tracks tightened, then she laid her cheek against the back of her hand to rest a minute.

Thomas got down on one knee and peered at her between the old creosote-soaked stanchions. "You okay, honey?"

"I'm fine. Just catching my breath."

Thomas tapped a timber with the tip of the machete. "I believe it's this one. It'll be on the uphill side, right close to the timber."

Cargie inched forward, and Thomas cut down the rest of the brush to let in the light. She used a flashlight to swipe at glistening spiderwebs—Cargie hated spiders—then she stuck her hand out into the sunlight and wiggled her fingers. "Trowel," she said, and Thomas handed it to her.

She scraped away a layer of gravel with the edge of the trowel. She kept scraping, shaving away the dirt as carefully as an archeologist unearthing fragile bones. Before long, the trowel scratched something besides loamy soil. Cargie shined the flashlight into the shadowy hole and began gently brushing dirt from oilcloth that still showed its red gingham check. "Lord God Almighty," she whispered.

She pulled the package from the hole and let the rotted cloth fall away. A leather pouch with a thin cord wrapped around it twice. She laid the pouch aside and reached into the hole again and pulled out a dirt-crusted bottle, the label still legible. Tennessee Sour Mash Whiskey.

"Do you see anything?" Thomas said.

"I found it. It's here."

She pushed the pouch and bottle into the sunlight and scooted back down the bank until she could crawl out where she had entered. Thomas was waiting for her and helped her get up. He bent over and brushed the dirt from her knees while she brushed at her elbows.

They walked to where Thomas had stood the bottle on one crosstie and laid the pouch on another. Cargie unwrapped the leather cord, which did not break, stiff as it was. She opened the flap and pulled out the money and the envelope. The money clip fell to the ground, but Cargie only glanced at it. Thomas picked it up. He worried the clip in one hand while Cargie opened the envelope with the Klan's seal, darkened with age, still affixed to it. "What does 'Non Silba Sed Anthar' mean?" she asked.

"'Not Self, But Others.' It's a Klan slogan."

Cargie pulled the letter from the envelope and read it aloud. When she had finished reading, she said, "There wasn't one of them brave enough to put his name on this, was there? Grand Wizard of the Invisible Realm my foot. This sounds like something little boys in a secret club would write. But they weren't children, were they? They were grown men, and violent ones at that. Reading this mess makes my blood boil, Thomas. This was wicked, wicked business. Through and through." Cargie stuffed the letter back into the envelope and handed it to him. "I say good riddance to the lot of them, especially that devil who was carrying this. You did folks a favor stopping him."

"Maybe so," Thomas said. "Maybe that man deserved the judgment of hellfire. Let's say he did, but whatever he had coming wasn't mine to mete out. I should've overcome evil with good that day instead of answering violence with violence. Maybe killing that fella wasn't the worst thing I did in this whole affair, or maybe it was—I don't know—but it *was* wrong. And I need to give an account for it."

"Then give your account to the Lord," Cargie said. "Not to a bunch of . . . not to a bunch of people who aren't worthy to judge you."

"Cargie, you know I'm right."

"The only thing I know for sure is you're about to resurrect something that's been dead and buried for half a century. You're a good man, Thomas. You are. But you're about to breathe life back into those racist old words, and you're liable to be living with them for the rest of your life. *We* are going to be living with them too."

After a moment, Thomas said, "You think I'm being selfish."

"I know you don't mean to be. But yes, honey, you are."

Thomas stared straight ahead. "If the Lord is working on my conscience and I don't do the right thing, well, I just feel like I might sear my conscience, Cargie. Maybe nothing bad will happen because of it, but something terrible might happen inside of me. Everything has to be reconciled eventually."

They sat in silence for a little while, then Cargie reached for Thomas's hand and entwined her fingers in his. "I don't like it," she said, "but I'm with you if you feel like it's what you have to do. I'm with you every single step of the way."

"Thank you, honey." Thomas squeezed her hand. "I reckon it's time we get this show on the road."

Chapter Sixty-Seven

Thomas pulled over to the shoulder of the road before they crossed the old drawbridge that spanned Lake Caddo from Mooringsport to the north shore. "Look at that rusted old thing, Cargie."

"It's seen better days." Cargie looked up through the windshield at the tall stanchions and said, "Looks like they took down the counterweights. There weren't many bridges built like this one, with vertical lift."

"You know about that?"

"My first year at Wylie, I roomed with a girl from Mooringsport. I went home with her one weekend, and here was this bridge—the most interesting contraption I'd ever laid eyes on. I loved to watch them raise and lower it. No telling what that girl and her family thought about me for getting excited about a bridge. Instead of boys."

"Gramps and I were going to watch them build it," Thomas said. "We planned to drive over here every Saturday to check the progress until it was finished."

"Did you get to?"

"No ma'am. They built it after I was gone." Thomas pointed to the water. "Just think, Cargie. That old Runabout's still under there."

Thomas turned into the parking lot of a small grocery store at Rodessa and asked if Cargie could use a cold drink.

"Yes sir. Sounds real good."

"Be right back."

Cargie sat in the truck, looking out the side window at two young boys wrestling in the yard of the house next to the store. They rolled around on the ground, and a dog on a chain barked at them.

The driver's side door opened, and Thomas got in. He handed Cargie an Orange Crush with a paper napkin wrapped around the cold, sweating bottle. He set his Coke on the dash, along with a stack of napkins. "Looky here, what I got." He placed a greasy paper sack on the seat between them, and Cargie smelled warm red-skinned peanuts.

"Thank you, honey."

They sat in truck sipping their cold drinks and eating the salty nuts. When Thomas finished his Coke, he laid the empty bottle on the seat next to him and wiped his hands with a few of the napkins. "Ready?" he asked.

"Not yet," Cargie said.

"No rush." He put the wadded napkins beside the empty bottle.

"Do you remember that book *The Velveteen Rabbit*?" she asked. "We used to read it to the kids."

"Yes'm. You brought it home when Becca was just a little-bitty thing. I think it was the first book you bought for her."

"It was, and I still have it. I kept it all these years."

"Every one of the kids loved that book."

"Do you remember what the story was about?"

Thomas nodded slowly. "Sure. A stuffed bunny that turned into a real rabbit."

"Do you remember how it happened?"

"Uh-huh. There was a fairy in a flower. She made the bunny real."

Cargie turned to face her husband and said, "Love made the rabbit real, Thomas." Then she asked him if he remembered the Skin Horse.

"Yes'm," he said.

"The rabbit asked the Skin Horse if it hurts to become real," Cargie said. "And the Skin Horse said that sometimes it does—the horse was always truthful—but when you're real you don't mind being hurt. Then the rabbit wanted to know if becoming real happens all at once, like being wound up, or a little bit at a time."

Thomas rested his hands on the steering wheel. "You remember the story better than me, even though I must've read it to the kids a hundred times."

Cargie went on, "The Skin Horse told the rabbit that becoming real does not happen all at once. It takes a long, long time. The Skin Horse was old and worn out himself, so he knew about such things."

"Uh-huh."

"Becoming real doesn't happen to everybody either. Usually, it doesn't happen to people who break easily or have sharp edges. And it doesn't happen to people who have to be carefully kept."

"I'd say we have avoided those pitfalls," Thomas said.

"Generally, by the time you're real, you're worn pretty thin from being loved so long. You get loose in the joints and very shabby."

Thomas laughed.

"But none of that matters one iota because once you are real, you can't ever be ugly, except to people who don't understand." And then Cargie Barre, who in all her years of marriage had never touched her husband in public, laid her palm against his cheek and said, "You made me real, Thomas."

He reached for her and they hugged each other as tightly as they could for a long time.

Chapter Sixty-Eight

When they left the little market at Rodessa, Thomas said, "I wanna go by Mama and Daddy's house one more time, if I can find it. And their graves."

"I assumed we would," Cargie said.

They drove a few miles, and then Thomas pulled over on the two-lane blacktop. "We've come too far. I must've missed the turnoff back there somewhere. It's been so long that everything looks different."

"Take your time," Cargie said.

Thomas made a U-turn and drove slowly. He stopped at a dirt track with a wide galvanized gate over a cattle guard. A no-trespassing sign was posted on the gate. "I'm pretty sure this is it," he said. He looked at Cargie. "Private property."

"Let's go have a look anyway," she said.

"Alrighty."

The unlocked gate swung easily on greased hinges, and Thomas stepped back to allow Cargie to hopscotch across the cattle guard. They walked side by side in the rutted dirt, with a grassy ridge between them. Cargie breathed the country air, more fresh air than she felt like she'd had in a month of Sundays. She'd kept her head in books and ledgers for too long. It was time to look around at what she'd been missing. "We need to start taking walks in the country," she said.

Thomas did not respond. The trail curved to the right, and he stopped. "It's straight ahead, through those trees." He led Cargie into the underbrush, here and there placing his heavy boot on a vine or a bramble so she could step over it. They came to a creek, which they followed to a spot where the bank had been flattened on both sides. The area had been strewn with gravel years before, and the gravel had long since mingled with the soil. But here and there, the pebbles had washed into long fingers that reached into the creek bed. "This is the old wagon crossing," Thomas said.

They followed the creek a little farther, then Thomas turned away from it, and before Cargie knew it, she was standing in the overgrown yard of the Walker home. Kudzu vines climbed the old clapboard walls and hung from the eaves, and a mature pine tree stood in one corner of the house, its trunk and branches breaking through the porch and walls and roof. Thomas climbed the steps onto the porch, and the old boards creaked. He stepped this way and that, testing them. "Feels pretty solid," he said. The front door was ajar. He pushed it open and went inside, and Cargie followed.

The house was empty except for broken bottles and rusting cans strewn about and piled in every corner. Thomas walked across the floorboards, testing them with each step, until he came to a doorway, beyond which Cargie saw an old sink. He pointed to the doorjamb and said, "Mama put me up against that doorpost every year on my birthday."

Cargie examined the faded pencil marks. They started at two and climbed the wood to seventeen.

"Put your back against it," she said.

Thomas obeyed, and Cargie saw the tick at seventeen was a little shorter than he was now, at seventy-two. "You haven't shrunk yet," she said, and Thomas smiled.

Cargie crossed the room to a window, and Thomas followed her. They stood quietly a long while, looking at the brush and trees. Cargie tried to imagine a bare yard and a boy playing there with his speckled dog. Her underlying aggravation with her husband melted, and she slipped her arm around his waist and leaned against him. "I'm so sorry this happened to you, honey," she said. "You were robbed of so much."

Thomas reached his arms around her, but he didn't say a word.

"Oh, Lord," Thomas said when he wheeled the truck into the gravel parking lot. The little church house, which Cargie was certain must have been white at one time, was the most colorful building she had ever seen. Every wall of the exterior had been painted with flowers and birds in psychedelic colors. People were painted on it in all different colors too. A thick purple cross encompassed the front door. It was curved, as if in dance, its crossbeams raised in praise.

"Was it like this the last time you were here?" Cargie asked.

"No ma'am. I drove up last spring—I always try to come up around Eastertime and put flowers on the graves. It was still painted the regular way then." Thomas turned off the ignition and the sound of a lawnmower drifted through the truck's open windows.

"Let's go have a look," Cargie said.

They got out of the truck and walked around the church to the graveyard behind it. A young man was mowing at the rear of the yard. His head was wrapped in a yellow kerchief above which bobbed a blond afro the size of a basketball. He tromped behind the mower in work boots, cut-off blue jean shorts, and a faded tee shirt on which Jesus Freak was printed.

Thomas paid the mower no mind and walked directly to a double headstone of white limestone. Patches of lichen grew on the stone, and the grass around it was freshly mown and fragrant.

"Lee and Blanche Walker," Cargie read aloud. She hadn't even thought to ask their names. "Where's your grandfather's grave?"

"He's buried in Port Barre with my grandmother."

"Barre," Cargie said.

Thomas turned to her. "Barre was the closest I could come to offering you a name that meant something."

"What about Thomas?"

"That was a little less weighty. When I was a boy, I used to pretend I was Tom Sawyer."

The young hippie who was mowing had cut the engine and was walking toward them, taking care to step around the graves. "Take your time," Cargie told Thomas. "I'll head that one off at the pass." She started walking toward the young man.

"Are you looking for someone in particular, ma'am?" he asked. He wiped the sweat from his brow with the back of his hand then wiped his hand on his shorts. His accent wasn't local.

"We found them," Cargie said. "The Walkers. Lee and Blanche."

"Did you know them?"

"My husband did."

"I'm Ricky," he said.

"Cargie. Do you mind if we give my husband some privacy?"

"This way," Ricky said, and Cargie followed him around to the front of the church house, where they sat on the steps.

"Where are you from, Ricky?" Cargie said, to get him talking.

"San Francisco. Have you ever heard of Haight-Ashbury?

"No sir."

"It's like this epicenter, where everything's happening all the time. Around the clock. Haight-Ashbury never sleeps."

"Why'd you leave?"

"I got clean, and I wanted to stay clean, so I had to get out of there." Ricky laughed. "Little did I know Louisiana is full of potheads and acidheads. The fields are white unto harvest around here. Lots of opportunities for ministry."

"There doesn't seem to be much of anybody around here," Cargie said.

"You'd be surprised. We have a camp in the woods. It's a whole community. We have a common garden and some fruit trees. We grow everything you can imagine, and we're canning a bunch of it for winter. We raise goats and chickens too.

"I reckon you can get through just about anything as long as you have fried chicken," Cargie said.

"Oh no. We don't eat anything with a face."

"I better go check on my husband," Cargie said.

She got up and walked to the corner of the church house to see how Thomas was getting on. She rounded the corner in time to see him struggling to get up from lying prostrate on his parents' graves. He knelt in front of the headstone and laid his hands on it. He bowed his head. She returned to Ricky, lest he take an interest in seeing what Thomas was up to.

"Do your folks know where you are?" she asked as she sat down again.

"Yes ma'am. They're trying to understand."

Thomas came around the corner, heading toward the truck. He did not look their way.

"Is he okay?" Ricky asked.

"He's fine." Cargie stood. "We'll be on our way. It was nice visiting with you, Ricky."

"You too, Miss Cargie. Um, before you go—I have to ask—do you know Jesus?"

Cargie had never been asked such a personal question outright, but she tried not to let her displeasure show. Ricky was young and forward, but his heart was in the right place.

"I do indeed," she answered. "But I find my comfort in believing that he knows me."

Chapter Sixty-Nine

Cargie was ready for a fight by the time Thomas pulled into a parking spot in front of the Miller County Courthouse. He turned off the ignition.

"Reckon I'm about to have my first conversation with a white man in over fifty years," Thomas said.

"What?"

"In all these years since that Klansman, I have never once spoken to a white. Not one time. I made a point of it."

"You've never met Bill Cole," Cargie said. How was that possible?

"No ma'am, I have not. Well, reckon I'm just stalling." Thomas reached across her and took the ancient leather pouch and his old pistol out of the glovebox.

"Why'd you bring your gun?"

"It was his, Cargie. I kept it."

"Leave it," she said. "Don't take it in there."

"It's evidence, honey."

"You've got plenty of evidence right there in that pouch," she said. "Leave the pistol in the truck. A gun changes everything."

Thomas thought about it for a few minutes, then he put the pistol back in the glovebox and opened his door. "I love you, honey," he said.

"I love you too, Thomas."

Cargie waited for him to come around and open her door. She got out and they trudged up the steps, side by side. Thomas opened the courthouse door and they walked straight across the lobby and into the sheriff's office.

All the desks were empty except one, and the deputy sitting at it raised his meaty crew-cut head. His neck bulged above his collar, even though the first button was undone and his tie was loosened. On the sides of his face, above his ears, arrow-straight lines creased the pink flesh, the work of wire-rimmed sunglasses that hung from a buttonhole in his shirt pocket. The name on the tag above his pocket read W. Bates.

Cargie's blood ran cold, in spite of her insurance.

"Morning," Thomas said.

Deputy Bates put his pen down. "Mornin', yourself."

"We're here to see the sheriff."

"Sheriff ain't here. What can I do for you?"

"We'll come back," Cargie said. "When will the sheriff be back?"

"Hard to say. He's been up at Little Rock since last week."

Without a word or a glance toward his wife, Thomas laid the ancient leather pouch on the desk.

Bates looked at it suspiciously. "What's this?"

Thomas unwound the cord and opened the flap. He pulled out the Treasury notes and the letter, its seal like a thick globule of blood. Then he took the money clip from his pocket and laid it on the desk with the Klan's emblem up.

Deputy Bates stood. "Where'd all this come from?"

"A Klansman had it."

"What Klansman?"

"I had a run-in with a Klansman at a little lake down below Doddridge. I was—"

"When?" Bates interrupted.

"The morning of October 18th, 1913. I don't know the time exactly. But I killed him, and I'm here to make it right."

The deputy hooked his thumbs between the protuberances on his utility belt. He looked around the room, as if searching for something. "Nineteen thirteen?" he said to no one in particular. He peered out the window at the street for a while, then he turned his attention to Thomas again and said, "You got a hidden camera around here or somethin'? This ain't funny. Killin' ain't no joke."

"I'm not joking. In 1913, south of Doddridge, I got into it with a Klansman and killed him. It was an accident."

"Where's the body?"

"The alligators took him. He's long gone."

Bates worked his mouth, drawing his lips in and pooching them out again. "Ain't no crime without a body," he said, finally. He waved at the pile of history on his desk. "Go on now and take all this mess with you."

"But the law—"

Bates walked around the desk and came chest to chest with Thomas, undaunted by Thomas's height or his evidence. "You listen, mister, and you listen real good. Today *I'm* the law in Miller County."

"C'mon, honey, let's go," Cargie said.

Thomas did not move. He seemed stuck, as if he were set on penance he was being denied.

"God Almighty!" Bates flared, flushing all the way to his khaki collar. He wiped spittle from his lower lip and collected himself. "I can understand y'all wantin' to do the right thing, but coming in here after half a damn century? In these times? You're gonna have to find your peace somewheres else, mister. Now, you take all this and clear out. I mean it. You got no debt to Miller County."

"Okay," Thomas said. "All right." He gathered the money and letter into the pouch and hastily wrapped the cord. They hurried out of the courthouse into the mild afternoon. Thomas stopped at the bottom of the steps and turned to Cargie. "What just happened?"

"Mercy," Cargie said. "Mercy just happened."

Chapter Seventy

1969

Mae had not seen Cameron, Louisiana, in twelve years.

To the day.

She arrived at the coast midmorning, having risen early to make the four-hour drive from Shreveport. She parked her sedan at a marina across from Monkey Island and walked down the wooden dock. In one slip was a pretty boat with *Millicent* painted in gold letters across the stern. A man in a captain's cap was hosing down the deck, and Mae asked if he would take her out on the Gulf, just offshore.

"Yes ma'am," he said. "Done fishing. Got nothing but time this afternoon."

Mae sat in the bow while the captain guided them out of the sheltered channel to open water. He pushed the throttle forward, and the boat plowed the buffeting waves. Mae hung on to the metal rail, riding high. Behind her stretched the empty beach, on which she and Hollister had enjoyed so many summer vacations, the last of which ended with them fleeing for their lives in the wee, dark hours.

"Stop here. This is good," She called to the captain.

He cut the engine. Suddenly it was quiet, with only the sound of waves slapping against the varnished boat. The captain descended the steps from the bridge and came to stand beside her at the rail. Mae hugged her cargo tight against her.

"Take as long as you need," he said. "I'll put down the anchor." When the captain returned, he stood with his back against the wheelhouse, giving Mae her space.

"Who's Millicent?" she asked.

"My wife."

"How long have you been married?"

He crossed the deck to the rail beside her. He wore a cap and sunglasses and a heavy, graying beard, so that his darkly tanned cheeks and nose were all Mae saw of his face. "We were married seventeen years," he said. "Been widowed twelve."

"Audrey?"

"Yes ma'am. Spent a day and a night in the deep, and my Millicent was torn from my arms. Our daughter too. Our son was sixteen and strong as an ox. He got through it in the top of a tree, same as me." The captain gripped the rail with both hands and put his head down. Then he sighed deeply and straightened up. He ran one knuckle up under his sunglasses. "Can't talk about it. Too raw. Even now."

"My husband," Mae pointed to the urn. "Hollister. We first came here in thirty-two. We were driving the beach road and happened on the Primeaux's cabins."

"Yes ma'am. We knew Tud and Flo. They perished as well."

"I don't believe they were ever found," Mae said.

"No, they were not. There was nothing left of their place."

"After Audrey," Mae said, "we started going to Florida. The Panhandle beaches were as white as sugar and just as fine, and the water was so clear and blue. We drove down there every summer and had a good time, but it never meant as much to us as this place."

"It does get in your blood."

"I remember one time—gosh, I haven't thought about it in years—one time, Hollister stood on the beach at high tide, right there." Mae pointed. "Right . . . just there."

She became quiet, remembering how he had looked. So handsome and young. Twenty-something and full of rye. Standing on the beach, just out of the waves' reach. A little bit drunk, as he always was.

After a moment, the captain asked, "And what did your Hollister do?"

"He pointed at the Gulf, at the whole Gulf of Mexico, and hollered, really loud, 'This far you may come, but no *farther! Here* your proud waves must stop!'"

"Book of Job," said the captain.

"Is it? I never knew that. I thought Hollister came up with it."

"This Gulf, she has a mind of her own. She doesn't obey God or your husband."

"No sir. Seems like most of life is of the same mind."

Hollister had gone so quickly that Mae didn't have a chance to say goodbye. They were in the kitchen—she was frying a chicken—

and he went down on the linoleum. Suddenly. "Good Lord," he said as he crumpled to one knee. He tried to catch himself on a barstool, and it clattered to the floor.

He rolled over and was unconscious by the time Mae got around the counter to him. She called for an ambulance right away, and she rode to the hospital in the back with Hollister and the attendant. The attendant paid no mind to her, but shouted to the driver, who relayed everything to the hospital on his radio.

"Jaundice," the attendant called, and it was repeated into a microphone at the end of a coiled cord coming out of the dashboard. Mae had tried to rouse Hollister on the kitchen floor. She had gone as far as lifting his eyelid, and the white of his eye had been as yellow as a daffodil.

Blood trickled from Hollister's nose. His mouth. His ears.

"Coagulopathy!" cried the attendant, and the driver stepped on the gas.

Mae laid her hand on Hollister's stomach, which had swelled like a pregnant woman's. When had that happened? They reached the hospital, and she held onto the gurney until it was shoved into a room she was not permitted to enter. A nurse directed Mae to a waiting area, where she sat and worried.

In a little while, a young doctor came out and sat beside her. "Mrs. Caine, your husband has suffered acute liver failure."

"Will he be okay?"

The doctor pressed his lips. Shook his head. "How long has Mr. Caine been an alcoholic?"

"An *alcoholic?*"

"Yes ma'am," the young doctor said mildly. Respectfully. "How many years?"

Mae thought about it, really thought about it, as she had never permitted herself to before. "All of them," she said. "All the years."

Mae declined the nurse's offer to call family and friends. Hollister would not have wanted anyone to see him like this. She sat by his bedside and held his warm and swollen hand until he expired a few hours later.

Mae took the top off the urn. It was hard to let him go. Many times since January, while she waited for this anniversary to come, she had opened the urn and breathed her husband's burnt mineral purity.

"Can't anybody or anything take him away from you," the captain said.

Mae nodded and upended the urn over the side. A flurry of ashes fell into the soapsuds water and quickly disappeared. The rest were carried away on the Gulf breeze. She shook the urn, then threw it as far as she could.

She turned to the captain. He had removed his cap, showing a forehead as fair and smooth as hers. He began to sing "Amazing Grace" in a clear choral voice. Mae joined him, and they did not let up until every word of every verse had been loosed upon the fickle sea.

"'Twas a sailor wrote that," the captain said. He settled his cap and went forward to raise the anchor.

Chapter Seventy-One

1972

Bill Cole finally went to the doctor when he was unable to shake off a cough that had persisted for weeks. The doctor pronounced that he was at death's door with lung cancer, even though he had not smoked a single cigarette in his life. "The doctor said it might've come from that mess we breathed back in the war," Bill told Cargie over their afternoon Spanish peanuts and cold drinks. "Or from all these dry-cleaning chemicals. Lord knows, I've inhaled enough of them." He munched peanuts as if it were any other afternoon. "But then he said maybe it was none of that. Might just be bad luck."

"Isn't there anything they can do?"

"He offered the chemotherapy." Bill paused and sipped his Coke. "But he did not recommend it."

Cargie was speechless. She did not believe she could have felt any worse if the death sentence had been hers. They sat a while, not counting the morning's money or receipts. Cargie opened the desk drawer, reached way to the back, and took out the diary. She placed it between them.

"Oh," Bill said. "I wondered where that got off to."

"It was wrong of me not to tell you. I'm sorry."

"I'm not," he said quickly. "To tell you the truth, Cargie, it was right nice knowing you took an interest."

Cole's Dry Cleaning and Laundry closed its doors when Bill died, and Cargie had no stake in the disposition of the business, having remained an employee through all the years. Neither did she receive the payout Bill made to the others who had worked for him, some for decades. She wouldn't have stood for it if he'd offered.

But there was one final reconciling that needed to occur, and that was the disposition of the partnership Bill and Cargie had created. The two of them had ridden the coattails of scores of companies that Cargie vetted. A few—Electric Boat, International Paper and Power,

Douglas Aircraft—had clawed their way out of the Depression, made money hand over fist during the war, and adapted to a new America afterward. All the while, the value of their equities multiplied like rabbits in spring.

Ever the fiscal guardian, Walter Addington was the one who had suggested the two entrepreneurs form a corporation to protect the wealth they were accumulating. Cargie conducted weeks of research and came to the same conclusion. "What should we call our company?" she had asked Bill.

"I've been noodling on that. I like the idea of working our names in. What do you think of Barre Cole."

"Sounds like we want to ban fossil fuel."

"Cole Barre?"

"Cole Pittman," Cargie said.

"Pittman?"

"That's my maiden name. Go on now. Write it down. Let's see how it looks."

Bill wrote Cole Pittman Enterprises on the back of a receipt. "It has a good ring to it," he said. "You sure about this?"

"Yes sir. I like it. Don't worry about Thomas. Trust me, he'll understand."

After Bill was planted and mourned, Walter Addington telephoned Cargie and asked her to come down to the bank. "We need to meet with the attorney," he said.

The morning of their meeting, Cargie stood on the sidewalk in front of First City Bank. A few years before, she would have been tackled by a guard if she had tried to waltz in the front door to do business with one of the tellers. Because Cargie had not been permitted to conduct transactions in person, the bank president himself had tended the savings account she opened there after the Crash.

But times were catching up with Cargie, even though she had not lifted a finger to help them along. She'd never darkened the door of a white-owned soda fountain, much less refused to leave in protest. She'd never insisted on sitting in the front of a streetcar or a bus, nor had she risked life and limb to march for the rights of black folks. Or women. Or anyone else, for that matter.

Cargie wished she had been as courageous as Shirley Chisholm, a black Congresswoman from New York—the first member of Congress to be both black and female. Chisolm had gone as far as

announcing her bid for the job of President of the United States—
President of the United States!—despite everyone knowing she
could not possibly win. Chisolm would lose, and she knew it, but she
fought the good fight anyway to inch folks closer to where they
needed to go.

As Cargie stood on the sidewalk in front of First City Bank on a
pleasant April morning, she concluded that her own journey had
been undeservedly easy. Every valley had been raised and every
mountain made low. Every rugged, impassable place had been
smoothed in front of her, thanks to the men in her life: Thomas
Barre. Bill Cole. Walter Addington. The pure kindness of these men
loosed Cargie's emotions. She ran into the bank, through the lobby,
and into the ladies' room, where she locked herself in a stall.

"Are you okay in there, honey?" a woman asked through the
door.

"I just need a minute," sputtered Cargie. She stayed put until her
hiccupy torrent subsided. Then she washed her face and went to her
meeting.

Mr. Addington's secretary stood when Cargie approached her
desk. "Mrs. Barre! We were a little worried about you. May I get you
something to drink? Would you like a cup of coffee or tea?"

"No ma'am. Thank you."

"In here then, please." The secretary opened Mr. Addington's
door. "They're waiting for you."

Cargie had not met Mr. Seele, the attorney who handled Bill's
affairs and drew up the papers for their corporation. The lawyer
popped up from his chair as if the Queen of England had walked in.
"Mrs. Barre! It's a pleasure to finally make your acquaintance."

"Pleased to meet you as well, sir."

"Please, Cargie, have a seat," Walter said.

"Your time is valuable, so I'll get right to it," said Mr. Seele. He
picked up a single sheet of paper from the edge of the desk. "Mr.
Cole signed this addendum to your partnership." He handed the
paper to Cargie.

"When?"

"Not long after you formed Cole Pittman. As you can see, it's
quite straightforward, stipulating that his interest transfers to you in
the event of his incapacity or death."

"What about Mrs. Cole?"

"Mrs. Cole?" Mr. Seele looked at Walter Addington.

"Vida Cole is well supplied," said Walter. "Bill set up a generous trust for her and other members of his family before Cole Pittman was ever conceived. Vida will never do without."

"Still . . . it doesn't seem quite right."

"Carrying out Bill Cole's intention is entirely *the* right thing to do," said Mr. Seele. "Legally and morally."

"For the record, Cargie," Walter said, "I concur without reservation. Bill always believed the company rightfully belonged to you."

Cargie was glad she had already cried all her tears. "Very well," she said, "but tell me about these trusts."

Chapter Seventy-Two

1987

On a Wednesday morning in October, when Thomas Barre was ninety-one years old, he put his hat on after breakfast and walked down the street to Lydie Murphy's house to have coffee and invite her to supper that night. The weather had been warming up since the weekend, and the sky was brilliant blue without a cloud in it.

Lydie answered the door. She had not found a live-in maid to her liking after Mavis passed. She had finally given up the search and hired two thoroughly tattooed former drug addicts, sisters, who cleaned houses and called themselves the Mopsy Twins. The twins drove a white van with a professionally painted logo on the side, and they did not mind coming out to Mooretown once a week to clean Lydie's mansion. Lydie paid them well, having a soft spot for down-and-outers trying to make a fresh start. After almost sixty years, the defiant swagger of Lydie's youth had mellowed, and she'd aged into an agreeably piquant matriarch. Thomas enjoyed her company immensely.

Lydie had taken to cooking. She raised her own vegetables and herbs in a large garden she planted in the vacant lot beside the mansion. She did not own the lot, but nobody made a fuss about her using it. It seemed to Thomas that folks avoided taking on Lydie Murphy.

Lydie took her cooking as far as attending a month-long course at Le Cordon Bleu in Paris. She took Becca, who saw and did everything there was to see and do in Paris while Lydie took her daily instruction. Thomas had to admit that Lydie came back a better cook than when she left.

Thomas and Cargie had traveled to France themselves. France was the first big trip they took after all the children were out of the house and following their own paths through the world. Many more vacations followed, so many, in fact, that the kids teasingly called their parents the Mooretown Globetrotters.

Cargie had mapped out a route through France that covered all the places she wanted to see. They rented a Renault and drove for miles through verdant farmland alongside the lazy Le Meuse river. Signs of the Great War were everywhere. Overgrown trenches and shell holes interrupted just about every plowed field. They saw crumbling German pillboxes too, in which the weary German soldiers had vainly tried to withstand French and American forces. A half dozen times, they passed rusted, mud-caked artillery lying beside the road. One farmer left his tractor and trotted across the field when he saw them get out of the car and walk toward the shells.

"No!" he hollered. "Danger!"

Thomas held up his camera. "*Image*," he yelled back, "*No toucher*."

The farmer nodded, gave Thomas a thumbs-up sign, and returned to his work. Thomas knelt to take a photograph of the three ancient shells lying in the soft grass.

Cargie knelt beside him. "The iron harvest," she said.

"Is that what they call it?"

"Yes sir. Read where one of these came into a plant with a load of turnips and killed three workers. Folks still dying every year from these things. Some of them are loaded with gas. Chlorine or mustard—awful stuff. Maybe these are, for all we know."

"Mercy," said Thomas.

They stayed at a fancy hotel in Sedan, and early the next morning they drove south to the Meuse-Argonne American Cemetery at Romagne-sous-Montfaucon. "I'm sorry Bill never got to see this," Cargie said. "Not just the cemetery. All of it, especially the countryside looking beautiful again. He would've liked that."

"He could've come over here."

Cargie sighed. "I reckon."

In the late afternoon, they sat in the cool inside the cemetery's memorial building, admiring the light coming through tall, stained glass windows. Cargie took Bill Cole's diary out of the big purse she brought on the trip. "I had in mind to read some of it here," she said.

"Sounds fine."

She opened the worn journal and read aloud.

11 November 1918, Le Meuse, France
Before daylight this morning we resumed heavy bombardment. I was with Wally and a 128th Infantry guy from Texas named Jesse. We were in the first advance. We scrambled from shell hole to shell

hole and got pretty close to a German trench. We saw the parapet when the star shells went off. Only thing was the Germans spotted us and laid down machine gun fire, pinning us in the muddy pit.

We lay low for a couple of hours. Dawn came on, and we wondered where the rest of the troops were. They should've been in the vicinity, but it looked like we'd advanced too far ahead and were stuck. The bombardment didn't get stronger after daylight as we expected. Instead the artillery and mortars and machine gun fire slowed down—like popcorn slows popping when it's done. We were in a jam. We settled into the mud because we'd get our heads blown off if we did anything else.

Jesse said maybe they were putting an end to it, and we ruminated on that while the front fell quiet. We heard men shouting, and we thought we heard singing, but it sounded like it was coming from the German side, so we weren't sure if that was a good sign or a bad one.

Then there was a volley of artillery and the whiz of shrapnel, and Jesse caught a fragment in the neck. Wally leaped over to him—he was closer than me. I guess that's all the sniper was waiting for because I instantly heard a shot and the thunk of a round hitting metal. Wally's helmet flew off, and I thought that was it for my buddy. He collapsed against Jesse. I scrambled to them and put my hand on Jesse's neck where Wally's had been, but my fingers kept slipping off because of the blood and mud.

I pulled Wally's face out of the mud with my other hand. I tried to find where he was hit but had no luck at all. After a minute he started coming around and feeling the back of his head. I reckon the bullet hit on an angle and ricocheted right off his helmet. I set to whooping, and pretty soon Wally started whooping too. Even Jesse was grinning.

I heard a rifle shot from behind us, and out of nowhere two guys jumped into the hole with us. One of them looked at Jesse's neck wound and said the fragment missed the artery and Jesse was gonna make it. He started hollering for a stretcher-bearer. The other guy said he shot the sniper. They were from the 128th, Jesse's company.

Turned out the Germans had called for a cease-fire, and the higher-ups made a symbol out of the time and day. They signed the Armistice at the 11th hour of the 11th day of the 11th month. I don't know if you could call it a real victory or if they just decided to call off the war. It should've been a wonderful day for us, and it was, except for what happened to Chaplain Davitt.

Chaplain Davitt really was about the best pastor I ever knew, bar none. To hear some people back home tell it, Catholics aren't even saved, but Father Davitt was a first-rate Christian and very brave too. He had just hoisted the American flag and gave a big whoop for the war ending when some lousy Germans fired off an artillery shell and killed him. Everybody knew the war was over, but they killed him anyway. Some of the boys went after the Germans, but they were long gone by the time our guys got across to their side. Chaplain Davitt had the same Christian name as me—William.

Wally and I and some of the guys sat on a parapet for a long time this evening and took a good look at No Man's Land. We never could get a look at the whole thing while the fighting was going on because of the snipers. Such a wasteland never ought to exist. All the earth between our side and theirs was burnt black and blasted full of shell holes. There was just nothing left except barbed wire and ruination, and men from both sides were combing every foot of it for the wounded and the dead and the pieces. Sitting on that parapet this afternoon was the first time the awful smell of the place didn't seem normal.

I reckon God alone knows the number of men whose blood defiles this land. If Abel's blood cried out from the ground, the scream from No Man's Land must be earsplitting. And who will answer for them? I have no idea how long it will take to make this part of France green again, if it ever can be. War is Hell. We said it a hundred times a day. We kept repeating it because it's true—Hell itself has nothing on the front line.

I heard birds singing this afternoon. I think they were in a stand of poplars behind the German line. A few poplars that survived the bombardments. They're all that's left of a forest that must've shamed the thick pines in east Texas and Louisiana. Poplars are pretty trees, very tall and straight. The bark reminds me of the sycamores back home.

Reckon I survived the war.

Cargie closed the diary and looked up. Her eyes opened wide when she saw the crowd of visitors Thomas had been watching collect in a semicircle around them. Cargie would scold him later for not letting her know, but he didn't because she would have gotten embarrassed and stopped reading.

The crowd stood in silence for a time. No one, not even the children, moved or made a peep. Then a woman began to clap, slowly and respectfully, and the rest of them joined in. Thomas knew it was a moment these folks would remember for the rest of their lives. A moment they would tell their families and friends back home about. They would tell their children and grandchildren too.

After the crowd broke up an elderly man came forward and held Cargie's hand. He had tears in his eyes. "*Merci*," he said. "*Merci beaucoup.*"

"You're welcome," said Cargie.

Thomas and Lydie had coffee in the sunroom. It was the room in which Rudy and Becca had played as children, the room in which they had fallen in love. As a teenager, Becca confided to her father about her blossoming feelings toward Rudy. She approached Thomas shamefaced because she thought she was confessing a sin. She thought Rudy was her brother, believing kinship to be a matter of proximity rather than blood. Becca was elated to learn that Rudy was no relation at all and could be hers. Thomas still chuckled every time he thought about that beaming face turned up to his.

Lydie drank Community coffee with chicory, and she turned up her nose at every other brand. That was Lydie. Most folks could not stomach chicory anymore, even in Louisiana, but Thomas liked the charred, bitter finish just fine. Lydie loved everything that included *lagniappe*. That's why she loved his Beef Bourguignon, although she didn't know it. "If you're makin' a Bourguignon tonight, I'll be there," Lydie said. "You make it better than those snooty cooks at Cordon Bleu." Lydie refused to call them chefs, even when she was in Paris on their home turf. That, also, was Lydie dead out. "You know you're gonna tell me your secret ingredients one of these days," she said.

"Yes'm." Thomas grinned. "Just not today."

When he got back to the house, Thomas spent half an hour spraying water on the yard and flower beds. It had been a dry autumn and warm. They had not had a freeze yet, and the bed plants were still going strong. Little Bit, a tiny piebald mutt who had shown up in late summer with more mats on her than meat, jumped and ran after the water so persistently that Thomas had to put her in the house to get the job done. He sprayed the dust off a row of crosscut pine rounds that marked the graves of the dogs they'd owned over the years. Seven of them altogether, beginning with Lazarus, and every one of them had died in Thomas's arms. Afterward, he always walked to the lumberyard and picked out a pine round to mark the grave. And he always thought about Huck.

As Thomas wound the garden hose back onto the holder that hung on the side of Pretty Mama's house, he noticed the mismatched shiplap on the corner. He always noticed it. It had bothered him for half a century. He sighed and straightened his back. "Too late to worry about it now," he said aloud. "Let it go, old man, will you?"

He went inside to get the Bourguignon going so it could simmer in the oven through the afternoon. He smiled when he took the brown sugar and cayenne from the pantry. So simple, these two ingredients, but they sure had given a lot of pleasure over the years. He'd tried them in just about everything he cooked at one time or another.

"Thomas, your fried chicken is the best. Better'n Mama's, but don't tell her."

"Daddy, make some of that sweet and hot bacon, *please!*"

"What did you put in these collards? They're delicious."

When the beef was in the oven, Thomas put away all the spices except the brown sugar and the cayenne, which he left out on a lark. He would not say a word about it, but he knew Lydie would notice. Finally, she would know his secret. What good were secrets anyway, if you never get to tell them?

He sat in his recliner to read, and Little Bit hopped up and settled into his lap. Thomas had learned to love poetry in the Wylie College library. One of his favorite reads was an autographed first edition collection of Robert Frost's poems. The children went in together and bought it for his ninetieth birthday. The book's pages were yellowed and brittle, but it was still a sight younger than he was. Thomas enjoyed reading from it because it contained many of his favorite lines of verse.

He rubbed the little dog's head and asked, "How are you feeling today, little girl?" She looked up at him with the same adoration he had seen in the eyes of every dog he had ever shown kindness. "Would you like to hear some good poems?" Little Bit did not object to the idea, so Thomas read,

> We stood a moment so in a strange world,
> Myself as one his own pretense deceives;
> And then I said the truth (and we moved on).

"I have a private interpretation of that one," he told the dog, "You don't mind if I skip around, do you?" Little Bit did not mind.

Whose woods these are I think I know.
His house is in the village though;
He will not see me stopping here
To see his woods fill up with snow.

The woods are lovely, dark and deep,
But I have promises to keep,
And miles to go before I sleep,
And miles to go before I sleep.

"Can you picture it?" Thomas asked Little Bit. "I stopped on a snowy evening like that years ago. In a place that wasn't mine." He tenderly turned the stiff pages.

I'd like to get away from earth awhile
And then come back to it and begin over.
May no fate willfully misunderstand me
And half grant what I wish and snatch me away
Not to return. Earth's the right place for love:
I don't know where it's likely to go better.

At odd times during the day, Thomas often thought about Cargie and what she was doing. Cargie, who never wanted to quit working, never had. Every weekday morning, she drove to the First City Bank building to work in the second-floor office of Cole Pittman Enterprises. Thomas imagined her in a sparsely furnished room—Cargie hated clutter—sitting at a desk poring over financial records, sizing up young companies and keeping a watchful eye on old ones. It was pure conjecture. Thomas had never been to Cargie's office. With respect to many things, their lives had been separate, but he did not think their hearts and minds could be closer.

Little Bit snored and coughed and woke herself up. "Am I boring you?" Thomas asked. He gently closed the book and laid it on the occasional table beside his chair. "Reckon we'll just have us a nap." He pushed back in the recliner until his feet were up. It was a peaceful, quiet afternoon, and it did not seem there was anything at all that needed doing, at least not until the Bourguignon came out of the oven. Thomas and Little Bit closed their eyes and nodded off to sleep.

Thus the thoughts of David Walker ended.

Chapter Seventy-Three

Thomas died in October, which seemed to be the popular month for big events in his life. Lydie came early for supper and found his body in the recliner, the little dog still curled in his lap. She turned off the oven and waited with him until Cargie got home.

"I need a minute," Cargie said when Lydie said she would call an ambulance.

"Take as long as you want. God knows he won't be hisself again after the undertaker gets hold of him." Lydie tried to pick up Little Bit, but she bared her teeth and snapped.

"Leave her," Cargie said. "She's afraid."

Sometime during the fuss of the ambulance fetching Thomas's body and Lydie Murphy hanging around until Cargie convinced her to go home, Little Bit peed by the back door. The tiny creature ducked her head and ran under the bed when Cargie found it. "It's not your fault," Cargie hollered toward the bedroom. "It's not your fault," she repeated quietly as she sopped up the mess. She dropped the rag and settled onto the floor, where she wept for a long time.

When Cargie collected herself, she finished cleaning up the mess and hunted around for something to feed the dog. In all the years since Lazarus had arrived—all the years of Thomas adopting strays that thumped their tails every time they heard his voice—in all that time, Cargie had not paid one bit of mind to how he tended to the dogs. She rummaged through every cabinet, searching for dog food, but she did not find any. She considered calling Lydie to ask if she knew where Thomas kept it, but that would only bring her back to the house to help. Cargie finally gave up and scrambled an egg in bacon grease. The smell brought the dog into the kitchen, and Cargie scraped the egg onto a plate.

"It's hot, Little Bit. Got to let it cool a minute."

Little Bit's tail wagged at the sound of her name, and she looked Cargie in the eye for the first time. Cargie placed the plate on the floor, and the dog gobbled the egg so hungrily that Cargie scrambled another one, this time with cheese.

That night Cargie put the dog up on the bed to sleep with her, but Little Bit would not stay. She jumped down and left the room, and Cargie found her in Thomas's chair with her head resting on her paws. "You're breaking my heart," Cargie said.

The next morning, the house filled up with children and grandchildren and neighbors, and Cargie and Little Bit retreated to the bedroom. Cargie pulled Thomas's clothes out of the hamper and off the hangers in the closet and piled them on the bed. She put Little Bit on top of the pile and watched the dog burrow in. Then Cargie lay down too and buried her nose in his scent. "How are we ever gonna make it?" she whispered. Little Bit did not have an answer.

Zion Rest Cemetery was not what it used to be, but Thomas and Cargie had agreed they wanted to be planted together in Mooretown, where their lives had been. So here Cargie stood, inside the rundown fence. A considerable crowd of mourners waited quietly for the preacher to begin. The air had taken on the chill of evening, and the sun cast long shadows.

Once the preacher got going, he talked and talked. This young pastor had a lot to say, and Cargie's thoughts drifted while he was getting it all out. What was she supposed to do now? Thomas had left her suddenly, without giving her a chance to get used to the idea of being alone.

The preacher finally finished and it was time to sing Thomas's favorite hymn. David stood and helped his mother to her feet, even though she could have stood up just fine by herself. Cargie was self-conscious about her singing voice, and she asked Thomas to forgive her for only mouthing the words.

> Amazing grace! How sweet the sound,
> That saved a wretch; like me!
> I once was lost, but now am found,
> Was blind, but now I see.

Cargie looked around in the dying light. Across the highway, the emerald rolling fairways of the Shreveport Country Club golf course caught her eye. Wispy white fog had collected in the low places. Vapors rose from the sun-warmed earth into the cooling air, making the golf course seem enchanted. While Cargie watched, shadowy specters appeared within the white mist. Thin and ethereal, they moved slowly toward one another. Congregating. Cargie closed her eyes, and the a cappella voices of Thomas's mourners continued,

> Through many dangers, toils, and snares,
> I have already come;
> 'Tis grace that brought me safe thus far,
> And grace will lead me home.

Cargie opened her eyes again. Her imagination had ceased its trickery, and the apparitions on the golf course had vanished. "Go on now, David," she whispered. "Go on home. I'll be along directly."

"What's that, Mama?" David, her son, asked.

"It's nothing, baby." Cargie slipped her arm through his. "Your mama's muttering like an old woman."

The visitation dragged on through the evening, and Cargie was distracted by the thought that she needed to go and get Thomas. He would be cold out there in the night. She knew he was past feeling the cold, but it still disturbed her to leave him there alone.

She and Little Bit retreated to the bedroom again, but Cargie was restless. She looked through Thomas's dresser drawers. She pulled boxes from the top shelf of the closet and opened them. One was filled with letters and cards from Zachary Tatum and a few from his brother Luke. Zachary's correspondence had arrived from all over the world. Luke's was from a rural box. She carried an envelope out to the hallway, looking for one of her children to get Luke Tatum's telephone number.

Luke came to see Cargie the very next day. He was no bigger than a minute and just as quick. His eyes twinkled when he talked, and Cargie felt as if she had known him all her life. The afternoon was warm enough for them to sit on the front porch, away from the horde that still occupied the house. Luke settled on the porch swing and Cargie took a rocker.

"Brought you somethin'," Luke said. He reached into his deep jacket pocket and handed her a tattered book. "Jacob taught me to read from that book. The very one. I wasn't much for learnin', but he got me through. It was no small job, I tell you." He laughed. "Anyway, I thought you ought to have it."

"Thank you, Mr. Tatum. This means more than I can say."

"Luke. Call me Luke."

"Luke," said Cargie. "Thank you."

Becca stuck her head out the door. "Just checking, Mama. Can I get y'all something to drink? We put on a fresh pot of coffee."

"No'm. Nothin' for me," said Luke. "Reckon I'll head over to the cemetery in a little bit. Got some flowers in the truck."

"Nothing for me either, honey," Cargie said, and Becca went back inside.

"Did your husband ever tell you how he came to be on our farm?" Luke asked.

Cargie smiled. "Eventually."

"I reckon that was quite a story," Luke said, but he didn't ask to hear it. He reached into his pocket again and took out a ragged, folded paper and handed it to Cargie.

Cargie opened it carefully. Its four quarters barely hung together. She laid the paper in her lap. "Missing," she read. "David Walker." She tried to make out what details she could from the faded image of the boy her husband had been before it all happened. "Was this the handbill your folks had?"

"No'm. They had one?"

"Yes sir. It was at the church house. Your mama figured it out right away."

"Mercy me. How 'bout that?"

"Where'd you get this one?"

"At the cotton gin in Baldwin. First harvest Jacob was with us, me and Zach run around the side of the building and saw this paper on the gin's board. We knew right away who the picture was of, and we took it down so's nobody else would see it. We liked Jacob real well by then, and we didn't want anybody takin' him away."

"Lord, Lord," said Cargie.

"We hid this paper under Mama's sideboard and never breathed a word to nobody. We was afraid they'd send Jacob away. We was mostly afraid of what Sherman would do. He carried a grudge back then."

"I don't think Sherman ever knew, but your parents did. They knew he was running, and they took him in. They probably saved his life."

"Reckon ever'body was pullin' the wool over ever'body else's eyes." Luke smiled and his eyes twinkled. "But the Lord was a workin'. He works in mysterious ways his wonders to perform."

"Yes he does," said Cargie. "He most assuredly does."

Chapter Seventy-Four

Victoria telephoned Mae to tell her Sissy had died. Mae wouldn't have known if her sister hadn't kept up with the Whitesboro crowd through the years. "Come to Fort Worth," Victoria said. "And we'll go to Whitesboro together for the funeral."

"Oh, gosh, Vic. Yes. Yes, of course. When is it?"

"Saturday afternoon. We have plenty of time.

"I'll come in the morning. I need to tear myself away from the television anyway. I've been on pins and needles ever since that baby went down that well. How can it take it so long to get her out?"

"I don't know. I had to turn it off. I can't take it twenty-four seven."

"Can't wait to see you, sweetie."

"I've got something else on my mind too, Maypearl. If you get a wild hair and decide to drive over tonight, come on. I'm here."

The choice between watching the rescuers in Texas toil through another night, seemingly in vain, and an evening road trip was an easy decision. Mae pulled a plastic dress bag over some hang-up clothes and packed everything else in an overnight bag. By seven o'clock, she was westbound on Interstate 20, driving toward a pink and azure sky.

The next morning, Vic treated her to breakfast at a neighborhood diner. The television in the diner carried the forty-eight-hour-old rescue efforts, reporting that the child had been heard singing nursery rhymes. "My goodness," said Mae.

"Tough little girl," Vic said.

When they left the diner, Vic drove to a quiet neighborhood with old houses and older trees, much like Alexander Avenue. She stopped the car in front of a two-story duplex, a fixer-upper, with a For Sale or Rent sign in the yard. It was a few blocks from the Texas Christian University campus. "C'mon, let's have a look," Vic said and got out of the car.

"What are you up to, little sister?"

"I've been thinking . . ."

"Uh-oh."

"Don't be a Wisenheimer. I was thinking that since Hollister up and left you and Dewey up and left me, we're kinda in the same pickle. Neither one of us has anybody to grow old with."

"We *are* old," Mae said, even though she could hardly believe it.

"To get *older* with, then. What do you think of this duplex? Dewey Jr. took a look at it for me. He says it's solid. We can get it for next to nothing, and he'll gut it and redo the plumbing and wiring. He can change the interior layouts to whatever we want. Heck, I'll even give you first dibs on picking a side."

"How can I refuse an offer like that?" Mae said.

Vic slipped her arm through her sister's. "C'mon. Let's walk." They strolled down the deeply shaded sidewalk. "This neighborhood's landlocked between the country club and the university. There's a really old Baptist church a couple of blocks that way. It's beautiful. We could walk to Sunday service on pretty days, like when we were kids."

"I don't have a letter anymore," Mae said.

"A letter? Do they still do that?"

"I don't know, but I refuse to be baptized again."

"Then we'll be visitors. At the end of the day that's all we ever were anyway."

That evening, the rescuers freed Baby Jessica alive and in one piece, and the entire country breathed a sigh of relief. Mae was surprised when the agitation she'd felt for two days remained after the news coverage had evaporated.

"I don't have a very good history in Whitesboro," Mae told Vic during the drive north to the funeral.

"Hmm." Vic glanced at her sister. "Well, at least it's ancient."

Mae saw Buster as soon as she walked into the church. He didn't look anything like she remembered, but somehow, she knew it was him. He recognized her too. He came over immediately and hugged her tightly. "Mae Pearl Compton! You are a sight for sore eyes."

"How are you, Buster?"

"Thin up top and thick in the middle, but still kicking. Come on, and I'll introduce you to my bride. I robbed a cradle up by Ardmore, Oklahoma."

Buster's bride of fifty years was not shy about telling Mae how they had met. "I was sixteen and wet behind the ears when this fella showed up on Daddy's farm askin' about drillin' rights. I tell ya, I'd been to three goat ropes and a county fair, but I hadn't *ever* seen a man as comely as this one. I set to work on him. Didn't much know what I was about, but I musta done somethin' right because the next thing I knew he was askin' Daddy for my hand."

Buster put his arm around his wife's shoulder and grinned. "Every word is true, and she's been my little Okie ever since."

Like Baby Jessica, Buster had survived his ordeal.

Chapter Seventy-Five

2012

Cargie kept Thomas waiting a good while longer than she intended, but she didn't think he minded. Thomas knew better than anyone that Cargie liked to take her time to finish a thing.

There was a spot on the second-floor gallery of her granddaughter's house, just outside Cargie's bedroom, that she liked particularly well. From it, she had a broad view of the pine forest south of Natchitoches and of the twisting river, flat and red. It was a view worth hanging around for.

Cargie heard her great-grandson talking on the phone before she saw him. These days, everyone communicated without pause. Even Cargie felt as if she'd missed something important if she spent an entire day off-line. Joshua stepped out onto the gallery in his dress whites, carrying his phone and a paper sack. "Mama C!" he exclaimed and spread his arms for a hug.

"Look at you, all spiffed up!"

"Whatcha think?" He spun around so Cargie could admire a three-hundred-and-sixty-degree view of his snow-white naval officer regalia.

"You're as handsome as they come."

"Look here." He set the paper sack on a table between two rockers, unfolded the top, and took out a bottle of Orange Crush. "For you. Nice and cold, like you like it." He twisted off the cap and handed it to her.

"Thank you, baby."

He lifted out a tall, thin can of Red Bull. "For me," he said and set it down. "And, for us." He took out a small white sack soaked with oil. Cargie saw the red skins of the peanuts through the translucent paper. Joshua pulled a wad of paper napkins from the sack, then flattened it and shook the peanuts onto it. They sat in the rockers on either side of the table.

"Mmm. Good stuff," Cargie said.

"Yes ma'am."

"So, how's the flight training coming along?"

Joshua wiped his hands and handed his cellphone to Cargie. "I tweeted this yesterday morning, 'First carrier landing in a jet! #rockandroll #flytheball #Goshawk.'"

"Go on now. Tell me everything. What's fly the ball? What's Goshawk?"

"Goshawk is the airplane I'm flying. Here, I'll show you a picture." Cargie handed the phone back to him, and a few seconds later, he held it up and showed her a fierce, red-tailed jet. "And this," He tapped the phone. "This is the ball. We call it the Optical Landing System."

"Tell me about that."

For the next half-hour, while Cargie chewed peanuts and sipped Orange Crush, Joshua told her every technical detail about flying the ball. Then he told her what still lay ahead in his training. "There's something else too," he said at the end.

"What's that, honey?"

"I met a girl. She's in the class behind me."

"Go on now."

"She's smart, and she likes to laugh. We have a good time together." He rocked for a while, and Cargie waited. Then he stopped rocking and said, "I might be in love with her, Mama C, but I'm not sure, you know? I'm not even sure if I *can* be sure."

"What's her name?"

"Gabrielle. I haven't told anybody else about her."

"It's yours to tell, honey. Or not."

"How did you know? I mean, how did you and great-grandad know?"

"I don't suppose we did. Love is a growing thing. After Thomas and I had been together many, many years, sometimes I'd look back and wonder if what we had at first was love or something else. I don't know what it was way back then, but it became love. I have no doubts about that. I'd have to say we *grew* into love. We did not fall into it."

Joshua resumed his rocking. "I wish I could've met him."

"You will. Someday you will. Wait here. I want to show you something." Cargie went into her bedroom and took a wooden box from the top of the closet. The box held her most precious memories, including Private William Cole's diary. She carried the diary to Joshua.

"Whose is this?" he asked.

"Bill Cole. He passed years ago, but he was my dearest friend, aside from Thomas. I thought you might enjoy reading this." Cargie turned the brittle pages to the entry about a young noblewoman and her Sopwith Camel. Adele, for whom Joshua's grandmother was named.

Joshua read the passage. Then he read it a second time. He closed the diary and said, "I *am* in love."

"Go on now."

"Yes ma'am." He pointed to the diary. "With her."

A bunch of the cousins were getting together that evening to kick off summer, and they planned to binge watch all the Star Wars episodes. Joshua invited Cargie to join them. "We'll start around four," he said. "What kind of pizza do you like?"

"Every kind," Cargie said.

A little before four, she made her way downstairs to the media room, which held a passel of her great-grandchildren and their friends. *"Mama C!"* they shouted in unison when she appeared in the doorway. Cargie thought that was Joshua's doing to make her feel welcome. The youngsters parted to give her the best seat on the sectional sofa. She received fist bumps and a paper plate loaded with pizza.

Joshua's younger brother Caleb, who had just finished his sophomore year of high school, said, "Mama C rocking Star Wars! Wanna try a Red Bull? Here, just try it."

Cargie took a sip. As far as she was concerned, the drink tasted like chilled cleaning solvent. She must've made a face because Joshua took the can away and fetched her a Coke.

They began watching Episode IV—Cargie's favorite—in the wee hours of the morning. When the first Star Wars movie had come out in seventy-seven, she and Thomas watched it at the Strand Theater, and they sat in the third row. Like everyone else, they marveled at the special effects. No one had ever seen anything like it.

After watching the *Millennium Falcon* jump to hyperspace, Cargie became interested in physics, and she read enough about Mr. Albert Einstein's Theory of General Relativity to put a handle on it. The notion that time and space were a single thing rather than two separate things came as no surprise to Cargie. The Bible spoke of "this present age" and "this present world" as if they were one in the same. While she munched pizza and watched the *Falcon* jump around in space-time, she thought about her Thomas taking the leap to another realm altogether. For the first time in her life, Cargie wanted to jump in after him.

"Way to hang with us, Mama C," Caleb said. "Are you getting sleepy?"

Cargie patted his hand. "Sleep will come soon enough, honey."

The next afternoon, Cargie scooted her ladder-back chair to the desk and jiggled the mouse, bringing her two computer monitors to life. Mr. Benjamin Graham's investing principles, which had served Cargie for years, had been overwhelmed by amateurs. Modern investors moved en masse as suddenly and unpredictably as schooling fish, and their sheer numbers drove the prices of individual equities and even entire markets up and down without any rhyme or reason. Nevertheless, Cargie still found amusement in dabbling, and she had a soft spot for companies that, like her, continued to put one foot in front of the other on the upward path.

She opened her favorite investing forum, where months before she had started a string titled, "Nineteen Hundred Reasons to Buy WHR." Early that morning, a regular named Paradigm451 had posted a question there. To Cargie. "Who *are* you?!?"

"Darth Vader," Cargie typed. She pressed Send, and her hand flew to her mouth.

"You are SO DOPE!" came the immediate response.

Cargie frowned. Then she Googled "dope" and discovered the word was now a compliment.

Chapter Seventy-Six

1926

By the time David Walker was thirty-one years old, he had worked in the library at Wiley College for nearly a decade. The knowledge he had gained during many Saturday afternoons in the library on Texas Avenue had prepared him to excel at his job. He was a master of the Dewey Decimal System and the acceptable methods for categorizing and cataloguing books. There was not a reference book or textbook or novel that entered Wiley during his tenure that he did not at least skim, and his knowledge of the authors and subjects the library housed bested any faculty member on campus. Professors consulted David, whom they knew as Jacob Tatum, an assumption that made life easier all the way around.

The university supplied David with room and board and an hourly wage. He supplemented these compensations by doing odd jobs for faculty members and their families and friends. There wasn't anything he could not repair or build. He became the campus pet, and as such, he enjoyed many good meals in the homes of his patrons. It was easy to save money, and David fulfilled his promise to Zachary to pay his tuition, even though David himself never attended a class.

One particular morning, which happened to be his birthday— David had not celebrated a birthday since he had done so with his parents and Gramps—he was in the stockroom going through a new shipment of books Wiley had received from Columbia University. Since he rarely felt the need to rush, he took his time thumbing through the pages of *Harlem Artists: A Mosaic*, *Studies in African American Heritage*, and *A Black Perspective on Southern Reconstruction*.

In the bottom of the crate, one last title presented itself. *Renaissance Men Volume 32: Caesar Carpentier Antoine*. Caesar Carpentier Antoine, or C. C., as David had known him, had been Gramps's captain during the Freedom War. Afterward, during

Louisiana's brief and glorious Reconstruction period, Gramps had worked with Lieutenant Governor Antoine in New Orleans.

David picked up the thin book and ran his fingertips over the image in the center of its tooled leather cover. It was the same painting that had hung over the mantel in Captain Antoine's house on Perrin Street in Shreveport, where C. C. had retired from public life. David had visited there many times with his grandfather. Often after their Saturday errands, Gramps and David enjoyed an early supper at Captain Antoine's table.

David opened the book and found a reference to Gramps, as he had hoped he would. Andrew Samuel Dyer, David's maternal grandfather, had spoken at Captain Antoine's funeral in 1921, and the eulogy Gramps's gave was quoted.

> C. C. Antoine was the most influential figure in my life. His generosity was equaled only by his commitment to an egalitarian Louisiana, a cause for which he worked tirelessly every day that he drew breath. Those of us who served alongside Captain Antoine in the Freedom War, those who served alongside Lieutenant Governor Antoine in New Orleans, as well as, the lucky few of us who did both—we all were given the gift of hope in the rightness, indeed the righteousness, of C. C.'s doctrine. Such hope guides us in the face of opposition, in the face of disappointment, even in the face of heartbreak. Such righteousness, in the end, shall prevail.

David read the words aloud and imagined hearing them in his grandfather's voice rather than his own. He read them again, and then a third time. There was a footnote that tightened his throat.

> Andrew Samuel Dyer. b. 11 February 1850, Port Barre, Louisiana; d. 15 November 1924, Caddo Parish, Louisiana. Union Army Corporal, 7th Regiment Infantry, Louisiana, African descent. Corporal Dyer, arguably one of the most highly skilled shooters on either side during the American Civil War, served on Lieutenant Governor Antoine's staff in New Orleans during Reconstruction. He retired to Caddo Parrish following the Democrats' return to power in Louisiana

State government. Corporal Dyer is laid to rest beside his wife, Lillian (née Cordova), in Port Barre, Louisiana.

Gramps was at last reunited with his wife and best friend. He had spoken of their reunion countless times. Pretty Mama, Gramps's pet name for the grandmother David had never met, had died of yellow fever before David was born. Oftentimes, David heard Gramps say, "When I see Pretty Mama again, I'm gonna tell her . . . ," or "I'm gonna ask her . . . ," or "Pretty Mama's gonna laugh when she hears . . . ." Gramps always spoke about his wife as if their parting were temporary, a brief inconvenience in a timeless friendship. David never forgot the certainty with which Gramps believed they would enjoy each other's company again. He was glad that Gramps and Pretty Mama were planted together in Port Barre, so they could come up together when the trumpet sounded and the dead came forth.

David thought about Gramps's passing for a long time. He thought about everything that had happened since the Indian summer day thirteen years before. In the quiet of a library stockroom on a December afternoon, David wept, as he'd done so many times before, and no one came to bother him at all.

After the Christmas break, when David and Zachary returned to the campus from the farm, David took an interest in a tall, thin girl who had frequented the library for several years. David could not explain why this girl, Cargie Pittman, suddenly commanded his attention after he had been indifferent to her comings and goings for so long. But one day he watched with interest as she came into the library, opened her book, adjusted the light on it, and began reading, running her finger across the text. David walked to her table and waited for her to notice him. Finally she looked up.

"Hello," she said.

"May I?" he asked, pointing to the chair opposite her. She nodded, and he sat down. He reached his hand across the table, and Cargie extended hers to meet it.

"I'm Thomas Barre," he said without a moment's hesitation. The name just popped right out.

She withdrew her hand before they touched fingers. Her eyes narrowed. "Why does everybody call you Jacob?"

"Let me buy you a milkshake, and I'll tell you how I came by that nickname."

Cargie smiled then. She had a good smile, full of mischief. And so they went for a milkshake that very night. And the next night. And the one after that.

Cargie Pittman listened to David's stories about everything from cotton farming to house building to tutoring college students. She listened patiently while he talked about his favorite novelists and poets. David listened while Cargie aired her opinions about her classes and the business practices she was learning. She had a memory like none other and could quote long passages from her textbooks.

She's a genius, David thought, as he sipped a malty chocolate milkshake and listened. He thought it would be an adventure to see what such a mind might do, given time and opportunity. Though Cargie was plain of face, though she was too tall and too thin, to David she was lovely, dark, and deep.

Winter led to spring, and Cargie's company became as familiar as David's own skin. In fact, he didn't quite feel like himself anymore when they were apart. Her presence comforted him, the way watching his mother fix supper had comforted him when he was a boy. David believed this was what love was, so he asked Cargie to marry him.

David and Cargie talked about practical things, such as where they would live. They kept their most deeply held regrets, desires, and dreams to themselves. They both believed a person's heart, like the past, ought to remain tucked away out of sight rather than worn on one's sleeve. But even though they did not voice them, their private longings thrived. Cargie dreamed about getting a job as a bookkeeper. David dreamed about his family, beckoning to him from a misty horizon. Waiting patiently for him to catch up to them.